Give Me Hell

THE GIVE ME SERIES BOOK 4

KATE MCCARTHY

Give Me Hell

This book is for Terrena.
"A best friend is someone who loves you
when you forget to love yourself."

Prologue

"Don't worry when I fight with you.
Worry when I stop,
Because it means there's nothing left for us to fight for."

Mac

Grace and Casey's party is in full swing. Their loft is a complete crush, leaving me stuck in the kitchen dispensing drinks. I'm busy making small talk but my mind is locked on the pregnancy test I purchased in a fit of panic on the drive here. It's buried deep inside my Burberry handbag. I haven't had time to take the test, but I can't stop thinking about it. At the pharmacy I grabbed the first one I saw and marched it to the counter, chin up like I was going into war and the test was my hand grenade.

When I was young having a baby was always in my distant future, but my entire life changed at seventeen. The life I imagined for myself got knocked off course. Marriage. Family. The white picket fence. A fairy tale—and one that was never meant for me.

I wrap an arm around my belly, wondering if my life is about to change. *Are you in there, baby?* I glare at my flat stomach. *If so, you're not in the plan.*

"Princess?"

The deep, husky tone infiltrates every part of my body. My head lifts and my heart lodges somewhere near the vicinity of my throat. Whiskey-coloured eyes look down at me with concern. I hate that I like seeing it. The way Jake Romero looks at me makes me ache. It always has, and it always will.

"I'm not your princess."

Not anymore. It's too late. I *wrecked* us. There's only so many times you can glue a broken vase back together. Our pieces don't fit back together anymore.

Jake ignores my retort. His gaze drops to my arm cradled protectively around my belly. He meets my eyes. "You okay?"

"I'm fine," I say sharply. My bitchy tone is a defence mechanism; it snaps in place like a rubber band whenever I talk to him. It's the only way to keep him at an arm's length, otherwise my hands will reach for him and I won't be able to let go.

Jake grinds his jaw. He wants to turn and walk away but there's a pull between us that makes it impossible for him. I know, because I feel it too.

I reach for a fresh beer and twist off the top. Tossing the lid in the nearby bin, I shove it toward him. Jake doesn't take it and leave the kitchen like I hope he will. Instead, he folds his arms creating bulges of tanned muscle. The coloured ink on his skin intertwines with dark images, forming beautiful works of art that sleeve both his arms. I remember those arms when they were reed thin and bare, when he was a boy on the verge of becoming a man. His hair was longer then. Golden brown strands rested against the back of his neck and fell in his eyes. It was the texture of silk, and I loved running my fingers through it. Gripping it in my fists when he did things to me that I never imagined possible. Jake said he'd always keep it longer just for me, but then I left and the next time I saw him it was buzzed short. It's been that way ever since.

"Are you sure?" Jake asks before I drown in the memories of who we used to be.

No. And I want to tell him that so very badly that I bite down on my lip to stop the word escaping. His heavy-lidded gaze drops to my mouth and heat flares between my thighs in an instant. *Damn him.*

"Take the stupid beer," I growl before I completely lose it.

With a sharp huff, he snatches it from my hand. He sets it on the kitchen counter and his eyes come back to me. Does he even know the heated way he looks at me? It burns me like a brush fire.

"Mac, I ..." Jake looks away, swallowing, and rubs a hand over his short buzz of hair. There's a war inside him. I see it on his face. Indecision. Frustration. Longing. The ache inside me intensifies. His gaze returns and he lets out a deep breath. "We need to start living more separate lives. I can't ..."

The pain of his words are a thousand rusty knives stabbing me straight in the heart.

I ignore the party going on around us and close my eyes for the briefest of seconds. The moment I do, his hand cups my jaw. The barest contact before it slides away. My eyes open, the rough touch of his palm lingering on my skin.

Why can't I unlove you?

"You're right," I force myself to concede.

Jake nods as if pleased with my response, which sends the knives deeper.

I snatch his abandoned beer and tip my head back, filling my mouth with fizzy alcohol. Then it hits me. What if I *am* actually pregnant? I can't drink this stuff. It sprays from my mouth like a ruptured fire hydrant. I turn and most of it lands in the sink rather than on Jake's shirt.

"Mac?" He takes the poor beer from my hand and once again abandons it on the kitchen counter. Then he grips me by the elbow as I'm trying to wipe at my face with a paper napkin. "You're not okay at all, are you?"

I breathe deep, lost in a sea of nausea and rejection. "Get lost," I rasp as I toss the bit of towel toward the bin.

"For fuck's sake," he spits, his hold on me tightening as he pulls me toward the bathroom. "Can't you lose the bitch for even a second?"

"No," I snap as I'm dragged alongside him. "It's who I am and I'm not asking you to like it. I'm asking you to leave me alone."

"You heard her," a deep voice growls from somewhere on my left. "Get lost."

My hackles rise further. Damn my meddling older brothers. Jared's green eyes spark fire as he glares at Jake.

"Stop interfering in my business," I hiss at Jared, poking him in the chest.

Jake smirks at my brother and arches a brow.

Jared's nostrils flare as he looks from Jake to me. He folds his arms, eyes narrowing on mine. "I wouldn't need to if you had it handled."

My fury climbs. "I *was* handling it, you asshole."

"Asshole is right," Jake adds.

I turn to him, mouth agape. "You're an asshole too! You want to end whatever the hell this is? Consider it *ended!*" I shout. With the thumping beat bouncing off the walls, no one around us pays any mind, not that I particularly care right now. "Now both of you can just go *fuck off!*"

I turn and disappear into a sea of people in my need to get away, leaving them to duke it out by themselves. The party has begun to wind down anyway. I'm tasked with dispensing keys to those who are sober, and it keeps me distracted and occupied.

When I'm down to the last set of keys in the bowl, I scan the room and don't see Jake. Casey's brother is one of the last to leave. He's been drinking all night and holds a fresh beer. I'm getting a death stare because the key to his Harley is being held hostage in my hand.

Kelly is a Sentinels biker with dirty blond hair, scary tattoos, and flirty blue eyes. He's the definition of trouble and so damn hot it rips the air from every room he enters. Even sick as I am, it's hard not to notice, yet it fails to stir anything inside me. Only Jake has ever managed to do that, and I hate him for it.

"You're not getting your keys, biker dude," I tell him in a firm tone. "No matter how hard you glare."

He glares harder. It doesn't faze me. He'll be thanking me in the morning when it isn't a piece of scrap metal wrapped around a tree.

I lift my chin, his keys tight in my grip. I'm not backing down and he knows it.

"They better still be there in the fuckin' mornin'," he bitches.

My gaze narrows. He seems to like it, and his bleary eyes drop, inspecting the decorative zippers on my tight black pants with serious intent.

"Or else what?" I bark.

Kelly pauses for a moment, weaving on his feet as he blinks at me. "Or else I'll be pissed off."

"Good one, Kelly," I snap, rolling my eyes. It's late. I'm tired. I'm also potentially pregnant for fuck's sake. I can't see Jake anywhere, and I'm pissed because it leaves me disappointed. I start for the living room, crooking my finger. "Come with me."

His flirty blue eyes light up. He leaves his bottle on the counter and follows me to the living area. Kelly has the wrong idea but if it gets him to the sofa where he can pass out, I can consider my duty done and leave.

I point to the couch. It's covered in blankets and pillows. "Lie down."

Instead of doing what I say, he peels off his shirt and stalks toward me like a lion. Then he pounces, planting his lips on mine. My hands move to his chest to push him off. He needs to remove his mouth before I punch his junk or barf on his face.

"What in the goddamn fuck?"

I leap in the air, a shriek escaping me.

Kelly pulls back and turns, affording me a glimpse of Jake standing behind him. His large hands are fisted so tight by his sides that thick veins pop wide over his knuckles. He isn't even looking at Kelly. His gaze is on me, his hurt so deeply visible it freezes me in place. He closes his eyes and when he opens them, they're blank. But it's too late. I've seen what he's trying to hide. And knowing I caused his pain burns like acid on my skin.

Don't cry. Do not fucking cry.

But I can't get any air. *Damn you, Jake, for coming into my life. For making me want things that were never meant to be. For telling me you wanted to end it all and then acting like I just stabbed you in the heart.*

We could have had everything. A whole different life. Yet in one fateful day we lost it all. The past swims in his eyes when I lift my chin and meet his gaze.

"Fuck this shit," he growls. He stalks to the door, rips it open, and slams it behind him so hard I flinch. The reverberating bang is a catalyst. The dam bursts inside me and a sob breaks free.

Kelly stares down at me, eyes round like a deer caught in headlights. His body is fairly vibrating with horror, which tells me he doesn't do tears.

"Fuck you," I mutter to him. *I don't do them either.* And yet here they are dripping down my face faster than a leaky pipe.

Kelly goes in for the awkward back pat. I dodge the advance. His huge pawing hands have done enough damage tonight. Snatching up my bag, I stomp toward the bathroom, wiping at my face.

Shutting the door behind me, I dump my Burberry on the bathroom vanity. Rifling through the contents, I find the brown package in the bottom and pull it out. Not bothering to waste time reading instructions, I unpack the stick, pee on it, and set it on the counter. There. Pregnancy test taken.

I exhale deeply and stare at myself in the mirror as I wait the requisite three minutes to find out my fate. My sheet of long blond hair is as limp as the rest of me, and mascara runs down my cheeks. I look like shit. Tired. Defeated. Not like myself at all.

When my time is up, I hold my breath and look down at the stick. Two lines look back at me.

Holy shit. My hands shake and my stomach rolls as I meet my gaze again in the mirror. The bright green of my eyes has always been fierce and sharp, never kind and loving like a mother's eyes should be. How the hell am I going to pull this off?

I grip the edge of the counter and set my jaw, glowering as I gather myself together. *You've got this, Mackenzie Valentine.*

I mean, really, how hard can motherhood be?

Jake

My jaw is tight as I drive along the quiet, dark streets after leaving the party. I'm tired. Tired of wanting the one thing it always seems I can't have. Tired of never being enough. I've been stuck on the fringes of Mac's life, waiting for her to find what it is she's searching for. Waiting for her to open her eyes and see what's standing right before her. But she never does. Whatever road Mac travels on, it never leads to me.

The knowledge burns like hell. I free one hand from the steering wheel and rub it over the tightness of my chest. My heart thumps painfully beneath it. How do you give up on the one thing that keeps you breathing?

You just do it.

With the car idling at a red light, I call up Henry Paterson's number on my phone and hit speaker. We met when *Jamieson* formed back in college. Despite being polar opposites, Paterson is my best friend. He's a flirty show pony, playing lead guitar and whoring his way through women like a man with days left to live. I prefer flying under the radar, smashing out my frustrations on the drums, feeling the pounding rhythm break me apart with its intensity. The thunderous beat and the wildness gives me peace, and the band—Evie, Frog, Cooper, and Paterson—is the family that gave me a home.

"Romero," Paterson answers groggily.

Shit. I woke him.

"What's up?" he asks.

"Never mind," I mutter as I take a left at the lights and hit the on-ramp for Sydney's Motorway 1.

"You've woken me now," he bitches. "What—"

I cut him off with the words I never thought I'd say. "I'm quitting the band."

"What the fuck?" he bleats. The shock in his voice is unmistakable. I don't make idle threats. In fact, I never say anything unless it's something worth saying. And I'm not impulsive. But leaving is my only option. I won't survive another minute living like this. "No. You're not quitting. Why? Where did this come from? Fuck, Jake. Way to drop a bombshell at two in the morning. I can't even right now."

Passing the sign that tells me Melbourne is eight hundred kilometres away, I gun the engine of my 1979 Dodge Charger. It's a car that Casey helped me lovingly restore over the span of three years. His girlfriend, Grace, smashed his own Corvette Stingray earlier in the year, and he's been making noises about stealing my Charger ever since. He'll be shattered to find out he's lost his chance.

"It's past time for a change," I tell Paterson.

"But—"

"Can you let everyone know?" *Coward.* "Box up the rest of my shit. I'll message you an address to ship it to."

Paterson's voice hardens. "You're not leaving."

"I'm already gone."

He huffs angrily. "Bullshit. You can't."

I jab the clutch and drop it down to sixth gear. Miles of dark road pass by me in a blur as I leave the outskirts of Sydney behind me. "Give me one good reason I should stay."

Henry doesn't hesitate. "Mac."

I stare at the empty road ahead of me, my chest aching. So much that I can't speak.

"You can't give up."

"I'm not giving up." I swallow the huge lump in my throat. "I'm just letting go."

"Then don't let go, asshole."

"It's too late, Paterson. I already have."

I hang up, dial another number, and put it back on speaker so I can drive.

It rings three times and then Mitch Valentine answers. "Are you good to go?"

"I'm good to go," I reply, my voice hoarse.

"Good. We're all set."

I exhale, my gaze hard on the road as I focus ahead.

"Romero?"

"Yeah?"

There's a pause. "You don't have to do this."

My hands grip tight to the steering wheel. "There's no other way."

"There's always another way."

I shake my head even though he can't see it. "Not this time."

"Good luck," he says quietly.

I hang up.

Chapter One

Mac

The beginning...

"Mac! Get your butt down here this minute!"

I ignore the command. My time is better spent cutting the hair off my Barbie. It's not that I don't like her long, voluminous locks. She's just too pretty. She needs an edge. A *rocker* edge. Which is why I drew tattoos down the left side of her arm and changed her name to Bon Jovi.

I wonder if we have any hair dye?

"Mackenzie Valentine! I asked you to chop those onions a half hour ago!"

The sound of heeled shoes clicking their way up the stairs reaches my ears. "Jared said he'd do it!" I lie quickly.

"No. I asked you."

My mother's firm voice is close now, and I turn my head. She's standing in my bedroom doorway, her arms folded and lips pinched so tight a screwdriver couldn't pry them loose.

"Why?" I growl. "Because I have a vagina?"

"Eww," Jared complains, choosing that moment to exit his bedroom, which sits opposite mine. He gives his floppy brown hair a flick, the style a lame version of Nick Carter a la Backstreet Boys. "Girl germs."

"Ugh!" I roll my eyes. "Find a more original insult, assface!"

Mum's intake of air is sharp and competes with the sound of my older brother's laughter. "Mackenzie!"

"Arrghh!" I launch Bon Jovi at Jared's head, and her booted foot catches him in the eye. A girlish shriek escapes his lips before they press in a thin line. He picks Bon Jovi up off the floor and shoves her down the front of his pants.

My stomach rebels when I realise where my poor doll now lies. I dry heave. "Mum!"

"Onions." She jabs her finger in the direction of the kitchen downstairs. "Now. And, Jared, please remove Mackenzie's doll from your pants."

I concede the battle but not the war. Tomorrow is a new day after all. I stomp down the stairs, passing by my other two brothers, Travis and Mitch, both of whom sit at the kitchen table doing homework. Mitch is the eldest at sixteen. With dark hair, tanned skin, and green eyes, he thinks himself God's gift. Trouble is so do the girls in his class, which reinforces his warped belief. Travis, with his blond hair and green eyes, is next at fifteen. Fortunately, he spends most of his time go-karting so he bothers me the least. Then there's Jared at thirteen. With brown hair and green eyes, this brother is the most evil of the three; my days are spent planning counterattacks and shoring up my defences against him. I'm the youngest at the sweet, tender age of eleven, but I'm also the only girl and in this house that makes me Ruler of the Kingdom.

"Do-gooders," I mutter under my breath as I pass by the dining table.

In the next second I'm flying through the air like a missile. I crash into the sideboard, rattling Mum's treasured china display.

"Mackenzie!" Mum whips out, turning. "What is *wrong* with you?"

I rise to my feet, ignoring the throbbing pain in my right hip. Mitch's smirk damns him as the culprit. Fool. *Oh dear eldest brother of mine, will you ever learn? Poker face is a weapon in this house, and you are yet to perfect it.*

"I tripped over the leg of the chair." I smooth my hair, tucking long blonde strands behind my ears. I feel Mitch's eyes burn into my back, waiting for the fallout as I follow Mum into the kitchen.

Soon, I promise silently and pick up an onion from the chopping board. "Mum, there's something I want to talk to you about," I say, slicing the ends off the vegetable.

"Mmm?" she murmurs distractedly, her back turned as she takes a tin of chopped tomatoes from the cupboard above.

"I saw Mitch kissing a girl by the school gate this afternoon." A total lie but Mum's attention latches onto the comment like a suction cup, her brow furrowing into deep grooves. "Does that mean she's his girlfriend? Are they having ..." I lower my voice to a whisper and widen my eyes "... sex?"

Mum sucks in a sharp breath, horror darkening the emerald green of her eyes. It's all I can do to hold in the burst of laughter as I peel the outer layer from the onion. I accidently take off three thick layers leaving half behind, but I begin to chop regardless.

"Of course not," she tells me and presses her lips in tight, white line.

"Because they're not married?"

"That's exactly right," she confirms, her eyes shifting to my eldest brother with a spark of determination.

Payback is a bitch, Mitch, I murmur silently, chuckling at my own rhyme as I go back to chopping, finishing when they're diced to Mum's specifications. As I'm leaving the kitchen, she doesn't just call in Mitch ... she calls in all my brothers. I hover for a few moments outside the door, eavesdropping as she makes a start on the birds and the bees speech for yet another year. Then I disappear up the stairs, happy.

Fifteen minutes later my brothers regroup in Jared's room and begin plotting my demise. I know because I'm hiding out in his wardrobe in the dark. It stinks in here like sweaty socks and old apples. I sigh silently, my ear to the door as I listen to their pathetic plan.

It's just another day in the Valentine household. Taking each other down is a long-standing tradition in our family. But while we stand against each other inside these four walls, outside of them we stand united. Our motto? *Never mess with a Valentine.*

"Kids, I've been called in on a case," Mum yells up the stairs. "Mitch, can you take over dinner for me?"

That means it will just be the four of us for dinner. Mum is a social worker and Dad works as a Chief Inspector for the Sydney City Police and he's on shift.

A quick peek through the crack in the wardrobe door shows my brothers putting their payback on ice as they leave the room. When I'm sure they're gone, I break free, gasping for fresh air. I spend the time before dinner hiding out in my room. When Mitch calls out for me to come down and eat, I flounce to the table in my brand-new dress. It's blood red—my favourite colour—with a stretchy bodice and tulle skirt. *Tulle* for god's sake. I bloody love it. The skirt is a bit short, but I can't help the fact Mum got the sizing mixed up. Nothing is stopping me from wearing this dress, not even a mundane Thursday night dinner at home.

Mitch glares at it when I pull out the chair next to Travis. "You can't wear that dress. Ever."

"Wrong, Stitch. I already am," I reply as I take a seat, using my nickname for him. Not only is it brilliant because it rhymes with Mitch, but it's named after Stitch, the extra-terrestrial genetic experiment— or *abomination*—out of Lilo and Stitch. Considering he's hideously handsome, the nickname helps bring his ego back down into the real world.

Travis glares at my dress too. Ever the diplomat, he at least likes to provide a reason before giving an order. "It's too short."

"No it's not." I pick up my knife and fork. "You can't see my vagina."

The subject of my girl parts never fail to make them back off. They don't like the reminder that I have one or that they have to defend it against future intruders. In any event, I utilize the topic sparingly. I can't have them becoming immune to its properties.

Jared, however, already appears immune. He, too, aims a glare at my dress. "Change."

My eyes drop to my plate. I rally for a moment and muster a tear. It spills out, plopping onto the overcooked pile of spaghetti. After taking a deep, shaky breath, I look up from beneath lowered lashes, my gaze encompassing my brothers.

"It was fr-fr-from Granny Mary," I stammer. Recently deceased, Granny Mary was Dad's mum's Aunt and a national treasure. Always a warm cookie to share and dollar bills slipped kindly into our moneyboxes. I bought my very first pair of ankle boots with that money.

Travis caves first, his eyes softening into green pools of regret. "Sorry, Mac." He takes my hand from where it rests on the table, clutching a fork. He gives it a quick squeeze before letting go. "You can wear it."

I blink away tears. "Thanks, Trav."

"Wait a minute." Jared's eyes narrow to slits. He half stands from his chair, eyes taking in my dress like a crime scene investigator. "That dress isn't from Granny Mary. Mum picked it up on sale at the markets last Sunday!"

Mitch's indrawn breath is so sharp he starts to choke on it.

Jared points at me. "Liar!" he cries.

An all-out war commences, going too far when Jared tosses his plate of food at my dress and shouts, "Well, let's just see you try wearing it now!"

"You ruined my dress!" I screech, glancing down at the spaghetti oozing into my beloved tulle. I look back up, murder in my eyes and knife in my hand. "Prepare to die!"

Mum interrupts my blood-curdling war cry. "What on earth is going on here?"

We all turn in unison toward the dining room entryway. Our mother is dressed in her caseworker outfit; blue and soothing, the material is soft but hardy enough to bear all manner of tears and tantrums. Her no-nonsense blonde bob hangs in a pretty sweep to her shoulders and her mouth is wide open. Such is my rage, I don't notice the boy standing by her side.

She looks to Mitch first because he's the eldest and therefore responsible for the situation. "Mitch?"

"It was Mac." His chin juts out, angered over my Granny Mary lie. Out of all of us, he'd been the closest to our dearly departed relative. Not to mention he hates when I lie. Mitch has high expectations when it comes to me. I don't know why. Maybe because I'm the only girl? He's the most protective of all my brothers. He's always the first one to bitch me out, but he's also the first to wade in if I've been done an injustice. Any hint of perceived bullying toward me will put you on his shit list for life. My eldest brother nurses a grudge like one would nurse a baby. "She started it with that stupid dress," he adds with a narrow-eyed glare in my direction.

Stupid dress? *Stupid* dress? "I hate you," I hiss at him, low enough for Mum not to hear. I'm over being told by my entire family what I can and can't do. "I hate all of you."

I straighten my shoulders and stand from the table. Storming from the room, I brush past the boy by my mother's side, not noticing the smear of spaghetti sauce I leave down the left side of his shirt in my haste.

Real tears burn my eyes as I stomp up the stairs to my room, my stomach growling. I had spent my time at the dinner table defending my dress rather than getting to eat a single bite.

I peel the so-called offensive outfit over my head. It sends sauce oozing over my face and into my hair. I drop it to the floor and move to my dresser. Clad in just a pair of panties and wrapping a towel around my torso, I'm intent on my next plan of attack when a tap comes at my bedroom door.

"Your mum said you'd help me find a clean shirt?"

A squeak escapes me at the unfamiliar male voice, and I spin around, my hands grasping at the towel to secure it tightly. It's the boy. He's plucking the damp, soiled shirt away from his side. He appears no older than twelve, and he's tanned like he spends most of his time outdoors. His hair is a light golden brown. It hangs in his eyes, leaving me unsure of their colour.

"Who are you?" I ask, my tone snappish because his concept of privacy is a complete joke.

"Jake," he replies and steps inside my room as if my question is an invitation. "Jake Romero."

"Get out of my room, Jake Romero."

His brows soar at my rudeness. It can't be helped. I'm hungry. "My brother's room is across the hall. He'll have a shirt in there to fit you," I force myself to say in a more polite tone.

"Right." With a roll of his eyes, Jake leaves and I think of him no longer.

Instead, I go and have a quick shower. Once I'm freshly washed and smelling of soap, I prepare to face off with my mother. She's in the kitchen, sighing heavily as she scrubs at the bottom of a burnt pan.

"How did you go, sweetheart? Did you find a clean shirt ..." Her voice trails off as she turns. "Oh. It's you."

"Who's Jake Romero?"

"He's—"

"None of your business, that's who."

I turn, taking in Boy Wonder himself. He's now outfitted in a clean tee shirt. "Touchy, Romero. Shall I tell my mother how you were in my room while I was getting changed?"

"Jesus Christ," he mutters under his breath. "You're a real piece of work, aren't you?"

Mum lets out another sigh, this one heavier than the last, and I know she heard him. The last time she sighed this hard was when

Granny Mary died. "Jake, honey, there's a plate of food for you on the dining table. You need to eat something."

Honey? *Honey?* He's the one invading my room and she smothers him with endearments?

"I appreciate it, Mrs. Valentine..." a sweeping gaze of contempt passes over me "...but I'm not hungry."

Boy Wonder's smile is forced. I know because it doesn't reach his eyes. They're deep brown with flecks of gold that I imagine would flicker with life at the right opportunity. Instead, they're flat and empty.

"Well, I am," I announce, shaking off the weird feeling I get from staring into his eyes.

Putting together a new plate of food, I set it opposite the table setting laid out for Jake in the freshly cleaned dining room. I'm shovelling in a fork load of spaghetti when he takes a seat, having surrendered to my mother's bullying tactics.

Jake picks up his fork and shifts the spaghetti around on his plate, ignoring me.

"Where do you go to school?" I ask, still feeling unsettled as I finish chewing.

"Banks Public," he says to his food.

"That's high school."

"Wow. You're smart."

I ignore the jibe. It's nothing compared to what my brothers dish out. My skin is Teflon after years of smartass remarks. "How old are you?"

"I just turned twelve." Jake finally looks at me, his head lifting slow as if it weighs a tonne. "You?"

"I'll be eleven soon. I'm having a pool party," I boast because surely that makes me cooler than cool. I have a brand-new swimsuit to wear too. "Do you want to come?"

His eyes drop back to his plate. "No."

"Fine," I reply, my hackles rising at his cool, disinterested tone. I don't know why I asked him anyway—a complete stranger. Looking at him is giving me weird jitters. I pick my plate up and stand from the table. "You wouldn't fit in anyway. It's for cool, fun people and you're a bit of an ass, aren't you?"

"Mackenzie Valentine!" I cringe at my mother's tone. "Upstairs now. I'd like a word."

I set my plate back down and follow her up the stairs and into my room. "I cannot believe you," she starts off then places fingers to her temples. "Actually, I can." My mother drops her arms and begins picking up my dirty clothes off the floor. "You're a rude, selfish little bully. I know your brothers goad you into trouble, but you need to be bigger than that. You need to find that sweet girl I know is inside you somewhere and bring her out. Jake is staying with us for a few weeks, and I want him to feel welcome." Mum sweeps from the room but not without one last parting shot. "After tonight's entire fiasco, I'm cancelling your birthday party."

I die a little bit inside. "Nooooooo! Mum—"

She gives me the hand. "Not another word, Mackenzie. After you apologise to Jake, you can make up the trundle bed in Jared's room for him to sleep on."

After stomping down the stairs, I offer Boy Wonder a stilted apology. He's still seated at the table, his plate of food uneaten and shoulders slumped. My heart gives a twinge, but I fight not to care. He ruined my birthday. It's a wonder I don't follow it up with a punch to his face.

Later that night I'm in bed asleep when an odd thumping noise wakes me. A curse follows. I scoot back on my bed, on immediate alert. My eyes scan the darkened room, focusing on a moving shadow. My heart pounds a furious beat. "Who's there?"

"It's me," comes the quick reply.

Boy Wonder. Of course. I glance at the clock. Two a.m. glares back in digital red. "What are you doing in my room?"

"I wanted to say sorry."

"Sorry?"

"About your party."

"And you had to say it *now*?"

There's silence for a long moment. "I couldn't sleep."

"So what?" I brush a mountain of long blonde hair from my face. "If you can't sleep, then stuff anyone else who's trying to?"

"God. You're like a damn cactus. I'm trying to apologise here."

"Well, you can shove it," I hiss, furious all over again. Mum is always bringing home random strays. Granted, the majority have been babies or toddlers so someone of Jake's age is something new, but I don't like it. I don't like him. He's managed to ruin my life in the space of one night. "I don't care about you or about your stupid apology because it doesn't fix anything."

"I guess you're right." Jake's tone is so flat my stomach squeezes into knots. "I'll see you in the morning, then," he says and bumps his way from my room, closing the door behind him.

I'm left feeling disquieted. He's made me angry for myself, but there's a sad kind of emptiness in him that tugs at my heartstrings. The ache of it is strong enough to keep me awake for another hour before I eventually find sleep again.

But when I wake, I don't see Jake in the morning like he said. He's gone and the ache that eased through the night begins to throb anew.

Around noon I chase Jared down in the living area to question him. "Didn't Mum tell you?" My brother pauses his game of Mario Kart and looks up. "The state turned up this morning and took him."

"Why?"

"He was only here because his father had a brain anyadoodlewhatsit."

"Anyadoodle what?"

He frowns at me like I'm stupid. "Aneurysm."

"Oh my god." My legs wobble and I sink down on the sofa. "Is his father okay?"

"I don't think so. I don't think his brain works right anymore. I heard they're going to admit him into some kind of care facility when he leaves the hospital."

"Why didn't anyone tell me?"

"Why would anyone tell you? It's none of your business."

"Well, if it's none of my business, how do *you* know?"

His expression turns smug. "I heard Mum and Dad talking about it late last night. He was going to stay with us until they tracked down his relatives, but apparently Jake doesn't have any. Anyway, he's probably going into some kind of boy's home."

"What about his mum?"

Jared shrugs. "I don't know. I didn't hear them mention her. Maybe she's dead."

Having given me the facts, Jared un-pauses his game and continues his race. I watch blindly, unable to move. My mind is on Jake. All I can picture is him getting taken away and facing a future alone, those eyes of his so flat and empty.

"I wanted to say sorry."

"Sorry?"

"About your party."

He was apologising over my stupid birthday party after his whole life had completely fallen apart. Guilt has my stomach rolling over.

"I'm such a bitch," I whisper.

"You got that right," Jared throws out cheerfully, focused on his game.

"Go fuck yourself," is my retort as I leave the living area for my bedroom. Taking a seat at my study desk, I sit down and pen Jake a letter. When I'm done, I fold it carefully, seal it in an envelope, and write JAKE ROMERO in block letters across the front.

"Mum?" I call out, jogging down the stairs.

"In the office!" she calls back.

She's sitting at her desk, tapping the keyboard when I drop the envelope in front of her. "Can you give that to Jake?"

Mum looks at it, then at me. "Oh, honey. I don't think that's a good idea."

"What?" I frown, folding my arms. "Why not?"

She releases a deep sigh, swivels her chair to face me, and takes off her reading glasses. "I worry about bringing these kids home. Here. Of you being exposed to their..." she pauses for a moment as if trying to find the right word "...troubles." Mum tilts her head, green eyes revealing concern. "I don't want you getting attached."

My chin juts out. "I'm not attached."

"Either way, it's not a good idea."

"Mum, seriously!"

She slides her reading glasses on and returns to the computer, re-focusing on her work.

"Don't ignore me, Mum, it's rude!"

Mum turns her head and peers at me over the top of her glasses. "No, Mackenzie, what's rude is *you*. I've given you my answer and it's final." She goes back to her keyboard and begins tapping. "Why don't you go swimming, hmm? It's a lovely warm afternoon. Your father's going to fire up the barbeque soon. We'll eat outdoors tonight I think."

With a frustrated growl, I snatch the letter and stalk back to my room, making sure my angry stomps are loud as I make my way up the stairs. I place the letter in the bottom of my underwear drawer and as the days and weeks, and then the months and years pass by, I never once get Jake Romero from my head.

Chapter Two

Three years later...

I take a sip of my drink and relax against the recliner by the pool. God bless the first day of summer holidays. No homework or assignments—just an endless stretch of sunshine, barbeques, and only one brother to deal with. Jared is holidaying on the Gold Coast with a friend and their family, and Travis is at a go-karting camp—the very idea so lame I couldn't even summon a laugh at his expense.

Drink in hand, I expel a deep sigh of pleasure and close my eyes behind the dark lenses of my sunglasses. After several minutes, I zone out in the heat of the day. Moments later a ball slaps me up the side of my face. I jump a mile in the air. Sticky cordial splashes down my front and stars dance in my vision. I raise a hand to my cheek, making sure it hasn't imploded from the impact.

When I'm sure there's no serious damage, I aim furious eyes at my brother where he's playing volleyball in the pool with friends. "Goddammit, Stitch!"

I know he threw the ball. The savage hit is payback for plucking away at the threads in the backside of his school shorts. It took all day, but they finally split right down the seam when the afternoon bus arrived and he bent over to pick up his school bag. It was brilliant. I laughed so hard I couldn't breathe. I can even say it's worth a punch to the face with a volleyball.

Still. I can't let this go. Setting my drink down, I grab the ball and stand. Stalking to the edge of the pool, I glare down at him bobbing in the sparkly blue water. His friends stare. Particularly Elijah Rossiter. I have teeny flourishing boobs and an itsy bitsy bright red bikini. The ensemble is enough to set my brother's lips in a thin line as I stand by the edge, palming the weapon between both hands.

My eyes flick to my brother's best friend. Eli is the son of Alan Rossiter, a big hairy deal in the policing world and one of Dad's closest friends. He's in the same grade as Mitch, and they've grown up together, forming a friendship that appears as unbreakable as iron. Eli is also hotter than the surface of the sun. His hair is blond with a slight curl, his skin tanned, and eyes a pale blue like the waters along the coast of the Great Barrier Reef. Dimples form as I spare him a glance. I'm not a particularly likeable person so his attention confounds me. Eli is eighteen and has the pick of any girl in school, yet that charm of his always seems directed on me.

My eyes warm and lips curve the briefest fraction in response to his grin. I simply cannot help it. He's like hot chocolate on a wintery day.

Then my gaze turns to my eldest brother and my fiery glare reforms. Without any warning, I peg the volleyball hard at his face. I'm aiming for his nose but a noise from behind distracts me and sets the ball off course. It bounces off Mitch's forehead.

"Nice aim," quips a male voice from behind me—a voice I haven't heard in three years.

"Not nice enough," I snap, irritated because that particular voice sets my heart off like a bongo drum. Turning, I come face to face with Jake Romero himself and freeze on the spot. Those flat and empty eyes of his are a little harder now. The reed thin arms are filling out, and there's muscle definition beneath the snug-fitting tee shirt that wasn't there before. Heat pools in parts of my body where I've never felt heat before. It leaves me dizzy and uncomfortable and completely unprepared. "Back so soon, Romero?"

Jake shrugs, a cocky grin forming on his lips. "Couldn't stay away, it seems."

I arch a brow. "Maybe I can help you with that."

"I'm sure you can." His smile turns mocking as he takes in my wet, sticky bikini. "But seeing you get all wet is too much fun, Princess, so I think I'll stay for a bit."

I bristle. *Princess?* I was fully prepared to offer Jake an apology for my childish behaviour from years ago, but I bite it back. That old letter I wrote is still sitting in my drawer. My new plan is to tear it into little pieces because my original instincts about him had been spot-on. Jake is a total dick.

My eyes narrow behind my sunglasses. "Stay away from me." I brush past him, muttering, "Party wrecker," which is lame but it's all I have.

"Nursing a grudge, I see."

I halt and turn. My eyes track slowly down the length of him and back up again. The gesture is meant to mock but judging from the amused expression, Jake notices the goose bumps rising over my skin. "I can nurse anything I like. Last I checked this was my house. What are you doing in it?"

"What are you saying? You didn't miss me?"

"Miss you?" I snort. "It's lucky I even *remember* you."

A loud splash comes from the pool. Both Mitch and Eli are hauling themselves out. They make their way toward us. Eli brushes wet curls from his face as they track pool water across the sandstone tiles.

"What's going on?" Mitch asks when they reach us. Eli stands beside him, his brow in a slight furrow and hands on his hips.

"You remember Boy Wonder don't you?" I say.

Eli's brows soar. "Boy Wonder?"

A scowl spreads across Jake's face, creating creases along his forehead that only serve to heighten his appeal. "My name is Jake."

"Romero," Mitch says, holding out a hand. "I do remember you."

Jake takes a step forward and shakes it. It has his shoulder brushing against mine. The move feels deliberate.

Eli holds out a hand next, a friendly smile forming across his face. "Elijah." He looks between the two of us as Jake shakes it, his eyes sharp with curiosity. "You're a friend of Mac's?"

"No," I answer at the same time Jake says, "Yes."

An awkward pause follows.

"Well, this reunion has been super fun," I say brightly, "but I have some reclining by the pool to do. If you'll all excuse me."

"Actually you don't."

I pause. Jake's declaration has everyone's brows rising in question, including my own.

"Mac and I are going skateboarding down at the local park."

My nostrils quiver with instant excitement. Enough to ignore the insulting *Princess* nickname Jake gave me earlier. My brothers have their own skateboards. I don't. It's not a *female activity*. Being the youngest and the only girl might make me mightier than Maximus Meridius himself, but it's zero fun. I'm not allowed to do half of what my brothers do. Instead, I get imprisoned in my little ivory tower and treated like glass.

I do admit to being a slight trouble magnet, but I can't help my nature. I don't have a death wish, I'm just determined to prove that I can do whatever my brothers can: whether that's shooting at the range, punching a school bully in the playground, or paddling out beyond the ocean break to surf the big waves.

There have been a few incidents over the years, like the time I shot Jared in the face with a paintball gun, but he taunted me by saying I couldn't hit him square in the nose from twenty paces. I might have missed, but not by much; my aim was a little too far to the left and he almost lost an eye. Then there were the suspensions from school for fighting … but I can't see how it's my fault for being honest. It seems people don't like hearing the truth about themselves. It makes them angry and violent. And while I don't like to start fights, I sure as hell like to finish them.

Mitch is already shaking his head at Jake and my blood boils.

"That's right," I say with a firm voice to my brother, corroborating Jake's story. "We're going skateboarding, which means there's no time for reclining by the pool. We have a park to get to."

Mitch rears up. "Oh hell no, Mac. You—"

Eli slaps a hand on my brother's shoulder. "Dude, let her go." He offers me a wink. "Be safe."

I grin in return before shooting sullen eyes at my brother. "Later, asshead," I tell him as I snatch up Jake's hand and tug on it, leading him toward the sliding doors that open to the back of the house. It's our first contact and my skin hums. It's like being attacked with static electricity.

"I'll be telling Mum about this!" Mitch shouts to our backs.

Anger twists my belly into a knot, yet I keep moving. It's Jake that stops and turns, forcing me to a grinding halt. "Actually it was your mother's suggestion," he tells my brother.

Mitch's eyes widen. He's completely dumbfounded. Even Eli appears a little taken aback. "It was?"

I am too. Skateboarding isn't a ladylike endeavour. It also goes against Mum's mantra of keeping me *unattached* from the strays she brings home. "It was?" I echo.

"No," he says in a voice low enough that only I can hear. His hand squeezes mine, and my breath hitches from the renewed sensation. "Just roll with it."

"It was," I say to Mitch, and just like that Jake becomes my very first co-conspirator in crime. "I know all the local parks." I don't. And I'm sure he knows it. "Mum probably thinks it's a good idea to get out of the house. You know, sunshine, fresh air..." my eyes narrow "...and an outdoor activity that doesn't involve smashing people in the face with volleyballs, which I'm sure she'd love to hear about."

My jaw still throbs. I rub at the sore spot and wince a little. Mitch's suspicious expression eases into one of contrition yet his arms still fold unhappily.

"Well, you split my pants."

"Prove it," I retort and pull Jake away before my brother can escalate the situation.

"Bring her back in one piece, Romero, or else!" Mitch yells to our retreating backs.

"Or else what?" Jake asks as I lead him through the back door toward the stairs.

"Eli and my brothers know how to shoot." I let go of his hand and climb the stairs to change, saying over my shoulder, "They're pretty damn good at it. And so am I."

Jake waits at the bottom, looking up at me with brows high. "No shit?"

I grin. "No shit."

Our trip to the park is an epic disaster. I struggle on the skateboard. It's humiliating and I hate to fail. At anything. But I like to consider myself bold and fearless, so I put my game face on and persevere. The heat of embarrassment leaves my cheeks when I eventually catch on. Hours later, the sun is setting and I'm tired and sore, but I've begun riding that skateboard like I was born to do it. I don't just impress Jake with my new ability, I impress myself.

Jake whoops and flies by me on his own board, encouraging me to heights of recklessness. A bolt of confidence shoots through me like an electrical charge. My legs take command of my body, forcing me to perform a manoeuvre my brothers would classify as insane.

My borrowed skateboard hits the ramp and I go up, speed whipping the hair around my face. My intention is to reach the rim and come back down, except I don't. I'm airborne instead. My insides lurch with adrenaline as I leave solid ground behind. I literally fly for a single, exhilarating moment that I'll never forget. It's an incredible rush, but I come down hard and my board goes one way while I go the other.

Now I'm splayed out on the cement, staring up at the dusky afternoon sky, trying to breathe because my body is broken in a million pieces.

"Mac!" Jake yells. I turn my head. He's running toward me, skateboard tucked under his arm and panic turning his eyes wide. His golden brown hair is mussed and cheeks tinged pink from the heat of the afternoon. Jake Romero is beautiful. How did I not see that before?

"I was awesome, wasn't I?" I croak when he gets close. "At least tell me that before I die."

Jake tosses his skateboard away and skids to his knees by my side, a hysterical sound of mirth leaving his lips. Rich, brown eyes scan me hurriedly. Hands reach out to prod down my limbs. "You're not going to die, Princess."

"I think I've proved I'm no princess," I rasp.

His gaze shoots to mine, his chest rising and falling with panicked breaths. He slows it with visible effort. "I think ..."

"You think?" I prompt when he trails off.

Jake's lips press together and something equalling affection softens his features. The gold flecks in his eyes come to life, just how I knew they would. He sits back on his heels and stares as though he's realised something monumental. "I think you'll always be my princess."

I suck in a sharp breath. Jake is infiltrating my heart in some kind of sneaky ninja attack. Is this a crush? Because it feels crappy and wonderful, and I don't like it one bit.

"What?" he asks.

I shift my arm and screaming pain shoots up the limb. I cry out. "It hurts."

He looks me over again. "Where?"

"My arm," I gasp. "The right one." I tip my head up, and we both look at it. The joint of my wrist is sitting at the wrong angle. Just looking at it has me breaking out in a sweat.

"Oh shit," Jake mutters.

"I'm broken," I whisper pathetically, my head hitting the pavement as it drops back down. I always considered myself a little invincible, but this has proved me otherwise.

"You are." Jake reaches behind and tugs a phone from the back pocket of his shorts. He flips the screen and dials.

"You have a phone?" I'm fourteen and still don't have one. My parents are fools that need to get with the times. "Who are you calling? God, not my mother. Please. She'll kill me. Ring Mitch."

Jake puts the phone to his ear with an expression of disbelief. "You're kidding, right? After the whole *'bring her back in one piece'* comment? I'm so dead."

"You can't tell my parents, Romero."

"They're going to notice a broken arm," he points out.

"They won't! I promise. I'll hide it under long shirts and hoodies."

Jake's eyes widen like I've lost my mind. "In the middle of a summer heatwave?"

He ignores my protests and calls for an ambulance, even holding me down when I try rising to grab at the phone.

With it on the way, Jake tucks his phone away and clears his throat. "So ... On a scale of one to ten, just how dead am I for breaking the Valentines' only daughter?"

"For me, I'd probably say an eleven, but for you my parents will probably go easy."

His eyes harden. "I don't need anyone going easy on me, Mac. I can hold my own."

"I'm sure you can," I snap, the pain making me extra snarly, "but after everything that's happened, they're hardly going to be assholes."

He stills. "Everything that's happened?"

"With your ... your ..." Shit, I'm not supposed to know.

"You know," Jake says flatly.

"No I don't."

"Yes you do."

"No I—"

"Did your Mum tell you? Because she's supposed to be like my lawyer or something and keep my business private."

I snort. "Mum's hardly a lawyer!"

"I never said she was. I said *like* a lawyer," he snaps.

"Jared overheard—"

"Whatever, Mac."

"Dammit, Jake. I'm trying to explain here." I shift and hiss. Despite our argument, his hand closes around mine and squeezes. The small contact is comforting. "You know, I wrote you a letter after you left."

"Funny." Jake cocks his head. "I didn't get it."

I close my eyes as the adrenaline wears off and throbbing pain escalates into agony. "I never sent it," I rasp.

"Oh?"

"It's still in the top drawer of the dresser in my room."

"Why did you keep it?"

"I don't know." But I do know. It was the only tie I had to Jake. A reminder that he existed out there somewhere, under the same sun and stars. It was comforting in a way that didn't make sense to me.

The ambulance arrives, minus the flashing lights and siren. It draws a small crowd. My cheeks are hot with embarrassment when I'm carted off on a stretcher for a broken wrist. I'm thankful though. Pain has me dizzy.

I'm given painkillers. Jake sits in the back with me as the pills begin to kick in. He takes my left hand and pets it like I'm his broken puppy.

Who gets to finally go skateboarding with a cute boy and ends up getting carted away in an ambulance? I'm a dick. A confused one. Because I was so caught up in our imminent adventure, I never thought to question why Jake asked me to go with him in the first place. We're hardly on the best of terms. "Why did you ask me to the park with you?"

"I don't know. Bored I guess. I might not like you that much, Mackenzie Valentine, but you sure are entertaining. Pretty to look at too."

It actually felt like Jake and I were becoming friends, so his answer stings. I huff. "Well, your hair is too long. It makes you look like a hobo." It doesn't. It makes him look glorious, as if he were Tim Riggins stepping straight from *Friday Night Lights* and into real life. "And I don't like you either."

The ambulance takes a sharp turn. Jake grabs hold of his seat and grins down at me. "Yeah, I kinda worked that out already."

Jake

When we arrive at the hospital, Mac is whisked away for x-rays. With her gone, I expel a deep, fortifying breath and phone the Valentine household.

I'm barely given the chance to explain before the cavalry are in the car and on their way here. In what feels like minutes later, Steve, Jenna, Mitch, and Eli, descend on the hospital. I stand from my seat in the waiting room, the instinctive urge to run kicking in. I should have done it the moment I called them. Just left the hospital and never looked back. It was tempting. And easy. I'm only staying with them because the home I was boarding with lost their funding. Jenna's taking me in a second time until she can find somewhere else for me to live.

I appreciate her help, even though I don't need it. I have friends I can crash with until I'm old enough to get my own place. But the truth is that I wanted to see Mac again. Now that I have, I don't want to leave, not until I have to, which isn't the smartest decision I've ever made. Mac and her pack of brothers spell trouble. No sane person would deliberately pit themselves against any of them.

Yet here I am, feet planted to the floor, unable to move. It only proves my lack of sanity. My heart pounds as I face the fierce glowers bearing down upon me. I've broken their little girl. Vengeance will be had in one form or another, I've no doubt of that.

Steve Valentine, Mac's dad, reaches me first. His presence is commanding, his body tall and wide. If you were able to choose your own father, he would be it. With sharp hazel eyes and dark brown hair, Steve is not the type of man who sits back and commands his troops. He's the one who goes out first, leading himself into the heart of battle. Fearless, shrewd, brawny. He intimidates the hell out of me.

I straighten my shoulders.

"Romero," Steve booms. People stop and stare at him for a moment. "Where's my little girl?"

"X-ray, sir."

His nostrils flare and he folds his arms—his silent, unhappy stance prompting me to add, "She's fine. Just a fractured wrist and maybe some bruising."

Jenna, Mitch, and Eli peel off down the hall, following the directions that lead to the x-ray room. Steve remains content to eyeball me. "Explain to me exactly what happened."

"Mac tangled with a skateboard, sir."

"And?"

"And the skateboard won."

Steve draws in a deep breath. I watch his wide chest expand beneath his folded arms and wait for the explosion. "Whose idea was it to go skateboarding?"

"Mine." I lift my chin, bracing for his anger. Only it doesn't come. He chuckles softly instead. It leaves me baffled. "Sir?"

Steve grasps my shoulder, giving it a squeeze, a sharp one that has me wincing. Fucking *ouch*. "You'll learn."

"I'll learn?"

He nudges my shoulder, pushing me into walking alongside him. "Trouble finds my daughter wherever she goes. Mackenzie is rash and irresponsible. I won't have you encouraging her into any kind of risky activity. She does better at more simple activities, like reading or erm ..." He clears his throat. "Well, reading is good."

Is he serious? "That's no way to live."

Steve halts me in front of the hospital vending machine, his hazel eyes hardening fiercely. "Are you questioning my duty to keep my daughter safe?"

"No, sir."

"Good." He gives my back a slap. Then he pulls out his wallet. He opens it, peels off a five dollar note, and tucks it into the top pocket of my shirt. "Here. Buy yourself something to eat."

With a nod, he walks off down the same hallway toward the x-ray room.

I shake my head and turn back to the vending machine. After inserting the note, I choose a packet of salted peanuts. Mac likes them. I watched her snacking on them by the pool before she got beaned by the volleyball.

"Really?" Mitch's voice behind me is packed with anger. "My little sister is lying in a hospital bed, bruised and broken because of you, and you're out here worried about your stomach?"

My eyes close for a brief second. *Princess, you better be worth it.*

I collect the peanuts and turn. "Dramatic, much? She's not on death's door, Valentine. She has a fracture."

The comment has Mitch visibly fuming. I cop a jab to the chest. "You need to stay away from Mac."

I know that better than he does. But it's too late. For some reason that knowledge has a grin tugging at the corners of my lips. I try fighting it, but not hard enough.

He fumes harder. "You think this is funny?"

"No. Actually, I agree with you. I need to stay away from your sister."

Mitch's eyes widen, clearly taken aback at my agreement. "Good."

"The thing is…" I wave the peanuts in his face "…I don't want to."

And with that I walk off down the hall toward x-ray, whistling lightly and wondering at my own idiocy.

Clearly, I'm screwed, but what the hell, right? Life is meant for living and nothing makes me feel more alive than when I'm with Mac.

Chapter Three

Mac

"It's the cast," I complain to Jake when I lose at another round of Deadliest Warrior, a video game I'm teaching him to play. After having had the plaster on for two weeks, I'm slowly losing the will to live. Who breaks their wrist in the middle of a heatwave? The combined itching and sweating has me on a rampage that no one, bar Jake, has been able to put up with. "It's wrecking my co-ordination."

A pathetic lie, but I've been playing this game forever and somehow Jake has beginner's luck. I've learned from long ago never to admit defeat. Not in this house. It's better to quit playing rather than risk losing another round, so I toss my controller on the sofa beside me and let my head loll back against the cushion.

"You don't want another round?" he asks.

"I'd rather have a tooth pulled," I mumble under my breath.

"What was that?" Jake's eyes crinkle with amusement. He heard me.

"You mean does she want another thrashing?" Jared snorts from the recliner beside the sofa. He reaches across and snatches my abandoned controller. "Mac, you suck at this game."

Straightening in my seat, I curl the fingers of my right hand around the cast and hold it up in a threat. "Come a bit closer and say that."

Jared laughs and leans forward, within swinging distance. I know his plan is to pull back at the last minute so I'll look lame hitting air, but Jake taught me a little something the other day about core strength and how it gives a punch more speed and power.

I tighten every muscle I have, plant my feet hard against the floor, and I jab with force. Sharp stabbing pain ricochets up my forearm, and Jared reels back. The controller clatters to the floor.

"Sonofabitch," he hisses, holding a hand to his eye.

"Holy shit!" I cry out, shocked at making contact. I want to bust out a victory dance, but I'm in a world of hurt. White lights dance across my vision and a cold sweat breaks over my brow.

"Mac!" Jake tosses aside his own controller and half stands from his chair on my left. I throw out my good arm, warding him off. "I'm fine," I bite out through gritted teeth as Jared flounders like a turtle on its back. "Just let me enjoy the moment."

"I don't think that's a good idea," he cautions.

Jake's right. There's no time for that. My brother is going to recover any second and launch a serious counterattack. "Let's get out of here."

We stumble over gaming console cords in our haste to leave the living area. "Mac!" Jared shouts at our rapidly retreating backs. "You are so fucked!"

"Jared!" Mum's yell comes from the kitchen just moments after I slam the front door behind us.

"How's your arm?" Jake asks, stepping off the patio behind me.

Throbbing like a bitch. "It's fine. That punch though, it was awesome, right?"

"Very impressive. Just like we practiced." He glances at me, a grin on his face and eyes squinting from the midday sun. "Remind me never to piss you off, ok?"

"You already do. Every day." He doesn't. "When are you leaving again?" I tease as we walk down the driveway. Our house is located in Balmain, an inner-west suburb of Sydney. It's an expensive area, but we aren't wealthy like most of the neighbours in our street. The house belonged to my grandparents. They passed away long before I arrived in the world, so it's the only home I've ever known. I can't imagine how Jake handles living in a bunch of different foster houses.

I glance across at him as we continue down the road, heading toward Mort Bay Park by the harbour. The grin has slipped from his face. The underlying reality is that Jake's stay with us is temporary and not something we talk about. "I can leave now if my staying here bothers you."

I nudge his shoulder with mine. "I was only joking."

Jake stops right in the middle of the road. He looks me in the eye when I stop beside him. "I know, Mac, but I'll be leaving as soon as another foster home becomes available anyway."

My stomach sinks at hearing my fear verbalised. "Leaving where?"

"Wherever." His eyes darken and I see weariness in their depths. "I don't get to choose."

"Maybe you can, Jake. Stay with us. Permanently. I'm sure Mum and Dad would consider—"

He cuts me off. "No."

"No? Just like that? You won't even ask?"

"No, Mac, I won't. It's not …" Jake's lips press together. "I can't ask them to do that."

My brows draw together. Why won't he even try? "Yes. You can."

"You don't get it, Princess."

"What don't I get?"

He glances down. I follow his gaze and see his palm held out in invitation. I slide my hand in his, shivering at the connection when his fingers tighten around mine. "That. How can I ask to stay when I feel this for you? It's not right."

I raise my head until our eyes meet and my heart skips a beat. He feels something for me? I have a sudden urgent need to know exactly what that is. "How do you feel?"

Jake pauses for a moment, his expression hard and intense. It makes him seem so much older than his fifteen years. "Like I belong to you, Mackenzie Valentine. That's how I feel."

Jake

I take a step forward and lean in close. Mac tilts her head upward and before I can think about what I'm doing, I press my lips to hers. They're softer than clouds and she smells so good, like a combination of sunshine and flowers. My head spins under the hot sun and my pulse skyrockets. I pull back quickly. I've never kissed a girl before, but kissing Mac is something I've thought about a million times—just not something I ever planned to do. It's like the saying "*don't bite the hand that feeds you*," though in this instance it's more a case of "*don't mess around with the daughter of the parents who house you.*"

Mac stares up at me, seemingly speechless for once.

"I'm sorry," I say on a rough breath.

"Sorry?" Her eyes drop to my lips before rising again. "Sorry for what?"

"For kissing you."

"I'm not," she says boldly. "Do it again."

"What?"

"You heard me. Kiss me again, Jake. I liked it."

She liked it? Mac *liked* me kissing her? I apologised because I figured she'd be mad for taking liberties, but if she wants me to do it again, I'm not even going to hesitate.

I put my hands on her hips and Mac puts hers on my shoulders, waiting. It's awkward, but it's also the sweetest, hottest moment of my entire life and I never want it to end.

My lips find hers again, and her hands skim over my shoulders, twining around my neck as her fingers trail through the ends of my hair.

I could stand here all day, but we're on the road. Even though it's a quiet street, it's possible we could get mowed down at any moment. The thought of putting Mac in the hospital a second time is enough incentive to have me pulling back.

"Don't leave," she tells me, her lips swollen and eyes unfocused in a way I've never seen before. Her slender fingers tighten their hold on me. "Stay."

I stare down at her and realise she doesn't mean right now in this moment, she means permanently. In the Valentine household. I want it so much I can taste it, but she's asking the impossible. She's asking me to do what I know is the wrong thing.

"I can't."

Mac lifts her chin. Frustration lines her brow. "You can."

"But I won't. I told you before, it's not right."

"Screw what's right." She steps back, anger flaring. "What about me? About us? What if they move you so far away I never see you again?"

I hesitate, my lungs squeezing at the thought. "They won't."

"You don't know that."

"You're right, I don't, but you don't have to think the worst."

"Expecting the worst means never being disappointed."

"That's not true. Just because you know something bad is coming doesn't make it hurt any less when it happens. Trust me, Princess."

"Don't lecture me," Mac snaps.

She turns, heading back toward the house. My eyes follow her as she stalks her way up the street. "You're just going to stomp off in a hissy fit?"

Mac spins around and walks backward. "Hissy fit? Screw you, Jake Romero."

"You still haven't grown up, have you, Mac?"

An angry growl escapes her throat, but she doesn't say anything. She just turns back around and keeps walking, leaving me standing by the side of the road.

"Well that went well," I mutter, coming to the realisation that kissing Mackenzie Valentine was stupid as fuck.

Mac

"Mac?" my mum calls out when the front door slams behind me. "Is that you?"

"Yeah," I call back, heading straight for my room. I need a minute to process that kiss. That *kiss*. Oh my god.

She walks out of the kitchen, wiping her hands on a towel. "Is Jake with you?"

Taking in her serious expression, I pause on the first stair. She's relaxed her rule of late on the *"getting attached"* issue, but I think it's mostly because I don't listen and she's tired of mentioning it. "No, why?"

"I just need to talk to him." She smiles reassuringly, an unconscious action she sometimes does to pretend everything is fine when it isn't. "Have you had lunch?"

"I'm not hungry," I mutter, hearing her sigh behind me as I jog up the stairs. It's the truth. There's a lump in my throat because Jake is going to leave and there's nothing I can do to stop it happening.

An hour later I'm sitting cross-legged on my bed, trying to focus on a book, but I can't. Instead, I feel Jake's lips on mine. The warmth of them. The softness. The heat that licked fire through my insides. I set the paperback aside when a tap comes at my open door. My eyes lift. Jake stands there, his expression passive. That's how I know and hurt rises swiftly in my chest.

"You're leaving."

"I'm sorry."

"No you're not," I mutter like a sullen child.

Jake walks into my room. The bed dips when he sits down on the edge in front of me. "I don't want to leave."

"When are you going?"

"In the morning. They have a foster home for me in Melbourne."

"Melbourne?"

I fight back the urge to cry. Melbourne isn't exactly a quick walk to the park. The city is a nine-hour drive south of here, and right now it's so far away it may as well be Narnia.

"Well, it's probably for the best," I tell him.

Jake pulls back a little in surprise. "It is?"

"It'll give me the opportunity to find someone who kisses better than you."

God, you are such a bitch, Mackenzie. First making him feel guilty for something he has no control over and now trying to make him jealous. What the hell is wrong with you?

I don't know! I tell the voice in my head. *I don't know what's wrong with me, but I feel like shit. And if I'm feeling like shit, I want to make sure he is too. I want to know I'm not alone in this.*

"The hell you will," Jake growls at me.

You like him, that's what's wrong with you.

NO! I don't want to. Not if he's leaving.

"The hell I won't," I growl back.

"You can't."

"Why not?"

"Because the thought makes me feel sick."

I try picturing an image of Jake kissing another girl, but my mind pushes it away before it fully forms like some kind of self-protection mechanism.

"I think ..."

"You think?" he prompts when I trail off.

"I think I might feel the same." *Goddammit.* Because where does that leave us?

Jake exhales deeply as if my response gives him some kind of relief.

"But what does it even matter?" I ask. "You're leaving."

"We can keep in touch."

He doesn't mean it because the smile forming on his lips doesn't reach his eyes. Jake is my partner in crime. He's the boy that makes me feel like I can do anything, and I'm losing him.

"Sure we can," I reply, but my voice is flat, and he knows I don't mean it either.

Chapter Four

Jake

Six months later...

It's three p.m. and my lips flatten as I leave the school gates. I'm not in a hurry to get home. There's no food there, and I'm starving. We've been without power for two days now and what little food we did have has begun to spoil. My foster carers are late paying the electric bill. Again. A cold, dark, hungry night stretches ahead of me. It's about as exciting as my history class this afternoon on the impact of migrants on Australian society.

The topic had been a waste of time. What does the impact matter? These people are human beings who need somewhere to live, and our country has the space. The end.

Besides, I know how they feel. Not having a home or a sense of belonging to someone or something is like being adrift at sea with no safe harbour to set down anchor. For a small moment in time, Mackenzie Valentine had been my safe harbour. I had belonged to her.

But like all good things, my time there came to an end. Jenna found me a foster home here in Melbourne. It's a nine-hour drive from Sydney, but there are few people willing to take in a fifteen-year-old boy. I had little choice but to move.

Mac wanted me to stay, and I wanted it too. More than anything. The Valentines are the definition of real family. They have a deep, underlying bond of love, loyalty, and protection. They don't believe family is important, they believe it's everything. Who wouldn't want to be a part of that?

But I didn't ask them if I could stay. My father had taught me respect and living under their roof while my hands and mouth were all over their daughter wouldn't have been right. Though now I'm wishing I stayed. Screw respect. Living here fucking sucks.

"Wait up, Romero!"

I half turn as I dawdle down the path outside the gates of school. Luke Fox is jogging to catch up, so I pause. He's in the same grade as me. We struck up a friendship based on a mutual love of cars, but he and his older brother, Leander, are in a local gang. I'm not one to get caught up in gossip mongering, but if the rumours are true, the Fox brothers are into the kind of shit I don't need to get caught up in. I barely have a roof over my head as it is.

"Hey, Fox."

He grins as he catches up, his eyes bright and blond hair mussed and sweaty from our afternoon practice of school football. Luke is a big guy for his age, but I'm bigger, and in football size is just about everything. That afternoon we'd played a scrimmage on opposing teams. Mine won. Mostly because whenever I had the ball, he was the only one willing to tackle me for it, and I had the ball *a lot*.

"Wanna go do something cool with me?"

"What, right now?" My stomach growls, reminding me that a body this size needs more fuel than it's getting. I begin to walk again and he follows alongside me.

"Yes, now. It's my birthday. Lee's taking me to get my first tattoo and then we're going out for burgers."

Goddamn. Burgers? I want to weep. "I didn't know it was your birthday. Sweet sixteen, huh?"

He shrugs like it's no big deal. "Come with us."

I swallow the bitter taste of envy. "I can't today."

A car rumbles to the kerb beside us and blares its horn. We stop and watch as the window comes down, revealing Leander. His hair is a shade darker than Luke's and hangs in his eyes. Black RayBans cover his eyes, and he's wearing a flannel shirt with the sleeves ripped off. He looks like he's stepped straight from the set of *The Outsiders*.

"Lee!" Luke hollers, his excitement barely restrained as he steps toward the car. Leander grabs a packet of cigarettes from the dashboard and taps one out before sticking it between his lips. He lights it and draws deeply.

I begin walking backward, my eyes shifting to Luke. "Happy birthday, mate."

"Wait," he orders and looks to his brother. "Romero is coming with us." I begin to protest, still moving away from them when he adds the words, "Lee can pay."

"Yeah, no worries," Leander replies and rests his arm across the open car window. "Get in."

Shit. I can't expect Luke's brother to buy me food. I'm not a charity case. I jab a thumb behind me. "You know, I should get going. I—"

Leander exhales a plume of smoke out the window and growls, "Get in, you fuckers. I got shit to do before we go get this tatt, and I'm running late as it is."

Luke holds the back passenger door open and raises his brows at me, his voice taking on a whiney tone. "Come on, Romero."

"Yeah, come on, Romero." Leander grins. The lit cigarette dangles from his lips. "Little Fox needs a big strong man to hold his hand while he gets the needle."

Luke scowls. "Get stuffed, Lee."

Lee laughs. So do I. And then I realise I'm being stupid. The Fox brothers aren't so bad and I'm hungry as fuck. What can going to get a burger with a friend from school hurt? With a careless shrug, I walk toward the car. "I didn't realise you were such a baby, Fox. Maybe I should show you how it's done."

Luke's dark brown eyes light up. "You could get a tattoo with me."

My heart gives a pang of longing. I've always wanted one. When I get a job, my first paycheque is going on ink. "Maybe next time," I tell him, shifting across the seat to make room. "Besides, you have to be eighteen for that, don't you?"

"Pffft," he says as I slide inside the car. "Lee is my official guardian. He can sign something that says I'm allowed. He can sign you one too."

Luke jumps in the back beside me. He shuts the car door and climbs through the middle to sit in the front passenger seat.

"But he's not my guardian," I point out.

"It doesn't really matter," Leander says. "I know the owner." He accelerates wildly, pulling out on to the street. "And it's Little Fox's birthday. If he wants you to get a tattoo with him, then I'll pay for it."

Disappointment flattens my lips. "I won't have the cash to pay you back anytime soon."

"It's cool." Leander lifts the sunglasses from his eyes and meets my gaze through the rear vision mirror. "You can owe me one."

After peeling off my shirt, I take my seat on the chair. The owner of *Ink My Life* tattoo studio hands me the red folder I was looking through earlier.

"Point the image out for me, mate."

I've already told him the number of the image. One six eight. Those three digits identify the first tattoo of my life. My heart pounds as I flip through the plastic-sleeved pages. When I reach the tiara halfway through the book, I tap my finger against it. The artwork isn't girly in the least. It's dark and filled with shadows of grey. The tips aren't edged with jewels but instead bear sharp points, some of them dripping with blood. "This one."

His expression is dubious. "You sure?"

Nothing represents Mackenzie Valentine better than this. It's perfect. A faint smile edges the corners of my mouth. "Sure as fuck."

"Righteo," he mutters, standing from the wheeled stool he was sitting on. "It doesn't get any surer than that."

Luke shuffles over when the ink technician begins his work, placing the tiara on my left pec, just above the nipple. Luke has just finished getting a fox placed on his right bicep. It's not finished yet. The tattoo has been bandaged for him to return another day.

I wait for the smart comment about my chosen tattoo as he watches. He doesn't disappoint. "Dude. You're getting a crown?"

"It's a tiara," I correct.

"Same thing."

"No it's not."

Laughter lights his eyes. "Is this part of your gender reassignment?"

"Bite me," I mutter, ignoring the irritating little jabs of the needle.

Luke studies the image for a long moment before looking at me. "What happened? Some princess break your heart?"

I snort. "Nope."

"Then what?"

There's no explaining Mac in one simple sentence. I don't even try. But I do correct his assumption. "She didn't break my heart. She stole it. It belongs to her now."

Leander rolls his eyes from where he sits on the counter behind us sucking on another cigarette. That shit he'd had to do earlier? A drug delivery. The heavy pounding of my pulse belonged to fear. I can be arrested for association. Not to mention being involved with drugs, or people who use them, isn't my scene. I justify it by telling myself that I'm not involved; tagging along doesn't make me a part of their world. Besides, I want that burger, and I want this tattoo more than anything.

"You're what, fifteen?" Leander huffs. "You don't even know love yet."

"Get stuffed," Luke tells him for the second time that afternoon. "Romero is almost sixteen, right?" He looks at me and I shrug in return. Sixteen is another five months away, but we can call that *almost sixteen* if he wants to. "You act like you're all that, Lee, but being eighteen doesn't make you the king of everything."

"I never said I was," Leander replies coolly, stubbing his cigarette out in the glass ashtray beside him, "but I do know that the girl Romero is getting crowned in ink for will be with someone else by the time he reaches his eighteenth birthday. Mark my words."

Mac and I made no promises, but Leander's cynical comment and the image it forms in my head has my fingers curling into fists. "You want to bet on that?"

His eyes spark with interest. "Sure."

"A thousand bucks." My self-assurance has just been rocked and now I have to fake it, but I've overshot the mark into reckless territory. I don't even have a dollar to piss on.

"Hardly!" Leander pushes off from the counter and walks over. "Ten thousand."

Luke folds his arms. "For fuck's sake, Lee. Romero doesn't have that kind of cash to throw around." He looks at me. "Do you?"

Leander cocks his head. "Relax, Little Fox. If I can have that kind of cash, so can he. If he wants to."

My nails dig into the foamy armrests of the chair. "You're saying that like I'm destined to lose."

"If I want you to lose, then you'll lose." Leander's eyes take a dark turn. "I'll make sure of it."

"Well, he's not eighteen yet," Luke advises, waving his arms like he's trying to disperse the crackling tension his older brother created. "He's got two years to win."

Leander's brow arches with cynicism. "Or two years to lose."

Or two years to get the hell out of dodge. Mac will have my balls if she ever finds out I'm betting hard cash on her affections.

Leander and Luke Fox deliver me home hours later. We pause for a collective beat of silence as they take in the worn timber cladding and sagging porch. The house is like a battered old work boot. The interior remains dark and as welcoming as a dip in the Arctic with a pod of killer whales. It's no surprise to see my foster carers left the electric bill unpaid today. Assholes.

I open the back passenger door and step out.

"I'll walk you in," Luke says quickly and jumps out of the car alongside me.

"Hey!" Leander calls from his open window as we walk across the front yard. "Don't forget you owe me one now, Romero."

That sounds ominous. Owing Leander Fox isn't one of the smartest things I've ever done, but I have a belly full of burgers and beer and I'm feeling magnanimous so I don't have the heart to care. I wave him off. "Yeah, sure. Whatever you need."

Luke stands on my left as I put the key in the lock of the front door. I don't want him to see how I live, but he's clearly curious. His eyes are focused on the darkened interior through the window. I pause. "You know, it's not a prom date. You don't have to walk me inside."

His gaze shifts to me and he grins. "And here I was hoping you'd put out."

"Pfft. In your dreams."

With a faint laugh, Luke looks back through the window. "It's dark inside. Folks not home?"

"Not my folks," I mutter.

"Oh." He nods as though he understands all about those three little words. "Fosters?"

"Yeah."

Knowing I can't stand here all night with the key in the lock, I twist it clockwise and shove the door open. Luke doesn't waste time. He pushes his way past me and inside. His hand goes straight for the light switch in the entry. The sound of a *click* renders the air but nothing happens. He flicks it a few more times. "Power's out."

"Yeah," I say a second time. "Must be an outage in the area."

He's nice enough not to mention the blinding lights coming from every other house in the street. "Well, I better go before Lee gets the shits and takes off without me."

The tension in my shoulders loosens a fraction. "Good idea. Thanks for the invite today."

"No worries." Luke starts for the door and pauses, half-turning to look at me. His forehead creases with apparent anxiety. "See you at school, yeah?"

Air leaves my lungs in a *whoosh* and my eyes find my feet. "About that ..."

An excruciatingly tense moment of silence fills the room.

"Christ!" he mutters. "Seriously?" Luke knows what I'm going to say before I say it. The words are either written on my face or he's heard it all before. "Get off your high horse, Romero. It pays the fucking bills, don't it?"

Luke flings the flyscreen door open and kicks it backward on his way out. It slaps angrily against the worn timber framework as he stalks outside.

"Fox! Wait!" I call, following him out.

"No, fuck it," he calls back without turning around. He's already jogging down the porch steps. His feet kick up dirt as he motors toward the car where Leander's fingers tap an impatient rhythm against the steering wheel. "No one wants to be friends with the brother of the local drug dealer, do they?"

His retort is sharp but the underlying hurt in his tone twists me in a knot for judging him. "It's not—"

Luke turns around, cutting me off. "I don't blame you." He takes a step forward until he's in my face. "But at least I have a roof over my head. And food. And decent fucking clothes," he says, sneering at the ratty school uniform I'm still wearing. After a quick flick of his eyes at the dark house behind me, he adds, "And at least I still got fucking family who gives a shit."

His words are an uppercut to the jaw. Swift and painful, they almost knock me backward. My hands fist. The short nails dig into the flesh of my palms, bracing me as I take the hit.

"Don't be an asshole," Leander calls to Luke through the open car window. Then he looks at me. "You ever need money, Romero, you come see me."

"Not sure he'd lower himself," Luke says to his brother while looking at me.

My jaw ticks. "I don't need money."

"Sure you don't." Luke walks around the front of the car, his hand going for the passenger door.

"Wait!" I call out. His hand lifts the handle before he pauses. "I'll see you at school."

I don't wait for a response. Instead, I turn, jog up the porch steps, and make my way back inside my own private hell. My plan is to fall facedown on my old, shitty mattress and revel in the feeling of a full belly, but I need to relieve myself first. My underage body has consumed enough beer to sink a battleship, and now it wants out.

The phone rings, the shrill sound diverting me from my path toward the bathroom. It startles me for a moment before I realise that the landline doesn't need electricity to work. The phone sits mounted against the wall beside the kitchen counter. I answer it with a tired "Hello?"

"Jake! Honey."

It's Jenna Valentine. Her voice is so familiar and so similar to Mac's that it hits me like a ton of bricks. My back slowly slides down the wall, the phone pressed hard to my ear.

"I've been trying to reach you for days."

Her lack of success is no surprise. I avoid being home. My afternoons are spent at the library. My grades are the only thing I can control. They're my ticket to better things. My ticket back to Mac. I can save some cash. Attend university in Sydney. Maybe Mac and I can go to the same one. Even move in together. If she hasn't forgotten me.

"Hey, Mrs. Valentine." I swallow the ache so she doesn't hear it in my voice. "How you doin'?"

"I'm good, thank you, Jake."

"How's Mac doin'? Does she—" It's an effort to halt the question. The last thing I should be asking Jenna is whether Mac ever mentions me. Of course she doesn't. "Does she still get into scraps like she did when I was there?"

"You know our Mac, honey." My fingers tighten on the phone. I did. And I want to know more. So much more. But it's not our time. Not right now. Perhaps I should accept the fact that maybe it was never but when you have nothing else except hope, letting go of it is like prying your fingers from the edge of a cliff.

"Actually, I was calling about your father."

"Oh?" I prompt.

I haven't contacted him since I left. Being here means being unable to visit him at the hospital every fortnight like I used to. I miss him, though mostly I miss who he used to be. There's no talking to my dad on the phone. Words are difficult for his mind to find and when he does, understanding them through the stuttering speech is just as hard. What is there to say anyway? *"Dad, you were the best, but I don't know how to communicate with you anymore?"*

He was the man who could do anything. At the age of four I spent a year refusing to go anywhere without my Superman cape. I was the hero sent from the planet Krypton and Dad was my Jonathan Kent. Between us, we were going to save the world. But everyone has to grow up sometime and as I got older, I realised he was just a man like any other. At least he was the good kind. The kind that raised me alone after my mother died giving birth. She didn't survive the emergency caesarean.

I know her only through photographs and stories from Dad. I have her laugh, and I have the same dimple that deepens my left cheek when I smile. I also have her eyes. Dad would look at me sometimes and flinch. Then he'd turn away, as if my image burned him. Some days I heard him talking to her. He would ask her what to do or tell her how I'd fallen off my bike that day and scraped my knee.

Dad never had a girlfriend after she died. He's only thirty-five now, and he never will. He's an empty shell of his former self, and I'm stuck here in this shithole without him. It's not a happy ending. Life has a way of ripping those out from underneath you and handing them to someone else.

"They're letting him leave the hospital."

"But ... Does that mean he's getting better?"

Jenna's tone turns sad. "No, honey. That's not going to happen. I'm sorry."

My teeth clamp together as I fight the tears. I know that. *I know.* But accepting it is another thing altogether. "So where is he going to go? They can't just kick him out!"

"I'm afraid there aren't many options. I'm trying to find a government-funded care facility that will take him," she advises, her voice taking on a soothing tone in deference to my obvious panic. "We'll work it out, okay?"

"What kind of care facility?"

There's a long pause. Jenna is hesitating. It makes me fear the answer, but I need to know. "Please. Tell me."

"Jake, honey, there might be an aged care facility available, but I just don't know. I think it's only partly subsidised. I have to look into it a bit more."

"Aged care?" I bend over on myself, my chest tight as hot tears roll down my cheeks. "But he's only thirty-five!"

"I'm so sorry. The government won't fund a private nurse and this might be all they have available. We tried to—"

I can't hear anymore. It's too painful. I stand and jam the handset back in its socket ending the call.

Moving down the unlit hallway, I find my way to the bathroom. I peel off my shirt in the dim light of the moon and face the mirror. My hair is mussed and my eyes red. Wet tracks mark my cheeks from the tears.

I wipe them away and drop my gaze to the square white patch across my chest. With shaky fingers, I snag the corner edge and peel it back slowly. My tattoo reveals itself. Angry. Red. Perfect. I stare at it until my harsh breathing calms.

"Do you miss her?"

Mac asked me about my mother. We were on the sun lounger by the pool and her eyes were on Jenna as she watched her own mother weed the garden bed in the back corner.

"You can't miss what you never had," I replied.

Green eyes of confusion shot my way. "But you do have her."

"Do I?" I waved a hand around. Sarcasm made my movements jerky. "Where? I don't see her, Mac."

Her expression was one of utter disgust, as if I'd just admitted to throwing little puppies off tall buildings. "You don't need to see her. She's in your heart, asshead."

I didn't believe her at the time. I still don't. Mac is the only one in there, and she takes up so much space it leaves no room for anyone else.

After dumping the bandage in the trash, I make my way to my room. Put in this same situation, Mac wouldn't sit back and do nothing. She wouldn't let this happen. So neither will I. My father needs a care facility, and I need to find my way back to Sydney.

"You ever need money, Romero, you come see me."

Leander Fox doesn't mean a hand out. No way in hell. I'll have to earn it, and the thought of how I'll have to earn it makes me sick to my stomach but the only other choice I have is to sit back and let fate take its course. And as far as I'm concerned, fate can go fuck itself.

Chapter Five

Jake

Luke dumps my stuffed satchel on the queen-sized bed. It represents everything I own in the world. He turns and waves his arms in a grand gesture. "This is it. What do you think?"

My eyes take in the room. It's big, with an airy window and walls the colour of stone. The walnut timber furniture is finished in a rich gloss, and the white sheets are bright and crisp. The best part? When I reach over and flick on the light switch by the wall, a warm glow fills the room. "It'll do."

The comment earns me a punch to the arm. "Get stuffed, Romero. This place is a palace."

In actual fact it's a four-bedroom brick home with a granite kitchen, stainless steel appliances, and an outdoor spa that Leander has christened the 'hot tub of love.' I won't be dipping my toes in it any time soon. God knows what lives beneath the dark, bubbling water, and he can keep that information to himself.

I reach for my bag and slide the zipper open, my mind going to my first tattoo. The memory will remain forever clear. The buzz of the needle had been an annoying mosquito; the sharp point jabbed repeatedly into firm muscle until I ached for it to end. The heat of the afternoon had been relentless, the sheen of sweat dampening my palms. Afterward, we'd sat in the courtyard of the local pub listening to live music and eating thick, juicy steak burgers dripping with barbeque sauce. The sense of fullness after eating for the first time in days had felt incredible.

Two, long hungry weeks later, I did what I had to do. I made the call and sold my soul to Satan. Now here I am, moving in to Luke and Leander's house. The money Leander says I'll earn is mind-blowing. I don't have to rely on the hope of there being food to eat or clean clothes to wear. I have independence now, and it's empowering.

I left no forwarding address with my foster carers. Despite the Government doing random checks on my placement, I don't believe they'll track me down. There are thousands of kids like me. They don't have the manpower to search out each and every one of us. To them I'll just be another kid lost to the system.

"Jake."

Luke's tone is impatient as if he's been calling my name more than once.

I half-turn, pausing from tugging worn clothes from my bag and placing them onto the bed. "Thanks, Luke. I appreciate this."

"Don't thank me." His eyes take on a dark, grim expression that ruffles my nerves. "You have tonight to get through first."

Tonight my fall into the underworld will be complete. According to Leander, I can't work for them until they're sure I can be trusted. In order to do that, an initiation will take place. "Right." I resume my task, removing the shaving kit and setting it on the bed. It's black leather and had belonged to my father. "What did you have to do?"

"I didn't."

That's cause for me to pause again. "Why not?"

"Because I don't do for them what you're about to do. Leander earns all the money. I just go to school."

The thought leaves me unsteady. I sink to the edge of the bed, a shirt bunched in my hands. The thought that at least Luke and I were in this together had bolstered my courage, but I'd thought wrong. I let out a shaky breath.

"You don't have to do this," Luke says, standing over me.

My head shakes vigorously. "I do."

"I can talk to Lee. We can work something else out."

There's no talking to Lee. The deal is done. I'd rather walk out in front of an oncoming bus than face what's coming, but I have to do this. My father needs me now. My throat tightens at the staggering responsibility on my shoulders. The new care facility bills are huge. And there's no one to pay them. No one but me.

I look up at Luke, my lips flat with determination. "There's nothing to work out, Fox." Standing, I toss my shirt on the bed and clap him on the back, forcing cheer to my voice. "Let's go downstairs and get a drink."

"You're gonna need one," he mutters beneath his breath as he jogs down the steps behind me.

"Ever fired a gun?" Leander asks as we stand in the kitchen later that night.

My gaze falls on his outstretched hand. He's holding one out toward me, his eyes zeroed on mine. Shit. Double shit. There's a difference between saying I'll work for Leander and actually *working* for Leander. "Once before. At a shooting range."

His expression is a smirk. "Well, now you get to do it again."

My heart pounds as I stare at the gleaming hunk of metal in his hand. I don't want to touch it knowing its purpose is not to protect but to threaten and potentially maim. *I don't want to do this.* My gaze lifts to Leander. "What do I need a gun for?"

He shrugs. "We're owed money and we're gonna pay the man a visit." He takes a step forward and shoves it at me. "Take it, Romero. It's not gonna bite your face off."

I think of my father. Of him sitting in a wheelchair staring out the window without a nurse to care for him. And I think of Mac. Of her soft lips and how her sassy attitude sets my soul alight. And as I do, my hand closes around the deadly weapon. The steel is cool and heavy in my palm. It feels wrong. My stomach knots and my lips set in a grim line. *I don't want to do this.*

"You alright?" Leander asks.

"Sure, it won't bite my face off," I tell him, holding the grip tighter to hide the trembling of my hands. It won't do for Luke's older brother to know that I'm shit scared. "It might shoot it off though."

Leander's laugh is loud and hard. "You'll be alright. Just don't point it at your face."

"Right," I tell him, watching as he grabs his own, checks the chamber like a professional, and tucks it into the front of his jeans. I'm not game enough to do that. I'd probably shoot my dick off. "I'll be sure not to do that."

He jerks his head toward the door that connects the kitchen to the garage. "Let's go."

I take a moment after he leaves to draw a deep breath of courage. When I go to follow, Luke rounds the corner of the kitchen and catches hold of my bicep, bringing me to a halt. "Romero," he hisses urgently, his tone low. "It's not loaded."

My brow creases as I stare at him, puzzled. "What?"

Luke yanks me closer, his mouth pressing close to my ear. "It's just a test. The gun isn't loaded."

He shoves me at the door, disappearing as quickly as he appeared.

We park in an abandoned driveway. It's further down the street from the house Leander pointed out as the one we'd be visiting. There's another vehicle parked in front of us, a plain black Mazda that looks like most other cars on the road. Average and indistinguishable.

Leander instructed me earlier on the gang I'm about to get involved with. Or join *if* I satisfactorily pass the initiation. They're named the King Street Boys. And they're not just some minor-league street gang, they're the biggest gang in Melbourne. The structure rivals a corporation. The hierarchy is extensive and has tentacles that wrap around the entire state including government members, political staff, and police. Leander tells me their reach is so vast they're expanding into Sydney and beyond.

Two burly guys alight from either side of the Mazda. After shutting their doors with mutual muted *thunks,* they walk toward us. Leander showed me photos so I recognise both. Ross is tall and bulky. His hair is short and golden brown with a slight curl, and his eyes a cold, hard blue. He's twisting a ring that sits on the middle finger of his right hand. The action highlights the thick muscle of his forearm and a singular tattoo of three letters 'KSB.' He's the gang leader.

My eyes slide to Leander with surprise. I'm expecting to be nothing less than a lowly foot soldier, so why would that attract the likes of Ross? Leander doesn't acknowledge my fleeting glance. His face remains blank. I pick up his silent cue and remove the expression of surprise from my face.

The guy beside him is Boyd, head of security and recruitment. His black hair is buzzed so short it's barely there at all, and eyes darker than night are busy taking me in without giving a single thought away.

They stop in front of us. Ross tips his head at me. "You're Jonah?"

His voice is rough, like he smokes a thousand cigarettes a day, but there's also a hint of surprise in it. I nod. The name change is for protection. Gang life gets dirty. I don't want any of this to come back on me later, or anyone I care about.

"You're how old now?"

I lift my chin, trying to hide the nerves. "Sixteen."

Ross doesn't appear displeased at my youth and continues to study me carefully. "You're a big boy for sixteen."

Bigger than both of them if they want to get technical. I shrug like it's no big deal but to me it is. Having a size advantage gives me confidence I wouldn't ordinarily feel otherwise. "I work out a lot."

"Eh ... Good for you."

Boyd takes a slight step forward and his head tips a little to the side as he looks at me. "Why do you want in with the King Street Boys?"

Money, for fuck's sake. Why would anyone want to join a gang unless it was lucrative? But gang members are brothers just like bikers are, aren't they? A unit. Mess with one, you mess with all. I could have had that once, with the Valentines, and I didn't take it. The knowledge is painful.

"Family," I lie, knowing it's what they probably want to hear.

Boyd nods as though he understands. "You in the system?"

"Not anymore."

"Good. The system is fucking useless."

We're in agreement on that. The system only gave me one thing. Mackenzie Valentine. And now I don't have her anymore.

Ross clamps a hand on my shoulder. The gesture is firm and brotherly but his voice is hard and does not allow disagreement or invite further conversation. "We're your family now."

He lets go and Boyd looks between Leander and myself. "You both good to go?"

Leander answers with a lift of his shirt. It bares the gun tucked in his waistband. Mine is on the passenger-side floor of the car. That's where I'm hoping like hell it ends up staying.

Boyd's forehead wrinkles. "Where's yours?"

My lips press in a grim line, and I tuck unsteady hands inside the pockets of my jeans. Shit is getting real and my legs are five seconds away from hauling me the fuck out of here.

"You leave it in the car?" Leander asks.

"Yeah," I mutter, as if it was an accident.

"I'll get it," he tells me and makes a move to leave. Boyd slaps the back of his forearm against Leander's chest, stopping him from going anywhere. After a shared glance with Ross, he says, "I'll get it."

Boyd walks away and Ross turns his attention to me with a fold of his arms. "Jonah, you ready for this?"

Not in the least. "I don't know what *this* is."

Ross points to a red brick house further down the street. It's nondescript—the type of house you'd never pick out from a line up two days later. "The man in that house is the worst kind of scum. A convicted paedophile. Instead of being locked up, he's out here stealing our drugs and watching Boyd's youngest sister from outside the school gates. We're here to deliver him one hell of a warning."

Disgust makes my stomach churn. Paedophiles should never be free, let alone allowed anywhere near the gates of a school. It explains why both Ross and Boyd are both here tonight instead of someone lower in the hierarchy. This is personal.

Boyd returns, gun in hand. He hands it to me, his dark brown eyes staring me down until I take it.

"What kind of warning?" I ask Ross, the weapon a heavy weight in my hand.

"The kind where we go in and rough him up, tie him to a chair, and you come in after and shoot him."

I jerk visibly. *Shoot him?* I don't think so. I don't *shoot* people, regardless of their criminal past. You can't just take justice into your own hands. My eyes shift to Leander, needing to assess his reaction.

"You can do this," he reassures me in a firm voice as Ross and Boyd start toward the house.

But I can't.

"It's just a test. The gun isn't loaded."

Is Luke telling the truth?

If he is, then it means this whole scene is a setup. The man in the house must be a gang member and not who they say he is. And this so-called test is for me to shoot him. If the gun isn't loaded, they'll hear the click and that will be my passing grade—an acknowledgement that I'd been willing to do as they asked. Once over, my place in the King Street Boys will be cemented.

But fifteen minutes later, I realise there's an issue with my thought process as I stand in front of the man. Neither Ross nor Boyd told me his name, but he's roughed up and tied to a chair like I was told he would be. Silver duct tape covers his mouth and his eyes are bugged out like a goldfish. His breathing is out of control. He doesn't look like a man who knows he *isn't* about to get shot. He looks like a man who knows he is.

"It's just a test."

Ross gives the order to shoot, his voice coming to me like I'm under water. I lift the gun, the move slow and painful. My heart thumps hard enough to pound its way from my chest as I look into the man's eyes. The fear in them is a living, breathing thing between us. Wild, like an untamed animal. I turn my head to Leander. He gives me a nod. *Do it,* his eyes say.

I aim for the right shoulder.

"The gun isn't loaded."

I take a slow, deep breath and pull back on the trigger. My finger moves at a glacial pace until a metallic *click* reaches my ears. For the briefest of seconds I feel aching relief. Then gunfire blasts through the small room. The bang is deafening like lightening has struck the ground at my feet.

Blood explodes outward from the man's chest, spraying my face. The gun still rests in my outstretched arm as the force of the bullet sends him backward in the chair.

My breathing stops, shock freezing me to the floor. The man lies unmoving, a river of red leeching from beneath his body.

Luke lied.

The gun was loaded.

I've just ended a man's life.

Bile climbs my throat, its onset so swift there's no time to swallow it back down. I bend over and throw up at my feet. My stomach heaves until there's nothing left.

I straighten, hands shaking. This is a nightmare and I want to wake up. But I know I won't.

My head turns to Leander. Blood smears the back of my hand as I wipe the side of my mouth. His face is white. But why? He gave me the gun. He knew this would happen. Didn't he?

Then realisation burns me in the chest like a hot poker. I'm no longer a petty criminal. These assholes have rendered me a murderer. The death of this man is their insurance that I'll never betray who they are or what they've done, because I've done it too.

There's no escape.

It means Mackenzie Valentine will never be mine. Not now. Not after this. I've taken a life and my soul is irrevocably stained. How can I ever expect her to live with me knowing I can never live with myself?

With a hand that takes everything I have to keep steady, I hold the gun out toward Leander. He stares at it, his eyes like dinner plates. "Take the damn thing," I growl.

Leander grabs it quickly.

With hard eyes, I hide the crushing ache deep down inside and stare each man in the room down until they look away. I'm in deep now, as deep as it gets, but I'm no one's bitch. "If anyone *ever* pulls this shit on me again, I'll find you in the dead of night and slice your neck from ear to ear while you sleep."

With that I leave, shoving passed Leander.

"Jonah—"

It's all I need to snap. With the force of a heavyweight boxer, I turn and punch Luke's brother in the face. He stumbles backward and no one steps in to help. With aching knuckles, I shake out the pain and glare. "Go to hell, Lee."

As I step out into the dark of night, I feel as dead as the man I've just shot in cold blood.

Chapter Six

Mac

2 ½ years later...

I close my eyes and fall back on my bed in the early afternoon. Today is my birthday. Seventeen years old and I will never be the daughter my parents want me to be. Sweet. Well-spoken. Reticent.

My father has enrolled me at Fleur Dreyer Halvorsen and no amount of temper tantrums or fake tears will change his mind. FDH, or Fucking Dick Head school as I like to call it, is a finishing college and a "wonderful opportunity" for me. In two months, my decline into the life of a Stepford daughter will begin. My parents are eager for the transition. Whenever Fucking Dick Head school is mentioned, their eyes light up like Christmas. They want me to make friends with other people of the female persuasion. I don't have any. Most aren't willing to suffer my forthright attitude.

FDH is going to teach me how to find them. It will also teach me to smile bright in the face of adversity rather than resort to petty words and violence. Instead, I can seethe on the inside like a winner. Kind words will become my new mantra. I will use them in response to bigotry, bullying, and dishonesty rather than pulling hair or calling out Renae Sanders in science class as a mean, obnoxious twat for spreading the rumour that Fern Jeffries slept with the teacher to get her A in our Theory of Evolution assignment. I might have also super-glued her textbooks to the desk and used the Bunsen burner to singe an irreparable hole in the pink personalised drink bottle she carries everywhere, but that's merely conjecture. There's no proof.

But no more. According to Fucking Dick Head school, I will graduate with the knowledge on how to groom myself. I will learn how to artfully arrange my hair and wear makeup, walk straight, exercise, and use a knife and fork. They will bestow me with the tools necessary to radiate positivity and lasting loveliness until the end of time. My new demeanour will *attract* people (i.e. new friends) and my warm, gentle nature will be remarked upon, as if being a Stepford daughter is something to be admired.

Fuck that.

I'd rather stab my eyeballs out with a rusty fork.

I want to *live*. I want to make a difference in the world the way my brothers plan to do. Mitch is already in the academy, and Travis and Jared are gone—living on campus at Charles Sturt University and following the family path of law enforcement. My brothers are badass. That should be me too. Instead, I'm stuck here: the youngest Valentine and last to leave the nest.

I will die in my pretty pink room, festering away from boredom. Rats will come and chew at my dull, insipid carcass until nothing remains but my artfully arranged blonde hair.

"Mac?"

Mum's voice echoes up the staircase and into my room.

"Come down for tea and cake!"

I roll over and give my pillow a solid punch, using the power in my shoulder like Jake had taught me so long ago.

"Mac!"

My pillow suffers through a few more jabs.

"MAC!"

"Arrghh!"

When my brothers' turned seventeen, they snuck out for late night beers at the local pub in Manly. And when I say snuck out, I mean "snuck out" because my parents knew and turned a blind eye. Boys will be boys, apparently. Meanwhile, I get crusty oolong with a side of Angel Food cake because Mum is on a gluten-free crusade.

With a huff that goes unnoticed, I heave my body off the bed and start downstairs. If I don't, Mum will only make her way up and drag me down. At least this way I can survive their birthday song with dignity.

Last year all three brothers were here for it, forcing me to suffer through their horrendous singing. Though for a bunch of wankers, they're surprisingly astute when it comes to choosing gifts. Not that I want to give them too much credit. I *am* easy to buy for; clothes, shoes, and bags are my Kryptonite. My closet is bursting at the seams with all three, but right now they feel meaningless. Does that make me selfish? Having all these things and not caring about any of it?

They don't fill the emptiness that gurgles in my belly as I eyeball the gluten-free creation in front of me. My parents begin the birthday song as the requisite seventeen candles blaze bright enough to burn down the house. Red Velvet is my favourite cake but it was banned ever since I made it at home and Mum saw the amount of red food colouring required, which even I admit was a bit gross.

When Dad's booming voice stops and Mum's feeble warble fades, I lean over and blow the candles out.

"Make a wish, make a wish!" Mum cries, clapping her hands as though what I wish for might actually come true. I close my eyes and with tears that burn the backs of my lids, I blow out the seventeen birthday candles wishing for Jake. I wish *so hard* that my throat aches and my jaw clenches tight enough to crack in two.

But wishes are complete bullshit because he never comes.

"You're going to love it, Mackenzie." Tomorrow marks the beginning of the end of my life. Dad confirms it as he sits on the side of my bed and looks down at me. He's taken to calling me by my full name over the past two months. No one uses a nickname at Fucking Dick Head school. It's not *proper*. "You just need to give it a chance."

"Chance schmance," I mutter.

"All the girls there will be just like you. You'll make so many new friends you won't know what to do with them all."

I glare. I remove my hands from beneath the covers, rest them on top, and I glare *hard*. "What do you mean *just like me*?"

Dad's eyes cut to the side and he shifts slightly on the bed. He looks utterly uncomfortable, as if answering my question is akin to getting a tooth pulled.

My lips pinch. "Dad?"

He offers me a shrug. "Just that they're ready to be transformed into little ladies, like you are."

His comment makes me so bitter it burns the lining of my stomach clean away. I'm not the daughter they wanted. But what about what I want? *I don't want to be a lady.* I want to be myself. Strong. Independent. Smart. Someone nobody will dare to mess with. And not because she has three beefy, overprotective brothers to do her dirty work but because she's lethal in her own right. Powerful and formidable. The game changer. The Queen on a chessboard.

"Dad?"

He sighs, his expression resigned. He's clearly expecting another argument. "Yes, love?"

My eyes fall to the suitcases standing by my bedroom door. Bright white with pink trim, Mum chose them just yesterday. I'd wanted the Samsonite hardcase range. They were like the outer skin of a toffee apple. Shiny. Red. Delicious. Mum had called them *harlot bags* and after a battle of wills, I ended up with something deemed more appropriate. We left the store on edge with Mum grinding her teeth and me sulking.

At least I know what I want and I'm determined to work for it, or in this case … argue for it. But clearly it doesn't count for anything. Raising a wilful daughter is hard work. They're tired of it. Of me.

It leaves me hollow, a state of being which I thought wouldn't feel much like anything, yet it hurts more than when I came off my skateboard and broke my arm. It's a throbbing ache of hopelessness. The emotion is foreign and unpleasant. My usual demeanour is titanium, like the song. I'm bullet proof. *Shoot me down, but I won't fall.*

But in this case I'm already down. The only way to get back up is to do something bold. Something wonderfully drastic. Something that makes my heart pound incredibly hard with both fear and excitement.

I have to remove myself from the equation.

I have to *leave.*

Once the realisation swims to the surface, the stifling thick blanket of control is gone and fresh air fills my lungs.

"What is it, Mackenzie?" my father asks again as I draw a deep breath.

I shake my head, my eyes moving from the suitcases and back to him. "I love you, Dad."

He leans down and presses a kiss to my forehead, visibly relieved. "I love you too." Then he pets my head like I'm a good little puppy. "See you in the morning."

His feet are silent on the thick carpet as he crosses the room. Turning, he offers a brief smile before flicking off my bedroom light. The door is pulled closed and darkness fills my room.

It will be the last time I see my father as the person I am now. When I eventually return, I will never be the same.

Chapter Seven

Mac

I'm headed in the wrong direction. Somewhere along the city outskirts of Melbourne, I've lost my way. It's taken me a whole hour to realise. *Asshead.* If I had enough money, I would have a phone. Instead I'm cursed with a paper map and I'm ready to gouge holes through it with the bobby pin in my hair.

After kicking a few rocks, I turn back the way I came. The heat is blistering my skin and the side of the road is gravelly and dusty, but I'm along the coastline and a cool breeze lifts from the ocean and flutters my hair, swirling my short dress around my thighs. It offers only a moment of respite.

Before I can stop myself, I stick out my thumb. Hitchhiking is stupid. I know that, but my legs are ready to fold like a bad hand at poker and the closest bus stop is a half hour away.

How did I get here? I can summarise it best with numbers: nine hundred and sixty-seven dollars of savings; one mobile phone, left by the side of my bed so I can't be traced and hauled back home; one overnight bag; two long bus rides to Melbourne, paid in cash; seven hours spent sleeping at the backpacker's hostel in the city suburb of St. Kilda; three pubic hairs found on the shared, unisex toilet seat—which made me question my adventure and my whole entire existence; four subsequent nights spent at the Travelodge Hotel next to Southern Cross Station; and seven hundred and twelve dollars expended on accommodation. It's money well spent in my opinion, to have a bathroom void of strangers' pubes, but my rapidly depleting funds will send me back to the hostel tonight.

The majority of my time here, besides sleeping, eating, and window-shopping along Melbourne's famous Chapel Street, has been spent looking for Jake. Finding my way around occupies the rest of my time. Public transport in this city is like navigating the Bermuda Triangle, but I'm determined. Jake Romero once said he belonged to me. Well he still does. And I'm here to remind him.

There will be no Fucking Dick Head school. I don't need to be a lady. I just need to be myself, and being here with Jake is where I'm going to do it.

The trouble with my plan is the lack of information on his whereabouts. The night before I left, I waited until my parents had gone to bed and the house was settled before creeping down the stairs and into the study. I made three attempts on the password, knowing it wouldn't be easy. Mum approached internet security as if the FBI were intent on cracking her entire system. On the fourth try, I typed in AzaeleaBush3 at random for the simple fact she had planted three of them in the front yard just two days earlier. I know this because I offered to help. She turned me down, not wanting to risk my fresh manicure in the countdown to FDH. The password worked and her screen came to life.

That was only the first hurdle. The second was finding out Jake's file also had a password. No amount of guesswork could get it open. My frustration reached critical levels by the eighth attempt when I heard a loud *clank* from the kitchen, followed by the soft *bang* of a cupboard door, then the *whoosh* of water gushing from the tap.

I was ten seconds away from getting found out. I utilised five of them to write down the name of Jake's file—Jake Romero, De Luca, Melbourne—and tucked it inside the pocket of my pyjama pants. I used the other five to shut down the computer. There would be time later to find out what the name of his file meant.

Mum's soft voice called out as I was leaving the study. "Mackenzie?"

She was standing at the kitchen entrance, glass of water in hand as she watched me approach. Her neat bob of hair was mussed and green eyes sleepy. My heart sank. I would miss my parents. They only wanted what they thought was best, but they were wrong and unwilling to listen.

Leaving was the only way.

"Hey, Mum."

"It's midnight," she told me, pointing out the obvious. "What are you doing up?"

"I thought I heard a noise. You?"

"I couldn't sleep." Mum set the glass down and opened up her arms. I stepped inside them, and she wrapped me up. The scent of Chanel No. 5 was subtle and enveloped me as warmly as her arms. "I'm going to miss you."

"Then don't send me," I muttered into the soft wool of her dressing gown, stubborn to the core.

She sighed. It was the exact same sigh Dad had made earlier that night and a reminder that they were tired of me and trying to change who I was. "Please, let's not argue about this anymore."

So I didn't.

I simply untangled myself from my mother's embrace, went upstairs, packed a small overnight bag and hid my bigger suitcases in the back of my closet. By the early hours of the morning I was gone.

I left them a note, telling them I had decided to leave for FDH early and caught a cab to the school. My explanation was that I didn't want any weepy goodbyes. Of course, they'll find out soon enough when the school calls to question them on my AWOL status, but I'm hoping by that time I'll be with Jake and have some kind of plan.

"Beeeeeeeeeeeeeeep!"

The loud horn blasts me sideways, jolting me from the memory. The receding car gets my middle finger as dust swirls up, coating my face and dress and filling my lungs. "Asshole!" I wheeze.

The rumbling engine of another car sounds in the distance behind me. I stick my thumb out as I rummage through my bag for a bottle of water, or gum, or whatever I can find to remove the dust from my mouth.

After some investigative Googling upon my arrival in Melbourne, I found out that De Luca isn't a suburb of Melbourne. It's a surname. A further search found only a few in the area. The small number was in my favour but after hunting down most with no luck, I'm left with one more shot. I don't have a plan beyond this. It's my last shot and it has to work.

My handbag search produces an old, furry eucalyptus lozenge. I'm almost tempted, but I toss it away as the rumbling car gets closer. It doesn't sound as if it's slowing down. I jab my thumb out a little higher.

It doesn't stop. The engine growls as it flies past. I spit a curse and choke on another cloud of dust. The car is a rusty vintage Holden, the body painted pale blue and the rooftop white. It's a death trap anyway. I lower my thumb. I don't need this. I need a payphone where I can call a decent cab and find my way back to Pube Hostel.

Ten metres ahead the Holden veers off to the side and screeches to a stop, skidding more dust and gravel in its wake. I halt on the spot, my gut giving me a fight or flight response. The male driver swivels in his seat. I feel his stare for several moments. I use the time debating whether to run in the opposite direction or walk toward the car. Just as I make the decision to turn and pretend I wasn't hitchhiking at all, a tattooed arm comes out of the driver's side window and opens the car door from the outside. A guy steps out. Dark aviators cover his eyes and silky brown hair falls in his face. He's wearing low-slung boardshorts, flip-flops, and a loose muscle tee shirt that shows off thick biceps and tanned skin.

He starts toward me. That's when I realise my mother's warnings about hitchhiking weren't helicopter parenting like I always complained but smart advice.

My hand tightens on my bag. I step back when he rips his sunglasses off and speaks as he walks closer. "What in the goddamn everloving fuck?"

A lightning bolt of shock zings through me as I look into a pair of beautiful dark brown eyes. My mouth falls open and my heart pounds a thunderous beat as he nears me. "Jake?"

"Hitchhiking?" he grinds out in a voice deeper than familiar. "Do you have a death wish?"

"I ... I ... No," I stutter, caught in shock as he reaches me.

Had I wanted to find him so badly that I'm now hallucinating? I blink hard, but when I look again he's still there. His chest rises and falls, and his pulse beats visibly in his neck. And those eyes. I know them. Stumbling across Jake along this road was sheer dumb luck. I can barely believe it. "I was—"

"You were what?" he shouts.

My eyes burn when I realise my mistake in coming here. In thinking it will be just how it was before. Jake is a stranger. His face has more angles and golden stubble lines his jaw. His frame is filled out. Shoulders rounded with muscle hulk over me, intimidating and overwhelming. Jake isn't the sweet boy I remember, but a harsh, aggressive man.

"I was looking for you," I answer.

Jake stares for an endless moment, his anger appearing to deflate. "Mac," he mutters gruffly, his eyes roaming over my face. "You were looking for me?" His gaze shoots over my shoulder, searching as if he expects my brothers to appear from nowhere. "By yourself?"

I open up my heart. "I missed you."

"Princess." With that word Jake changes from a stranger to the boy I used to know. Joy washes over me. "Are you crazy?" he asks then shakes his head. "What am I saying? Of course you are."

"No crazier than you," I retort.

Jake's eyes drop to my lips. "There's that smart mouth I remember." He crooks a finger. "Come closer."

I take a step forward and he grasps my jaw with his thumb and forefinger, tilting my head upwards. He turns my head slowly left and right for a thorough inspection. "Goddamn, Mac." A broad grin stretches over his face. It steals the breath from my lungs. "You haven't changed a bit."

Jake has. So much I barely recognise him anymore.

He lets go of my chin and steps back, eyes dropping to my chest. "Well, maybe a little," he adds. "That flat chest has grown some tits."

I fold my arms, which only serves to push them up higher. The *tits* are small and don't appear to be growing any larger, but better some than none at all. "You like my tits?"

Amusement flickers across Jake's face and his eyes rise to mine. "I do."

"So do lots of boys," I taunt. My anger over him leaving is irrational, but it doesn't stop the flood from rising. Jake might have had no choice, but he didn't *fight* to stay either.

"You let them touch you?" His lips press into a thin line. "You know what?" Jake grabs my bicep in a rough grip and marches me toward his car. "We're not doing this here on the side of the road." I struggle to push Jake away, but his strength is ridiculous. He yanks open the passenger door and shoves me inside. With my body half sprawled across the seat like a sack of potatoes, he leans down and looks me in the eye. "If that venomous mouth of yours has shit to spew, it can wait until after I've had something to eat. No one should be forced to battle your anger on an empty stomach, Princess."

The door slams shut, and he disappears. I wind down the window and stick my head out, yelling, "Screw you, Boy Wonder!" as he walks around the back of the car.

Jake opens the driver's door and slides in, giving me a sideways smirk. "I'm hardly a boy anymore. You'll have to come up with something better than that."

"Asshead," I mutter.

"Seriously?" He turns the key in the ignition and the car rumbles to life. "That's the best you've got?"

"Yes! I'm tired." My stomach roars like a wounded bear. "And hungry."

"Well, let's go eat."

After ten minutes of driving in tense silence, our windows down and hair whipping in the wild breeze, Jake turns onto a busy street teeming with people and cafes. A car pulls out ahead, and he whips in to the empty space, parallel parking like a boss. Slight resentment steals over me. I'm a shitty driver; there were fights in our household over who had to take me out for parking practice.

Finding a table outdoors in the sunshine, we each order a big breakfast. I sit back in my seat when the waitress leaves, sunglasses jammed on my face as I stare across the table at Jake. "Over two years, Jake. So much for keeping in touch, huh?"

"I know, but we both knew that wasn't going to happen." He rests his elbows on the table. "Me leaving was for the best."

Hurt swells in my chest. "Why?"

Jake turns his head and stares across the busy road, his expression sombre. "Because I'm not good for you."

"Nice of you to make that decision for the both of us," I snap.

"It was the right decision, so tuck your little quills away, Mac. You've got a bright future ahead of you and a family who loves you."

"You do too. My family has your back. They always have."

Jake shrugs. He sits back in his seat and pulls a pack of cigarettes from his pocket. My jaw tightens as he taps one from the packet and puts it to his lips. After lighting it he draws in deep before exhaling a long plume of smoke. "They did have ..." he acknowledges. "Once. But they don't now. I'm not their problem anymore, Princess. It's best just to leave me where I belong. In the past."

Jake brings the cigarette back to his lips. Rising in my seat, I reach across and snatch it from his fingers. His brows wing up. "Get over yourself," I hiss and toss it out on the street, barely missing two pedestrians strolling by. I turn back to Jake with a hard glare as I sit back down. "If I'd known you were planning a pity party, I would've ordered cake."

His lips twitch and my nostrils flare.

"You think this is funny, Mr, I'm No Good For You? You have the exact same future I do, Jake Romero. And if you want to throw it away because you think you're not good enough, then feel free. Just don't expect me to stick around and watch you do it."

I stand and collect my bag. The waitress chooses that moment to deliver two steaming plates piled high with bacon, eggs, sausage, toast, and beans. The delicious scent sets my nostrils quivering. My attempt at fighting my hunger is pathetic. I don't *do* starving. It makes me irrational and lightheaded. I lose the battle and sink back in my seat, setting my bag on the ground by my chair. "Well it would be a shame to let this go to waste. I'll eat first. Then I'm leaving."

"Mac?"

I glance up, fork already in hand and poised over a rasher of bacon. Jake's eyes are soft as he looks at me, and I know right then and there that I'm not going anywhere. His voice is a little hoarse when he speaks. "I missed you too."

Chapter Eight

Jake

The words leave my lips before I can halt their escape. *Moron*, I curse silently when pleasure lights Mac's pretty face. She's somehow managed to drop from the sky and into my lap. I can't believe it, and I can't deny how good it feels to have her with me again, but she can't stay. It's not safe for her. *I'm* not safe. "But yes, you're still leaving," I add.

She shrugs and stabs at a slice of bacon with her fork.

The nonchalance doesn't fool me. "Alright?"

I need to be sure. *Say the words, Mac.*

"Of course. Leaving. If that's what you want."

"Actually, what I want is to know how the hell you got here in the first place." The very mention takes me back to finding her ambling along the road, blonde hair tangled and gleaming bright in the sun, the skirt of her dress swirling around those pretty tanned thighs. My temper riles. "And what the hell do you think you were doing hitchhiking?" I feel a rant coming on and try to pull back, but my anger is like a steam train with faulty brakes. "You were this close..." I growl, holding up my thumb and forefinger an inch apart for emphasis "...to being picked up by some serial killer and having all the skin peeled from your body. If I hadn't—"

"Jake, don't be dramatic."

What in the actual fuck? My knuckles whiten around the knife and fork in my hands. I stab a piece of grilled mushroom and shove it in my mouth, chewing furiously.

"It's hardly *Wolf Creek* territory here in Melbourne's outer suburbs," she adds, snorting.

Her cavalier comment makes me livid. I suck in a sharp breath and a piece of mushroom lodges in my throat. "Arrghh!"

Mac stands and leans across the table. Her little fist thumps my back with surprising force. "...and besides," she says, still chattering as she delivers her mighty wallops, "I can take care of myself."

The mushroom flies from my mouth and lands on the table. Mac ignores the offending object and calmly takes her seat. She picks up her fork and spears another rasher of bacon.

I stare at her from across the table. "How can you be so smart and yet so mentally challenged all at the same time?"

And so damn pretty it takes my breath away? Mackenzie Valentine is evolving into a great beauty, the kind so imposing it hurts if you stare for too long.

Her brow furrows. "Why are you mad? If I've learnt one thing, it's to never sit back and let life come your way. You have to get out there and fight for it. So that's what I'm doing."

I can't refute her assertion, but there's a right way to go about fighting for it and then there's a dumb way. Mac chose the latter. And now she's here when she shouldn't be, and I'm a selfish asshole because I don't want her to leave.

"Besides, each day is a gift," she adds. "Special. We should live it accordingly, and ... and ..."

A crack forms in Mac's *tough girl* veneer. She looks away, not wanting me to see it, but it's too late.

"And?" I prompt.

Her eyes drop to her feet as if she's found something interesting in the pavement below. "And no day is special without you."

My heart flips over in my chest.

I want this girl.

I want her for me.

A desperate ache thumps in my chest. I need to stop this now before I do something crazy, like grab hold of her and never let go.

"If that's what you think, then you have no concept of real life."

Mac winces. She finally shows me a piece of her heart, and I crush it.

"You know, initially I thought you'd changed, but you haven't." Her gaze narrows on mine. "You're still a moody bastard."

"And you haven't changed a bit either. You're still a spoiled, sheltered brat, Mackenzie Valentine. You have a family that shields you from life's bullshit. They give you everything and like the wilful little girl you are, you take it with one hand and complain about it with the other." I shake my head and reach for another cigarette as I stand. After lighting it, I exhale and force coldness to my eyes. "You haven't grown up at all, Princess. You just made your way down to Melbourne expecting me to be the same and for us to go back to who we were. Well, we can't because you're wrong. I *have* changed and the world I live in isn't one where you belong."

Mac puts her knife and fork down. They clatter on her plate as she stands, our little altercation drawing the eyes of those around us. "What a complete load of bullshit. I belong wherever the hell I choose, and I choose here, with you."

My eyes flatten. "Wrong choice."

Her gaze narrows in return. "I'm tired of people telling me what I can and can't do, Romero. Don't you start too."

"You can do whatever you want, Princess. Just not here with me."

"Fine. I'll leave." Mac shoulders her bag and walks away, leaving almost a full plate of breakfast behind. That's when I know she's seriously hurt, and I hate the very idea of it. Mac is strong. I want her to always be strong.

I throw some cash on the table and chase after her. "Mac, wait!"

She walks straight passed my parked car and keeps right on going.

"Where do you think you're going?"

"Away from you!" she yells back without turning around.

I follow at a light jog to catch up. "When I said you could do whatever you wanted, I meant *go home*."

"And when I said fine, I'll leave, I meant *go fuck yourself*."

A shout of laughter escapes me. Mac is pure fire, and I love her. Even after all this time. I'm still hers.

"Laugh it up, chuckles," I hear her mutter as she motors down the street.

What the hell, right? Life is meant for living. "Mac, stop."

She keeps walking ahead of me. "No."

"Stop!"

"No."

"Remember when I said I belonged to you?" I call out. Pedestrians glance at me, but I don't care. When she stops and turns around, others do too.

Her green eyes soften, and I know she's remembering. Our first kiss. First love. I want her to be my first everything.

"I still do," I say. There's no denying that particular truth.

"I know, Romero," Mac says and starts back toward me. "Why else do you think I'm here?" Her chin lifts. "But there's one thing you don't know, and I never told you …"

"And what's that?"

"I belong to you too."

"Can you hold up the towel?" It's more a demand than a question as Mac jams the bright flowery towel at my chest. Later that afternoon we're in the mostly deserted car park at the beach, both standing by the passenger door I just opened for Mac. We'd spent the day catching up on the two years that had passed between us, and before taking her back to my house we decided to go for a swim at the beach. Me because I need to cool off. Being around Mac again has me itching to do things I shouldn't be doing. And her because she's on a mission to *live life to the fullest* and *make each day count.*

I take the towel and hold it up. "What are you doing?"

She doesn't answer. Instead, she turns, leans inside the car, and rummages around in her bag. Finding what she's after, Mac backs out and faces me. "Not that way." Mac huffs and grabs the towel. She rotates it sideways and hands it back. "That way."

Satisfied I'm holding it in just the right position, Mac takes a step back, picks up the hem of her dress and peels it over her head. It drops to the ground.

Holy shit.

I choke.

She isn't wearing a bra.

"Mac!" I bark and come at her with the towel— but not before I take in every inch of naked skin and commit it to memory. I wrap it around her front, effectively straight-jacketing her with it and hugging her at the same time. "Don't do that here where people can see you."

Amusement flashes across her face. "No one's looking. There's no one here."

"I am, Mac," I say wryly. "By *people,* I mean me."

Her lips curve. "But you're allowed to look. Don't you want to?"

"Yes." There's no hesitation in my response. "Hell yes," I add, just so she knows how much.

She grins. I duck my head and effectively kiss it right off her face. It's a quick press of my mouth to hers, but it's enough to draw a ragged moan from her lips when I pull back. It sends blood pumping so hard through my veins it hurts.

"Is that all you've got?"

Mac's taunt has me leaning close, my lips a mere inch from hers. "You want more?"

"Don't you know me by now?" she breathes against mouth. "I want it all."

I kiss her again when I know I shouldn't, but there's no stopping myself. Her lips are on mine, and I feel it down to my toes. Heat and need surge together, a desperate war that has me pushing her back against my car. My tongue slides inside her mouth. Mac returns the touch and a groan climbs the back of my throat.

Tomorrow, I vow. *I'll send her home tomorrow.*

Her hands slide around my neck, fingers tangling in my hair.

"Now, Jake," she pants, pulling back. Her lids are lowered and eyes glazed. "I want you now."

"Now?" *Here?* My mind scrambles. I search the parking lot. It's mostly deserted. Why am I even contemplating this? It's crazy. We only just reunited *this morning,* after *years,* and even though it feels as if we've picked up right where we left off, it's too soon for something like this. "No. We can't."

Mac doesn't listen. She opens the back passenger door instead. She climbs in and turns around dropping the towel. "We can."

I can hear her say something, but the words don't register. My eyes are on her tits. They're small and round, her pale nipples beckoning like pink cotton candy. My gaze lowers following the trail of smooth golden skin to the pair of red lace panties. Mac is only seventeen. Sexy underwear like that should be wrong, like a girl trying to be something she's not, but on Mac they belong. They hug her skin like gift wrap waiting to be torn off.

A whimper escapes me and my voice becomes weak. "You don't play fair."

"I never have," she says. "And I never will."

Mac leans forward. She takes my hands and pulls me onto the backseat of the car. I let go, bracing my palms on either side of the seat so I don't fall right on top of her. "Not like this, Princess."

My voice is a rasp and her lips curve. She knows she has me. "Exactly like this."

"Would it be ..." I trail off, the question in my eyes.

"My first time? Yes," she answers without hesitating.

My heart threatens to beat right out of my chest. "Me too," I answer. I've never been able to bring myself to look at another girl. How can I when I belong to this one?

"Jake."

She speaks my name in a throaty whisper and it has me trembling. I lock my muscles tight, fighting against the instinctive urge to take what I want. "It should be special."

"This *is* special. Finding you like this was meant to be. *We* were meant to be, and I don't want to wait. I don't want any obstacles getting in our way ... or doubts. I just want you, Jake, and you want me too." Her fingertips trail down my straining biceps as I hold myself up off her. Shivers break out across my skin. "I can feel it, and see it." Mac sounds so fanciful. Not like herself at all. And yet her words are catching hold. Like a brush fire, they're sweeping me up and burning me to ash.

She takes the hem of my shirt and pulls it up. I take over grabbing the back of the neckline in my fist and dragging it over my head. Mac's breathing escalates when I throw the shirt to the side. Then her soft, warm hands are on my chest. They lower slowly and her eyes fix on the ink above my left nipple.

Her hands freeze as she stares, silence beating thick and heavy between us. "This is a tiara," she states, her voice scratchy. She clears her throat and drags her eyes upward. "When did you get this?"

"When I was sixteen. It was my first tattoo."

Mac covers the image with the flat of her palm as though absorbing it into her own body. "It's me, isn't it? You marked me onto your skin."

"It's not on my skin, it's beneath it ... just like you are."

She exhales loudly. "That is unbelievably hot."

A laugh escapes me. "You think?"

"I know," she corrects. Her gaze dips to where my cock strains against my shorts. Her eyes widen. "I can't believe how much you've changed." A huff of laughter leaves her lips. I'm not sure if the sound is one of disbelief or apprehension. "So much."

She puts her hand flat on my dick. Her fingers curl around the fabric of my shorts, squeezing. I jolt in surprise. "Mac!"

"For fuck's sake, Romero. Touch me."

I want to, but I fear the moment I do it will be all over for me. She makes the decision for me and grabs my hand, slapping it on her breast. *Oh god.* An involuntary groan escapes me when firm, warm flesh fills my palm. I squeeze. *Oh holy mother of god.* Mackenzie Valentine is beneath me, mostly naked, my hands are on her body, and my cock feels ready to blow. I scrunch my eyes closed, fighting to breathe. How ridiculous it feels to be so jaded in life and yet so innocent in this.

"Let's lose these shorts," she says over the roaring of blood in my ears. "I want to see you."

Her hands fumble with my button and zipper. I unlock the tight grip I have on her boob and bat her away. "Don't."

Not one to be denied, Mac keeps coming at me until my shorts and boxer briefs are shoved down and my cock fills her small hands. White spots dot my vision. "Oh god," I breathe.

Mac's eyes are focused on what she's holding. "You're so hard and warm and smooth." Her breath is coming fast. "I like it."

I do too. Hell yes, I like it too.

I watch her watch my cock in her playful hands, trying to keep my wits but it's too late. My ship has sunk. I lower my head and take a nipple between my lips, sucking it deep inside my mouth.

Mac lets out a squeak. I look up. Her head has fallen back, her eyes glazing over. Mac is beneath me, *finally under my control.* A powerful, primitive surge overtakes me. My mouth shifts to her other nipple and bracing on my knees, I grip the sides of her panties and shove them down. "Oh god." She's panting now. "Touch me," she orders.

I rear up over her, my head lost deep in lust. "When we're together, and we're doing this, don't ever tell me what to do. I'm in charge." My palm lowers down her belly as I loom above, my eyes on hers. When I reach between her legs I delve inside. She's slick and wet and so deliciously hot, I want to weep from it. "Got it?" A moan leaves her lips. I pause my fingers, my gaze locked on hers. "Do you understand?"

Relief sweeps across her features, as if relinquishing control is everything she needs. "Yes," she breathes, nodding. "I understand."

Mac

For what feels like the first time in my life, I let go. I just ... *let go*. Of everything. I put my whole world right in the palm of Jake's hand, and he stepped up taking it on instinct.

There's always a fight inside me. It's constant and exhausting, but it's who I need to be to survive, to show I can stand on my own two feet, to prove myself. In a singular, monumental instant, Jake has taken that fight away, freeing me. The liberation leaves me lighter than the clouds in the sky. Even if it's only just for this moment, it's enough.

My eyes burn as his fingers began moving again. Pleasure floods my body, white-hot and consuming.

It isn't just his touch that has me burning hotter. It's the intimacy of what we're doing, his body and mine so close and feeding off each other. My breath comes faster and my heart beats harder. An orgasm rips through me like a freight train. I cry out, eyes closing as I get caught in the waves of it.

"I've got you, Princess."

And he does. Jake has me.

My eyes burn as the pleasure takes me to another place.

Then I feel him. The intrusion. He's pushing his way inside my body. It's incredibly surreal. His cock pulses as he pauses, gritting his teeth. My hips push upward, feeding my instinctive need for more.

"Move again," he says through gritted teeth, "and I'll spank your pretty little ass."

The very thought leaves me dizzy and fevered. I want him to. I *want* it. What the hell is wrong with me that I want to feel the sting of Jake's palm on the naked skin of my butt? My body is more than on board with the idea, but my mind balks. Either way, my hips are moving of their own accord. Jake groans and surges forward until he's fully inside me. I suck in a breath at the sharp stab of pain.

Sonofabitch! Ouch!

"I told you not to move."

"I couldn't help it."

"You'll pay for that, Princess."

Jake draws back a little. The friction hurts and I hold still. "I think I already am."

"I'd stop. Let you adjust," he rasps, pushing back in and pulling out, "but I don't think I can."

He thrusts again, and my body responds as the pain slowly recedes.

"That felt good," I say on a moan, my insides squeezing him tight around me.

"Too good," Jake mutters, and this time when he drives forward, he doesn't stop. Three deep, forceful thrusts and he's groaning long and hard, hips grinding and face buried in my neck.

So this is sex.

My first time was at the beach in the back of Jake's car. A grin spreads across my face. He feels my mirth and draws back to look down at me.

"What?"

My grin widens. "We just did it on the backseat of your car."

"Shit," he mutters. "This was not how I ever imagined making love to you, Mackenzie Valentine."

"You imagined this?"

"All the time."

"Even after years of not hearing from you at all?"

Jake closes his eyes for a brief moment and swallows before he opens them again. "Can we not do this right now?"

My eyes spark fire. "What, now with your cock inside me isn't a good time for you?"

Chapter Nine

Mac

I just had sex. Me. Mackenzie Valentine. I squirm a little in the front passenger seat, my body parts sore and throbbing. We're driving back to Jake's place and with the humidity rampant, both windows are down. A wild breeze blows through the car.

I turn to look at him as he drives. One tattooed arm controls the steering wheel and the other rests outside the open window. Jake looks mussed and sexy and completely carefree. A wide grin splits my face.

"What?" Jake asks, glancing across at me before turning back to the road. A grin curves the corners of his lips.

I shove the windblown hair off my face.

"Nothing," I reply when right then it's *everything*.

I turn my focus out the window, unable to stop smiling. I'm alive. Relaxed. *Happy*.

Sex is not how I imagined it. It's messy and awkward, but it's so *intimate*, as if in a single moment we became one person. Jake is right. It should have been special. Planned. But with him all my plans seem to get tossed right out the window. I become reckless and lose my mind. It's a good feeling.

"I can't believe we just did that," he says without taking his eyes from the road.

"Me either."

"We should do it again."

Again? The idea sends my body into overdrive. I've always imagined my first time, but it never went further than that. Now I'm quickly realising that this is something we can do *every day*. My insides quiver and the throbbing between my legs intensifies at a rapid pace. "When?"

Jake indicates before turning left into a tiled driveway. A frown forms. The house is unexpected. It's imposing and beautiful despite the front lawn being overrun with cars. The gardens are chaotic, but the scent of jasmine in the stifling heat is rich and sweet. The address is also not the last house on my list. If I hadn't stumbled across Jake while hitchhiking, I would never have found him.

He turns off the ignition and looks at me with heat in his eyes. "Now."

My heart rate escalates. "Now?"

Jake reaches behind and plucks my bag off the back passenger seat. There's no centre console in his car. The front seat runs all the way along and when he opens his car door, he grabs my hand and pulls me out his side.

The front door is timber and wide. It swivels inward as we step inside and through to the living area. The space features three long leather couches. They're black and occupied by three guys who are passing a joint around. The air is thick with smoke and makes my throat burn.

One of them glances up at our arrival and does a double take. He's built with blond hair that hangs in his eyes. He exhales a deep plume of smoke, his green eyes widening on my face.

I know him, though I have no idea what he's doing here. He spent one year at my high school before disappearing like smoke. He used to hang with a crowd of motorcycle heathens, the kind my brothers would lock me up for if I were caught talking to them.

"Luke," I say. "Luke Fox."

His gaze drops, assessing my hand clasped inside Jake's. A furrow creases his forehead when he looks back up. "Mackenzie Valentine."

"You two know each other?" Jake asks.

Luke's gaze shoots to Jake, his eyes wide. "*She's* your princess?"

"Wait, what?" Jake had mentioned me?

Brows rise all around the room and I don't understand it. Luke passes the joint toward the guy next to him and gives Jake his full attention. "Does this mean you win the—"

Jake's grip on my hand tightens. "Not now, Little Fox."

"Little?" I almost laugh. Luke is *huge*.

Jake points to Luke. "Little Fox." Then he points to the guy beside him. An older version of Luke with cool eyes. "Big Fox."

"For the record..." Luke's palm goes to his junk and he winks "...I'm not little."

Jake rolls his eyes as if he's heard the line a thousand times before. "So how do you know each other?"

"Luke went to my school. We were in grade seven together."

"Small world," Luke adds then cocks his head, eyes crinkling curiously. "How did *you* meet Mac?"

Jake's response is unexpected. "We used to be neighbours."

"Didn't know you lived in Sydney, Romero."

Jake shrugs. "I used to."

"Didn't know it was the famous Mackenzie Valentine who stole your heart either. I should've known. I tried pinning the girl down all school year, but her brothers guarded her like she was the crown jewel of England." Luke's gaze shifts to me and he winks again. "Isn't that right, sweetheart?"

My hackles rise at the endearment. "I'm not your sweetheart."

"I guess you aren't." He looks at Jake. "I'm impressed, Romero. You've got balls the size of King Kong to take on the Valentine clan and survive."

Neither of us mention that my so-called *Valentine clan* don't quite know I'm here. From the way Jake squeezes my hand, I figure I should keep quiet about it too. "I guess that's something you wouldn't know about, is it, Luke?"

Jake snorts with laughter. Even Luke cracks a grin. "And a pity that is too, isn't it?" He gifts me with a wistful sigh as his eyes trail down my legs and back up again. "We could've had it all, you and me."

"Put your dick away," Jake retorts before I can say the exact same thing. "Mac doesn't want your STDs."

Laughter fills the living area. "Don't listen to him, Mac," Luke says in an overly serious tone. "I'm still a virgin."

My cheeks warm in an instant. Luke is only teasing, but I'm not a virgin as of an hour ago and the reminder makes me hot.

Jake squeezes my hand again. I turn my head. He's looking at me, his eyes hotter than my cheeks. We share a small smile that can only be described as goofy.

"Well this was fun," Jake says and leads me down the hallway of the house, away from Luke and the smoky haze.

"Say hi to your brothers for me, Mac!" Luke yells after us. "I remember them fondly!"

I follow Jake up a set of stairs and inside his room. He sets my bag on the big bed and scrambles to collect random clothes that are strewn about the floor. Sheets are spread across the mattress in a haphazard fashion and empty bottles litter the bedside tables. Jake tosses the clothes in the corner and scratches the back of his neck, shrugging.

"It's a bit of a mess. Wasn't expecting company, you know?"

"I don't care about the mess."

Jake straightens and gives me a look I can't decipher. "Well, it's just for one night, right?"

"One night?"

"You're going home tomorrow, Mac. You can't stay here. I mean..." he waves his hand about "...look at the people I live with. You don't belong here." My nostrils flare as he grabs another shirt from the floor. The reason I'm here is because I don't like being told how to live my life, and now Jake is trying to do the same thing. "You need to go—"

"Not this again, Jake. I belong wherever the hell I choose."

Jake pauses in his attempt to fold the tee shirt. He bunches it in his hands and sighs deeply, his eyes fixing on the open window. "Why with me? I'm not anyone special. I don't have anything to offer you. You have so many opportunities to live a crazy and exciting life. Who would throw all that away for some guy they used to know a long time ago?"

My eyes burn. Since when did Jake become so defeatist? I move toward him and take the shirt from his hands, tossing it to the floor. With his hands free, I take them in mine. "I'm not throwing anything away. I *want* to live a crazy and exciting life. I just want to do it with *you*."

I push up on my toes and press my mouth to his. He responds, his touch heartbreakingly tender. It sends my pulse rocketing clear through the roof. "This is a bad idea," he mutters against my lips. Then his arms snake around me in a fierce hold and lift me until my feet leave the ground. "But I don't know how to be smart when it comes to you, Princess. You make me stupid."

A smile pulls at the corners of my mouth. "Then we can be stupid together."

He laughs and the sound is beautiful and light. "I can't argue with you. You have an answer for everything."

"So don't argue."

His expression darkens. "We can talk about it tomorrow."

"There'll be no talking tomorrow…" my eyes drop to his lips "… and you know it."

Heat replaces the dark, and he tosses me on the bed. I know then that I have him and giddiness consumes me. Laughter spills out as I bounce on the mattress. Jake jumps on the bed above me, hair falling in his face as he grins down at me. "You'll always be mine, Mackenzie Valentine, won't you?"

"Yours," I confirm.

His smile sobers as his eyes search my face, serious in an instant. He tucks wayward strands of blonde hair behind my right ear with care. My lungs constrict at the intimate gesture. Literally. I can't get any air. "I don't deserve you."

I wake the next morning with Jake wrapped around me. His body is warm and heavy. I love it. Happiness settles in my gut. I was right coming here. Jake is the man for me. No distance, time, or age, will change that.

A knock comes at the door. It opens without invitation.

"School, fuckface!" Dark brown eyes settle on me. "Well, well. The rumours I heard downstairs at the breakfast table were true."

I pull the sheet high from prying eyes as Jake stirs behind me. "And who are you?"

The guy grins, hand resting on the door handle as he gives me the once-over. "I'm Rowan, sweetheart. Lead singer and stud for hire, if you're interested."

My eyes frost over. "Do I look interested?"

"Not yet, but I can change that."

"I'm with Jake in case that escaped your attention," I snap.

"I can change that too."

Jake groans from behind me. "Get lost, Rowan. It's school holidays."

Rowan gives a mock pout as he throws up his hands and turns to leave. "Fine. I get it. I'm not wanted."

I roll and face Jake. His eyes are a little puffy and stubble lines his jaw. He's sexy and all mine. My lips curve. "Good morning."

His eyes light with warmth. "Morning, babe."

"Oh, I'm *babe* now?"

I poke his naked chest.

"Yeah." Jake laughs and wraps his arms around my head. My face gets stuck in his armpit and the hair tickles my face. His grip tightens when I try squirming free. "You don't wanna be my babe anymore, babe?" The big dork chuckles at his own joke. "Didn't realise you were so fickle."

I'm slowly suffocating in a haze of man smell and warm skin. I manage to rip my head free and sit back on my knees, dragging air inside my lungs. "Oh, you wanna fight?"

Jake grins. The sight sends my heart into jackhammer mode. "Give it your best shot, *babe*."

Before he can do anything more, I have him flipped over, his right forearm pinned behind his back while I reach for the left. "Holy fuck," he mutters into the pillow where his face is now mashed. "I'm so hard right now."

I laugh. My hold loosens enough that he gets free and rolls beneath me. "Jesus, Mac." Jake's expression sobers as my hands rest flat on his chest. His heart is pounding an erratic beat beneath my fingers. "Don't look at me like that."

"Like what?"

"Like I hung the goddamn moon."

"It feels like you did, Jake, because I love you."

Jake swallows and his eyes shift somewhere over my right shoulder. "You might think you do, but you don't."

I pull back, hurt welling in my chest at the rejection. "You're going to tell me how I feel now?"

I roll off him, scoot my way from the bed, and reach for my clothes.

"Stop being so prickly."

"Oh my god!" I yell, spinning around as I yank on my underwear. "Would you just stop telling me what to do!"

Jake sits up in bed, the sheet pooling at his waist. Frustration lines his forehead. My body gives a jolt of longing. *It would be easier to be mad at him if he didn't look so good.*

"Damn you," I hiss. "Don't you have school like Rowan whomever said anyway? Go do that. And who is he anyway, lead singer of what? The Muppets?"

"He sings in my band."

Half-dressed, I pause. "*Your* band?"

"The band I'm in," Jake corrects.

"*You* are in a band? Since when?"

"Since a year ago," he tells me, moving off the bed and getting to his feet, naked. He yawns and stretches. Meanwhile my gaze lowers until it reaches what my hands itch to wrap their fingers around.

It begins a slow rise as though saying hello.

"That's quite the greeting," I manage to get out, utterly fascinated and impressed all at the same time.

"It's because you're staring at it."

My gaze flies up. "You got hard because I looked at your dick?"

"Um, yeah?" he says, his tone sardonic as if it's something I should already know. "Feel free to touch it."

Jake mustn't have been expecting me to actually do it ... because when I wrap a warm, slender palm around it and squeeze, it gives an almighty jerk. Jake groans and tips his head back, his eyes closing.

"What do you play?"

"Play?" he hisses when I give a firm stroke.

"In your so-called band, The Muppets."

"We're not The..." His breath catches when I stroke again. I like his body's response. "The Muppets."

"Well ...?"

"The drums," Jake manages to say through his heavy breathing. "I'm the drummer."

"Are you any good at it?"

"The best. You should come watch us one night."

My hand keeps up its ministrations. I love how much Jake enjoys my touch. "When do you play next?"

"The ahhh ... the weekend."

Jake takes my hand and peels it off. Then he turns me around, and I'm pushed down on the bed in just a few fast beats of my heart. He bends and touches his lips to my chest, his touch lighter than a feather. They trail down, lower and lower, until he's peeling the panties down my thighs, his face now hovering between my legs.

I can feel his breath puffing against my skin and fight the urge to squirm. When his tongue snakes out and touches me there, I almost jolt straight off the bed. *Oh my god, is this even real?*

"It might mean me staying more than one night," I gasp, which is a bonus for me because I've decided that Jake's head now has to live between my legs.

He moans and licks me again as though the taste of me is better than ice cream. "Okay."

Chapter Ten

Jake

"Mum?"

Mac's voice is a low whisper as we lie in bed. It's early, the sun barely breaking across the horizon, and it's been three days since her arrival. A war has raged inside of me each of those days. One side fights for her to stay, the other for her to leave. I'm at a stalemate. Mac can't be here. Even though our house is reasonably safe—we don't invite the King Street Boys for dinner—we're still a part of their world. A gang of undesirables, criminals, and murderers. It makes me sick to the stomach to be included in that. To know I'm not good enough. She deserves better. But I'm selfish. Mac is mine. *My* family.

Right now she's calling Jenna. Believing I was asleep, Mac took my phone from the bedside table and began pressing buttons. I wasn't, but knowing she was voluntarily calling her family, I played possum. Let her think she has the privacy she's seeking. I've been badgering her to call them. They need to know where she is. That I'm with her and looking out for her. Most importantly, they need to know why she left.

Mac had explained Fleur Dreyer Halvorsen, and I'm still gobsmacked. Don't they know their own daughter? Yes, her spirit is wild. She's argumentative and troublesome. But is it any wonder? Her parents control her every move. Her brothers do the same. For her, it's a daily battle to be heard and a constant fight to take back her own life. As an outsider to the Valentine clan, it's easy for me to see. As a consequence of their behaviour, Mac has a need to be in control of any situation … with anyone, and it's consuming her life.

"I'm okay," she says into the phone.

There's a pause. Jenna is talking on the other end but I can't hear what she's saying.

"I'm not in any trouble. I'm fine, I promise," she answers.

Another pause.

"I'm not coming home. I can't go to that stupid school, Mum. I'll wither away and die."

Mac shifts closer. Curling into my side, she rests the side of her face on my chest, the phone pressed to her ear. It brings the conversation closer and Jenna's voice becomes audible to my ears. "Don't be dramatic, Mackenzie. We've talked about this. About how good this school will be for you. They're still holding your place."

"Well tell them to un-hold it."

"I can't do that. We paid a fortune."

"Then you should get a refund. I'm not going. Not ever."

"I don't want to argue about this, honey."

"So don't. I only rang to let you know that I was okay. I didn't call so you could spend the time convincing me about how much I need this finishing college. Why are you trying to change me?"

The hurt in Mac's voice is so sharp it stabs me right in the chest. I can't play possum any longer. My arm curls around her back squeezing her closer. She shifts her head upward, eyes finding mine. "I love you," I mouth.

My announcement is terrible timing, but she needs to hear it. Her eyes close and her lips press flat in response as they fight a tremble. My chest expands. Yep. She needed it.

"Oh, honey. We're not trying to change you. We just want you to be the best version of you that you can be."

"Oh my god." Mac jolts upright, hurt evolving to fury. "You're giving me the brochure spiel?"

"I'm not! I ... Oh hell, I didn't realise. Mac ..."

There's a long beat of silence between the two. Sitting up, I splay my palm on Mac's naked back and begin a long, slow rub. I hope it's soothing. I don't know what else to do.

A sob breaks free on the other end of the phone. "I'm sorry." I realise then that Jenna's been faking her strength and can no longer pull it off. "Forget the school. Just come home."

Mac exhales deeply, her back rising and falling beneath my palm. "I can't. It's too late, Mum." Her voice cracks. "It's too late."

"Please, honey. Tell me where you are."

Mac's voice is firm. "No."

"Why, Mackenzie? Why are you doing this? We've given you everything. We *love* you. And you turn your back on all of it and run away? I don't get it, honey."

Mac lowers her voice to a hoarse whisper. "I never wanted anything." She turns her head to the open window, her green eyes lost as a single tear tracks down her cheek. I shift closer and swipe my thumb across the soft skin, wiping it away. Mac looks to me as she speaks into the phone. "I just want to be free to be myself. I just want to be free."

A sniff comes through the phone. "Oh, honey, your brothers, your father, I know they're a little stifling. They're just trying to protect you."

Her tone rises. Bitterness gives it a sharp edge. "I can protect myself."

"You can't. You're a sweet, young girl who doesn't need to worry about such things."

"I can! You don't believe in me. None of you do. And you never listen. Not even now. This whole entire conversation is pointless."

"Mac—"

"I have to go. I'll call you again. I promise."

Mac hangs up the phone and leans over to rest it on the bedside table. She hasn't told her mother where she is, but she hasn't thought about them tracing the call. I don't mention it for the simple fact they can't. It's a burner phone. With the life I lead, I can't be traceable. Even the payments made toward my father's care facility are from an anonymous account. From the moment I left the De Luca foster home, I ceased to exist. I left no trail behind. I got new identification and changed schools. It's better this way, and yet here Mac is having stumbled her way back into my life through sheer, dumb luck. Why does fate keep throwing us together?

Shifting back on the bed, Mac straddles my hips. Such is her strength, all trace of sadness is gone from her face. What remains is a fierceness that sets my blood on fire. "Promise me something, Jake."

"Anything."

"Love me just the way I am. Don't try to change me."

"I don't want to change you."

"And I want you to believe in me."

This isn't just important to her. It's everything. "I do."

"*Always* believe in me."

How can I not? What Mac doesn't see is that I'm her greatest protector of all. "I'll always believe in you."

Her lips curve slightly. She's satisfied with my response and lies down beside me, curling into my side. I hug her close and press a kiss to the top of her head.

"Tell me about your life, Jake. I want to know everything."

Mac can't know everything. Ever. The type of man I've become is not the man she needs, so I give her the edited version. "I was born Jacob Rhys Romero on May tenth, at Westmead Hospital."

"You're a Taurus."

My brows rise. "Yeah, I guess. I didn't pick you as someone that's into that kind of thing."

"The easiest way to read someone is to work out their sign. Everyone knows that."

"Oh?" A smirk plays upon on my lips. "Read me, then."

Shifting to her side, Mac rises on her elbow and rests her head in her hand. "You're a bull. That makes you a stubborn, hard-headed dick," she says, returning my smirk. "You're also strong, romantic, and possessive, and you like pretty things. You're quick and clever, but underneath it all hides true talent and hard work."

"You think I'm all that?"

A grin curves her lips, and she shrugs her shoulders. "Mostly just the stubborn part."

Grabbing the pillow beside me, I use it to whack her on the head. She shrieks, laughing. I use the diversion to my advantage and roll on top of her, pinning her arms to the bed.

"And strong," she gasps.

I shift a little, taking some of my weight from her body.

"Tell me more," Mac says. "All the facts I have are that you were born and your father had a brain aneurysm."

My stomach sinks. I hate to talk about my father. It's a reminder that the man he used to be is not the man he is today. Scooting off the bed, I reach for a pair of shorts from the floor. "What more could you possibly need to know?"

I stand and slide the shorts up my legs as I scan the floor for a shirt. I'm a messy bastard, I know. I need to work on that.

Mac's voice hardens. She's getting annoyed. "Don't be evasive."

I find a crumpled shirt half hanging from the drawer of my dresser. I grab it and turn to face Mac. She's sitting up in bed, long hair tousled and bed sheet pulled to her chest with one arm holding it in place.

She's utterly enthralling, like a butterfly come to rest on my hand. I want to stand here all day and absorb her beauty, even though she'll soon fly away. That will be my next tattoo—a butterfly on my hand, complete with wings of absolute fire.

"What?" she asks.

I've been staring. "What do you mean what?"

"You're staring at me."

The shirt is bunched in my hands. I shake it out and tug it on. Then I walk over and dip down, pressing my lips to hers. Pulling back a fraction, I give her a grin. "I was just thinking of how beautiful you are."

"Oh …" Pink warms her cheekbones. "It's what's on the inside that counts."

"Accept the compliment, Princess."

Her green eyes sparkle and she concedes. "Thank you, Jake. Now stop being evasive."

With a deep sigh, I turn and sit on the edge of the bed. "You know my mother died, so it was just me and my father. We lived in a normal house. I went to school, came home, watched TV, played computer games. It was all completely ordinary and boring."

Mac shifts until she's sitting beside me. "What did your father do before he got sick? And where is he now?"

"He is … *was* a music professor. He taught music history, composition, and performance at the Academy of Music and Performing Arts in Sydney." I swallow bitterness. "Now he's in an aged care facility."

Her slender palm reaches for mine. She takes it and gives me a comforting squeeze. "He must have been an incredible musician."

"Not so much. He knew everything about music but when it came to instruments, he was a jack-of-all-trades and master of none. He loved the violin best. When played right, he said the sound was clearer than glass and purer than snow."

"And you end up playing the drums."

"Yeah." A laugh escapes me. "It was always my favourite. Dad liked to joke that my first word was *rhythm*. I could find it in anything—banging pots, slapping tables, cardboard boxes. When I was seven, I discovered I could use different parts of my hand to get different sounds." Letting go of Mac's hand, I hold mine up and point to the base of my palm. "This part gives you a low beat." I point to the middle of my hand. "This gives you a higher pitch. And here..." I point to my fingers "...gives you fast rolls and pops."

"Why do you like it so much?"

I give Mac a grin. "Because you get to hit things. And they don't hit back."

She laughs. It's a light sound and I like it. I lean in and rub my nose against hers. Mac is close enough for me to see the flecks of gold in her eyes. "They're also fun," I say. "And when I play them I feel happy."

"Did you have a drum kit when you were young?"

"Dad bought me one when I was ten."

"Is that the one you use now?"

"No." I draw back and stand, scanning the floor for some shoes. We've barely left my room since Mac got here and it's time to get outside and enjoy some fresh air. "We should go do something."

Mac doesn't budge. "Not yet. I want to know more."

She's a dog with a bone. Heaving a deep breath, I turn to face her and fold my arms. "It was sold when he got sick. His insurance only covered so much, you know?"

"I'm sorry," Mac tells me. "About what happened. I wish I wasn't such a bitch to you that first night."

"You didn't know." My jaw ticks, fighting back the ache. It throbs like a fresh wound in my skin. When does the pain get easier to bear? "I barely felt a thing that night anyway, but now ..."

"Now?" she prompts.

My throat feels raw and I swallow. "Now I don't know how to feel. It's like he died, Mac, but he's still here."

Mac stands. The sheet falls away, revealing her naked body. She's confident in her skin and doesn't care. It's beautiful. She walks toward me and slides her arms around my waist, pulling me tight against her.

"It hurts," I admit, returning the hug. It hurts like holy fucking hell, but Mac is here in my arms and it feels so good I don't know how I'll ever let go.

Chapter Eleven

Jake

"I want out."

Leander, Luke, and I are sitting at the round breakfast table in the nook by the kitchen. Mac is in the shower, and I'm tapping my fingers against the pale timber, anxious to have this conversation before she gets out. I've been thinking on it for weeks. About how I'm not good for Mac. But maybe I can be.

If I got out, we could have a future together. I have a load of cash saved. Enough to get me through university and still pay for my father's care. After that, I could get a job. A real one.

Luke's brow pulls together in puzzled lines. "Out?"

Leander isn't confused. His expression is one of resignation. "You can never get out."

"Oh Jesus," Luke mutters when he realises what I'm talking about. His head tips back and his eyes close as if I'm dead already.

"Goddammit!" I tug fingers through my hair. "I'll just leave. They don't know my real name. They'll never be able to find me."

Leander shakes his head. "You aren't a ghost, Romero. They'll find you."

With a low roar that rumbles through my chest, I jerk to my feet. My chair skids backwards on the tiles. "Then fix it." I jab a finger at Leander. "You got me into this. You get me out!"

The accusation isn't fair, but I can't think straight. I can't be tied to the King Street Boys for life. *I can't.*

The night I shot that man, I left that house and wandered for hours. When I eventually came back here, my steps were heavy as I walked the stairs to my room. Luke had been sitting on my bed, waiting.

"What are you doing in my room?" I growled.

He was paler than the crisp white sheets he sat on. "Lee told me what happened. Holy fucking shit, Romero. I didn't know. I swear to god. The gun wasn't loaded when you left here. It wasn't fucking loaded."

My teeth ground together, stopping me from throwing up a second time. "I killed someone."

"I know."

I kicked the bag on my floor clear across the room. The force sent it crashing into a lamp. It smashed to the floor, the bulb shattering. "I fucking killed someone!" I yelled at him.

"I'm fucking sorry!" he yelled back, rising from the bed. "I didn't know!" His voice cracked, like he couldn't bear knowing what I'd been forced to do. "I didn't know."

Standing still, I stared at him, my eyes burning, and I believed him. He was my best mate and I trusted him with my life. Luke wouldn't have lied. Not about that.

"Leander says Boyd must have loaded the gun when he got it from the car. After you left he tried finding you. He drove around for an hour. Then he came home and he's been yelling into the phone ever since. He's pissed."

I didn't give a shit about Leander at that point. He could go get fucked for all I cared. "How do I live with myself?"

Luke shook his head. "I don't know."

Neither did I, but somehow I did. The first few days after were a bad dream, one I prayed to wake up from. They had me do small jobs at first that grew to bigger ones. I hated it. I hated the gang. I hated being trapped. But like I told them, I was no one's bitch. My rule was no more guns. They relented. I was given the least violent jobs. But it was a waste, Ross told me, eyeing my size.

I still played school football. It was an outlet. A stress release. But then I was introduced to Rowan, who played in a band at The Bar—an original name for a huge tavern by the beach. It was a hopping place and when they needed a drummer, I stepped in. I'd found my happy place there and a small measure of peace. It was there I'd found a way to live with myself.

"I'll talk to Ross," Leander says, dragging me from the past. "If you want out, I'll find a way. We'll make this work."

I give him a short nod. "Good." As I start to walk away, I turn and narrow my gaze. "By the way, you owe me ten thousand dollars, asshole."

Leander laughs. It's a rare sound. I don't know what happened to the Fox brothers. They don't talk about it. But with the way Leander is, I know it was bad. Real bad. "Is she eighteen?"

"Not yet," I concede.

"Then hold your horses, mate."

"What are you going to do?" Luke asks him. "Set Rowan loose on her?"

Rowan can talk a nun out of her underwear, but his charms washed right over Mac. My smile is smug. "He already tried that. Didn't work."

"I could set Luke on her. He's always had a thing for Mac."

I look at Luke, my glare promising death.

He holds up his hands. "Fuck that, Lee. I prefer my balls attached. You both keep me out of your stupid ass bet."

"What bet?"

We all turn. Mac is standing in the doorway. She's wearing the same pale lemon dress she wore the day she arrived. Her hair hangs in a wet curtain down her back.

"Just some bet on the horses," I say in an offhand voice.

Luke snorts in his chair, muttering under his breath, "Horses? Damn, you are so dead if she finds out."

"What do you want to do today?" I ask, knowing Mac hasn't overhead us. If she had, she'd be setting fire to the house and watching us burn.

"I want to get my hair cut," she announces, moving into the kitchen. Checking the water level in the kettle, she flicks it on and turns around, leaning against the counter. "I wasn't allowed to cut it before. You can't 'artfully arrange' short blonde hair at Fucking Dick Head school," she air-quotes.

Leander and Luke know all about FDH. Mac is bitter. And she showed them the website. It looked like a pretty prison for Barbie dolls. If she'd gone there, she would have snapped eventually and slashed everyone's clothes with a machete in the dead of night. No dress would be spared. Every female in the college would wake to a wardrobe of ribbons. I know this because she told me exactly that with very solemn eyes.

"Alright," I tell her. "I'll go shower."

"I'll make you a coffee," she yells behind me as I climb the stairs.

"Make me one too," I hear Luke say.

"Get stuffed, Little Fox," she replies, turning his favourite phrase against him. Mac already has his number, and it makes me chuckle as I walk to my room.

Mac

It's Saturday night and summer holidays. Jake and I are at The Bar where his band is playing tonight. It's my first time here and watching Jake play is more fun than a trip to Disneyland. Humidity is high and his shirt came off an hour ago. It's tucked into the back of a worn pair of jeans. Drumming is a physical activity. Sweat beads on his chest and muscles ripple as he hammers the drums with his sticks. His rhythm gives life to the song.

"Cheap bastard," I bitch to the bartender when he hands over my drink. It's supposed to be juice, but all I see is ice and a dribble of pale, orange liquid. His response is to snatch the glass back, tip out two cubes, and add a squirt more juice.

I exercise considerable restraint in not leaping the bar, grabbing the squirty juice gun, and blasting it in his face.

Instead, I take my drink from the bar and return to my table, running fingers through my hair. It was freshly shorn this morning, cut in a short, choppy style just below my ears. It feels fun and light. And my outfit is inspired. I'm in short, ripped denim shorts, knee-length brown boots, and a tee shirt with Miss Piggy printed on the front. Unfortunately for Jake's band, I'm still calling them The Muppets and it's begun to stick.

My stomach rolls as I sip at my drink. I've barely eaten a bite all day. Jake keeps throwing me concerned looks from his perch behind the drums. Each time I wave and smile, and I swallow the bile climbing my throat. It must be a virus but in this humidity, it's hard to tell if I'm fevered or slowly dying from heatstroke.

When they begin a cover version of "Drive By" by Train, Jake chimes in with back-up vocals. My ears perk up. I haven't heard him sing before. His voice is deep and strong.

I stand from the table, needing to be closer to the stage. My eyes watch him as I shift through warm, moving bodies. He's looking at me. Chills ripple my skin as he sings, "I was overwhelmed, and frankly scared as hell, because I really fell for you," as though it were meant just for me.

I hold my hands above my head and bop my hips to the beat. He grins, liking it. Moments later, harsh screams tear right through the music.

Jake's beat falters.

I turn.

Something hot zings by my neck.

"What the hell?" I mutter, my heart hammering as I hold a hand to the burnt skin.

The scent of fear permeates the air. Bodies surrounding me push and shove, creating pandemonium. The guy next to me stumbles and falls. People step over him, and on him, booted feet unintentionally kicking him as the crowd rushes the exit. I drop to a crouch beside him and someone's knee catches me in the head.

"Hey!" I shout, but they're long gone, lost in the crush of stampeding bodies.

I grab the guy's arm, trying to help him up. By this time the music has died. The only sound I hear is yelling and panicked screams and a sharp whistling *ping* sound above me. I know that sound. They're bullets. Oh my god! What the hell is happening?

"Mac!"

The shout comes from Jake, his voice loud and frantic.

"Here!" I yell back as I yank on the bicep in my grip. My shout is cut short as my hand slips. I fall backward, landing on my ass with a thump. Then I notice my hand and stare in shock, paralysed for a single second. My palm is covered in blood. I look back at the guy. He's staring at my palm too, his eyes glassy and face pale.

"Those fuckers are shooting at us!" I shout.

I need my backpack. It's in the room down the hall behind the stage. All our shit is kept there while the boys play. *Important* shit. Shifting to my knees, I make another grab for the guy. We get to our feet and I begin dragging him with me. He struggles, trying to run the other way, toward the front exit.

"Don't be a dick!" I yell at him and yank on his arm. "That's where the shooters are. You want them to put another hole in you? Jesus!"

"Mac!"

I turn back and Jake smacks into me. "Out the back," he orders and makes a grab for me. Then he pauses, his face blanching as he takes in the smears of blood covering my right arm and coating Miss Piggy's face.

"It's not mine," I yell, evading him with a quick sideways shuffle. "It's his." I shove the guy at him. "He's been shot."

Not turning to see if they follow, I race down the hall, adrenaline firing my blood. Jake's band is in there grabbing at cables and shoving guitars into cases. "Are you all crazy? There's no time for that shit!"

They keep at it, ignoring my shout. I leave them to it and make a beeline for my bag.

"Mac! Get to the car!" Jake yells behind me.

Finding what I'm searching for, I load the handgun with steady hands and engage the slide. Straightening, I turn, raise both arms, and aim it toward the hallway door. "I'll hold them off," I say, countermanding his order.

"Holy shit." Rowan pauses in his grab for a bass guitar. He looks from the gun to me, taking in my proficient use of a weapon and cool demeanour. "Who the hell *are* you?"

I can't resist and narrow my eyes. "I'm your worst nightmare."

Rowan's laugh is nothing short of hysterical.

"She really is," Jake mutters. "Put the gun away, Mac."

"Don't be ridiculous. There are bandits on the loose and you're telling me to holster my weapon?"

Jake stares me down, eyes hard. "This is not the Wild West."

"I wanna see what she can do," Rowan interjects.

He doesn't sugarcoat it. "Mac is a shitty shot."

I gasp.

Rowan is standing near my line of fire and cups his junk.

"That was *one* time!" I retort, outraged at the reminder of our family trip to the shooting range. I'd been keen to impress Jake with my skills, but when I lifted my arms and took aim, he came up close behind me. His breath had been warm on my ear and the heat of his body set mine alight. For a single second I'd thought my knees would give out beneath me. The shot went wild, and I haven't lived it down since.

The guy we dragged to the back room with us begins to moan like an old woman. He weaves unsteadily on his feet. Moments later, the lights go down and booted feet hit the hallway as if a veritable army is coming for us.

"Go!" Jake bellows.

"Jake—"

"I'll be right behind you!"

I don't know what comes over me in that moment, but a shutter slams down. Everything inside me switches off leaving behind cool, clear focus. My body has taken over, and I can't stop it, not even if I wanted to.

"You go," I order. "I'll cover you."

"Mac!"

My name rips from his lips, wild with panic.

"Go!" I shout, evading his capture as I run toward the hallway door. Arms raised, I fire blind shots into the inky darkness and pray at least one will find its mark. The scuffling and the cadence of booted feet stop instantly, but there are no shouts of pain.

"Are you crazy?" Jake grabs my arm. With the injured guy in his other grip, I'm dragged through the back room and out the door into the heat of the night. We're nearing the van where the band is tossing equipment in the back when I turn my head. My heeled boots catch in the gravel. I curse, stumbling as I catch sight of a gunman right behind us. Jake loses his hold on me.

He stops, making a grab for me. I shove him forward as I right myself. "Go!"

But the sound of heavy breathing hits my neck. Whoever it is, I'm about to be caught if I don't do something quick. He's too close for me to simply turn and fire my gun. It would be knocked from my hands before I could take aim.

Reaching the van, I tuck my handgun in the back of my shorts and snatch the nearest guitar case. Spinning, I slam it into the head of my pursuer.

He goes down like a sack of potatoes. My feet skid on the gravel from the momentum as cheers erupt behind me.

I pause for a moment, wide eyed as I realise I just felled an attacker with a guitar case. It's still in my outstretched arms as my chest heaves. I stare at him, wanting to smash his teeth down his throat and leave him to choke on them. He shot at me. *At Jake!* I take a step toward him and he lets out a moan.

Jake pulls me away and the case is pried from my white-knuckled fingers. My stomach lurches when I'm launched into the sky, my body airborne. Jake has hauled me up and hefted me over his shoulder, growling, "Have you lost your everloving mind?"

With adrenaline eclipsing all else, all I can do is grin, breathless, as he runs toward his car. This, right here and right now, is my proof that fate has a way of intervening. I didn't ask for this. I didn't *ask* for violence and chaos. It finds me, no matter where I go or what I do. I'm simply following the path created by destiny. I didn't *choose* the badass life, the badass life chose *me*.

"I do believe I have," I answer as I'm shoved into the back of Jake's car. Moments later, the bloodied body of the injured guy is dumped beside me. The very second Jake and Rowan slide in the front, the car careens out of the parking lot behind the van. Dust and gravel fly out behind us as we fishtail out onto the road.

Leaning forward, I untuck my gun, check the chamber, and rest it on my lap. My gaze slides to the guy beside me. He's sitting as far from me as possible, eyes shifting like a ping pong ball from my face to the gun and back again. He looks *terrified*. "Who *are* you?"

Rowan hoots from the front. "Don't you know? She's your worst nightmare."

I hold out a hand toward him. "I'm Mac."

He doesn't take it. We literally just saved his life, and he's staring at me like I'm about to shoot his face off. "Are you like, the police or something?"

"Or something," I snap, my eyes dropping to his wound. "Rowan, give me your shirt." Moments later, I'm handed a warm bunch of cotton. I shove it toward the guy. "Here. You're bleeding all over Jake's car."

He takes it and presses it to his wound, hissing.

Catching a meaningful look between Jake and Rowan, my eyes narrow. "What the hell *was* that back there? What's going on?"

Jake's eyes fix on the road, his car eating up distance at warp speed. Rowan responds. "A robbery, maybe, I don't know."

I'm sceptical. It felt like we were specific targets. "Jake?"

"What Rowan said." His voice is raspy, and he clears his throat. "The Bar does a rocking turnover. Lots of cash in the register."

What he says makes sense, yet something feels off. I sit back in my seat, my hands linking together when I realise they're trembling. Why am I shaking? Why is my stomach still pitching like its adrift at sea? Bile climbs my throat. It rushes upward at a burning pace, faster than I can swallow it back down. "Pull over," I garble.

"What?" Jake half turns, taking his eyes from the road and glancing at me.

"Pull over!" I boom, heaving on the words.

Jake eases off to the side of the road. Sliding my gun to the seat, I give the injured guy a sharp look. "Touch that and I'll cut you." The words are meant to be harsh, but I expel them in a shrill voice with my desperate need to purge everything from my body.

"Mac? Are you okay?" Jake asks.

There's no time to give the obvious answer. Shoving open the door, my legs give out. I drop to my hands and knees and hurl in a violent fashion. Rowan winds down his window and sticks his head out. "No rush, Mac," he says mildly. "We only happen to have a guy in the back seat who's been *shot*. But if you feel the need to puke, take your time. He doesn't mind bleeding out all over the—"

"Shut the fuck up, Rowan," Jake growls from somewhere near my ear. Then his hands are under my armpits and he's lifting me. "Princess?" he says softly, cradling me against his warm chest as I breathe through another wave of nausea.

"I'm fine," I slur, but in the dark recesses of my mind I know I'm not. There's something wrong with my body. I've been off my game all week.

My eyes flutter closed and I hand control to Jake. I trust him with my life.

"Rowan, you drive," he orders.

Jake slides into the passenger seat that Rowan quickly vacates. His hold is tight, and we drive to the hospital with me curled in his lap. It feels warm and safe. I drift in and out. When the car comes to a complete stop, my eyes open to mere slits. Headlights shine bright in the darkness, illuminating the side of Jake's house. They switch off and night surrounds us.

"We're home?" I mutter tiredly.

"We're home," Jake answers, his voice choked for reasons I don't understand. Rowan is already out of the car and a quick glance shows an empty back seat. "What happened to—"

"He's fine. He's at the hospital."

I'd slept through all of it. Why am I so tired?

Opening the car door, Jake slides out managing to hold me tight against him. When he stands, I'm still in his arms, his heart beating a soothing thump against the side of my face.

"I can walk," I protest, though I make no move to stand.

"Let me carry you, Mac." His grip tightens, and he brushes a kiss against the top of my head. "Please."

Chapter Twelve

Jake

I'm standing in the living room, having carried Mac upstairs and left her sleeping in bed. When I come down, Rowan is perched on the edge of the armchair, filling Leander and Luke in on the night's events.

Besides being a lead singer, Rowan is a friend and knows of our involvement in the King Street Boys. And he really is a stud for hire, just like he told Mac. He escorts his services out to any woman foolish enough to pay for what he gives away free every other night.

"What the hell is going on?" he asks, dragging fingers through his dark hair when he finishes the recount.

Leaning back against the wall, I fold my arms and fix my gaze on Leander. He's watching me, eyes dark and serious. "You spoke to Ross, didn't you?" I ask him.

He nods.

"About what?" Luke interjects.

Leander rolls his eyes. "For fuck's sake, Little Fox."

Luke looks at me. My stance is rigid and tension is rolling outward like gamma rays. "Oh," he says. "Oh shit."

"Oh shit puts it mildly," I reply.

Leander snatches a packet of cigarettes from the coffee table that rests between us. Tapping one out, he puts it to his lips and lights it.

After a long plume of smoke is exhaled, he says, "They'd rather see you dead then let you out."

It's the worst possible outcome. I'm a marked man. Mac could be killed simply by association. Or caught in the crossfire. Apprehension sends jitters through my stomach. Despite trying to quit the filthy habit, I reach for the cigarettes. If there's ever a time for a nicotine fix, now is it.

Lighting it, I draw on the end. My chest expands and fills with smoke. It expels past my lips as I speak. "What did Ross say when you spoke to him?"

"He asked why." Leander shrugs. "I told him you wanted the straight and narrow. That you don't want to do this forever and that it's better to get out now while you're still young enough to find a better life."

"Did you mention Mac?"

His expression is withering. "No, I didn't mention Mac."

"They shot at her," I tell them all, my hand trembling as I bring the cigarette to my lips.

"And she shot back." Rowan looks at me, shaking his head in wonder. "Your girl looks like some kind of angel, but holy shit she's got some balls in those panties of hers!" He hoots. "She almost shot me in the junk!"

Luke's brows wing up. "She *what?*"

"Don't be dramatic," I tell Rowan. "She didn't shoot anywhere near you."

"How does Mac even have a gun anyway?" he asks.

"Because she's a Valentine," Luke informs him as if that says it all.

Rowan is clueless. "Who are the Valentines?"

"They're like the Avengers of Sydney. Don't ever get on their bad side," he cautions.

Rowan shakes his head as if he can't believe it and looks at me. "How did you end up with her?"

"Really?" My temples begin to throb marking the beginning of a painful headache. "After everything that's gone down, these are the questions you find the most important to ask?"

Rowan shrugs and gives Luke a look as if to say *"I thought it was pretty damn relevant."*

"You should see Mac with a gun," Rowan mutters to him. "It's hot as fuck."

"It's not hot." I jab a finger at Rowan with the hand holding my cigarette, furious all over again at Mac's rogue behaviour. "It's stupid."

Rowan holds up both palms. "Whatever, mate."

My gaze cuts back to Leander. "What are you thinking?" he asks me.

"I'm thinking they all know where I live. If they wanted me dead, I'd already be six feet under."

He nods, agreeing with my assessment.

"Holy Jesus," Luke moans, clearly stressed. There's a bottle of Jack on the table and four empty shot glasses. Rowan must have set them out before recounting our story. Luke pours them out and picks one up. Tipping his head back, he tosses the contents down the back of his throat. Hissing, he sets the empty glass down and reaches for another. He tips that back too.

"Are you okay, Little Fox?" his older brother asks.

"I'm not sure," he gasps, rubbing his chest.

"Can I get you anything? Some smelling salts, perhaps?"

Luke opens his mouth, spouting his predictable reply, "Get stuffed, Lee."

We all chuckle lightly, except for Luke. He's busy reaching for another shot.

"What I'm thinking," I say as I lean down, stubbing my butt out in the glass ashtray, "is that it was a warning. Next time will be the real deal."

Rowan expels a sharp puff of air. "Fuck," he mutters. "What are you going to do?"

I grab a shot from the table and drink the scotch down in one, quick gulp. Fiery warmth spreads through my chest. "I'm going to have to talk to Ross. Tell him I thought I wanted out but I was wrong."

"You know what else you're gonna have to do," Leander says.

All three of them are watching me. I nod, appearing calm. On the inside I'm anything but. Heat prickles my skin as anger and frustration build. Mac is the only thing in my life that matters and I have to let her go. She's going to deem it the ultimate betrayal. She's going to hate me.

My mouth clamps shut before I can roar my outrage. When I eventually speak, my voice is gravel. "I'll go make the call."

Mac

When I wake in the morning, I'm alone. I roll to my back and fix my eyes on the ceiling. My belly feels ready for another purge but there's nothing left. I have no fever. No headaches. No pain. No nothing. Then my eyes go wide and I know. I just *know*.

I launch from the bed, pitching stomach be damned. I can't hold this news in for a single second. Jake needs to know. Giddy, I conduct a thorough search of the house. It's deserted, which is unusual for this early in the morning.

Goddammit, this is so typical! I'm bursting to deliver the news of my life and there's not a soul in sight. I walk to the front door and peek out. Jake is on the porch seat in the early light of dawn. He's hunched over. His elbows rest on his knees and his eyes are locked on the riot of colour across the horizon. Red, orange, and pink blend prettily in the sky as the sun rises on another day.

The beat of my heart accelerates, and a cold sweat chases the warmth from my skin as I reach for the handle of the door. *I'm nervous,* I realise with surprise. I don't know how he's going to react.

Jake turns his head as I step out. His eyes on mine are troubled, and he's cracking his knuckles. An ominous feeling settles in my gut, and my gut is something I've always trusted. It's about last night. I know it is. I went a little crazy but I'll rein it in. My hand goes to my belly. I have to. It's not just about me anymore.

"Jake? What are you doing out here alone?"

He blinks rapidly and his nostrils flare. It's how he gets when he speaks of his father, so I know he's trying hard right now to hold himself together. "I couldn't sleep."

My brow pulls together. "You sat out here all night?"

He nods and looks away, his eyes returning to the sunrise.

"Why?"

Jake doesn't tell me why. He shakes his head as if he can't even speak. A heavy beat of silence passes between us. His gaze shifts to his hands. "Whatever you do," he eventually says, "promise you won't hate me."

Oh god. My stomach sinks and fear rises in an instant, sending a chill over my skin. My voice is an accusation. "What did you *do*?"

In the still of the morning, the crunch of gravel reaches my ears. My head turns toward the sound. A car is pulling in the drive. The colour is a deep royal blue with white racing stripes on the bonnet and wheels that could flatten a dinosaur. But none of that matters. What *does* matter is that I know the car. I know it well.

It comes to an easy park in the driveway. The engine switches off and the door swings open. I shield my eyes from the early morning sun as Mitch steps out.

I stare at my eldest brother as betrayal steals my voice. He's striding toward me, whipping off aviator sunglasses and tucking them in the neckline of his shirt. The action reveals enough raw emotion in his gaze to wipe out a small nation—love, support, and overwhelming relief. They narrow as he gets closer and reveal the wrath of a thousand warriors, and retribution so fierce an ordinary person would fear for their life.

Hurt and anger swallow me up, and when I take a step forward, my legs almost give out from the force of it. I take hold of the stair railing and turn my head to Jake. His beautiful eyes are fractured, wavering between pain and regret. Good. I hope it chokes him to death in his sleep.

"You don't want me to hate you, but that's asking too much," I say in a crushing whisper.

His eyes close as if my words have ripped apart his entire world. "I'm sorry."

"You don't get to apologise," I hiss.

There's so much more I want to say, but I'm damned if he deserves to hear any of it. Instead, I take a deep breath and lock the pain away so deep inside I vow it will never see the light of day again. "You held my heart in the palm of your hand and you've just thrown it away." My voice is cooler than the arctic, and he flinches at the tone. "If you want a promise from me, it's that you'll never hold it again."

When I turn back, Mitch is there in front of me. He folds me up in his arms, squeezing so hard my ribs scream in protest. "Mac," he mutters near my ear, not letting go. "Are you okay?"

"Yes," I whisper, but the word is a lie because I'll never be okay again.

"Good." His voice hardens. "Because I'm going to fucking kill you."

I've heard the threat a thousand times before, but this time there's a wealth of hurt in the words. Tears burn. I blink them back. I'm not going to cry. "You can kill me later," I whisper. "Just get me out of here. Please, Mitch." My voice cracks and when he draws back to look at me, he nods once, his face pale.

He was expecting trouble over getting me home and my lack of fight has him worried. "Get in the car."

I step around him and walk toward it. I don't look back. And I don't breathe. I can't. My chest is too tight.

Elijah is standing by the open back passenger door. The closer I get, the easier it is to read the relief in his eyes. "Why did you come?" I ask, reaching the car.

"I came because I care about you, Mac."

I nod. Eli has always been another brother figure in my life. When I go to slide inside the car, he stops me with a hand to the shoulder. "What were you thinking?"

My jaw tightens as I look him in the eye. "Excuse me?"

"This stunt was childish, Mac."

"I don't need a lecture from you."

His lips mash together as though he's carefully considering his next words. "You're right. You don't need it. But you hurt a lot of people, including me."

Elijah's eyes are pained and remorse fills me. "I know. I'm sorry." *But if I had the choice, I'd still do it all over again.* My actions in leaving were rash and impulsive, but they were worth it.

His hand squeezes my shoulder before letting go, and I climb inside the car.

Jared occupies the driver's seat, and Travis sits in the back. They both swivel their bodies to face me as Elijah slides in. I scoot into the middle to give him room as my brothers sit tense, their shoulders tight and mouths pressed in grim lines. They're expecting me to cause a scene. I want to. There's an urge inside me to scream until my voice gives out, but I don't. I've been defeated in a battle I didn't see coming. Now I just want to huddle in a ball and will this hideously painful ache to go away.

I look through the front window. Mitch is talking to Jake. I don't know what they're saying, and I don't care. Getting out of here is my number one priority.

"Mac," Travis begins.

I cut him off before he gets another word out. "I don't want to hear it."

"We don't care what you want," Jared adds, his tone furious. "You're—"

My brother's statement is the equivalent of poking an injured bear. I turn my head to look at him, my eyes narrowing to slits. "Of course you don't *care* what I want," I hiss, rejection burning a hole right through me. My gaze shifts to Travis. "Neither do you. None of you do!"

And Jake least of all.

My heart squeezes.

"Assheads," I mutter, wiping at my eyes. *Do not fucking cry*, I order myself. *Don't do it.*

"Mac," Travis tries again.

I hunch over, hiding my head in the palms of my hands, and burst into tears. My sobs are loud and ragged, their intensity so deep it hurts my chest. Shock fills the car in a thick cloud. I can't see it, but I feel it.

Elijah drags me toward him. His arms lock around me, anchoring me to him. "Jesus, Mac," he mutters as I soak his shirt with my tears.

Travis leans down and tips my chin up with his hand so he can meet my eyes. "Of course we care. You're our little Mactard. A fucking Valentine. When we found out you were gone we—"

"We were terrified," Jared cuts in. My eyes open to swollen slits and see the sincerity on his face. Then Mitch gets in the front passenger seat. He looks at Elijah, Travis, and Jared in turn, giving them a sharp nod.

"All good?" Elijah asks.

Mitch takes me in. The distress on my face is brighter than a neon sign. His eyes turn hard before he looks at them again. "All good." Then Jared starts the car and we drive away.

The ache inside grows bigger the further we drive, until the pain becomes so unbearable I feel I'll explode.

My brothers last twenty minutes before the lecture begins. I sit there dully, tuning them out as I stare out the window. We hit the freeway and the scenery is a blur as the miles between Jake and I grow bigger, and the cracks in my heart grow wider and deeper.

"Love is such bullshit," I mutter to myself, finding my anger. It fills up the hollow ache in my heart.

"Don't say that," Elijah whispers beside me, his hand falling onto my knee in a soothing gesture.

"Jake can go to hell," I vow with steely determination, ignoring my brother's best friend. "I hope he falls face-first in a pile of fire ants. I hope his precious rusty car spontaneously combusts. With him in it," I add snidely. "I hope—"

"Are you even listening to us?" Mitch asks, his voice high with incredulity as I mutter away to myself.

I turn my head. My brothers are staring, and Jared is throwing concerned glances my way from the rearview mirror. The pressure of their censure, along with my compromised emotions, weighs on me like a smothering blanket. All of a sudden I can't breathe. It leaves me lightheaded and reckless. The sudden lapse of sanity has me blurting out the one thing guaranteed to shut them all up. "I'm pregnant."

The words are flippant. A diversion attempt. And I put them out there without giving a single thought to the ramifications. Four pairs of eyes widen like dinner plates, and Elijah's hand freezes on my knee. Time stands still as they absorb my shocking announcement. Jared clearly struggles the most because the car veers right off the road.

"Jared!" I shout as we hurtle toward an embankment at high speed.

He curses wildly and grapples with the steering wheel. Mitch yells at him to brake. Jared jabs at the brakes, but his timing is all wrong because we've just reached loose gravel. Tyres spin beneath us and any control Jared has on the car is gone. We begin to skid and the back end flies out behind us in a dizzying circle. My hands grip the headrest in front of me, and I hold on as we spin with a force so strong it steals my breath.

"Get your foot off the motherfucking brake!" Travis yells.

Jared does and the car slows but it's too late. "Fuck!" he shouts. "We're going to flip over. Everyone brace!"

There's no time for panic. It all happens too fast. The wheels lift from the ground with wild momentum. Travis slams his arm hard across my chest, pinning me back in the seat as the world rolls before my eyes. My neck and back jolt with sickening force, and the crunch and screech of grinding metal reach my ears when the car slams upside-down on its roof. We roll again and again, the windows around us shattering. Glass splinters the air and cuts my skin like razor blades. A sharp sliver gouges my brow and blood fills my vision.

"Mac, close your eyes!" Eli orders.

I scrunch my eyes closed, blonde hair whipping around my face as blackness descends.

Jake

One hour earlier...

Mac will thank me for it later. At least that's what I tell myself as Mitch reaches her side. They hug for a brief moment, her brother muttering something before she pulls back. He looks down at her, jaw tight as if he's restraining the urge to wrap her in cotton wool and carry her away. Instead, he nods and Mac steps around him, reaching Elijah by the car. He's looking down at her like she belongs to him and I bank the rage with massive effort.

I force my gaze back to Mitch, watching his eyes harden like granite. I brace and Mitch comes out swinging, though it's not with fists like I expect. He attacks with words that do more damage than any punch can do. Physical injuries can heal, but words find the deepest part of your soul and they live there for an eternity.

He steps up on the porch. It brings us to eye level.

"You made the right call," he says.

My voice is like sandpaper. "I know."

"You're not good enough for my little sister."

I don't need Mitch reinforcing what I've known all along. "I know that too."

"You want to know why?"

Mitch has a steely look in his eye that Mac gets. It means he's going to spell it out for me whether I want him to or not. "I know why."

"I don't think you do, so I'm going to do you a favour and tell you." Mitch steps in my space, nostrils flaring. "My little sister is a lone wolf. Fierce and unpredictable. She's pretty much untameable, no matter how much my parents try. She has more worth than the rarest diamond, more heart than the strongest lion, and she's smarter than any of us give her credit for. And here she was, prepared to give all that to you, and you just let her walk away."

My head fogs with confusion. "I ..."

His finger jabs me hard in the chest. Twice. "You didn't fight for her, douchebag. That's how I know you're not good enough."

I take a step back and fold my arms, brows tight with tension. "I'm doing the best thing for her. We're too young. She should be home with her parents, shopping with her friends, going to movies, choosing a university out of all the offers she got. She shouldn't be at some ridiculous finishing college, and she shouldn't be here with me, pissing her future away. I thought we'd be in agreement on this."

"We *are* in agreement. Coming home is the best thing for her."

I throw up my arms. "Then what the hell!"

"Love transcends everything, asshole. The only man good enough for my sister is one who would fight to keep her no matter what." Mitch shakes his head, and he's right. I'm not fighting to keep her. But I *am* fighting to save her from myself. "You screwed up, Romero. Big time. There's no coming back from that."

Mitch starts down the stairs and pauses, turning to look back. "Oh, and one more thing. Stay the hell away from her. If we find you back in her life, Travis will dig a nice big hole in the ground, Jared will hunt you down, and I'll bury you in it."

Chapter Thirteen

Mac

Two years later...

I wheel my suitcase down the hallway until I reach the numbered apartment I'm searching for. Letting the handle go, I straighten my shoulders and stare at the door. It's been a long road to get here after leaving Melbourne. After the car accident.

My life irrevocably changed the day I woke up in hospital. Even now, when I'm doing everything I can to move on, it plays out like a movie in my mind.

"Mitch?" I turned my head on the pillow of my hospital bed so I could look him in the eye. "Did you talk to Jake?"

My brother just stood there grinding his jaw, his right arm in a sling from a wrist fracture.

"Did you tell him about the accident?" I prompted. Then my voice lowered to a raspy whisper because the words were hard to speak aloud. "Did you tell him that I lost ... that I ..." I couldn't finish. Jake lost a child before he knew he was going to be a father. A lump formed in my throat. It was painful to swallow. I didn't care that he pushed me away. This was bigger than our rift. It was bigger than anything. The pain had eclipsed my entire world.

Jake would want to know. And I needed him right now, more than I'd ever needed anyone.

Mitch looked away, fixing his gaze on the wall to my left. "I told him."

But Jake wasn't here. "And?"

His gaze came back to me. "And nothing, sweetheart."

"What do you mean *and nothing?* Why isn't he here?"

Mitch's expression was stony. "He wanted a clean break."

"No ... Mitch, he wouldn't do this." Tears threatened and my voice turned shrill. "He wouldn't stay away." I swung my legs over the edge of the bed, panic building like a storm. I rose to my feet. "He wouldn't."

My brother just stood there like a dumb, useless lump. I planted my hands on his chest and shoved. My legs were unsteady and it caused me to stumble backward.

"You're a liar!" I cried, grabbing the mattress to keep me upright. Mitch tried to help with his one good arm and I batted him away. "Where is he? Where's Jake?"

Mitch shrugged, helpless in the face of my rage. "I'm sorry."

"Fuck your apology!" I screamed. "Fuck you!" My fingers found the IV in my inner elbow and I ripped it from my skin. I was going to leave the hospital and find Jake. And when I did, I was going to beat the everloving shit out of him for abandoning me like a loser.

"Calm down." Mitch grabbed my shoulder and pushed me back toward the bed.

I slapped and shoved at his chest. "I won't calm down. Fuck you!"

My shouts drew Elijah and Travis to the room. "Mac!" Travis barked. "What are you doing?" Mitch had my shoulder and Travis grabbed at my torso, trying to push me back in bed without using too much force. "Get back in bed!"

"Don't order me around!" My breath came in frantic pants. I fought like a wildcat, and the three of them worked at pinning me down as I thrashed and screamed. "Let me go!"

They wrestled me onto the bed and Eli got in my face, blue eyes panicked and blond hair falling in his eyes. "Mac! Please," he begged. "You can't—"

"Get the hell off me!" My legs kicked out forcefully and my back bowed in an attempt to buck them off. A male nurse rushed into the room to help.

He jabbed a needle in my arm but I didn't see it. I rolled to my side and curled in a ball, a deep sob ripping from my chest. I wanted to die. "Just leave me alone," I whispered.

I was defeated. They must have seen it because the room slowly emptied, all except for Eli. I turned my head and looked into his eyes. He stared back silently and after seven pained breaths, my eyes closed and I drifted away.

We returned to Sydney three days later. Mum and Dad were relieved to see me home, but they treated me like a shattered picture frame that had been taped back together. We downplayed the accident so as not to worry them, and they didn't know about the baby. I made my brothers promise to keep it quiet. I wanted to mourn the loss in private and move on. That's what I came home to do.

I spent the next few days in my room, leaving only to shower and eat. Weeks into my convalescence, I made the trek outside to the pool. I sat there for an hour and stared at the rippling water, thinking of nothing. I returned the next day, and the next. It gave Mum hope. She came out and sat beside me, brandishing university brochures. I'd been accepted to five exceptional institutions, having applied for them before I left. The applications had been a last ditch effort to escape finishing college.

I grabbed the first brochure I saw. "This one," I told her so she'd stop talking.

Mum took care of the enrolment. She was thrilled to see me making a decision. She had no idea that I didn't care which university it was. I couldn't think about my future. It was too dark and bleak.

Over the next two years, I became the Stepford daughter they always wished for. The funny thing was, no one seemed to like it. My parents hovered more than ever. My brothers, including Eli, returned from their studies at Charles Sturt whenever they got the chance.

Once again, I was smothered, though this time it was for different reasons.

At the end of my second year of university, I discovered I barely knew the people I studied with. I barely knew my campus. And I didn't have a single *real* friend. None of them really knew me at all. I hadn't been living for two whole years. I'd simply been existing. The realisation hit me harder than a jackhammer. It was time to move on. And I couldn't move on at home.

I told my parents. I expected an argument but instead they gave in with equal expressions of defeat. Perhaps they thought it would help. They were desperate to see me return to my normal self, but I'd forgotten who that was.

Arrangements were made and my enrolment was transferred to a Melbourne university. I wasn't sure why I chose to return there, but something pulled me back. The city held such bad memories, but it held the best ones too. I loved hard and I lost deep, but I lived so much in that short period of time with Jake.

A shout comes from behind the apartment door. It jolts me from the memories of my past.

You're here to move on, I remind myself. *To remember who you used to be. Find that girl again. And if you can't, fake it until you do.*

I raise a fist and give the apartment door a sharp rap. A female voice filters through in a shout. "Hussy, get the door!"

"It's your turn, Sandwich," comes the pissy reply.

A loud smacking noise follows, like the sound of a ball hitting a wall. "You're so lazy!"

"And you're a greedy bitch."

The response is a wheezy gasp as though someone is caught in a chokehold.

"I am not!" comes the indignant, yet strangled reply.

I rap again.

"You ate all my Doritos, Evie!"

"Not *all* of them."

A loud squeal results.

"Ooomph! Get off me, Henry!"

There's a loud thump. It sounds like a body hitting the floor. Annoyed with waiting, I try the handle. It twists easily beneath my hand. The door isn't locked. I push it open. The girl, whom I'm assuming is Evie, is on her hands and knees on the floor. Her face is stuffed full of corn chips, her cheeks resembling a chipmunk. Her hair is the colour of dark caramel, her skin like nutmeg with a dash of rose, and her wide eyes the colour of chocolate. She's wonderfully exotic and beautiful, even with the thick layer of orange seasoning that covers half her face and lips.

The guy behind her must be Henry. He's cute. His hair is so blond it's almost white. His eyes are bright blue, and his bared muscular chest is currently sporting four blood-red scratches. He's busy pulling a chunk of Evie's long hair. His other hand is mashed into her back, pinning her down. An open packet of Doritos rest on the floor beside them, chips strewn carelessly across the floor like casualties of war.

"Spit them out," he growls.

She makes a garbled sound as if trying to say no.

He uses the hand fisting her hair to shove her head down further. "Spit them out, Sandwich."

The manoeuvre is aggressive, and Evie sputters. Two corn chips break loose from her mouth. They drop to the floor along with a string of saliva.

"And the rest," he growls again.

A muffled sound escapes her mouth. It sounds a lot like "Fuck off."

The scene reminds me of the relationship I had growing up with my brothers. It leaves me feeling at home in an instant. Armed with the knowledge I've chosen the right apartment and the right roommates, I wheel my suitcase inside and slam the door behind me.

They freeze in position, their eyes sliding my way. A brief pause ensues while we all stare at each other. It's followed with a loud crunch, which draws a glare from Henry. Evie swallows hurriedly, wincing as the solid mouthful forces its way down her throat.

"I'm your new roommate," I announce, because they don't know it yet. Their ad was pinned to a board in a local university pub named The Elephant.

ROOM AVAILABLE

Looking for the best, ass-kicking roommates that ever lived? Then we are your people. We have a great apartment near campus. We are both undergrads at Melbourne University and our interests include music and food.

YOU: must share similar interests, be financial, not steal food, be a good cook, be able to operate a thermomix, excel at maths, dislike country music, exhibit hygienic tendencies, and not lick windows.

PS we're not racist but no vegans need apply.

I unpinned the sheet of paper before anyone else got to it and wheeled my suitcase directly to the address listed. Finding an available room near campus is the equivalent of God turning water into wine. I'm not giving them a chance to say no, so I stare them down with brows high, daring them to refute my statement.

From what I can see, the apartment is fairly ordinary. The furniture appears pre-owned but clean. The windows are oversized and let in an abundance of light. The walls are beige but the floors are timber, and my small heels made a pleasant clicking sound when I walked inside.

With one last shove into Evie's back, Henry gets to his feet. He rubs a hand along the scratches on his chest with a wince. "Can you cook?"

"No."

He looks to Evie. She's getting to her feet and brushing hair from her face. She shrugs and both pairs of eyes return to mine. "Do you eat meat?"

"Your inquisition is unnecessary," I state coolly. "I'm your new roommate and that's that."

They purse their lips at the same time, like peas in a pod.

With an impatient sigh, I hold out a hand. "I'm Mac."

My gesture is ignored.

"She didn't answer your question, Evie," Henry says. His brows draw together in a wobbly line of worry. "I don't think she eats meat."

Evie clears her throat, drawing my attention. "You can't be vegan. We love bacon and we won't tolerate death stares while trying to eat it. It gives us indigestion."

"I eat anything," I tell them.

"Can you operate a thermomix?" Henry asks.

"What's a thermomix?"

Evie slaps the back of her hand against Henry's bared stomach. He has lovely washboard abs, but I'm immune. Men are not on my radar. "I told you that stupid appliance was a waste of our savings."

"It's supposed to do everything!" he protests.

Evie sets her lips in a grim line. "It does nothing but sit there gathering dust because you don't know how to use it," she hisses.

"I can chop things," I interject, fascinated by their argument. They act like brother and sister, yet they look nothing alike. It makes me wonder who they are to each other.

"Like?" Henry prompts.

I huff. It's a ridiculous question. "Like carrots and onions."

"That works," Evie says and offers me a grin. "I'm Evie Jamieson and this is Henry Paterson. Welcome to our humble abode, Macklewaine."

I arch a brow. "It's Mac. Mackenzie Valentine."

Her grin widens. "Mac Attack."

"Mactard," Henry offers.

My gaze pins him to the floor. My brothers use the nickname liberally. At least they did. I haven't heard it much in the past two years. The reprieve had been nice. "Henrietta."

"Yes!" Evie hisses loudly and jabs a finger at Henry. "I love it! Perfect for the times when you're acting like an unwaxed vagina."

His jaw locks. "I've never acted like a vagina in my entire life. Waxed *or* unwaxed."

An argument ensues, causing my head to pound. The two of them clearly need a parental figure to keep them in line. It seems that figure is going to be me. I clap my hands together smartly. "People!"

They pause for a breath.

"Perhaps you can show me where my room is?"

Evie leads the way. Henry follows, scooping his Doritos from the floor. He munches on them as I'm showed to the third bedroom. I wheel my suitcase inside and take it in. It's not much but it's furnished. A double bed fills the majority of space, and I have one bedside table and a built-in wardrobe. One acoustic guitar and two electric ones occupy the bed. We eyeball them for a moment.

"We're musicians," Evie offers.

"Oh?" I prompt.

"We have a band," Henry adds.

"Called?"

"The Futons."

I snort.

Evie and Henry look to each other and then back to me. "No good? We came up with that this afternoon."

"While you were sitting on one?"

"Well ... yeah," Henry says, and shovels a load of chips inside his mouth.

My lips mash together. *Be nice,* I tell myself.

"You don't like it?" Evie asks, hands on her hips.

Fuck it. Being nice is for dogs. I tried it once but it just didn't stick. They can either like me as I am or not at all. "It's a shit name," I tell them, "but we can work on it. Where do you play?"

"We don't," Evie says, not seeming bothered at all by my blunt honesty as she reaches for one of the electric guitars. "Not yet."

"You don't have any gigs lined up?"

They both shake their heads.

"We can work on that too."

My welcome to the apartment begins with a mini party. After spending a half hour unpacking my suitcase, the three of us go shopping for snacks and alcohol.

It takes two painful hours as I quickly get to know the two people I'll be sharing living space with. Evie is indecisive when it comes to food purchases. How long does it take to choose between crinkle cut or thin and crispy? I'll tell you how long it takes. *Ten whole minutes.* Do we want salted cashews or the mixed nuts? *I don't know, but let's stand in the supermarket aisle and discuss it for an hour.* Henry is no help. He's clearly used to her indecisiveness and entertains himself on his phone. Frustrated with her antics, I start grabbing at the items she can't choose between and throw both in the trolley. It's piled high when we reach the checkout. The total cost is tallied and it's beyond our budget. It's my fault apparently. Evie has deemed me too excessive. We spend another lifetime choosing which items to put back before we make our escape and arrive home, exhausted.

"I'm never going to the supermarket with your indecisive ass again," I announce to Evie.

"Yeah?" she retorts, dumping our shopping bags on the kitchen counter. "Good. Because we can't afford to take your excessive ass."

I set the bag of alcohol down. "Let's set a schedule and take turns."

Evie nods as if my suggestion is brilliant. "That's a great idea."
I pull a bottle of vodka from the bag and set it on the counter. "You know what else is a great idea?" she says with a grin.

"What?"

She whoops. "Getting this party started!"

We set our snacks on the coffee table and line the kitchen with spirit bottles, juice, an assortment of fruits, and a blender. I've never made a cocktail in my life. It would have been the one good life skill I could have taken with me from Fucking Dick Head school. With the price my parents were prepared to pay for my attendance, it would have been an expensive skill too. Thankfully, they were issued a refund. The money is helping pay my living expenses here in Melbourne.

I grab a bottle at random and pour with a flourish. Done, I screw the lid back on and reach for another.

Evie watches for a moment, giving the impression she's as clueless as I am. After throwing in a handful of ice cubes, I put my hand on the lid of the blender and flick the switch. It comes to life with a frightful revving noise, and my ears go into shock.

"Right," she says, startled into life by the sound. "I'll chop some fruit."

Henry walks in, rubbing his hair with a towel after having a shower. His lips move.

"What?" we both shout.

"What are you making?" he yells.

"Mai Tai's!" Evie screams helpfully.

I nod because I have no clue. It looks like the right colour for a Mai Tai. I flick the switch off and unclip the jug attachment. My ears ring as the apartment settles into relative stillness.

Henry stares at the contents, appearing doubtful. "You don't need a blender for those."

"These ones you do," I say and thrust the jug toward him. "Take this into the living room."

"You're bossy," he informs me as he walks the short distance to the couch. Henry sets the jug down and goes to choose some music. Moments later a thumping beat fills the apartment. He fiddles with the volume and the walls begin to vibrate.

There are no screaming parents here to yell, *"Turn it down!"*

I grin, picking up glassware while Evie throws the makings of a fruit salad into a bowl. "Get used to it," I yell over the music, feeling almost normal.

I take a seat on the couch. Henry and Evie pull up cushions on the floor. We pour drinks and add random pieces of cherry and orange. I'm watching Henry and Evie joke with each other when it hits me harder than a basketball to the face. I haven't thought of Jake in three whole hours. A lump rises in my throat. I swallow it down with the icy concoction I created.

"I've met someone," Evie announces before I can give the realisation any more thought.

Henry flinches, appearing alarmed.

She blinks rapidly, her chin jutting out. "He's really cute."

I get the impression this is not good news. Especially when I see Henry finish his entire drink in one swallow. He's yet to speak a word.

The song ends and Evie fills the silence as he pours another drink. "He's nothing like Wild Renny or Asshole Kellar."

Her reassurance doesn't ease the thick haze of tension that fogs the room.

"Explain," I order. I want to know what's going on. The two of them don't appear to hold any unrequited love for each other, so I can rule out jealousy.

When Henry leans over and tops up my glass, I know it's going to be good. "When Evie was sixteen," he begins. Evie gets up from our little circle and stumbles slightly as she reaches for the jug. She walks away, muttering something about more alcohol. "She lost her mum in a car accident..." he takes a sip from his glass and whispers "...and she went off the rails."

I'm wrong. It isn't good. It's bad. Very bad.

"I'm so sorry," I say to Evie as she sets the empty jug on the counter.

She waves a hand as though it's nothing when it's clearly not nothing.

"Renny was into motorcycles. One night they went out drinking and decided to take the bike out on the open road. It didn't end well. Evie wound up in the hospital and Renny disappeared. Just … poof!" Henry spreads out his fingers, mimicking a vanishing cloud of smoke. "He walked out of that hospital and left her there."

"Oh my god. What a dick!"

He nods knowingly. "Right? And Kellar was a drug dealer." My mouth falls open. "Evie didn't know." The blender switches on and Henry's voice rises to be heard. "He slipped something in her drink at a party. There was a raid and the cops found her climbing up the railing of the third balcony in an attempt to fly."

If that were me, my brothers would have hunted the asshole down and put a bullet in his kneecaps. That was if I didn't get to him first.

"Can you see why I fear for her life when she says she's met someone?"

"I do." Swallowing the last mouthful in my glass, I set it on the coffee table between us. "She likes the badasses."

Henry sighs. "She does."

"The bad badasses."

"Yep."

"She needs a different kind of badass. The kind that fights for good, not evil."

Evie returns with another full jug. She fills our empty glasses and we settle in, talking about our lives as we get to know each other. I learn that she has an older brother, Coby Jamieson, who sounds just like mine. Henry has three sisters. Two are twins and Grace, the sister he was closest with I'm told, is a model. He shows me images of her stored on his phone. One shows Grace walking the catwalk at Milan fashion week. *Milan.*

"But she's so young," I exclaim, admiring the floaty black designer creation she's wearing, though her hip bones jut from the outfit, pronouncing a thinness that looks unhealthy.

"I know but she seems happy." Henry shrugs but there's sadness in his expression, making me think he misses her. Perhaps Evie fills the void.

The room has begun to spin as we keep drinking. My glass is receiving another refill when the front door flies open with considerable fanfare and noise. My back is to the entrance, but I hear drunken, stumbling footfalls make their way inside. Evie whoops loudly. "All hail the Rice Bubbles!"

I hiccup. "The *Rice Bubbles*?"

"Snap, crackle, and pop," she tells me. "The rest of the band. They live just across the hall."

"Say it ain't so," whines a male voice. "You're partying without us?"

I half-turn in my seat. My eyes land on the guy closest. His hair is black and silky, and his eyes are dark pools of ink. Evie points at him with her drink. "Meet Cooper."

Cooper's gaze slides my way. "Sandwich. Paterson ..." he says as he stares at me. "Why didn't you tell me the most beautiful girl in the world was alive and well and not just living in Melbourne but *partying in your apartment?*" He moves closer, presumably for a better look because he's squinting. Or possibly trying to wink. I'm not sure. It brings me to crotch level and a smirk curves his lips. "While you're down there ..." he trails off suggestively.

"While I'm down there what?" I ask, my voice as pleasant as pie. "I can punch you in the junk?"

Cooper cups the area with a wounded expression.

"Back off, Cooper," Henry orders. "You're not touching her. This is our new roommate, M—"

"Mac."

My gaze shoots to the owner of the shocked male voice.

Oh my god. No. Just … no. How can this be? I suck in a mouthful of air as I drown in whiskey-coloured eyes.

The rest of the band, Evie's voice echoes in my head. *They live just across the hall.*

I convinced myself I'd never see Jake again. If I did, it would be at a point in my life when I'm older, mature, and it wouldn't *hurt.* Now is too soon. The hurt hasn't had time to heal. The wound is still there. It's not even a scar yet. Or scabbed over. Nor is it even fresh. It's still an assault. I know because it's stabbing me in the chest right now.

My heart gallops harder than a wild horse as I look at him. Two years has added more muscle to his frame and tattoos to his arms. Yet his hair—the glorious silky brown strands that turn to spun gold in the sun—is no longer the same. It's buzzed short. He promised me he'd never cut it short.

I moaned throatily, powerless to restrain the sound. Jake's head was between my legs. My fingers tangled in his hair, tugging it in my fists, as his mouth sends me over the edge. He kissed his way up my body until he hovered above me, a playful smile on his lips. "One day you're going to rip all the hair from my head if you keep doing that."

I smirked. "Well maybe you should just cut it all off."

"Never." That same hair tickled the side of my face as he bent his head, pressing slow kisses to the side of my neck. "It's how I know you've let go of yourself. That you're lost in the moment. It's how I know that you're mine, Mackenzie Valentine. All mine."

The words echo in my head. *Mine. All mine.* But not anymore. It sets off a tightening in my chest like heartburn after eating too much curry. I hate curry.

My gaze narrows on Jake. His eyes roam over me, eating me up like a last meal. He can't get enough, but neither can I. The urge to escape takes hold. I'm not one to run from confrontation, but fury is taking root. That asshole *abandoned* me. Right when I needed him most. If I don't leave right now, I'm going to throat punch him in front of everyone.

"You two know each other?" Henry's voice comes from far away.

Jake opens his mouth, but I beat him to it. "No."

The solitary word erases him from my life completely, wiping away years of friendship, love, heartache, and memories.

He jerks visibly. My response has cut him to the bone. Good. I twist the knife in further. "I'm sure I'd remember you."

"I guess you look like someone I used to know," Jake says, ire burning in his eyes as if he has the right to be angry. *Is this how it's going to be?* his expression asks.

I set my jaw. *Yes. I don't want to remember you so it's easier to pretend I don't know you at all.*

Cooper waves his arms between the two of us like a robot. Everyone looks at him apart from Jake and me. We're too busy staring each other down. I don't care if it's immature. I won't be the first to look away. I'm not the one who did wrong here.

Cooper keeps up his jerky moves. "The tension is killing my party vibe."

Jake looks away first but my triumph falls flat. There are no winners here.

He tucks his hands into his pockets and mutters, "I'm just gonna head out." He turns and leaves. The apartment door closes behind him with a soft click.

Chapter Fourteen

Jake

Not slamming that door takes every ounce of my control. Mac wants to play it like we don't know each other? *Fine.* Does she want to hold a grudge for eternity? *Okay.* I get it. I hurt her. *Bad.* But if that spoiled bitch is pretending to herself that I never meant anything at all, then I'm damn well going to remind her.

Except … I can't. It's been two years since the Valentines made sure I removed myself from Mac's life permanently. I received a phone call from Mitch Valentine the day after she left.

"How is she?" I asked because I was in absolute hell. With Mac gone it felt as if my life was over.

"You don't get to ask that question. Mac is none of your concern anymore."

My hand tightened on the phone, nostrils flaring as I leaned my back against the bedroom wall, letting it prop me upright. "It's a simple question. All I want to know is that she got home and that she's going to be okay."

"She's going to be fine," was all he said after a long pause.

"Okay." I drew in an aggravated breath. "Then to what do I owe the pleasure of this call?"

"We know."

Mitch had always been a man of few words. It was frustrating as fuck. "Know what?"

"We know all about your life since you left Sydney, Romero. After you gave us your address to come and collect Mac, Dad did a little digging." Of course he did. Damn Valentines sticking their fingers in everyone's pie. "I just got off the phone with him. He had a lot to say."

Sure he did. After some careful questioning with Mitch, I realised they knew just about everything. "Is there a point to this call?" I eventually asked, because if Mitch had one, he hadn't reached it yet.

"Yes there is."

"And?"

"How's your father doing?"

What the … "He's fine," I snapped, annoyed at the change of subject. "Why? Do you know something?"

"I know he's the reason why you're caught up in the King Street Boys. We found the lump sum payment you made for his care. Two years' worth. That's a lot of money."

I made the payment a week ago. It was part of the original plan in leaving with Mac. I wanted to make sure Dad was taken care of if something happened to me. "I had to do something."

"I know. But you don't have to live this life anymore."

"What do you mean?"

"We can get you out."

I turned around and pressed my forehead to the wall, closing my eyes. I hated that they knew my business. But what I hated more was hearing Mitch offering to help. I wanted to leap at it. At this point I'd do anything. Even accept the offer. But I couldn't because it was too late.

"I already tried." My voice cracked and it was embarrassing. I cleared my throat.

"And you failed," he said as I walked to my bed. Sinking down on the edge, I pressed the phone to my ear with one hand and held my head with the other. "With these people, Romero, it's not what you know, it's who you know. If you want out, consider it done. Just say the word."

"How?" I asked. "Who is it you know?"

"Does it matter?" At this point, no, it didn't. "Just say the word, Romero."

"Goddammit." I took a deep breath. "Get me out."

So they did. But freedom comes at a price. And we all know the cost. Stay away from Mackenzie Valentine. Except somehow we've been thrown together again. How am I supposed to do the right thing and keep my distance when fate keeps making it impossible?

Walking inside my apartment across the hall, I swipe the half empty bottle of Jack from the counter. Tipping it back, I swallow easily as I wonder what Mac is doing here in Melbourne.

Her face swims in my head as the alcohol burns through me. *Fuck.* I'll never dig her out from under my skin. I swig another huge mouthful of whiskey and choke, sputtering it everywhere. How am I going to live across the hall from her in a constant state of *look but don't touch.* It's going to send me insane.

Spinning, I throw the bottle against the wall. There's no satisfaction in watching it shatter everywhere.

"Dude," Frog says as I wipe my mouth with the back of my hand.

My head is fuzzy. I'm drunker than I realised. Jason Froggatt, my bandmate, roommate, and the best bass guitarist I've ever had the pleasure of hearing, stands in the doorway with his hand still resting on the handle. He looks so much like our other roommate, Cooper, they could pass for brothers. Frog's brow is wrinkled, his dark brown eyes forlorn as he stares at the shattered bottle. Alcohol pools on the floor amongst shards of glass and clumps of dust.

"Why ..." he starts and then trails off as if he can't speak. The waste of a Jack bottle is simply too much for him to comprehend.

"It slipped from my hand," I lie.

His gaze drops to my hand. He's inspecting it for lube. The last time booze was dropped in this house happened when Frog was drinking and rubbing one out at the same time. With the excessive amount of lube he somehow managed to get all over himself, the bottle glided right out of his slicked up hand and hit the bathroom mirror. The loud crash had Cooper and me running. We opened the door and found Frog standing naked in a pile of mirror shards, dick in hand, wailing about the seven years of bad luck about to rain down on his head.

"What was that about back there?" he asks as I open kitchen cupboards, looking for something to clean the mess with. The empty shelves stare back at me as I think about how to answer Frog.

Oh that's just Mac once again reappearing in my life. You know her, right? Except he doesn't know her because I never told anyone I let the best thing in my life slip right through my fingers without a fight. No point explaining to anyone that I'm a stupid sonofabitch. But I'm a sonofabitch that sleeps at night knowing she's better off without me, right? *Right?*

I have no idea what I'm going to do, but I can guess what the Valentine brothers will do. The minute they get wind of our inadvertent reunion, shit will hit the fan. I'll be in for the beat down of my life.

I slam the kitchen cupboards closed. There's nothing to tidy the mess with. When you're at the shops with limited funds and it comes down to either booze or cleaning supplies, what kind of chump buys a dustpan and broom?

"It's nothing," I tell Frog, when it's actually everything.

The truth is that I see Mac everywhere. I catch her walking down the street, sundress on and hair tousled from swimming in the ocean. Then she turns around and it's a stranger. I see her sitting in my lecture, three rows down. I stare at the back of her head for minutes at a time, missing everything my professor says. Then she laughs and tilts her head and her face is all wrong. A trapdoor opens and my heart plummets, each and every time.

It leaves me feeling like I'm losing it.

"You're losing it, man," Frog cautions, somehow stumbling onto the same conclusion. He staggers his way to the bathroom and unzips his pants to take a piss with the door wide open.

"Don't I know it," I mutter.

"What?" he shouts over the noise of him urinating into the bowl.

I don't answer. Instead, I search for my wallet. It's wedged down the back of our ragged old sofa. I tuck it into my back pocket. "I'm going out to get another bottle!" I call out, heading for the door.

"Fuck that," Frog says, zipping his jeans as he walks back in the room. "Stop being a killjoy and come back next door." His words are slurred. Whatever he drank over there, it's taking effect. "They have plenty of booze to fix whatever's going on in your head right now."

I'm not admitting to what's going on in my head right now. Or ever. I met this merry new band of friends two years ago, and if I've learned anything since then, it's that they pry into everything. No topic is too big or too small, and the term *too much information* does not exist. Your business is their business, your success their success, and your problems their problems.

It actually makes them the best kind of friends to have. They always have your back, even when they know you're wrong.

For example, Frog slept with another guy's girlfriend last month. It wasn't the coolest thing to do, but Frog believes in his right to fuck any living, breathing female that crosses his path. And he can be persuasive. The boyfriend found out. He came looking for Frog like a wounded bear charging prey. He had friends at his back and a knife in hand, fully prepared to cut Frog's dick off and shove it down his throat.

We knew this day would come eventually, so we might have been drunk and barely seated upright on our bar stools, but there was no element of surprise. We came out swinging, no holds barred. The showdown ended in a bar brawl, six stitches to a wound in Cooper's back from a switch blade, two broken chairs, and a lifetime ban at the bar we brawled in. It also ended with Henry getting diarrhoea because we got stoned afterward and dared him to eat a giant lump of wasabi.

No doubt my friends will come in handy when the Valentine brothers came to hunt me down and bury me in their dirt hole, but even *that* isn't incentive enough to share my stupidity over losing the girl who is everything I never deserved.

So when I open the apartment door and look at Frog, I keep my expression blank. "There's nothing going on in my head."

A loud burp escapes his mouth and he laughs. "You said it."

I roll my eyes. "Whatever, asshole."

Frog shuffles me across the hall. He opens the door and I'm pushed inside. I don't offer much resistance. To be honest, I'm not sure I can keep away. It's only been a few minutes, and I already want to see Mac again.

But she's not here. All I see are Henry, Evie, and Cooper. The three of them are yelling over the top of each other as Cooper struts in front of the television. He has heels on his feet and boobs underneath the white tee shirt. It's stretched tight from the new additions, revealing a hint of the orange balloons with black skulls underneath. They're leftover from our Halloween party last year. I know because I'm the putz who got stuck blowing them up. I gave up halfway through when it left me gasping like an asthmatic. I made the resolve to ditch the cigarettes, which I still plan to do. Soon.

I walk over and cup Cooper's chesty balloons. I've no doubt they've been playing Truth or Dare and he's chosen the latter. It's what we do when we drink.

I give his new additions an amorous squeeze and wink. "Show us ya tits, love."

Cooper smacks at my groping hands.

"Nice." Mac's comment is sharp and biting, like a rubber band flicking my skin. I turn around.

"I thought so," I reply in a mocking tone.

There's nothing more either of us can say without revealing our past connection, so I stare. Mac's hair has grown. It's piled in a messy topknot leaving her slender neck bare. She's wearing a baggy shirt and sweatpants. I can't remember her ever looking so good.

"See something you like?" she asks, folding her arms. "Because I don't."

"Burn," Cooper says from behind me and sniggers. It makes me feel ten years old. Frog pays no notice to either of us. He jabs at Cooper's chest like a punching bag. Popping sounds render the air and a loud argument ensues.

Fuck it. Mac and I can't be at each other's throats every day. No one can live like that. I walk toward the hall, holding her eyes until I pass. I know Mac will follow. She sees the intent on my face and is never one to back down from a challenge.

Knowing the guest room will be hers, I walk inside, turn around, and fold my arms as I wait. Mac doesn't disappoint. She joins me moments later and closes the door behind her with a discreet *click*.

It encloses us together and the battle to keep my emotions in check begins. I can already feel my jaw ticking as we glare at each other. I'm angry. She's not supposed to be here. I can't keep my promise to her brothers like this. "What the hell are you doing in Melbourne, Mac?"

She mirrors my actions and folds her arms, creating a standoff. "How dare you! I'm attending university here just like every other student." Her nostrils flare. "I'm not following you, if that's what you think. I'm not that pathetic to chase after a guy who doesn't want me."

A protest climbs my throat. I choke it back down.

I want her. *God, do I want her.* My hunger is palpable. It rages through my blood like an inferno, savage and hot. It's all I can do not to reach out and grab her.

I fist my hands by my side in a fight for control, but my voice is hoarse. It betrays me. "You think I don't want you?"

She cocks her head, entirely too calm and in control. I know it's an act. The colder Mac becomes, the deeper her agitation runs below the surface. "I used to think that, but I'm watching you now, Jake ..."

She steps toward me. Lifting a finger, she rakes a nail slowly down my chest, never taking her eyes from mine. I suck in a breath. Her lips curve coolly. She heard it. "... and I'm thinking you do. You want me. I see it in your eyes." Her finger trails down until she's cupping my rapidly filling cock. She squeezes and my pulse ignites. "And I feel it here."

I take her hand and move it away. "You think you can toy with me now?"

Mac smirks, tugging her hand free from my grip. "I don't think I can. I *know* it."

My chest expands with anger. "I'm not your plaything."

"I don't plan on playing with you. I plan on reminding you that we always want what we can't have. And you," she says, taking a step backward as she holds my eyes, "will never have me."

My restraint snaps. I hate her coldness. I *hate* that it's directed toward me.

I grab Mac's arm and turn her, twisting it behind her back. She struggles as I push her against the bedroom wall, face-first. She turns her head sideways, growling curses. I take immense satisfaction in her loss of composure. "You're wrong," I hiss in her ear. "I've already had you." The familiar scent of her fills my nostrils, and I completely lose my mind. I forget every promise I made, both to the Valentines and myself. That's what she does to me. "I'll continue to have you whenever I damn well please. In fact, no one will ever have you the way I have you. Got that?"

"Fuck you," she spits out.

My cock is harder than an iron pipe, and I grind it up against the sweet, round cheeks of her ass. "Anytime, Princess."

"No," Mac says with force. My hold goes lax and she turns. Sparks shoot from her eyes. "No, damn you. *I don't want you.* Being in the same room as you makes me want to puke. I never belonged to you, Jake. And you never belonged to me. I just thought we did. I thought I had an idea of what love was, but I was young and stupid, and you ... well, you were just stupid."

The venom she spews is like little jabbing darts to the chest. It hurts. "Mac, what I did was the right thing to do. You know it is."

"You don't get to speak," she hisses, her hate so strong I can barely stand beneath the weight of it. "And you don't get to wrap up what you did with a self-righteous little bow to make yourself feel better. You're just some loser who had the chance at something great and didn't have the balls to take it."

With that Mac walks to the door, flings it open, and leaves.

She's right. She's so very right that it eats away at me every single day. I had the chance at something great. But I couldn't take it. And now it's too late.

Chapter Fifteen

Mac

Three months later I'm happily settled in what we refer to as the *party apartment*. I fit neatly into the new dynamic *and* I have friends. Evie, Henry, and I balance each other out. If yin and yang were a triangle, that would be us.

Jake has made himself scarce wherever possible. When we get stuck in the same room together, he sits far enough away that my laser death stares don't scorch giant holes in his head. It's the smartest thing he's done since our unfortunate reunion.

With my dominant personality, it's natural for me to take on management of the band. The vote had been unanimous (and by unanimous I mean all but Jake). I have a knack for telling people what to do, and they need someone to tell them what to do. It's a match made in heaven. The first thing I do is change the name from *The Futons* to *Jamieson*.

Management of a band is not as easy as one would think, though. It's a nightmare. And stressful. My initial idea had been to upload videos of them playing their songs onto YouTube. In theory, it's an effective plan to help build an audience and a following. In reality, it's more complex than long division. The band members are like little kids thrown inside a play centre. I had moved to Melbourne and literally inherited four giant babies. And Jake. The biggest asshead that ever lived.

Cooper tried calling me "Momma Mac" once. I shot him down faster than a fly lands on shit. He avoided me for a whole week, slinking his way around like a whipped puppy.

Eventually I get them all together to record, sober, body parts intact, clothes void of food and alcohol stains, and they knock it out of the park.

Evie's smoky voice gives me chills, the boys' guitar playing sets the strings alight, and Jake, well ... it's good he sits at the back. I can watch him uninterrupted. My eyes travel the length of his straight nose, along the stubbled line of his jaw and down where his massive biceps flex and release, over and over. His hands fist the wooden sticks, and he pounds the drums like the beat is alive inside him. He's fantastic. My vagina thinks he's fantastic too, throbbing away to the same beat like it's a siren song. I literally have to clench my pelvic floor muscles and drag my eyeballs away.

After uploading the videos and spreading the word, *Jamieson* gets five bookings. They played their first on the Friday night just gone. They were a huge success. An epic bout of drinking followed. I could barely remember my own name when we stumbled home at five a.m.

It's later that day, near lunchtime on the Saturday, when a little bit of hell breaks loose.

Henry, Evie, and I are lying prone in the living area. Evie is splayed on the couch. Henry is on his back, calves resting on the arm of the couch and head tilted so he can watch music videos. I'm a starfish on the floor. We're hung over, starving, and incoherent so when the knock comes, the several feet it takes to get up and answer the door is the equivalent of a journey to Middle Earth.

Our arms shoot out simultaneously, fists closed. A quick rock, paper, scissors commences. Evie loses like she always does. She staggers off the couch and hobbles her way to the door. Each step is no doubt setting off little explosions in her head.

She flings the door wide open. Losing control, it flies back and hits the doorstop with a *clank*. She's so hung over her body has forgotten how to function. We wince at the noise. Henry mutters a quiet, "Fuck."

But then I see who's standing on the other side of the door. My heart thumps in excitement. Jared is here. My brother has changed since the accident. It brought us closer. We still have our fights, but they're good-natured. He also defends me to our parents. I have a suspicion he talked them into my move here. I'm thankful. We message each other daily now, but his visit is a surprise.

"You must be Evie," he says to my roommate as I roll to my belly in a pathetic attempt to stand.

Evie doesn't speak.

"Can I come in?"

No answer.

I push up on my hands and knees.

"I'm Mac's brother Jared," he offers as I get to my feet.

Evie is clearly unhinged as she guides him to the living area. Her body is moving but her synapses are not firing. I tuck that interesting bit of information away for later and run at my brother with a squeal. Henry mutters another quiet "Fuck" as I leap into my brother's arms.

Jared catches me. The last time I did that, our timing was painfully off. He'd spread his arms wide at the same time I leaped. Scrambling to catch me, he came away with a fistful of my hair and I came away with bruised butt cheeks.

Jared sets me carefully on my feet and palms my face with both hands. He smushes my cheeks together. "How's my little Mactard?"

I smack his hands away. "Fuck off, shit lips." Grinning, I turn. Evie has disappeared, but Henry remains. "This is my brother Jared," I tell him. "Jared, my roommate Henry."

Jared walks over and Henry partially stands to shake my brother's hand. Then he falls back on the couch with a pained groan.

"Wait." Jared looks between us both. "Are you two hungover?"

"No," I say quickly.

"Yes and we're dying," Henry gasps at the same time.

Thankfully, Evie catches everyone's attention, diverting Jared from his questioning. She races by in a flurry of bags, scarves, and jingling bracelets. Reaching the door, she hops about putting one shoe on after the other.

It's an embarrassing spectacle of the like I've never seen from her before. Her smile is bright. Knowing her insides are curled up in the foetal position like mine currently are, it's clearly false. The smile takes in all of us, though with Jared her eyes skim vaguely above his head. She offers a vigorous wave before disappearing out the door. All without a word.

We remain silent for a long moment, processing what has just occurred. Then I realise I have to explain what that was. I can't have Jared thinking I room with drunken oddballs or he'll rat me out. We might be getting along, but it doesn't mean his protective instincts died. He will happily ruin this for me if he thinks shitty roommates are compromising my living situation.

I open my mouth to explain when he beats me to it.

"Pears."

"What?" I whip out. Has the whole world gone mad?

Jared is staring at the door Evie flew out of, one hand on his hip, the other scratching the back of his neck.

"Pears," he repeats with impatience as if I know what it's supposed to mean.

"What about them?"

"Good for a hangover," he mutters. His tone is vague as he drags his gaze from the door and finally looks at both of us.

It's clear he's distracted, and by Evie no less. This is fantastic. He hasn't even mentioned the fact that for me to be hungover, I had to be blind drunk the night before. The possibilities of this unexpected development have me giddy.

Of my three brothers, Jared would be the perfect one for Evie. Not Mitch. He's too responsible. And not Travis, he has a level of sweet that would be lost on Evie. But Jared … he has just the right amount of wild to appeal to her dark side, mixed with enough forcefulness to rein her in when she gets too out of control.

I almost beam but don't want to freak Jared out, so I pull my lips into a thin line.

"Nothing cures hangovers better than a bacon and egg McMuffin," Henry argues with careless disregard for the consequences.

It earns him a withering look from Jared. My brother suffers a health-food affliction. A potentially life-threatening one because he pushes this affliction onto everyone he meets. He's trying to change the world, one bunch of kale at a time. Soon enough it will get him killed.

God knows I've imagined shanking him in his sleep several times after going to bed hungry. His turn at cooking dinner is the stuff of nightmares. Take his open lentil burgers … it's basically a lentil patty with a side of salad. The "open" part means there's no bun. I remember smushing that patty so hard in his face he had lentils coming out his nose for days.

"A McMuffin?" Jared folds his arms. I brace, aware that a lecture is imminent. Henry sits there clueless. A babe in the woods. "Do you even know what's in one of those?"

"Sure I do." My poor oblivious friend reclines back on the couch and pats his belly, his expression dreamy. He's picturing one in his head right now. "Bacon," he states first, because it's the most important ingredient. "Cheese." I risk a glance at my brother. His nostrils have begun to flare. "Egg," Henry continues.

The apartment door opens and the Rice Bubbles enter the room. All three of them. Holy mother of shit. Jake's gaze hits Jared and his eyes widen swiftly. Without missing a beat, he backs straight out the door, his steps soundless.

"Keep going," I say to Henry before Jared can give the new arrivals his attention. Unfortunately, it means throwing my friend under a bus. I have no other choice.

"Errr ..." Henry's gaze flicks to Jake, brows drawing together with confusion.

"Focus!" I snap my fingers in his face. His cloudy gaze comes back to me. "Egg ..." I prompt.

Poor Henry. I feel guilty enough to consider doing his laundry for a whole week. Not that I would, but I considered it.

"Uh, a muffin."

With Jake blindly stepping backwards, he stumbles into a pair of shoes by the door. Jared starts to turn.

"What else?" I yell, and Jared's attention is back on us.

Henry's eyes shift from me to my brother and back again. "That's it, isn't it?"

Cooper and Frog stand there mute, clearly trying to follow what's happening. They look between the three of us and mostly settle on Jared because they don't know who he is. That's too bad. There's no time for introductions right now. Jake is almost out the door.

"No!" I'm looming over Henry now, panicked. I have a sweet set up here. All will be lost if Jared finds out about Jake. My friends. My independence. My management of the band. It's brought me back to life. I need this. I *need* them. "That's not it!"

Henry looks up at me from the couch. "It's not?"

"Love, dude," Cooper interjects, saving me.

I point at Cooper. "He's right. How could you forget that, Henry?" Oh my god, this conversation is ludicrous, but I'm all in now. There's no going back. "In every single McMuffin there's a sprinkle of love."

"Mac!" Jared's face pales in horror.

Jake's palm is wrapped around the handle and he's slowly closing the door as he backs out. *Forget the damn door, you twat,* I try telling him with my eyes. *Just run.* I turn on my brother, widening my eyes with feigned nonchalance. "What?"

He huffs and levels his gaze on Henry. "That *McMuffin*," he spits the word as Jake is almost out, "contains liquid margarine, which has genetically modified ingredients like hydrogenated soybean oil."

We all stare at my brother. His folded arms convey both tension and enthusiasm for the subject matter. Even Jake stares for a moment. I glare sideways. *Get out already, asshole.*

"It's basically a trans fat," Jared continues. "Which is linked to cancer, heart attacks, diabetes, asthma, and more. Then there's the muffin. At least eight genetically modified ingredients there, including some which are banned in certain countries. They're linked to issues like heart disease and IBS."

"*IBS?*" Cooper and Frog mouth silently to each other.

"The cheese, eggs, and bacon?" Jared shakes his head. Right then I know he's about to ruin McDonalds. Not just for me, but for my friends. "That highly processed cheese comes from unhappy cows injected with synthetic hormones."

"Aww, man, not unhappy cows," Frog comments, his shoulders slumping.

"Unhappy chickens too. The eggs don't come from little hens that frolic happily in grassy fields. These ones are kept in cages with no room to spread their wings, their little eyes never having seen sunlight. The pigs? They—"

"Dude," Cooper rasps as the door closes behind Jake with a soft *click*. "You gotta stop. My poor heart." He rubs his chest. "I can't take it."

"Jared," I snap, safe now that Jake finally cleared the room, having gone back to the bowels of Hell from where he'd sprung. "Enough. You're scaring my friends."

"Good." His lips flatten. "They should be scared. That kind of garbage isn't doing their body any favours."

My eyes hit the ceiling. When I find calm, I introduce Jared to Cooper and Frog. Then I drag him away before he does any more damage.

"What are you doing here?" I ask as we do a quick tour of the apartment. It's a pointless question. I know why. Jared is here on behalf of the entire Valentine clan to check up on me.

"I'm here to check up on you," he confirms.

What I love about Jared, and all my brothers, is their inability to tell a lie. No matter what, they're always honest with me, and if I never have anything else, at least I have that.

"Of course you are," I say as we wrap up the tour. It took all of thirty seconds. I lead him to the kitchen. It's crowded in there. Frog has the fridge door open. He's half inside it, rummaging through the shelves. Cooper and Henry are standing at the counter fighting over the last slice of pepperoni pizza.

"Be thankful it's me and not Travis or Mitch," he tells me.

"I got it!" Frog yells over the top of everyone. He backs out of the fridge, waving a bottle of hot sauce in the air. I snatch the bottle.

"Oi!" Frog cries.

Cooper and Henry have drawn battle lines. I lean between them and snatch the last pizza slice. They halt mid-argument, watching open-mouthed as I waltz from the kitchen.

"Why should I be thankful?" I call to Jared as I make my way to the living area. I turn and brace. My three friends come out, murder in their eyes. My own narrow in response. I know how to fight for food. Especially pizza.

Cooper takes a step forward and hesitates at my intimidating stance. I almost laugh. Several hairs were ripped from his head the last time he stole something from my plate and he's remembering the incident. He whined about his sore scalp for two whole days.

"Because I'm not as stupid as you seem to think I am," Jared calls back, catching my attention. "If it had have been Mitch or Travis here, they would've just killed him. No questions asked."

My mouth snaps shut with a *clack*.

Does he have eyes in the back of his head?

"Yes I do," he tells me.

Did I say that out loud?

"I see everything, Mackenzie Valentine, and you have some explaining to do. But first," he says, starting for the apartment door, "there's something I need to attend to across the hall."

I throw the pizza slice in the general vicinity of my pursuers and make a grab for Jared. He moves too fast. He's already in the hallway before I catch up. "Will you just stop!" I shout, careful to shut the apartment door behind me.

"No."

Raising a fist, he bangs on the door opposite ours.

I shove at him.

He doesn't budge.

"Stop interfering in my life," I hiss.

Jared faces me, hands fisted by his sides and fury burning bright in his green eyes. "We would stop interfering if you had your life under control, but clearly you don't. So I'm here to do it for you."

Rage builds so quickly I can't breathe. When I exhale it comes out as a howl through clenched teeth. I'm going to throat punch my brother so hard he won't be able to talk for a week.

Then a light dings on. "Wait a minute." My nails bite into my palms. "How do you know Jake lives here?"

"Because we know everything."

Oh. My. God. *My asshole brothers!* Snooping into my life. Snooping into my friends' lives. I'm sure they even performed a background check on the stupid bird that squawks in the tree by my window every morning. The same one that squirts its crap all over the glass. I'm sick of cleaning it.

Jake is the whole reason Jared is here. Not me. My brothers already know he lives across the hall. Just like I'm sure they know he's the drummer for *Jamieson*. They simply sent brother number three as a representative to deal with the issue.

Just to round out my shitty weekend, the apartment door opens. Jake stands there, shirtless as usual. I eyeball every inch of inked, tanned skin until I'm dazed. What is he doing? Growing muscles on his muscles? He looks ridiculous.

I scowl at him. "Put on a damn shirt."

Jake huffs in a breath. His massive chest rises like the sun. He huffs it back out, his gaze moving from me to Jared. He gives my brother a chin lift and steps back, opening the door wide. "You may as well come in."

Jared steps inside. When I follow behind, my brother turns and plants a hand in my chest. "Oh no, little Miss Sunshine. You're not invited."

"You can't—"

That's all I manage before the door slams in my face. The *thunk* of a lock clicks in place. The urge to kick the door is strong. I resist.

Picking up the phone and raging at Mitch and Travis will achieve nothing. Calling Mum and Dad to bitch them out will simply draw attention to a situation that I'd prefer remained under the carpet.

I stand in the hallway gnashing my teeth as I figure out my next move.

A slow smile pulls at the corners of my lips when I realise exactly what it is.

The plan of all plans to rid myself of my brothers for good.

It will take time.

But the best plans always do.

And I can be patient when required.

I'll have them out of action without them even realising what's happened.

Chapter Sixteen

Jake

I'm surprised it's taken one of Mac's brothers this long to pay a visit. The Valentines are not only resourceful, they're smart, and their contacts stretch to all four corners of the globe. I'm sure they've been keeping tabs on me since the fateful phone call I had with Mitch two years ago.

I click the lock in place and Jared turns.

I fold my arms. "I've been expecting you."

Mac's brother nods, absorbing that piece of information. *That's right, bud. I'm not stupid either. I know how you all operate.*

"Then you'll know why I'm here."

I manage not to roll my eyes. "Yeah, I have a fair idea."

"Good." His eyes scan the apartment, taking in the cheap furniture and open textbooks strewn across every surface. We actually do try and study once in a while. The next words from his mouth have my brows soaring in surprise. "Got any beer?"

My phone buzzes as I'm reaching for two bottles from the fridge. I hand one to Jared and keep one for myself. Whatever he has to say will go down a damn sight easier with a beer in hand.

Collecting my phone from the breakfast table, I read the message as I tilt my head back and swallow the beer.

Princess: Tell Jared we're having lunch with Evie and to get his ass over here

Jake: Tell him urself

"So …" Jared leans himself against the kitchen counter behind him and twists the lid off his bottle. "Do you really think being in this band is a good idea?"

My nostrils flare. "Because Mac manages it? You know, this band was formed before she came in and started taking over. I've been here for two years. She's been here three months." I hold up three fingers to emphasise my point. "Three! So if you think this happy little reunion is anything but coincidental, then you're all idiots."

My phone buzzes again.

Princess: Asshole

Jake: Bitch

"Oh, we know it's coincidental." Jared cocks his head, his expression smug. "We know everything, in case you forgot that."

I return his smug expression. "So if you know everything, then you'd know why Mac is here."

His brow wrinkles in puzzlement. "Because of the scholarship, of course. Transferring in her final year was last minute, but this university has the best business program in the country."

"That's what she told you," I mutter.

"Sorry?"

"She came here to get away from all of you," I flat out tell him.

"Rubbish. She—"

I cut him off, done with the conversation already. "Look, it doesn't matter. You're here to deliver the warning to stay away from Mac so get it done and leave."

"Actually that's not why I'm here, but since you mention it…" his green eyes turn hard "…stay away from Mac."

My phone buzzes once again. Ignoring his threat, I flick the message open.

Princess: I'm going to throw a brick through your bass drum while you're sleeping

She will too. Mac doesn't deal in empty threats.

Jake: Fine. I'll tell him

I put my phone down and look at Jared. "So why *are* you here then?"

"Because of *Jamieson*. You'll get recognised."

A snort escapes me. "Hardly. We've played one gig."

"Two things, Romero. The first is that I saw the YouTube videos Mac's been posting. The band is beyond good. The second is that I know my sister. She's determined and she's not afraid of getting her hands dirty. She'll have you bigger than *U2* in less than a year."

"You're getting ahead of yourself, Valentine. Besides, even if we did make it big, no one recognises the drummer. Sitting behind a set of drums, I don't get seen."

Jared's expression remains sceptical as he downs a mouthful of beer.

"I'm not a target anymore, and I'm not quitting the band."

I can't. It's all I have.

My phone beeps another message.

Princess: Did u tell him?

Jake: Impatient much?

Princess: I'm trying to help you out here

Jake: Sure and I'm the tooth fairy

"Fine," Jared says, setting his empty bottle down on the counter. I get him another. "Just don't die on my watch."

"On your watch?" My brows pull together. "Just how close are these tabs you're all keeping on me?"

"Close enough. I'm just here to deliver a warning. We got you out, Romero, but Ross has contacts too. Don't let him drag you back in."

My phone gives another impatient *beep*.

Princess: Brick. Bass drum

I sigh. "Mac says to hurry up. You're supposed to be having lunch with Evie."

Jared jerks forward, his eyes going from hard to bright in a split second. It's like seeing light illuminate a dark room. "Evie?"

"Yeah. You met her, right? Mac's roommate. Long brown hair. Smart mouth."

Jared seems exceedingly interested in the new direction of our conversation. "She talks? I mean, I heard her sing on YouTube, but ..."

"Well, yeah."

"What else do you know about her?"

Jared's unexpected distraction has me thumbing open a new message to Mac. I start tapping keys.

Jake: You sneaky bitch

Princess: Rule number 1 ... Always have a plan.

A smile of admiration tugs at the corners of my lips. That girl has a spirit no one can break.

Looking up from my phone, I say, "I know she's waiting on you and Mac for lunch. Better get a move on."

"Right." Pushing off from the counter, he finally opens the fresh beer I gave him and points it at me. "Don't get dead," are his parting words before he sails out the door, closing it behind him.

Mac

I sit down at the quaint table outside the café. Leafy trees rustle in the breeze and fresh pink roses rest in a little round vase. Their scent swirls around us headily. It's the perfect setting—sweet and romantic.

At my demand for Evie to join us for lunch, she's dragged her brother along too. I've met Coby since I moved here. He's two years her senior and a typical older brother. They look alike. He has rich dark hair and brown eyes, a rose tint to his tanned skin, and a smattering of freckles across his nose.

So it's now become a table of four, which foils my plan to bow out early. And with the way my brother is openly staring at Evie, and the way she's busy looking everywhere but at him, this is not going to be easy.

But so help me god, I'm going to fan the flames of this attraction into the size of a bonfire you can see from space.

That will leave one brother down, two to go.

Then I'll be free to live my life.

I totally have this.

Chapter Seventeen

Mac

In the weeks and months following that fateful Saturday lunch, something miraculous happens. Seeming to share common goals and interests, Jared and Coby Jamieson become fast friends. Deciding to join forces, Coby moved to Sydney and they formed a consulting business with Travis named *Jamieson and Valentine Consulting*.

In my opinion, *consulting* is a loose term for what they dabble in. Their firm contracts to various government departments, collaborating on hostage negotiation, kidnapping and ransom, and other highly specialised services. They're building a reputation as being cool under fire—the guys you call in when everything goes to shit. The *experts*.

The new business is right up my alley. I'm smart, keep my head under pressure, and can shoot a bullet through the eye of a needle. My leadership game is strong, my body is fit (sort of), and I can handle all kinds of assholes. I know I've proved this over the years. In short, I'm the perfect candidate.

As part of the Valentine clan, I wait for my invitation to join the firm. Mitch has been asked, but he's already angling for lead detective in the homicide division with Sydney City Police. He has other fish to fry. I don't.

But the invitation never comes.

I wait.

And nothing.

The exclusion is absolute and leaves me seething. Having a goddamn vagina is ruining my life.

How can they not see that gender is irrelevant? I can look after myself better than they can. At last count, Jared has been knifed twice, Travis shot once in the shoulder, and their newest partner—some rogue cowboy I've yet to meet named Casey Daniels—has been involved in a full-blown car chase down Sydney's Motorway 5, resulting in rolling his car. Evie christened them the *Badass Brigade*, which would be a fitting name if *I* were part of the team.

There's only one thing left to do. Move home to Sydney, dragging the band with me.

It will mean a return to the smothering fold of Valentines, but it will put Evie right in Jared's line of sight and me in a better position to demonstrate my flair for badassery, thus gaining me a role in their firm.

With graduation just three short months away, I gather the band into the living area of our apartment for a meeting.

Evie is the last to sit down, having kissed her current boyfriend—aptly nicknamed Beetle Bob for his extreme interest in insects—goodbye and sending him on his way. The pair have been seeing each other for over two months. I let it slide because I know Jared scares her. Evie's past relationships were dire and Jared's done nothing but prove he's trouble. But she doesn't see how perfect they are for each other. I do.

My brother is laying out the charm like a besotted boob, and Evie is being reeled in but the pace is glacial. At least they're friends. I know because I've snooped in her phone. They're messaging each other every day. Bob might have her physically, but it's Jared she shares her shit with. It speaks volumes.

With her nerdy off-sider removed from the equation, I begin my first order of business. It's also the only order of business. "Right," I say, standing before them. "After graduation, the band is moving to Sydney."

An uproar commences.

My gaze finds Jake. He's seated on the floor in front of the couch, knees pulled to his chest and tree-trunk arms wrapped around them. He's studying me as if he's trying to figure out my agenda.

A smirk crosses my face. *You'll never find out.*

My eyes follow the path of his tongue as it runs along his bottom lip. *Try me.*

It's as if a blistering fireball has shot from the sky and slammed me against a wall. I'm hot in an instant.

Jake grins. He knows what he just did. He rarely grins but when he does it lights his face. Amusement flickers in his eyes and a solitary dimple pops. He's enjoying this.

The chatter dies down and I drag my gaze away. Henry speaks first. His role has evolved. He's not just lead guitarist anymore. He's also a kind of mediator between the band and me. "Why?"

"Because it's the music hub of the country," I inform them all, which isn't a lie. Before I made the decision to move, I researched. I want to ensure the band gets the best possible future from the change in location. There may be an ulterior motive in play, but the move is in their best interests too. "Sydney will put you in the face of the best producers in the industry *and* the best venues. I already have a contact with the White Demon Warehouse, and they pay *a lot*," I tell them, watching their eyes widen. As they should. The Warehouse is a leading venue for up and coming indie rock bands. It's also well known as a place where the big record company scouts visit regularly. "I've reviewed our bookings. There's enough funds to move us there and arrange a bond. As long as I can start getting you bookings now for Sydney, finances won't be an issue. If you want to make a real go of this, then it's my job as your manager to make it happen, and the best place—the *only* place to do that, is in Sydney."

My speech finished, I wait.

"We should put it to a vote," Evie announces.

"All right," I concede. "All those in favour of moving to Sydney, raise your hand."

Four hands fly up at once. Henry, Evie, Cooper, and Frog, vote to move. That leaves Jake. He's sitting there like a big, useless lump, his arms not moving. "You plan on staying behind?" I ask him.

"I think the vote should be unanimous, don't you?"

I arch a brow. "So you want the deciding vote?"

"I don't see *your* hand raised, *Mackenzie*."

Smug bastard. I want to slap the smirk from his sexy lips. "It's not raised, is it?"

His brow furrows. "You won't be moving with us?"

I pause. There's worry in his expression and it makes my chest ache. *Don't look at me like that, Jake. You don't have the right.*

I raise an arm. "Yes, Jake. I'll be moving too."

Jake exhales in a *whoosh*. Then he gives me a single nod and lifts his arm. "Looks like it's unanimous."

My heart leaps. *Don't you dare,* I rage at its foolish notion. *Jake abandoned us. He left right when we needed him the most. There's no forgetting what he did and there's no forgiving it.*

My spine snaps straight and I force a smile. "Right then." I clap my hands together. "Let's have a drink to celebrate!"

"Mac, is everything okay?"

I pull my gaze from Jake and smile at Evie. "Everything's fine."

Her eyes drop to my empty drink. It's been one of many. "Can I get you another?"

I don't need more alcohol, but today has been a bad day. Jake had cut through my defences like a swift blade. I need those defences. They keep me strong. "I can get it."

I leave her side and make my way to the kitchen, my head fuzzy. As I stand at the counter pouring a glass of wine, the scent of spiced soap sets me alight. Heat lines the length of my back and Jake's lips tickle my ear. I shiver. "Tying one on tonight, Princess?"

"Back the fuck off," I bark, setting the bottle on the counter. I pick up my glass and turn, forcing Jake to back up a step. The step isn't big enough to give me any breathing room, but my eyes remain cool. I swirl the tawny liquid in my glass and take a sip. He watches with glittering eyes. "So what if I am?"

"You can do what you like, but all that alcohol you're downing tells me I'm getting to you."

"I can do what I like?" Disbelief makes my tone so snide my eyes water. "Thanks for your permission, Romero, but considering how you went behind my back, deciding *you...*" I take a step forward and jab my left finger in his chest "...knew what was *best...*" jab "...for *me...*" jab "...your statement rings a little false. I'm sure you understand. As for you getting to me? Well, I'd have to have a heart for that to happen."

And I don't because you broke it.

"No heart?" Jake cocks his head and smirks. "Doesn't that make you the lion from *The Wizard of Oz*?"

My knuckles turn white as I tighten my grip on the wine glass. "No it doesn't, *asshead.* It's the Tinman who doesn't have a heart. Perhaps *you're* the lion. He's the one searching for courage, which is fitting, isn't it? Or maybe you're the scarecrow in search of a brain, hmm? Either way, it seems you're lacking both."

Jake's expression hardens. "You get off on being a bitch, don't you?"

"To you? It just comes naturally."

Henry appears beside us. "Is everything okay here?"

"Everything's fine," Jake says, even though the tension in his body is obvious. It fairly crackles in the air around him.

"I was just teaching Jake about the moral of *The Wizard of Oz*."

Henry doesn't bat an eye over the subject matter. He simply stands there, beer in hand and a puzzled expression. "There's a moral to that movie?"

"There is," I say, taking another sip of wine.

"What is it?" he asks.

"That men are stupid."

Jake scowls.

"That's funny," Henry says. "I don't remember getting any of that from the story."

"You're right," I concede. "I must have been referring to the movie about that girl who thought she loved a guy. But it turned out she actually didn't. It was all just a big mistake."

"Oh … What's that one called?"

My lips press flat as I stare at Jake. "*The Betrayal.*"

Henry's forehead wrinkles. "I don't think I've heard of it."

"Probably because it's shit," I tell him.

Jake shrugs. "I heard they planned a sequel so it can't have been all that bad."

"A sequel?" I snort. "Titled what?"

"*I Screwed Up and I'm Sorry.*"

"That kinda sounds like a long title," Henry interjects.

We both ignore him. My silent glare is too busy telling Jake he can stick his title where the sun doesn't shine. "It also sounds a little too late," I add to Henry. "I mean, what's the second movie about anyway? How she forgives him? Because that would never happen."

"Forgives him for what?" Henry asks, trying desperately to keep up with our conversation.

"For fucking up the best thing he ever had," Jake replies as he looks at me.

My palms sweat as I cling to my wavering resolve. I take a fortifying sip of wine and pray the glass doesn't slip from my fingers.

"Christ. That sounds like a chick flick. No thanks." Henry guzzles the last of his beer and waves the empty bottle at us. "Time for another. You both good?"

"We're good," Jake answers, "but I think Mac needs some fresh air."

My bicep is grabbed and I'm marched toward the apartment door. Unfortunately, I'm drunk; the room spins and escape proves elusive. "*You've* decided I need fresh air? Funny, but that doesn't sound like a man on the road to his redemption. It sounds to me like he hasn't changed a bit."

"Don't be a smartass," Jake growls. "The pretence of fresh air is so I can get you alone. We need to talk."

"And what if I don't want to talk?"

His eyes heat in an instant. My antagonistic words roll right off his back. "Then I'm sure we can find something else to do."

My body is on board with *that* plan. I don't have to forgive him to sleep with him. In fact, I don't have to like him at all. My gaze runs the length of his back, following the bunch and flex of muscle moving beneath his shirt.

Would sleeping with Jake be such a bad idea?

Yes! my inner voice shouts with force. *A monumentally bad idea.*

Why? I argue as my gaze drops lower. His waist is trim, his ass round and firm. *Jesus.* I know he works out. I see him come and go from the university gym every day. It makes eyeballing his body this close an exercise in restraint.

Do I need to list out the reasons why? There are too many.

Jake opens the door to his apartment, oblivious to my internal struggle as he pulls me along. He shuts the door behind us and lets me go.

I stand in the living area watching him move toward the kitchen with fuzzy eyes. "So what else did you want to do, then?" I ask him. "Because I have an idea."

Jake pauses in the act of setting his beer on the counter. He turns and looks at me. I still have the wine glass in my hand. I lift it to my lips and tip it back, swallowing the last half in one go. Then I set the glass on their little coffee table with a *clank.*

With my hands now free, I take the hem of my tank top and peel it off, mussing my hair as I toss it on the nearby sofa.

My intentions cannot be any clearer.

The pulse point in Jake's neck throbs visibly. "I want to talk." His tone is rough as if saying the words pains him.

My chin lifts. "There's nothing to talk about."

"You're wrong."

"I'm never wrong."

"So what?" His eyes darken. They run down the length of me and back up again. My body aches, the need inside me rising to a level so strong I'm drowning in it. "You want to ..."

He trails off as I start toward him, reaching behind to unclasp my bra as I get closer. "To fuck?" *Good. That's good, Mac,* my inner voice croons. *Keep emotion out of it. Nothing more to it than just a physical reaction.* "Yeah."

I drop my bra to the floor, now clad only in a pair of denim shorts.

"Mac ..." His protest is weak. "Please. Can we just talk for a minute?"

"I don't want to," I say, reaching his side.

I take his shirt and tug it up. He reaches behind and peels it off. "What *do* you want?" he asks, his question a hoarse whisper of need.

"You."

Jake puts his hands on my shoulders. He runs the calloused palms down my arms and presses his forehead to mine. "I want you too. So much."

I hate you for this, Jake. For making me want you after everything you did. My body trembles and my eyes burn from the wild emotion. I close them, finding that space where I can let go and give myself over. I need this outlet, desperately. "So take me."

Jake's grip tightens at my submission, and his lips press against mine.

Oh god. The light touch is so intimate my legs almost give out. His kiss is the equivalent of spending days in the desert and getting your first sip of cool water. My mouth opens with invitation. Jake doesn't disappoint. His hot, hungry tongue sweeps in and rubs against mine. A hand fists in my hair. My scalp stings from the force of it.

A breathless moan escapes me.

Jake breaks the kiss, panting as he draws back. He lets go of me and skates his hands down my chest until he's cupping my breasts. His touch isn't enough. It's too light. His grip firms as if hearing my need. He runs his fingers over my nipples, pinching them. I moan again and he pinches harder. A subtle sliver of pain shoots through me, igniting my blood. It sends a rush of heat between my legs. "Oh god," I groan.

"You like that?"

My eyes flutter open. "More," is all I get passed my lips.

"Fuck," he mutters, heat flaring in his eyes.

Jake walks me backward until I reach the sofa. He pushes me down. My ass hits the soft cushions, and he takes the button of my shorts and flicks it open. The zipper slides down and my shorts are tugged off.

My panties follow quickly. Jake yanks them down with force, his expression almost brutal with its intensity. Kneeling between my legs, he grabs my thighs. His fingers dig in as he wrenches me toward him. "I can't be gentle with you, Princess," he cautions, his eyes dark and hungry. "Not right now."

My stomach knots with pain. *You'll always be my princess.*

Oh my god. I still *love* him. The shocking realisation leaves me sick. How can you still love the person who left you when you needed them the most? What is wrong with me? I'm strong enough to withstand a goddamn apocalypse.

So why can't I withstand you, Jake Romero?

I glare. "Good. I don't want gentle from you. Ever."

Because that will be too much.

Jake

My heart is raw from the punches Mac keeps pulling. I endure them. As long as I can have her, even like this, it's enough. For now.

I lower my head and stroke her with my tongue.

A soft breath escapes her lips. But I want more. I want her crying my name.

I take her clit in my mouth and suck hard. So hard it probably hurts. Her back bows from the couch and her head falls back. My cock throbs at the sight.

I keep it up. Mac wants rough. She likes it. I lick and suck hard, giving her what she wants.

Taking her left leg, I lift it and hold up the back of her thigh with my hand. It exposes more of her to my eyes. She's beautiful everywhere, and so fucking *hot* it's almost unbearable. I slide a finger down the silken skin of her pussy before I slip it inside, moving in and out.

"Fuck," she pants, her hips moving with me.

I push in another.

"Oh god, yes," she hisses, biting her bottom lip.

My head dips and my mouth finds her again. My fingers continue to drive in and out. The rougher I become, the harder she breathes and the more her hips grind against my mouth.

A shudder racks my body. If I'm not inside her soon, I'm going to blow in my shorts. I draw back, letting her leg drop so I can get them off, but I'm too impatient. I'm aching too much to have her. All I can manage is to shove my shorts down.

"Get down here," I growl with a rough breath, tugging on her leg.

She slides until her ass hits the floor.

I spread her legs and the little restraint I have left snaps. Leaning forward, I line my cock with the entrance to her pussy. Fuck condoms. At this point I'm too far gone to care.

"Condom," she pants.

"Why?" I glare, holding my position. "Have you been with anyone else?"

It's a ridiculous question. It's been *years*. Of course she has. But I haven't. God knows I've tried. There have been more opportunities than I can count. But it always felt wrong, and I would stop before it reached the point of no return. I didn't care that my friends thought me mad shunning numerous advances. I wasn't going to sleep with a girl just to look good in their eyes.

The pain of losing Mackenzie Valentine had been too raw. It still is. She's all encompassing. Like the sun. She rises and sets, but she never dims, and no matter what I do, I can't block her out.

"Fuck you, Jake," she snaps in answer to my question. "Put one on or this isn't happening."

I draw back and jab a finger. "Don't move."

I stand and kick off my shorts as I walk to the bathroom. The box inside the cabinet beneath the sink is almost empty. I grab one, tearing the wrapper open with my teeth and sliding it down my cock as I walk back.

Satisfaction is a hot surge when I see Mac still there, right where I left her. I kneel back down, and she looks at me for a long, pained breath.

"Not like this," she says.

Mac turns over and gives me her back, then leans her forearms on the couch. My eyes travel the sweet curve of her back and down to the round cheeks of her ass. My cock twitches. Her *ass*. "You want ..." I almost choke. "You want me to fuck your ass?"

"No." She pushes back against me. My hips surge forward of their own accord, and I rub my cock between her cheeks. "I want you this way."

Her head lowers, waiting, expectant.

And then I know and my heart aches.

Mac can't look at me. She wants to pretend it's not my cock inside her body. She doesn't want me, she wants a faceless fuck.

With an angry snarl, I grab the soft skin of her hips and pull her close. Guiding my cock, I slide inside, inch by inch, until she's full of me. Her round cheeks rest against me as I hold her tight. "You don't want to see who's fucking you?" Reaching forward, I take a fistful of hair and wrench her head back and to the side. The angle ensures she can't miss seeing me, and what I'm doing to her. "Too bad."

I draw out and drive back in. *Hard.* And then I do it again. And again. And again.

Fuck. I can't last at this pace. "I should give you that spanking you deserve for the way you talk to me."

There's no *should* about it. I let go of her hair and my hand connects with her ass cheek in a light slap. Mac's eyes close and I'm rewarded with a long, slow moan as her skin turns a faint shade of pink.

My cock tingles and I'm ready to explode. I grab her hips and stop, trying to think of algebra and old Mrs. Lawrence who taught fifth grade. She was ancient and never shaved her legs. The manlike hair would poke through the beige stockings she wore.

Mac whimpers and pushes against me, begging for me. "Harder, Jake. Please."

Oh Christ. I'm done for. I slap her again without even thinking about it. Harder this time.

She cries out and the flush on her ass colours to a deep rose. God, why does that feel so good? And look so hot? Combined with the sweet taste of her on my lips, it's sensory overload. I'm about to come like a freight train.

I wrap an arm around her waist and press my chest against the bare length of her back. It allows me to reach her clit. I find it and rub as I drive in and out, silently begging her to come so I can let go.

She does. Mac gives out beneath me. Her pussy contracts and shudders, forcing me to explode. My cock pulses. I wrap both arms around her as I ride the enormous wave of sensation.

Emotion overwhelms me. God, I love this girl. *So much.*

Mac mumbles something I don't catch.

"What?"

She pushes backward. "Get off me."

My brow furrows as I draw out slowly. I tug the condom off and tie it in a knot. Rising on unsteady legs, I walk to the kitchen and throw it in the trash. When I return, Mac is half dressed and reaching for her shirt.

My stomach dips. "What are you doing?"

Her response is cool. "Leaving."

Fuck. That hurts. "Mac …"

She pulls the tank top over her head and twitches it in place. When she's finished, she looks at me. "Jake, you were an itch. I scratched it."

Mac walks to the door and takes the handle. She turns, taming her mess of her. "Thanks."

Then she leaves.

I'm left standing naked, staring at the back of the closed door as I wonder what the hell just happened.

Chapter Eighteen

Mac

Fifteen months later...
ANZ Stadium Sydney

After arriving for sound check, Evie and I walk on the stage, taking in the huge stadium of my home city. It's late January and the afternoon sun is bright and hot. The arena is empty, minus the stagehands rearranging barriers, sorting cables, and doing everything else they need to do in order to ensure a smooth, successful concert.

Evie wears oversized sunglasses, yet she still has to shade her eyes as we stare out over the cavernous space. I glance at her, seeing both pain and triumph on her face. As the person who pushed Jared and Evie together, I feel responsible for both. The past year has been nothing less than turbulent. My beautiful friend has been dragged through hell and it isn't over yet.

Jamieson and Valentine caught a case involving two criminal brothers. Jared shot and killed one. The other, Jimmy, remains at large, revenge now his sole purpose in life. He's determined to get his hands on Evie and exact similar retribution. She's being watched around the clock by the Badass Brigade and yet months later, Jimmy still eludes the authorities.

We're all on edge waiting for him to strike again. It's exhausting, and yet every time I try taking matters into my own hands, I get thwarted. Mostly by Travis and Mitch. Jared's sole focus is on Evie.

She breathes warm air deep inside her lungs. "How did we get here?"

"The limousine brought you here, Sandwich."

She huffs at me with affection. "You know what I mean."

I do. I'm just trying to lighten the moment. Jamieson is on the road to achieving everything they've ever dreamed of. I've worked hard, *so hard*, to get them to this point, but it's come at a cost. Having focused all my energy on the band, there's nothing left over for me. My dreams are on hold, but my determination has never wavered. I'm interviewing for an assistant next week. It will give me someone to hand the reins to when I make the switch from band manager to professional badass. I have my eye on a girl called Quinn Salisbury. I've seen her work the reception desk at Jettison Records, the same label about to sign the band.

My lips pinch together, hiding the smirk of satisfaction. Quinn is perfect. Not just for the job either. Travis is going to fall harder than a tonne of bricks. That will make it two interfering brothers down, one to go. It doesn't make Mitch lucky last. He's simply a tricky case. I know the girl meant for him. They were together in college and so in love it was painful to stand on the sidelines and watch it all fall apart. I don't know what happened. Mitch's girl went underground and my eldest brother has struggled to move on ever since.

"What?"

The word cuts through my thoughts. I turn my head. Evie is looking at me. "What do you mean, what?"

"You're scheming something. I can see it on your face."

My eyes widen. "Me? Scheme? Really, Evie. Sometimes I think you don't know me at all."

She does though. Except I like to think of them more as plans than schemes. Like my plan to convince Jared and Evie of the wonders of babies. Those sweet frilly outfits I've been eyeing won't buy themselves. Though it's not just an opportunity to shop for cutesy little dresses. It was Mum's reaction when I'd selected a pink, fluffy bunny jacket from the rack—tiny enough for a doll—and held it up. Her intake of breath had been sharp, and her eyes had *burned* with emotion. A grandbaby. *A grandbaby!* Not only would I make the perfect aunt—teaching her how to shoot and shop, and showing her the importance of ambition and confidence—she would be a tiny little human for Mum and Dad to fuss over.

"You're practically my sister now, Mac. I know you better than you know yourself."

I abandon my cute baby thoughts in favour of a grimace. Guilt burns a hole in the lining of my stomach. Evie's right. We've become closer than sisters, but what kind of sister keeps so much from the other? Jake is such a huge part of who I came to be, and who I am now, and she knows nothing of it. None of them do.

But I can't tell them. They won't understand why he did what he did, the same as I don't. And while we're all a little family, they're his *only* family. No matter what he did in the past, I find it impossible to rip that out from under him by saying anything. So our history remains buried deep down below where the judgement of others can't touch it.

I turn and see Jake behind me. My heart gives its familiar leap. He's wearing a cap set backwards, his shirt off and tucked into the back pocket of worn jeans. He's bent over, pants stretched tight as he shifts a drum into better position. My eyes lower. Jake's butt is the stuff legends are made of. When he was born, God said, "And so it will be, that this human shall be blessed with the greatest posterior in all of the lands. There will be no greater."

And so it was. Round, firm, squeezable. Dimples on either side highlight the powerful muscle underneath, and the rich golden tan of his back leads down to paler skinned cheeks, quite like trailing your eyes down the path to the Holy Grail.

Jake tilts his head, catching my eyes pinned to his ass. He gives me a wink. It's not an affectionate gesture. Nor is it flirty. It's a cool and detached acknowledgment.

Sleeping with him that night in his apartment caused a hurt I never expected. There have been more moments between us since. Angry sex. Nasty words. Hateful behaviour. But underneath it all exists a love just about damaged beyond repair. There's a pulse but it's faint and slowly fading. We're killing it. But I don't know how to stop what we're doing. I can't hold on, and I can't let go.

Dragging my gaze away, I do my best to ignore the flare of pain and give Evie my attention. She's been chattering the whole time and I've missed all of it.

"How are you feeling?" I ask when she takes a breath.

"Sick as fuck," she mutters.

It's no surprise. There was an incident last night. Evie landed herself in the hospital after being drugged and placed in a compromising position. Jared had, naturally, jumped to idiotic conclusions and took off in a childish tantrum. I've been trying to contact him since without any luck.

I tap the button on my headpiece and speak. "Someone get our lead singer a glass of water. With ice," I add, because the sooner that crap is flushed from her system the better.

"Thanks," Evie mutters, her expression grim, and I know her thoughts are on my stupid brother.

I give her a pat on the back. I'm not the best at soothing gestures, but it doesn't mean I don't care. "I'll try calling him again. In the meantime, go to the dressing room and shut your eyes for a few minutes, okay?"

She leaves and I walk to the side of the stage where Travis stands. "Heard from Jared?"

Travis's lips press in a flat line as he checks his phone. He shakes his head. "He'll be okay, Mac."

"I know, Travis. If only he would just check in so we could sort this freaking mess out."

"He'll show up," he says patiently.

I think my brothers sucked all the patience genes from our mother before I was born because I don't have a single one in my body.

"Yes, yes. I know he will eventually and love will prevail and I'll finally get my little niece, but I'm not the most patient of people, Travis."

He snorts. "No shit."

"So any idea of what this Jimmy asshole might do tonight?"

Jake

We're wrapping up our second last song of the night when Mac disappears. She's not by the side of the stage giving orders like she usually is. My stomach knots, and my instincts already scream that something's wrong.

Everyone is so focused on watching Evie that they're blind to the real danger. Jimmy is after *retribution*. While all of his recent attacks have been focused on Evie, none of them have caused serious harm, and maybe they aren't supposed to. Maybe they're a distraction. Retribution is like for like. Jimmy's brother for Jared's sister.

It's entirely possible that *Mac* is the real target.

And she isn't here.

The show ends. We conclude our post-concert wrap-up in the dressing room and still no sign of her. I've tried calling her phone but we're always so pissed at each other, knowing it's me she's unlikely to answer anyway.

Travis sticks his head in the door, eyes scanning the room. "Where's Mac?"

"We don't know," Evie answers. "She's not out there?"

He shakes his head. "When I got off the phone, one of the roadies was asking me where she was because they're doing the pack-up and they need her."

"Have you tried her phone?" Henry interrupts. "She mentioned a few industry bigwigs were stopping by tonight, so maybe she's caught up schmoozing."

Evie tries calling but she doesn't get an answer either. My heart thumps hard with real fear. Travis opens the door wider and moves into the room.

"When did you last see her?" Coby asks.

Travis pauses for a moment and rubs his chin. "Right before the last song. She mentioned something about picking up an unscheduled delivery for Jamieson at one of the gates. I can't remember her returning."

Meaningful glances are exchanged before the two leave the room. Evie stands to follow. I snag her wrist. "Sit down," I growl. "You aren't supposed to be going anywhere without either of those two." I push Evie back down at the same time I stand. "I'll go."

We conduct the search best we can, but there are thousands of people out there. It's like the proverbial needle in a haystack. Travis tries tracking her phone. She never goes anywhere without it. It shows nothing.

The rest of Jamieson is sent home with Coby, and we continue the search. Mac runs the entire show and hasn't submitted a list to anyone of the names manning each gate. We have to check each one individually.

The clock is ticking and frustration is ripping me apart. "Where the hell was the unscheduled delivery?"

"I don't know!" Travis growls, his own fear and frustration no longer under wraps.

Casey Daniels comes running toward us. He's the other partner in *Jamieson & Valentine Consulting* and forms part of our security detail on occasion. We have a mutual love for old muscle cars. Casey owns a Corvette Stingray called Marjorie that I'd give my left nut for. The car is so lovingly restored it's almost a crime to drive it.

"Gate E!" Casey shouts. Before he's even finished we're running in that direction. "That's the entrance where the delivery was supposed to be. George is stationed there."

It's the farthest entrance from the stage and not a public entry or exit. Access is via a solitary road littered with trees and shrubbery. We're breathing hard when we reach the gates, only to find them unmanned and wide open. There's blood on the ground. It's a splattered pool that coats the road, its copper tang thick in the air around us.

Terror rips through me, white-hot and intense.

"Mac!" I roar, turning, eyes scanning, frantic.

"There!" Travis yells.

He's pointing to a copse of trees by the left of the gate. A smear of blood lines the patchy dirt, dots of it covering dead leaves that scatter the ground. Underneath a pile of branches peeks the base of a shoe.

Travis reaches the area first and rips the shrubs away, exposing a body. Casey and I reach his side and I stare down at the sightless eyes of the security guard. The nametag on his shirt confirms him as George. He hadn't died instantly. There are two bullet wounds in chest that coat his uniform in blood. It's smeared over his hands as if he tried compressing the wounds after being shot. My gut rolls and I clamp my teeth together, forcing harsh air out my nostrils.

Travis and Casey are straight on their phones. There's a man dead at my feet, a man who *suffered*, and all I can feel is a wild sense of relief because it's not Mac. The feeling lasts a scant second. Whoever shot George has taken her and now Mac is in the clutches of a murderer—one who continues to evade even the best detectives the country has to offer.

So I fucking lose it.

Travis is tucking his phone in his back pocket when I pull back a fist and smash it in his face. My knuckles connect and a sick crunching sound renders the air. Pain shoots up my arm. "This is your fault!" I yell, rage pumping through me so thick I can barely see.

His head snaps back but it doesn't stop me. I grab his shoulders, shaking them as I yell. "You were so damn focused on watching Evie you never saw that Mac was the true target!"

Travis, an all-round good guy and always calm under pressure, loses it back. He's no doubt already drowning beneath a huge weight of guilt and fear. He needs my accusations like a hole in the head.

"Fuck you, Romero!" he growls. He rears back a fist and returns the favour. His massive blow sends me staggering backward.

Casey grabs both my arms and secures them behind my back. His tone is furious as I struggle against the hold. "Lock it down. Both of you!"

"No!" I break free and go for Travis again. My punch catches him in the gut and he doubles over. It's almost like it's not me hitting him. I'm standing outside myself and I can see what I'm doing, and that it's wrong, but I can't stop.

"Most of my life you told me to stay away from Mac. All of you!" I shout, my tone so violent it makes me hoarse. "I came from nothing and she had everything. She was always too good for me, but it never made me want her any less! The moment I joined that fucking gang it was over for me. I never wanted that life but I was young and stupid and backed into a corner. Then she showed up and it was amazing. I thought it was meant to be, so I tried to get out but it almost got her killed! I sent her away. I thought it was best. For her!" I spit blood in the dirt as Travis grinds his jaw, fury in his eyes. I don't care. I'm *done*. "But everything's changed. You might have got me out, but I'm the one who turned my life around. I'm not the same person I used to be. And I'm tired of you all telling me we can't be together. Mac is mine and I'm going to fight for her," I vow. "And that fight starts *now*."

Instead of coming at me like I expect, Travis bends and rests his palms on his knees. He stares down at the ground for single beat before he looks at me. His green eyes are dark with regret as though the weight of it holds him down. "I'm sorry."

I stand, dizzy, not sure I've heard him correctly. "What?"

Travis straightens. He wipes the trickle of blood from his nose with the back of his hand and shakes his head. "You don't even know."

"Know what?" Mac's brother can't even look at me. "Know what, dammit?"

Whatever he's talking about, it can only involve Mac. That makes it imperative that I know, and that I know *now*.

"You ladies can fight this out later," Casey snaps with impatience. "We need to go."

"She wanted you too. She *asked* for you. And we took that from her." Travis sways, his eyes on me defeated. "You broke her, Jake. But we did so much worse. We *destroyed* her."

"You ..." I can't make sense of what he's telling me, but I know it's bad. My chest constricts as I stare at him. "What did you do?"

The headlights of a car shine over us, bright and blinding. With the squeal of tyres, a vintage Porsche comes to a wild halt beside us. Jared is at the wheel. The car is ridiculously small, something we constantly give him shit for, but that tiny piece of machinery can *move*.

"What did you *do*?" I shout, getting in Travis's face.

Jared opens the door, unfolding his big body from the tiny car. "What the hell? Now is not a good time for a girly pow wow!"

"Fuck you, Jared," I yell, not looking at him as he walks toward us. My eyes are on Travis. "What did you do?" I whisper.

A painful beat of silence surrounds us. Jared breaks it. "Aw hell, Trav."

Travis swallows, stoic. "He deserves to know. They both do."

Jared's jaw clamps shut and he looks away. He can't look at me either.

"Now is not the time for confessions," Casey says. "As much as we all know Mac can take care of herself, she can probably do with some backup right about now."

Jared turns disbelieving eyes on his brother. "He knows?" Then his gaze cuts to Casey. "You know?"

Casey shrugs.

"Would you all just shut the hell up and tell me what every other motherfucker seems to know but me?"

Travis looks at me and speaks. "That day we came and got Mac, we were in an accident. The car rolled four times before landing upside down in an embankment."

Jared was behind the wheel that day. I turn to look at him. His face is whiter than snow. "I was driving too fast," he admits. "I lost control of the car."

My mouth opens and snaps shut. "Why the hell did no one tell me?"

"That's not all," Travis interrupts. Jared bends his head and rubs the back of his neck. Casey steps up beside me, his shoulder brushing mine. "Mac was ... She ..."

My heart is pounding harder than a jackhammer. "Spit it out, Travis."

"Mac was pregnant and she suffered a miscarriage from the impact."

My lungs squeeze and blackness edges my vision. The world slowly tilts beneath my feet.

"She was going to tell you about the baby, Jake." Travis keeps talking but it's hard to hear over the buzzing in my ears. "But you never gave her that chance."

"I never gave her that chance?" I whisper.

"She was about to tell you when we turned up to collect her."

And it's my fault because I sent her away. The guilt overwhelms me. I drop to a crouch and hold my head in my hands, unable to stand the weight of it.

Mac was going to have a baby. *My* baby. My heart is breaking, and I can't breathe over the pain. "Why didn't she ever tell me?"

"She tried," Travis chokes out. "In the hospital when she woke, she asked for you. She wanted you to know. She wanted you there. We ..." He lets out a shaky breath. "We told her that you knew. That we'd told you."

My eyes burn. Mac, who never needed anyone, needed me and I wasn't there. *Because I didn't fucking know.* I rise slowly to my feet. My hands fist by my sides, but I hold my chin high. "You goddamn interfering motherfuckers," I bite out. "You let her think I knew?" My voice rises to a shout. "Why? Because I was never good enough and this was your chance to shut me out of her life for good?"

"We thought it was for the best," Jared says, his voice low and gruff.

"You." My nostrils flare as my eyes cut to him. "You were driving the damn car and you just lost control?"

"I'm sorry," he whispers, taking a step toward me.

My back stiffens and my voice comes out broken. "You killed our baby."

Jared clamps his jaw shut, his breath coming out in harsh puffs through his nostrils. He's on the verge of losing it but I don't care. I'm caught in a world of pain. Nothing can stop it. It's a freight train slamming into me without warning.

Casey puts a hand on my shoulder, squeezing. "Jake—"

I shrug him off and back away from all of them. "Don't touch me."

My breathing is heavy as my mind traces over our every interaction since the day she left. Mac's hostility. Her *anger*. It all makes sense. It's a testament to her strength that she's still standing, putting one foot in front of the other each day. That she even *speaks* to me at all.

She's the only person I've ever loved and look what I did to her. What *we* did to her. She was going to be a mother. We were going to be *parents*. A family. And now we're nothing at all.

The stab of loss is excruciating. A sob climbs my throat. I swallow hard in an effort to keep it down.

"Jake?"

The sound comes from far away.

My head swings slowly. Casey has hold of my bicep. He's saying my name as he drags me toward the car. His lips are moving. "Mac needs you," they seem to say.

He opens the passenger door of Jared's Porsche. I slide inside. Numb. He shuts it behind me. Jogging around the front, Casey slams into the driver's seat and guns the engine, roaring off before he even has the door fully shut.

"Jared is going with Travis in his car," he explains without me asking the question.

Good.

I can't be around the Valentine brothers right now. Violence simmers under my skin, ready to unleash on any one of them without notice. A single punch to each brother in the face will make me feel better. Every day. A punch a day, until they add up to the number of days since they started this shit.

My eyes focus outside the window. The night is dark but the traffic lights are bright. I stare, watching them blur into each other as we speed through the quiet streets.

"Where is she?"

Casey glances across at me. I feel his concern. It's like a thick fog blanketing the interior of the car. "I don't know." At least he's honest. "But we'll find her," he vows.

The light of dawn is hitting the horizon when we finally get a break on Mac's location, though it isn't the kind of break we're hoping for. A phone call between Casey and Travis confirms that Evie, supposedly on lockdown at the duplex where we've been living on the seaside suburb of Bondi Beach, has gone rogue.

Mac clearly taught her well. Evie disappeared just a half hour earlier, spiriting her car out of the driveway, along with the gun Mac keeps in a locked box on the top shelf of her walk-in robe.

At least we have her on GPS. All the manpower we had tracking down leads is now zeroed in on Evie's Hilux truck.

I glance at the speedometer on the little dashboard. The speed limit is eighty. We're doing a hundred. "Can't you go any faster?" I bark at Casey.

Casey shifts gears with a grim expression and pushes his foot down harder. We're hitting one-twenty when his phone rings, the sound barely audible over the growl of the engine. It's sitting in the centre console and lights up showing Jared's name.

"Answer it," Casey orders, his eyes glued to the road.

I pick it up and hit the green button. "You're on speaker," I say to the phone and rest it back in the centre.

"He's got Evie." Jared's voice is hoarse. "He has my sister and now he has Evie."

I tip my head back against the seat, eyes unseeing. It's impossible to think about whether Mac is hurt or dead. And now Evie. I can barely function as it is.

"Dammit," Casey mutters.

"We have an address where the Hilux stopped five minutes ago." Jared rattles off a residence in the south of Sydney. "We're ten minutes out. You?"

We're maybe fifteen minutes at the least. Casey and I share a mutual glance before he accelerates further.

"We're right behind you," I tell him.

"Jake, I—"

"Don't. Let's just focus on getting Mac and Evie out safe."

Jared huffs a shaky breath. "Right."

I end the call and drop back in my seat. My hands are shaking. I fist them and rest them on my knees.

"She's going to be fine."

"I know," I tell him, but I don't. He doesn't either. I can tell by the tone in his voice.

Mac is a loose cannon. There's no telling what she'll do in any given situation. But if anything, she'll fight with every breath she has. Mac was forged in fire. She'll give him hell.

I check my watch. *Ten minutes out.* Why has time slowed to a snail's pace? It's unbearable.

"Jake ..." Casey begins and then stops as though he's thinking about how to say what he wants to say. Whenever there's a pause like that, it's never good. I brace. "You can't tell Mac that you know."

"What?"

"About what happened. With the car accident. And the ... baby."

Is he serious? I shoot Casey an angry glare. "Why not?"

"We don't know what she's been through tonight. If you tell Mac what really happened, it will put a huge wedge between her and her brothers. She'll shut them out in an instant, which is not what she needs right now. She's going to need her family, Jake."

My teeth clamp together as his advice sinks in. I come to the same realisation—one I would never have reached without him pointing it out.

"Fuck!" I yell, slamming a fist on the dash in front of me. "This is bullshit. Damn you, Casey."

His voice is low. "I'm sorry."

But he's right. We both know it.

"So I have to keep being the bad guy."

"You're not the bad guy," Casey tells me.

"I've always been the bad guy," I mutter, frustration making my chest tight. I glance at my watch again. *Seven minutes out.* Time has slowed further.

We're almost there, Princess. Please be okay.

"If you were the bad guy, you wouldn't be in this car right now. You wouldn't be fighting like you are. You would have given up."

"I can't give up."

"And Mac will see that. When the time is right, you can tell her and she'll see that you were always there fighting when a lesser man would never have tried."

"I hope to god you're right, Casey."

He shrugs, forcing a grin that doesn't reach his eyes. "I'm always right."

"Except when you're wrong."

A light chuckle escapes him. He nods his head. "Except when I'm wrong."

Five minutes out.

Three minutes out.

I stare out the window, focused on breathing.

"I love her, you know."

Casey's voice is soft. "I know."

I swipe a hand across my face, exhausted and on edge. My cheeks are scratchy with five days of beard. Mac likes the facial hair but when it gets to the point of being itchy, I always get the shits and shave it off. Maybe this time I'll keep it.

"How do you know?" I eventually ask, wondering how Casey sees it when no one else does.

"Because you stand up to her in a way no one else does. And she lets you."

Two minutes out.

"I never noticed that."

"I did."

"You notice a lot of shit, Daniels."

"I do."

"Do you think what Mac's brothers did was right? You knew and you never said anything."

Casey shakes his head, downshifting gears as we turn a sharp corner. "I think they were so blinded in their duty to protect Mac that they didn't think about how much damage it would cause. Travis feels a lot of guilt. He told me. And Jared still struggles with the knowledge of what he did. It was an accident, Jake. A stupid, horrible accident, but the fallout was huge."

"Damn straight it was huge."

"You have to let them put things right."

One minute out.

"Maybe in some other lifetime," I mutter.

Thirty seconds.

Casey floors it around another corner, fishtailing onto the street of the address we were given. We can both see the house we're aiming for. It's white weatherboard. A dilapidated, rundown heap of shit set in a neighbourhood you wouldn't send your worst enemy. Three cars are out front. The one in the drive is an old Mazda hatchback. Parked on an angle in front of it is Evie's bright blue Hilux. Right in the middle of the street sits a souped-up black Subaru WRX, both doors wide open. Black tyre tread marks the road behind it. The car belongs to Travis.

"The glove compartment," Casey barks urgently.

I seize the handle, ripping it open. Two handguns rest inside. I take them out and check both with practised efficiency before handing one to Casey.

He brings the Porsche to a screaming halt in the street. I'm out of the car and running without missing a beat, my heart in my throat. I vault the porch stairs and tear through the front door, my gun in both hands, breathing out of control from panic. Casey comes up behind me. We're moving quietly through the front section of the house when I hear the sweetest sound of my life. It rings out loud and clear.

"Goddamn asshead!"

My legs almost give out beneath me. I can't lock the emotion down. I'm not trained for this shit.

"Thank Jesus," Casey mutters from my right.

Jared yells in response. And Travis. But I hear nothing from Evie.

We abandon all stealth and run through a large archway toward the back of the house. I come to a dead stop, absorbing the scene before me in a single second.

Jimmy is on the ground, a bullet in the middle of his forehead and blood pooling beneath him. Across from him lies Evie, flat on the floor. Both Jared and Travis are kneeling on either side of her. Both shirts are off and pressing against Evie's chest. She's covered in blood. It's splattered across her face and chest, her hands, her legs. It's *everywhere.*

"Fuck!" Jared's agonised roar fills the room. "Where are the fucking paramedics?"

My gaze finds Mac. She's strapped to a wooden chair with clear plastic cable ties. Blood drips down the side of her face from a split brow, her right eye is almost swollen shut, and her wrists and ankles are bleeding and raw.

The pretty cream-coloured blouse she paired with dark jeans for the concert is torn and filthy, covered with grime and sweat and blood.

Her eyes are on Evie, but they shift to me when we come in the room. "Jake," she mouths, her jaw trembling. She clamps it tight, holding herself together.

I tuck the gun in the back of my jeans and move quickly.

"Nice of you to show up," she mumbles as I crouch in front of her.

"We got here as fast as we could, Princess," I reply as I check the ties that bind her hands to the arms of the chair. She flinches at my ministrations. Her skin is a bloodied mess from where they cut in to her.

"Well, I had the situation handled, just so you know."

"Of course you did." My voice is muffled as I shift lower to inspect her ankles. "I need a—"

Casey waves a pocketknife in my face.

"—knife."

I flick the blade and make quick work of the ties. Mac stands on shaky legs, sucking in sharp, pained breaths as I peel them from her wrists.

"Baby," I whisper, staring at the damage.

My eyes lift, finding hers. Her entire body has begun to shake. Shock is setting in fast. She holds my gaze as she trembles, her expression tortured. "Evie's going to be okay."

She says it as a statement but I hear her need for reassurance. I nod, cupping her cheeks in my hands. My voice is firm. "Evie's going to be fine."

"That sonofabitch shot her. Twice. I told her not to come."

"Would you have not come if the situation were reversed?"

Her voice wobbles yet she stands strong. "No."

"Then don't even go there."

Mac nods, swallowing. I take my hands from her face and wrap them around her. My hug locks her arms by her sides. She buries her face in my neck for a moment. I died a thousand deaths in the hours she was gone.

The faint sound of a siren cuts through the air.

Casey leaves to direct the ambulance officers while Jared and Travis push down on Evie's wounds. She's breathing but it's erratic. There's nothing we can do short of getting in the way, so we stand together and wait.

"Jake," she whispers hoarsely, shivering.

"Mmm?"

"Don't let go."

My arms lock tighter, my eyes burning as I hold on. I don't want to let go.

I let out an unsteady breath.

Don't ever ask me to let go.

Chapter Nineteen

Mac

I wake, blinking open gritty eyes to a warm summer morning. The sun streams through an open window. Sheer white curtains billow in the soft breeze, bringing with it the salty tang of the nearby ocean. Moving my head on the pillow, I realise I've slept in my own room for the first time in three nights. My bed is a soft fluffy cloud, so much nicer than the rock they call a mattress in the doom of Ward 2A.

My room here is decorated in white. Cool, crisp sheets, fresh painted walls, white-framed photographs. No colour. Not in my private space. Colour is fine to wear, but here I need no distraction; white is quiet, inoffensive, and gives me no bullshit.

I was in the hospital overnight, suffering minor wounds and dehydration. The second night I slept in a chair, refusing to leave the Critical Care Unit where Evie was stationed. She fought a hard battle through the first night, but she won, surviving two gunshot wounds that should have been fatal. You would think Jared would be rejoicing, but he's moping around as though she's in a coma with days left to live. It makes no sense but that's my brothers for you. They're unpredictable dickheads.

A bang comes from my left. I turn my head. Jake is carrying a timber tray in both hands, using it to push open the bedroom door. His eyes come to me once the tray is stable. He assesses me with a careful scan as he walks in.

Seemingly assured I'm alive and breathing, he sets his burden on the white-washed timber bedside table. It has my belly rumbling. Juice, coffee, toast heaped with poached eggs and a pile of bacon high enough to feed all the animals of Africa. I glare at the addition of a yellow rose in a little white ceramic vase. It's not red, but it still screams *romance*.

"What's with the flower, Nurse Betty?"

He straightens and folds his arms. "You're a grouch when you're injured, Princess. Thought it might cheer you up."

Jake has been unusually solicitous since my kidnapping, as though another abduction is imminent. The hovering is downright aggravating, but I can't ignore the benefits. Jake has brought me food, dressed solely in a pair of football shorts. That singular scrap of clothing makes his miraculous body appear all the bigger.

My eyes shift from the wonderment of his chest and back to the rose. It has no doubt been snipped from the neighbour's yard in an attempt to add a little happiness to my morning. It's in the prime of its life—petals the colour of sunshine unfurled and glistening with morning dew. It's bright, cheery, and annoying. Yet warmth steals over me, ripping away my usual morning churlishness.

I force a scowl. "Do you think it worked?"

"Yes."

His chin lifts, daring me to tell him his efforts have all been for nought.

"It's pretty," I mutter, reaching for my coffee. The stretch pulls on the bandages wrapped around my wrists. I wince.

Jake grabs the mug before I can reach. "Would you sit up?" he barks. "If you try drinking hot coffee while lying down, you'll tip it all over yourself and end up with third-degree burns."

"Oh my god, you sound like my mother."

"For fuck's sake. I do not," he argues, indignant. With my beverage in one hand, Jake uses the other to shove pillows into a pile behind me, forcing me into an inclined position. Once satisfied that I'm suitably vertical, he holds out the mug. "It's just logic and gravity."

"Gravity, schmavity."

Jake huffs, sitting down on the edge of my bed. "Do you always have to have the last word?"

"Of course." I breathe on the black liquid in my mug, cooling it before taking a sip. Warmth floods my system, bringing me to life. Jake is a master at brewing the perfect blend. The coffee is strong as an ox. Black, rich, and sugar free. My toes all but curl with pleasure. "You should bring me this exact coffee in bed every day."

"Suck my dick every day and I will."

I roll my eyes. "You're so crude."

He snorts. I have everyone beat when it comes to hurling obscenities, but Jake is a close second.

"Suck your own dick," I add.

Jake reaches for a slice of bacon from the plate. "I would if I could."

"That's my bacon."

He shoves the whole rasher in his mouth. Eyes flash with defiance as he chews the huge mouthful.

I glare as I sip at my coffee.

When Jake finally swallows, he says, "I made enough for two."

He picks up the plate and sets it on my lap. Then he climbs on the bed, his big body shifting until he's settled in beside me, our shoulders brushing.

I glance sideways. "What are you doing?"

Jake snags another rasher and gives me a wink. "Lying here with you, eating breakfast."

"I'm not going to be abducted from my bed," I point out as he munches his way through my food.

"I know, but I like this."

"Like what?"

"This." Jake waves the remainder of his bacon in a little arc over our laps, anointing my sheets with tiny droplets of grease. Then he pops it in his mouth, chews, and swallows. "Being with you." He turns his head. It brings us so close our noses almost touch. "You smell good."

"I've been in a hospital," I argue, enjoying the interaction. I like this too. A lot. It feels … *right*. "I smell like antiseptic ointment and disinfected sheets."

"No, it's not that." Jake leans in and rubs his nose along my neck. His breath tickles my skin. "It's like the scent of you is plugged into some fundamental part of my brain." His tongue snakes out, trailing a hot path toward my ear. My breath hitches when he nips at my lobe. "And the taste of you." He pulls back, looking at me with hooded eyes. "You're a drug, Mackenzie Valentine. One I can't quit."

But you did quit me.

The reminder has me crawling back inside myself.

"Don't," he says, his voice gruff.

"Don't what?"

"Don't do that. Every time we get too close, you shut down and we end up fighting."

"Because I can't forget, Jake," I answer honestly. "And I can't …"

"Can't?" he prompts.

My heart aches. "I can't forgive," I whisper.

Grief flits across his expression, and he bows his head. His wide shoulders sag. Damn him. He makes this so *hard*.

"I'm sorry, Jake."

"I don't want an apology when I'm the one who's sorry." He shakes his head, lifting his gaze. "I just want you to try."

"It's too hard."

"I'll make it easy for you. I promise." Jake shifts closer, his calloused palm rising to cup my cheek. His eyes darken, beseeching. "Please."

A small smile finds its way to my lips, and he covers it with his mouth, kissing me. The touch is tender. Light. Impossible to deny. My body responds, nipples tightening to painful points and heat licking its way down my spine.

Jake feels it and our kiss hardens into basic need. He needs my touch. I need his. My mouth opens and our tongues meet, rubbing and tangling together. Kissing him makes me dizzy and wet. A moan climbs my throat.

Before it escalates any further, Jake draws back and presses his forehead to mine.

A lump fills my throat. "What if I can't?"

"Don't even think about that. Let's just take each day as it comes. And then one day it will become easy and there'll be nothing between us. No past. Just you and me, together." He kisses me again, a soft press of his lips. "I love you, Princess."

"I—"

Jake shakes his head. "Don't say anything. I just want you to know."

The loud clearing of a throat interrupts us.

I jerk wildly. Coffee tips from the mug I forgot was in my hands. It splashes out, staining my sheets.

"Shit," I mutter, seeing Casey leaning against the doorframe. An amused glint lights his eyes as he looks between the both of us. "Jake was just … He brought me breakfast."

Casey waves an opened packet of Doritos, seeming to think nothing of Jake's and my close proximity. "I was just doing the same thing. Looks like he beat me to it."

Jake's tone is unamused. "You were bringing her *Doritos* for breakfast?"

"What?" Casey looks at the packet in mock confusion. "It's cheese. And corn. Part of the food pyramid."

He tosses a chip in his mouth with a loud *crunch*.

"What did *you* bring her?" His flirty blue eyes fall on the breakfast tray before moving to the plate in my lap. "Wow. A full-cooked breakfast. Bacon. Eggs. Coffee. Food of the Gods." He nods, looking at me. "That right there is the actions of a man in love."

"Dude," I mutter. "That is *not* what this is."

"Fuck you, Mac," Jake mumbles under his breath. "That's exactly what this is." Louder, he says, "What do you want, Daniels?"

A cheeky grin forms on Casey's lips. Damn, but the man is powerfully sexy, and I'm not blind. Short, dirty-blonde hair, tall and built, he has an infectious attitude that draws you in like a moth to flame. "I was checking to see if the Mac Attack needed anything, but clearly you've got her bases covered. *All* of them."

"I do. Mac doesn't need anything you've got to offer, mate."

A laugh flies from my mouth. His statement is almost absurd. Any girl would *beg* to have what Casey has to offer. Even if it *does* only come in Dorito form.

Indignation flushes Jake's cheeks. "Did you just *laugh*?"

"No."

"You did."

"I did not."

"Well, if I'm not needed," Casey says, interrupting our squabble, "then you ladies will have to excuse me. I've got shit to do."

He leaves quickly and we hear the sound of him jogging down the stairs moments later. I turn to Jake. "Do you think he knows?"

"Knows?"

"About us?" I clarify with an eye roll.

Jake

How Mac is letting me stay in her bed, I don't know. Scratch that. I do. She's vulnerable after what happened. Do I feel guilty about taking advantage of that vulnerability? Fuck no. She's going to have to suck it up and get used to me being in her face. Short of telling her *everything* that went down the night of her kidnapping, being like this is the only way to cement a future together as a happy, albeit hostile, couple.

I like the hostility, the rabid interaction we have. It keeps me on my toes. Keeps me wanting more. Being on stage, hammering a wild, heavy beat as the rioting crowd swells into a single living organism is nothing compared to having Mac naked beneath me. Or here beside me, bickering as she likes to do.

"So what if Casey knows, or anyone else for that matter?" I answer. "Would that be so bad?"

Mac lifts her chin, the stubborn bitch. "Yes."

"Why?"

She pauses for a moment as if scrambling for a reason. "Because it's unprofessional. We work together. I'm the manager. You're the talent."

I snort. "Try again."

"Because I don't know how to explain the history we've kept hidden from everyone all this time."

"I'll explain it," I say, shooting down her second reason.

Her brows snap together. "Dammit, Romero."

"Your reasons are thin, Princess. Try again."

Mac huffs and exhales sharply through her nostrils. The truth is in there, bubbling beneath the surface of her skin. It will come out because I've succeeded in pissing her off by digging for it.

"Because I'm not ready."

And there it is. I hide my disappointment by reaching for her mug of coffee. I take a sip. It's a punch to the eyeballs. The liquid is dark, bitter, and blacker than night. It's also lukewarm. I set it on the opposite bedside table.

"Okay then," I reply and force a smile.

"That's it?"

"I can't make you do something you're not ready for," I explain patiently.

"That's right. And it's not like we're even together," she goes on to say, her words a blow to the heart. *Not like we're together? I can't live without you!*

Despite the inner turmoil, my external voice is calm. "We're anything you want us to be."

As long as she wants us to actually be together.

I'm a fool for listening to Casey. Mac should know what her brothers have done. They're the ones who deserve her anger and forgiveness. But there's a small voice in the back of my mind that whispers, *What happens when she does find out? Will it all become water under the bridge, or will it be too late for the two of us to recover what we lost?*

Forcing Mac to rest for the majority of the day is impossible. Her parents and friends have been visiting on and off since we finished breakfast, so she got nothing done regardless.

It's late afternoon and she's in the shower when Jared puts in an appearance. I've avoided her brothers since the night of the kidnapping. My tolerance for them is zero, and I can't see that increasing any time soon. So when the knock comes at the door and I open it to find him on the doorstep, my blood pressure hits the roof.

His brows wing up. He's surprised to find me here. Perhaps he was hoping to avoid me too. The duplex we live in houses the six of us, though Mac, Evie, and Henry live in this side; Frog, Cooper, and I live in the other. It's basically the same set up we had in Melbourne, except we're two joined houses on one property with a shared back deck and yard. It's the perfect arrangement, except for times like now when I have to face Jared standing at the door with the expression of a guilty chump.

"What do you want?" I growl for the sole purpose of being difficult. It's clear he's here to see his sister.

Jared flicks his sunglasses up and rests them on his head. His green eyes are worn, the skin beneath them bruised from apparent lack of sleep. "Can we talk?"

"Is there anything left to say?"

"Yes."

I grind my jaw. "You mean there's more you've kept from me?"

"No. There's nothing else we've kept from you."

I turn and walk into the kitchen, leaving the door wide open. It's a clear indication that he can come in without me having to be solicitous about it. He steps inside and follows, dumping his keys, wallet, and sunglasses on the kitchen counter while I help myself to a beer from the fridge. I don't offer him one. It's his sister's place. If he wants a drink, he can get it himself.

He notices the slight with an audible exhale through his nostrils. Good. My emotional position has been made clear. I'm still *angry*.

Using the bottle opener, I flick the top from my beer and toss it in the bin. Tipping it up, I take a hell of a long sip before I acknowledge him with my eyes.

"Talk already," I mutter when I'm done, realising that drawing this out is making the situation more strained than it already is.

"I want to apologise," he says.

"Is that it?"

"I understand why you're angry."

"Good for you."

Jared's brows snap together. "Dammit, Romero."

"You want me to make this easier for you?"

"I just want to explain what happened."

"No, you just want to come here and say you're sorry to make yourself feel better," I point out. "But apologies are just an acknowledgement that you stuffed up. They don't fix shit." My mind goes to the child Mac and I made together. Was it from the first time we made love? We had argued. Then she told me she belonged to me before laughing in my eyes as she peeled off her dress. It's the best memory ever. So wild, unpredictable, and incredibly beautiful. To think of losing a child, a son or daughter, just like her makes me ache in the most painful way possible. It's torture. "It doesn't bring back what was lost," I whisper hoarsely, unable to hide the onset of grief.

I need to share it with Mac. I want to wrap my arms around her and just hold on while I howl because the pain is too much.

Jared breathes in deep, his expression clearly distraught. It doesn't stop me saying what needs to be said. "I think about how I feel right now, and then I think of what Mac must have felt when it happened. And to not be given the opportunity to cry with her, grieve with her, and hold her through the worst of it kills me. It fucking kills me," I choke out. "You took that from us and that's something you have to live with."

"I don't know how to explain how sorry I am." Jared swallows, but he stands strong, holding my eyes as he bumbles through his apology. "We lied to you by not saying anything. By telling you to stay away from Mac. And we lied to Mac by telling her you knew about the accident, and losing the baby, when you never knew at all. It was a horrible mistake, and I—"

There's a sharp intake of breath behind us.

We both turn.

Mac is standing on the bottom stair, feet frozen and face stripped of colour. A beat of strained silence falls before Jared takes a step toward her.

Mac moves back in response and fumbles as she hits the stair behind her. "What did you do?"

Her voice is a low accusatory sound that rips my chest wide open. A shaky hand comes to her mouth and her eyes seek mine.

"Princess," I mouth, my vision blurring.

"They never told you?" she croaks.

Mac's gaze follows me as I walk toward her. She's on the step above when I reach her side and it brings us to eye level. "No, sweetheart. I didn't know. I found out the night you were kidnapped."

Her jaw trembles.

My voice comes out a harsh whisper. "We lost a baby."

She nods, her lips pressed together as if she'll lose it by speaking.

The ache in my heart is heavy as I stare at the girl who's been through hell and yet stands tall and strong in the face of it. My insides feel like flimsy glass ready to shatter. How has she not broken like the way I feel I'm about to? "I'm so sorry."

"Why didn't you say anything when you found out?"

"It was the last thing you needed to hear under the circumstances."

Fire sparks in her eyes. "Fuck the circumstances," she snaps, holding her jaw tight to stop the trembling. Her eyes cut to Jared. "And fuck you."

Her brother tucks his hands inside the pockets of his jeans. "Mac, we thought—"

"You don't get to speak," she hisses, her body vibrating with anger. "I don't want to hear what you have to say. I don't want to see you. I don't want to talk to you. I want you to leave. Now."

Chapter Twenty

Mac

The fire of betrayal burns my skin to ash. My fingers curl into my palms, the sharp nails digging into my skin. It keeps me from falling apart as my brother closes the front door softly behind him. My gaze returns to Jake. For the first time I notice the dark circles that lie beneath his eyes.

"How much did you hear?" he asks.

I run my tongue along my lips. They're dry and in desperate need of lip balm. "Enough," I tell him, stepping off the stair and toward the kitchen where my handbag rests on the counter.

"Mac."

Ignoring Jake, I reach for my bag and rummage through the contents, not finding any. "Goddammit, where is it?"

"Where's what?"

"My lip balm," I mutter, my chest feeling tight. Why is it so hard to breathe right now? Am I having a goddamn heart attack? "Everyone's always bloody stealing it," I gripe. My lungs squeeze as I grab the bag and upend the entire contents over the bench top.

Crap scatters everywhere: bits of paper, lipsticks, pens, tampons, and my current sheet of birth control pills. "It's not here!" I half-shout, spreading my hands through it all in a frustrated search.

"Mac!" Jake shouts.

I shove it all off the counter, my chest heaving as I fight for another breath. Everything clatters to the tiled floor and scatters every which way.

My shoulders are grabbed in a vice and Jake gets in my face, shaking me. "Stop it!"

"I can't," I gasp.

"You can!"

"I can't! I can't breathe!" I press a hand to my chest. "I'm too young for a heart attack. I'm too young." A few wheezy pants escape my mouth. "This is my brothers' fault. They've gone too far now. *Too far.*" I jab a finger in Jake's face to emphasise my point. "And now I'm going to die."

The world tilts as Jake picks me up, cradling me to his chest. My body jostles as he walks us to the living area. "You're not going to die, Princess."

God, my chest *hurts*. "I am."

"You're having a panic attack."

That's insulting. I look down my nose at him. My tone is imperious but its effectiveness is ruined by my wheezing. "Fuck you, I don't *do* panic attacks."

Jake has the audacity to look amused. "You're doing one right now."

"I'm not."

"You are."

"I. Am. Not," I enunciate.

We reach the couch and he sinks down, bringing me with him. His arms tighten around me like a steel band. The tight entrapment usually has me straining to disentangle myself and he knows it, but instead I feel cocooned, as if anyone trying to get to me will have to break Jake apart first.

"You're bottling everything up inside you." He touches his nose to mine. "This is your body's way of trying to get rid of it. Let it out."

Let it out, he says, as if it's just that easy. I almost snort, but I'm basically doing that anyway as I suck oxygen in through my nose.

"If you don't let it out, I will instead," he warns me.

I can't let it out. I buried it deep long ago. It's sealed in a vault where there's no escape.

We stare at each other for a long, painful beat as he waits.

I give him nothing so Jake does the talking for both of us. "I was wrong," he admits. "I let you go and I was wrong."

My eyes close. It aches to hear his confession. He *was* wrong. We should have stayed together, no matter what.

"Breathe, Mac," he orders.

My chest is burning. A harsh rasp of air leaves me as I open my eyes.

Jake keeps talking. "I watched you walk down those steps. Not once did you look back. I betrayed your trust and in a single instant, I was wiped from your life. I didn't realise how much it would hurt. It fucking *hurt,* Mac." Jake shakes his head, his eyes distant. "But at the same time I was so proud of you. Your back was so straight as you walked away from me and toward the car. So true. Like the edge of sword." His gaze finds mine. "That's what being with you is like, Mackenzie Valentine. One wrong move and you feel the blade slice you wide open, so swift and clean it's done before you see it coming."

"You let me go, Jake. Why would I stay?"

"The baby."

Fire burns my throat. "You think I would honestly keep something like that from you? I was going to tell you, but you didn't give me the chance. And when you gave me up so easily, I realised you didn't deserve the chance."

Pain reaches his eyes. "You think I gave you up so easily?"

My response is a stony stare.

"I haven't slept a proper night since. Every damn night I lie in bed and all I see is you walking away from me. I work myself to exhaustion hoping that just once there'll be a night that my head hits the pillow and I'm out cold, but it never happens. And now…" Jake swallows hard "…now I see you walking away carrying my child and it kills me."

"Why did you do it?" I ask, for the first time being able to force the question past my lips.

"Why did I …" Jake trails off. A grim *whoosh* leaves his lungs. His hold loosens; one arm lets go to rub over the short buzz of hair on his head.

Seeing his struggle makes me wish I could retract it. I fight his embrace, realising I'm not ready to hear the answer. To hear him say *"I didn't want you."*

He turns his head, his voice firm in my ear. "Don't."

I still, unable to look at him.

"Please."

Jake

"You were everything to me, Mackenzie." A lump fills my throat. "You always were. You always will be. That's why you had to leave."

"Don't give me that convoluted, cryptic bullshit, Jake. I get enough of that from my family."

Mac is fighting so hard to hold herself together. After everything we've been through, I owe her the truth. The *real* reason I sent her away. But I'm scared. It will change the way she sees me. Forever.

"Give it to me straight," she demands, her chin jutting out. She's bracing for the hit.

So I give it to her like a neat shot of whiskey. "I killed someone."

Mac scrambles from my lap and the loss of her warmth is sharp. She rounds on me, her eyes wide with shock. "Jake."

"I shot a defenceless man in cold blood."

It's finally out there. I feel no better for it. Admitting what I've done to the person I love above all others just about breaks me.

Mac is looking at me as if she doesn't know who I am. I'm a stranger to her now.

"Why?" Her voice is sharp, almost shrill. "Why would you do that?"

"He wasn't supposed to die!"

I stand and she steps away from me. I'm already losing her.

"I got caught up with some bad people, Mac." I shake my head, feeling sick. "The King Street Boys. I never wanted you involved. I've done things I'm not proud of. Things that earned me a lot of money. The cost of my father's care was something I couldn't afford. Not when I was sixteen fucking years old." I scrub hands over my face. Frustration rises until I'm drowning in it. "He can't even talk properly!" I cry. "How was he supposed to fend for himself? I know it's not an excuse, but I felt I had no choice."

"You always had a choice!" she screams, fury burning red streaks high across her cheekbones.

"I didn't!"

"You could have come home! You could have talked to me. To my parents. We could have worked it out!"

"You don't understand."

"You're right." Her eyes are like ice now. "I don't."

My hands clench, itching to take hold of her and force her to understand, to bridge the gaping fracture in the earth between our feet. It's opening wider with every breath she takes.

"And the man you killed?" Mac asks, her voice stony.

"They were testing me. They wanted to be sure I'd take orders. So they gave me a gun. It was supposed to be empty. At least Luke thought it was, but it turns out it wasn't," I say, my tone bitter. "And a man died. That made me a murderer, Mac. And they knew it. They bought my loyalty to the gang with fucking *murder*."

Mac swallows and shakes her head as if my words are incomprehensible. And they are because it's been years and I still can't comprehend them either.

"Then you show up out of the blue in Melbourne, and I knew you couldn't stay. It wasn't safe. But I wasn't strong enough to make you leave. So I had the great idea to get out."

"And they didn't like it," she says, smart enough to put the puzzle pieces together.

"That night at The Bar was their warning. Leave and we won't just shoot you, we'll shoot your girlfriend too. So I rang your brothers and the next morning you were gone."

Mac wraps her arms around herself, hugging her upper body. It makes me ache that I can't do that for her. "You could've told me. Instead you kept me in the dark. You made the decision to get rid of me."

"They would have killed you!" My shout is so loud she flinches. Why can't she see that I was just trying to keep her alive!

"I can take care of myself!" she shouts back. "You're just like my brothers. You think you know what's best for me, but you don't." Her entire body is trembling now. I take a step toward her, and she steps back again. "You have no idea!"

"I'm sorry," I implore. "I was young, Mac. And stupid. I thought I was doing the right thing."

"You thought," she throws out. Her voice is harsher than the black coffee she drinks. "You. You. You. What about what I thought?"

"I'm sorry," I say again. "I was wrong."

Mac tilts her head back. An abrupt laugh leaves her lips as if my apology is ludicrous. The sound dies out and she shakes her head. "Sorry doesn't even begin to cover it." Her eyes fill and she blinks. "What a goddamn clusterfuck."

Emptiness engulfs me. Coming clean was the right thing to do, but at what cost? "Can we just put this behind us and move forward? I know it won't be easy, but we have time on our side. I love you."

Mac steps back again and the fracture at our feet is so wide now I fear it irreparable. "There's no moving forward, Jake. Only moving on."

She turns and plucks a set of car keys from the bowl by the door. Then she leaves without speaking another word.

The duplex settles into painful silence. The kind so loud it roars in your ears. I sink back on the couch, trying to convince myself it doesn't hurt. That maybe she's right. Moving on might be the only way.

The front door flies open with a bang.

My head jerks up.

Mac is standing there, eyes on me. Her mouth opens and closes. "I ..."

Hope rises in a heady rush. I stand.

Her eyes darts to the kitchen, her body skittish. "I forgot my bag."

"You don't need your bag."

Her brows soar high. "I don't?"

"No. Because you're not going anywhere."

"Jake." She shuts the front door behind her and moves on legs that appear unsteady.

Give me something, Princess.

Please.

Anything.

"I love you too."

The impact of her words hit so hard my eyes close for a second. I absorb them like the warm summer sun on a cool blustery day. How can she still feel the same knowing what I've done? I don't deserve it, but I don't care. We've gone through too much and come too far for me to not grab that love with both hands.

Mac is still there when my eyes open, her declaration lingering in the air between us. I close the distance and grasp the lapels of her leather jacket, pulling her against me. Her hands cup my cheeks and I mash my lips down on hers. Heat shoots straight to my belly.

Mac doesn't hold back. Her mouth is warm and eager. I part her lips with my tongue and sweep inside with aggression. My hands loosen on her jacket. They slide underneath and span her ribcage.

The kiss feels endless yet it's not enough. I draw back, giving us a moment to breathe. Her hands slide from my face and she moves backward. My arms fall away. The expression on her face gives my gut a jerky twinge.

"No, babe. Whatever you're thinking, stop it," I demand, my voice hoarse. "Right now."

"I can't."

"Can't what?"

"I love you, but I can't do this," she whispers.

"You can," I argue. My anger grows until I fear my chest will explode.

Mac holds her head high. "I'm sorry, Jake. Too much has happened. Too many lies and secrets. I can't get past it. I just can't."

I breathe deep, fighting for calm, but I lose. "Goddammit!" I roar. Mac flinches.

I turn and kick the small side table beside the sofa. The force has it skidding across the floor upending against the wall near the stairs. One of the legs splinters on impact. It doesn't ease the rage and frustration. Grabbing the glass bowl off the cabinet by the door, I throw it across the room. It smashes against the wall and punches a hole in the plaster before shattering into a rain of glass shards across the floor.

"Stop it!" Mac shouts, her voice piercing the red haze.

I've never had anything worthwhile apart from music and Mackenzie Valentine. But I'm a fool, because I never had her. It seems destiny has decreed I never will.

I try to say something, anything, but words stick in my throat.

Mac speaks instead. Her tone is soothing. "Remember that summer when we were kids and we snuck up on Mitch and Eli in the backyard with the hose?"

Of course I remember. It was hot as blazes, and Mac still had that damn cast on her arm. She couldn't swim in the pool and every shower required her wrapping it up in garbage bags. We wrapped it up again after lunch and lay under the sprinkler on the front lawn to cool off. Mac had been in the throes of planning a revenge attack against Mitch. He'd tipped out her new, expensive shampoo a week earlier and filled the bottle with dishwashing liquid. Her hair resembled straw for two days afterward until Jenna had him coughing up hard-earned pocket money to pay for a deep-conditioning treatment at a salon.

It hadn't eased Mac's bitterness. She was busy griping as we lay on the lawn, drops of water sprinkling intermittently over our bodies. Then an idea hit me. Mitch and Elijah were seated at the table out the back, frantically pulling together their summer essays at the last minute before school started back. I suggested we hose them.

So we did. Creeping around the back of the house, Mac hid behind the hedge of shrubbery while I stood by the tap waiting for the signal. Turning the dial to *jet* and taking aim, Mac touched her earlobe and then held up two fingers telling me she was good to go.

I twisted the tap and ran, reaching her side just as she turned the hose on Mitch full force. The blast had loose papers and books flying off the back table in a flood of complete and utter devastation.

The fury Mitch turned our way should've set our hair on fire. He stood like the Terminator, eyes red with a vengeance that would not be stopped. Mac had muttered an "oh shit" and dropped the hose, leaving it to gush water over the grass.

Grabbing her arm, I dragged her off until we were running around the side of the house, our hands clasped tightly together and laughter tearing from us until my eyes blurred and my sides hurt.

Mitch chased us all the way down the street before finally giving up. When we eventually risked returning, we found he'd locked us out of the house. We sat side by side on the front stoop waiting until Jenna returned home from work.

"We sat on that damn stoop for over two hours as the sun set," Mac says, pulling me from the memory, "wet and getting colder by minute."

"I remember," I mutter gruffly.

"I jostled your shoulder and you looked at me. The colours of the setting sun were bright in your eyes, and I'd never seen anything more beautiful. You laughed at me and I realised I was staring. Then I told you that I'd never had so much fun or felt so free as I did when I was with you. That you were my best friend."

The lump in my throat is huge. "And I said that you were my best friend too. The only real friend I ever had."

Mac's head tilts back. She's desperately blinking back tears. When she has them under control, her eyes return to mine. "I want to go back to that. I love you, Jake, but I need time. Time to be your friend again like we used to be. Can you give me that?"

She's right. There have been too many secrets. Too many lies. Betrayal. And so much hurt that we both need time to mend the wounds. As much as I want to be with her, we can't force the healing process.

"Okay," I croak and hold out my hand. "Friends?"

The front door flies open as she's taking my hand in hers. "Friends."

We shake on it.

"Holy shit!" Cooper announces from behind Mac. He's staring at us, at our joined hands, and then back at us. Frog steps in beside him.

Both of them take in the scene before them, which includes smashed glass, splintered furniture, and the contents of Mac's handbag strewn about the kitchen.

"Holy shit!" Frog exclaims.

I let go of Mac's hand. The smooth warmth of her palm slowly slides away from mine as we ignore our friends. My lips curve because for some reason it feels good. Like we've been through a wild cyclone and were standing in the aftermath. Survivors. Mac's lips curve in response.

"Has Armageddon arrived?" Cooper bleats as he walks further inside, hands on his hips as he inspects the damage.

"I don't know," Frog replies, "but I feel all wrong. Like I stepped inside an alternate universe in some kind of monumental cosmic accident." He actually steps back outside and looks to the sky, eyes searching.

"What?" Cooper says. He walks out to stand beside Frog and looks up.

"I'm checking for a tear in the fabric of time."

Cooper scratches his head. "Isn't that for time travel? I thought a parallel universe was like radio waves or something."

Mac clears her throat. "I'm going to go visit Evie at the hospital."

"Alright." My gaze sweeps over the evidence of my tantrum. "I guess I'll clean this up."

Chapter Twenty-One

Mac

To say our family dinner the following Sunday is a cold affair is to say water is a little bit wet. It's as if a blizzard has blown through, leaving a layer of frost on everything it touched, including me.

"Can you pass the salt?" Mitch asks from my right.

Ordinarily, their bullshit puts me in a rage and that saltshaker will find itself pegged at his head. Instead, I pick it up in silence and set it to my right, looking at no one.

I can't bring myself to talk to any of my brothers, let alone look at them. My trust in their honesty has been destroyed, levelled to rubble like a building in an earthquake.

"Mac, honey, are you okay?" Mum asks from across the table.

My eyes flick up from the food I'm pushing around on my plate. "Never better."

The flat response doesn't appease the concern in her eyes. She tilts her head. "How's Jake?"

"He's good."

"And Cooper? Frog?"

"They're all good, Mum."

"Well then." She smiles with false pleasantness, trying to lift the dark mood that has settled in around the table. "I saw Evie today." Her gaze shifts to Jared seated beside her, lines forming on her forehead. "She told me—"

Jared clears his throat loudly, and she stops talking. "That I'm leaving tomorrow," he says in a pre-emptive strike. I already know. Evie was a broken-hearted mess thanks to my douchebag brother. He's leaving because of what happened. Jared blames himself for her getting shot. His ludicrous solution is to remove himself from the equation, leaving Evie safe from danger. I can't even begin to list all the things wrong with his plan. It's evidence of his assumption that he's doing *what he thinks best for her*. Meaning he hasn't changed a bit. "For work," he clarifies.

"Don't you mean running away?" I mutter snidely under my breath.

Dad's brows pull together. "For how long?"

"A few months, maybe."

"Good riddance," I mutter again.

Mitch gives a saddened sigh. He heard me.

"I'm taking Casey's place overseas for the training workshops."

Mitch turns his head toward me. He speaks softly, not wanting to be heard above the conversation taking place around the table. "Mac, can we talk? Outside?"

"No."

"Please?"

Of all my brothers, Mitch is the most considerate. The *wisest*. His moral compass is so strong a hurricane can't blow it off course. It makes his inclusion in the betrayal all the worse. "No."

His voice comes out as a low growl. I'm trying his patience, which is not an easy feat. "Now, Mackenzie Valentine, you'll hear what I have to say."

"I couldn't give two shits about what you have to say."

He ignores my snide tone and reaches across the table in front of me for the pepper grinder. His arm bumps my glass of wine. It tips toward me, making a loud *clink* as it hits my plate. Conversation halts as merlot spews out in a giant arc, dousing my face and chest.

My hands fly up, a loud gasp leaving my mouth as I look down at my pretty lemon dress. It's a Collette Dinnigan. An absolute classic. A treasured masterpiece of fabric that makes my tired skin glow, my legs appear longer, and cheers me up better than a block of chocolate.

"I'm sorry," Mitch says, abandoning his quest for the pepper as he takes in the disaster he created. "I'll buy you a new one."

If I were ever going to *do* tears, now would be the time. "This one isn't in her collection anymore."

"Then I'll buy you a hundred new ones."

Mum comes racing toward me with paper towel. "A hundred?" I echo.

"Sweetheart," Mum mutters at Mitch as she blots at the mess. "You can't buy a hundred new ones. This is a Collette Dinnigan."

His face remains blank. "So?"

"So you may as well just buy me a Ferrari instead," I snap. "I'll take one in red, thanks."

"Maybe I'll just replace the one dress," he mumbles.

"Honey, quickly go upstairs to your old room and get this off," Mum instructs as she steps back to survey the damage. "We'll get the stains right out, I promise."

I do as she suggests. I'm just sliding on a pair of old sweatpants when Mitch appears in the doorway. He leans against the frame and folds his arms.

My eyes narrow. "You ruined my dress on purpose."

He shrugs. "I did. I'm sorry. To be fair, I thought the wine would just spill onto the food you weren't eating anyway. I didn't realise your glass was so full."

"Well it was, so thanks a bunch, asshead. You can take me shopping tomorrow."

"Done," he says quickly. *Too* quickly. "Whatever you want. It's yours."

My eyes narrow further, to mere slits. "You can't buy forgiveness, Mitch."

"I know that, but you've been through a lot in the last week. More hell than some people go through in a lifetime. You deserve some time out to focus on something frivolous like shopping."

It's a sentiment I can't deny, and Mitch is vulnerable right now. I should be taking advantage rather than getting my knickers twisted in a knot. Leaning back against the dresser behind me, I fold my arms and contemplate my traitorous brother. "I want matching shoes to go with the new dress."

"Done."

"And a matching clutch."

"Done."

"And jewellery."

His brows rise a fraction, but he agrees nonetheless. "Okay."

Hmmm, what else? My stomach rumbles, putting in its two cents. "And buffet lunch at the Marriott."

"You—"

"No wait. Lunch at Mr. Chow's. You better ratchet up the charm so you can get us a table at such short notice."

"I can—"

I cut him off again. I'm on a roll now. Full steam ahead. "We can follow that up with a trip to Zumbo's patisserie. I've got a hankering for a donut soft serve cone." That shit is an orgasmic diabetes attack. "With sprinkles."

"Okay," Mitch says slowly. "Can I talk now?"

My stomach sinks. I don't want to talk. Mitch is always too reasonable, and too easy to forgive. I want to stew in my anger for years to come. I want to hold this over my brothers until the goddamn end of time. The apocalypse can bring zombies, acid rain, and the implosion of earth, and I will still go to my catastrophic death happily clinging to my wrath. They deserve no less.

"I'll let you talk," I say, and he opens his mouth to speak, but I'm not finished. "On one condition."

His mouth snaps closed for a moment. Then he concedes with a nod. "Okay, what?"

I give him a level stare. "Jake comes with us tomorrow."

If Mitch hesitates, I'll know he still doesn't like the thought of Jake and me together, and any kind of apology he gives will be moot.

"Of course." Mitch smirks. "That's if he actually *wants* to go shopping with you."

There was no hesitation in his answer, and my heart thaws the slightest fraction. "Okay. Talk."

"Mac, honey?" Mum calls out. Her voice gets closer as she makes her way up the stairs. "Do you have the dress? The sooner we get to that stain the better."

Mitch steps to the side, allowing our mother through the bedroom door. I collect the dress from the timber rung of my old bed. She takes it, talking as she walks back out, expecting us to follow. I give my brother a sardonic shrug as I follow her while she chatters. "I got you a fresh plate of food and your father opened another bottle of wine. It's resting on the table so get yourself another glass."

"Tomorrow," Mitch says from behind as he follows us down the staircase.

They always say tomorrow never comes, but to me the statement is illogical. Last night, 'tomorrow' was Sunday, and now it's Sunday. Hence tomorrow came.

And here we are, the four of us—because Jake readily agreed to the shopping trip and somehow Elijah got included too. It feels uncomfortable, like I'm wearing the wrong-sized jacket. I roll my shoulders, trying to disperse some tension.

The day isn't going well. In fact, it started out strained and is rapidly declining into downright torture.

Mitch is being so obsessively accommodating it's making my teeth grind. Jake is ignoring Mitch. When he isn't, he subjects my brother to angry glares. And every time we walk inside another store, he heaves a resigned sigh. Shopping clearly makes him miserable. Too bad. This is what I do with my friends. If he doesn't like it, he can find the nearest exit.

And Elijah is being ... well, weird. His expression toward Jake when he thinks I'm not watching is downright calculating. I don't understand it. But with me he's being overly solicitous, as if I'm an invalid on leave from the hospital.

All of them are being painful, and I haven't found a single dress I like. I'm ready to give up when I find *the one*. It's deep red, yet still rich and vibrant. Strapless with a sweetheart neckline and barely breathable waistline, it drapes over my hips until it reaches the floor. Trying it on is a delicious *Pretty Woman* moment that I want to revel in until the end of time. Or at least a few more minutes.

"Can I help zip you?" the sales lady calls through the door of the fitting room. Though, *fitting room* is an understatement; it's large enough to hold a small settee, on which my handbag rests.

"Give me a minute," I call back.

I slide the dress up my legs. Holding the back of it together, I use my other hand to unlatch the door. It opens but the saleslady has disappeared. Instead, Mitch steps inside the spacious enclosure. His big, stupid bulk makes the room claustrophobic.

"What are you doing?" I hiss, grabbing the gaping front of the dress to make sure it covers my front. It causes the fabric to fall and gape at the back instead.

"Zipping you," he says, shutting and latching the door behind him. "Turn around."

I turn and face the mirror, shoulders tense. My brother stands behind me. He's a head taller than I am so I can see him clearly. He makes quick work of the dress, zipping me together from my waist upwards in one swift movement.

When he's done, he rests warm palms on my bare shoulders and looks at me in the mirror. A faint smile rests on his lips. "It's perfect."

An evil glint lights my eyes. "It's six thousand dollars."

He flinches yet holds strong. "What can you do? The dress was made for you."

It was. My gaze runs the length of the dress and back up again before returning to Mitch. His eyes have softened and my heart gives a tiny bleat, causing my shoulders to slump a fraction. "You don't have to buy it, Stitch."

His eyes soften further at the nickname. The use is familiar. Friendlier. Damn him. He does this all the time. His dumb soft heart is hard to deny.

"I do," he counters.

"It's too much. I would never really expect you to spend that kind of money."

"You look beautiful, Mac. I'm buying it."

My eyes shift back to the dress again. "Where would I wear it?"

"Let Jake take care of that part."

I turn and his hands fall away from my shoulders. "We're just friends."

Mitch has the nerve to laugh. "That's a crock and you know it. Jake was made for you, just like that dress was."

The comment has the breath catching in my throat. It's a statement I never expected from my brother. "Why do you think that?"

"Because only a man stronger than Hercules could ever handle you, and his right hook just about put me in the ground."

"Jake *punched* you?" Of my three brothers, Mitch has the bulkiest muscle, the coolest temperament, and the strongest loyalty. Hurt what he loves and nothing will save you. You won't even go down swinging because you'll be too busy running for your life. Jake had managed to *punch* all that and come out unscathed? "Holy shit," I breathe. "When did that happen?"

"The night you were kidnapped," Mitch replies, shifting around me toward the settee. "In the hospital parking lot. After he punched out Travis too."

"The night I was …" Shoving my oversized Burberry aside, he sits and stretches his legs out, crossing them at the ankle and making himself comfortable. "What are you doing?"

"Talking."

"Now?" I bleat, my mind still caught on Jake's violent rampage.

"Yes, now," Mitch replies mildly. "We're meeting Jake and Elijah at the Tavern in a bit so we have time."

"In a bit?"

"Yes, in a bit."

"So they get to avoid shopping and your blabbering mouth and go toss back a beer, while you hold me hostage inside a fitting room wearing a six thousand dollar dress I can't get out of?"

"Basically, yes."

"I'm glad Jake punched you," I hiss. I'm fuming at the trap, so when a light rap comes at the door and the sales lady calls out, "How's it going in there?" I reply with, "Actually it's not going so well."

"Oh?" she prompts.

"I can't seem to get the full effect of the dress without wearing heels," I call out over the door. "Perhaps some Louboutins would help?"

Glee tinges the edge of her reply. "We have a few in his latest collection that would suit. Shall I bring them?"

Setting my jaw, I fix a hard glare on my brother. "Please."

Her footsteps are soundless on the plush carpet as she leaves. Silence settles around the fitting room as my gaze falls to my brother.

"I'm sorry, Mac," Mitch says quietly. "I interfered in your life. We all did. You're our little sister. No matter how strong or capable you may be, it's our instinct to protect you. Sometimes we do that without thinking clearly. And at that point, straight after a car accident in which our little nephew or niece was lost …" He pauses. He sits forward in the seat. "Any one of us could have died, and we all kind of lost it."

My brother links his hands together and rests his elbows on his knees. "I know Romero told you he had people who wanted him dead. Just being around him was dangerous for you. Add in your fixation for danger, and it made you and Jake a volatile match. We feared for your life. So we acted in the only way we knew how. The only way we figured you would let it go without a fight." He sighs heavily. "What we did wasn't right. And it's weighed on me, on all of us, ever since. But it was done. And yet somehow you and Jake managed to find your way back to each other. So no matter what we did to intervene, fate has determined otherwise for the two of you."

His apology doesn't sound rehearsed. It's sincere and irrefutable. I knew his words would worm their way beneath my skin. His ability to charm is effortless. It's no doubt the reason Mitch was sent as a representative for the three of them.

"Damn you," I mutter. "Apologies don't change shit, Mitchell Valentine."

"They don't. But in my opinion they're pretty damn important. Don't you think?"

They are but I don't want to concede too quickly. I shrug and turn back to the mirror, studying the red dress with hands on my hips. "It's a start."

A light tap comes at the fitting room door. "Are you ready for some shoes?"

My eyes light up. "That's a yes."

Mitch stands and tugs his wallet from the back pocket of his worn jeans. "And that's my cue to get out of here." Grabbing my hand, he turns it over and slaps the wallet onto my open palm like manna from Heaven. My fingers curl around the soft leather as he tells me his PIN for access. "Don't clean me out, sweetheart," he mutters as he opens the fitting room door and walks out.

The sales lady fumbles the shoeboxes in her hand as she stares after him. She emits a longing sigh.

I clear my throat purposefully.

She spins quickly and loses her hold on the boxes. They tumble out in every direction. "Sorry," she mumbles, crouching to collect the boxes. I go to help but I can't bend in the dress for fear my organs will cave in. "Your boyfriend looks like someone familiar, that's all."

"He's not my boyfriend, he's my brother."

"Oh." She stands, eyes alight, her name badge proclaiming her as *June*. "Well maybe you wouldn't mind passing on my—"

I cut her off quickly, my mind going to Gabriella. Mitch has always belonged to her. Soon enough he'll be reminded of that. My eyes narrow. *It's too late for you, June.* "He's taken."

June's shoulders sag. "All the good ones are."

Jake materialises when June finishes boxing the dress. Combined with the buzzed hair and fitted vintage shirt, the leather jacket and the jeans, he looks like a thug. A *sexy* thug.

Jesus Christ, Mackenzie Valentine. You're trying to be friends again. Not sex him up.

My sales lady emits another longing sigh and I swallow a growl. I angle myself to block his view as the last of the material disappears beneath layers of tissue paper. For some reason I don't want him seeing the dress.

"Almost done?"

"Just about," I say with glee as June enters the payment into the EFTPOS machine.

He gives me a faint smile. "Spending all your brother's money?"

"Doing my best."

"Good."

"I thought we were meeting at the tavern when I finished. Am I taking too long?"

"Nope. There was something I had to do." June hands over the machine and I tap Mitch's bank card to the Paypass device as he speaks. "I haven't made it to the tavern yet."

My interest is piqued. "Oh?" I punch in the PIN and hand back the device. "What did you have to do?"

He clears his throat. "Just some personal business."

I can't stand being kept out of the loop. "What kind?"

June hands over the boxes and credit card. She interrupts our conversation to inform me the receipt is tucked inside with the dress. Jake takes them from her before I can.

"Thanks, June."

We walk off as I tuck the credit card back inside the wallet and pop it in my handbag.

"Hope to see you again soon," she calls out behind us.

"The kind that's none of your business," he tells me, tucking the boxes under his left arm. He uses his right to link arms with mine.

I huff. My shoulder brushes his as we make our way to the tavern. "Well, why mention you had something personal to do if you aren't going to tell me what it is?"

He gives me a mysterious smile, the cheeky kind that makes the reckless place between my legs throb like a bass drum. "You'll find out in good time."

"Damn you, Jake Romero."

His grin deepens. "Keep talking dirty to me, Princess. I love it."

The throb escalates. "Yeah? Maybe I should tell you about how I think of you at night when I'm in bed touching myself."

Jake stumbles and I shout with laughter.

"Jesus Christ," he mumbles. "I need a cigarette."

My top lip curls in a sneer. "Fuck your cigarettes, Jake."

"I'd rather you fuck me," he mutters beneath his breath.

I can still hear it. Try and be friends again first? Yeah, that's working out just great.

Chapter Twenty-Two

Mac

The next few months bring a new kind of trouble to our door in the form of Quinn Salisbury, our new band assistant.

Considering trouble is my middle name, I'm all in. It's a fresh start in my quest to become a member of the Badass Brigade. My brothers may be untrustworthy, lying wankers, but my dream to work in their firm hasn't diminished.

Though having three of them to deal with has me wondering what you call more than one wanker, in the same way you call more than one duck a *gaggle* of ducks. Henry, Evie, and I argued about it late one night with a few vodkas under our belts. A festival of wankers was our conclusive verdict. *Wankfest* for short.

Anyway, the trouble with Quinn started not long after Jared returned from overseas and proclaimed his undying love for my best friend. He bought Evie a house in Bondi—a pretty beachside suburb north of our duplex in Coogee—and she folded like a cheap lawn chair.

Clearly she was wearing her dick goggles because it was a shit house. I teased her about it profusely. *"Blinded by the dick,"* I crooned in her face to the tune of "Blinded by the Light" by Manfred Mann's Earth Band. Henry would too. It was especially fun to do it while drunk. Evie would try to slap us but missed as we danced out of reach. She doesn't know that Henry and I found the song under a secret playlist on her phone. It includes other such gems as "Africa" by Toto and "Don't Stop Believin'" by Journey.

Henry and I scream with hilarity each time we find a new song's been added. Frankly, though, we're just relieved she's still around for us to tease after the shooting. It brought us closer together. Not close enough to share the past I have with Jake, but closer nonetheless.

Jake and I reach some weird kind of limbo. It's slowly becoming clear that we're trying to go back to something we'll never have again. Too much has happened. Not to mention the sexual tension. It's hot enough to blister my skin. Our frustration levels peak. We snap at each other every other day. It doesn't go unnoticed. But I don't have time to deal with it. Work is too busy. The band has signed with Jettison Records, and Quinn has begun her employment. It gets off to a smooth start, but her life slides into a decline soon after.

Quinn has a violent stepfather who was recently released from prison. A bitter, angry man, David hated my assistant. His plan was to show her just how much.

We helped her arrange a Domestic Violence Order, but its protection is minimal. It wasn't safe for her to live alone. Considering Evie had recently moved to the shit house in Bondi, we moved Quinn into her old room.

It's not until the night before our flight to appear at the Melbourne Music Festival that I discover the level of trouble she's in.

It starts with me waking at three a.m. to an unusually loud *thud.* I sit up in bed, pushing hair off my face as I cock an ear, listening intently. A shriek soon follows, along with a banging crash.

I roll to get up and encounter a huge lump of naked man. "Oomph!"

The moonlit room reveals Jake. He's sprawled like a starfish across every square inch of mattress. The giant tool promised he would get up and leave. I didn't mention how much I wanted him to stay. Jake's presence in my bed feels *right.* His dominance overpowers the room, and his warm heavy body lulls me into a restful sleep. Clearly Jake feels the same. He's far too comfortable, and far too busy sleeping like the dead, to move. He would be useless in a midnight home invasion.

I shoot him a dirty look as I climb over his body. My naked skin slides deliciously against his, yet he sleeps on, undisturbed.

My satin slip is crumpled on the floor. I put it on. The cream fabric skates over my body until it reaches just below the curve of my backside. When I'm done tugging on the panties that had been flung clear across the room, I pad out the door to investigate the sound.

Jake

My body ascends slowly to consciousness. Sex with Mac does that to me. It knocks me right the fuck out. I swipe a hand over my face, and my eyes open to tired slits. It's still dark out. Good. That means it's safe to sneak back next door without getting caught.

I roll to my side. My plan is to glide my palm down the naked length of Mac's back until I have a juicy handful of ass to squeeze. It will have to tide me over until our next sexual happenstance. My hand encounters air and falls flat, landing on cool sheets.

Lifting my head, I frown and wrinkle my brow.

Mac is nowhere to be seen, and the blinding glare of the clock shows a little after three a.m. in the morning.

I snap to a sitting position when a female shriek renders the air. Fear sends my heart pounding. Heedless of being caught coming from Mac's room, I leap to my feet and snag my boxer briefs from the floor. I barely have them on as I fly out the door.

I hear a fight in progress coming from Quinn's room. I race along the upstairs hallway. Henry, Frog, and Cooper stand just inside her bedroom door.

I push between them, my chest heaving from the rush of adrenaline. I stop and stare, blinking. Quinn has Mac pinned on the floor beneath her while the boys watch on, stupefied.

Mac's arm is outstretched. She's grappling for the phone above her head. It lies just out of reach.

"No!" Quinn yells as she claws her way over Mac.

Our band assistant is clad in just her underwear. With her white-blonde hair, tiny stature, and brown eyes big enough to rival Bambi, seeing her in a sexy black bra is quite the jolt.

What's worse is Mac wearing just her slip and panties. The same pair I ripped off just hours earlier. They're black and lacy with cream polka dots. They're also completely visible to every eye in the room.

Her slip rises as Quinn makes a grab for the phone. Mac's flat, tanned belly is now exposed. The wrestling sees it rise further. Underboob is just a scant inch of fabric away, and I'm transfixed.

"*Arrghh!*" Mac squeals when Quinn's elbow catches her in the eye.

"Sorry," Quinn mumbles. When her hand encircles the phone, she gives a shout of relief. It's short-lived when Mac rolls her over, pinning her to the floor. That tight ass rises, and my dick gives an almighty *jerk*.

It's then that I realise everything I'm seeing, the boys are seeing too. That's my princess on the floor, and she's for my eyes only.

"What the hell is going on here?" I bellow.

The girls freeze and both heads turn toward me.

Cooper elbows me in the side. "Shut up, idiot. Naked chicks wrestling."

Right. But one of those *naked chicks* belongs to *me*. "Cover your eyes," I mutter, avoiding their twin looks of incredulity.

Mac ignores us. She turns back to Quinn and growls, "Give me one good reason why I shouldn't ring Travis right now."

Quinn's eyes flutter closed. A tear escapes and falls down her temple. She whispers something I can't hear. Something that turns Mac's face white. She scrambles off her.

"I'm sorry," Quinn chokes out, opening her eyes. They're filled with tears and take in all of us. "I'm so sorry."

Mac nods toward the door. "Everyone out."

None of us move.

She arches a brow. "Did I just speak Klingon? Out. Now."

I shoot Mac a look. *You better tell me what the fuck is going on.*

She gives me a nod that no one else sees. *Later.*

With the four of us leaving the room en masse, I have no choice but to return next door.

The next morning when we board our flight to Melbourne, I muscle my way in front of Henry and Evie and snatch the seat beside Mac. With three seats on each side of the plane, she's stuck in the middle and an elderly man has the window. It leaves me with the aisle seat.

It judders as I sit and my shoulder accidently shoves Mac into the old man. He gives a little yelp and she tries to straighten. It's a big fail because my shoulder now takes up half her seat.

"What are you doing?" Mac hisses as if I'm causing a commotion that every passenger on the plane has stopped to watch.

"Sorry," I mutter. It's unbelievable how airlines actually consider these things *seats.* It's like sitting in a toddler chair. I'm too wide to fit them properly. My shoulders cop a hit whenever a flight attendant moves down the aisle with their food and drink cart. Aisle seats are something I avoid for that very reason, but trapping Mac on this flight is likely my one opportunity to find out what went down last night.

Quinn comes toward us, wheeling her little carryon. Her slight body is getting shoved by careless passengers in their rush to get seated. Travis is stuck about five bodies down, brows drawn in a pissed expression.

I stand and block everyone who's trying to come or go. Sometimes my size comes in handy. "Where's your seat, sweetheart?"

Her brown eyes scan the aisle numbers above. "Ahh, behind you."

I snatch her carryon. Lifting it with ease, I tuck it into the storage compartment above.

"Thanks, Jake," Quinn says and takes her seat behind me.

"No problem."

I sit back down. Mac gets knocked sideways. The old man gives another yelp. I sigh. "Sorry."

"Next time I'm telling Quinn to book business class," she mutters.

"Hell yes." I tuck my shoulder in as a guy bigger than me makes his way down the aisle. We shoot each other a mutual look of sympathy before he moves on. "Surely the band is earning enough now to afford that."

"And then some."

"No shit?" I'm impressed with how quickly our star is rising in the music world.

"No shit," she confirms, satisfaction gleaming in her fierce green eyes. "If this keeps up, one day the band will have its own jet."

And all I have to do is keep doing what I love. It seems too easy. How had I managed to turn my life around? As much as it grates, I owe a lot to the lying bastard Valentine brothers. They got me out of the gang. To this day I don't know how. All I had to do was pack my bags in the middle of the night and leave. I haven't seen or heard from Luke or Leander Fox since. It's hard not to search for them. Luke had been my best friend. But I don't. It's my past. It's best I leave it there.

Our plane taxies into the sky, and I turn my head toward Mac, keeping my voice low. "So tell me, what was all that about last night?"

She shoots a quick glance over her shoulder between the gap in the seats. Clearly Mac doesn't want either Quinn *or* Travis, who's now sitting beside her, to overhear our conversation. She tilts her head close to mine and speaks quietly. "You know how David was released from prison? Apparently he's gone underground because he owes people money."

"Okay." But it doesn't explain why the two of them were wrestling last night for the phone. "So?"

"Well, if they can't get their money from him, who do you think they're turning to next to get it?"

Quinn Salisbury. His stepdaughter.

"Jesus," I mutter. "How much?"

She rattles off an impossible sum.

My head falls back against the seat in disbelief. "What's the plan?"

"Plan?" Her eyes widen. For several moments she doesn't blink.

It's Mac's tell that something is going down, and that something means A: chaos and reckless idiocy are sure to ensue, and B: shit will hit the fan as a result.

"Mac," I growl. "Does Travis know?"

She huffs at my question, making it obvious there's a tight little loop and her brother is being kept out of it.

Mac flicks her black-framed oversized sunglasses down from her head to cover her eyes, and she folds her arms. "The plan is that we're just going to tell them we don't have the money next time they ask. Jake, she was planning on disappearing in the middle of the night, scared of getting any of us involved or hurt. It's lucky she even told me. I woke to the noise of her trying to wrestle her suitcase down from the top shelf in her wardrobe." Her chin juts out. "I tried phoning Travis to tell him, and we will ..." she adds hastily when she sees anger rising in my eyes, "but for now, we're just going to take it one step at a time, and that step is to inform them that we aren't going to play along. By god," she mutters angrily, "they can't just demand Quinn hands over that much in cold hard cash. It's not her debt!"

My eyes close for a moment as I pray for calm. It goes unanswered. I'm wholly riled. The blood in my toes is boiling upward until my head starts feeling hot. The flight attendants choose that moment to thunder up the aisle behind us with their drink and food cart. My shoulder is rammed hard enough to dislocate bone. "For fuck's sake," I mutter under my breath.

They pause their violent march. One attendant places her hand on my shoulder. "Sir, I'm so sorry." Bending slightly, she offers me a conspiratorial wink. "Can I offer you a beverage?"

Mac leans in and lifts her sunglasses to rest against her forehead. "God yes," she declares loudly. "Is it too soon to drink? I think I need a vodka."

"Me too," Quinn announces from behind us.

Travis butts in. "Quinn, what the ... It's ten a.m!" He sounds scandalised. I'm sure he'd be sounding a lot worse if he knew even a tenth of what those two girls are up to. It prompts me to ask the question, "Who else knows?"

"Sir?"

"Just a juice, please." I need a sugar hit because I have a feeling it's going to be a long day.

"We've got apple, orange, pineapple, guava—"

"Orange is fine," I blurt, eager to get them moving along so we can continue our conversation.

Mac leans in again. "Do you have any cranberry?"

I raise my brows at her.

"What?" She shrugs. "It's for the vodka."

"I'll have the same," Quinn pipes up again from behind us. "And maybe a cookie too?" She sounds apologetic. "I can't drink on an empty stomach."

The attendant's eyes narrow. She's annoyed she stopped to offer a solitary drink in apology and is now getting inundated with orders from surrounding passengers.

With a quick, efficient *flick*, she has my food tray down and piled with juice bottles, clear plastic cups, napkins, enough plastic-wrapped cookies for all of us, and mini bottles of vodka.

"Bless you." Mac flicks her sunglasses back down to cover her eyes and offers a smile.

It's lost on the attendants. They're already thundering the rest of the way up the aisle and away from us.

"Who else knows, Mac?"

"Just give me a ..." She's trying to twist in her seat to hand Quinn her requested order. It's quite a feat considering half my body is in her way and the old man on her other side keeps *harrumphing* every time she takes a breath.

Frustration has her half standing and flinging the bundle over our seats. A *thunk* and a growl confirm Travis has copped a glass bottle of juice to the head.

"Mac!" I bark.

"Okay! Fuck!" she shouts, drawing the attention of everyone around us. "I'm just trying to have a damn vodka, asshead. Is that too much to ask? I need this."

"Talk."

Her nostrils flare. "Fine." After snatching a clear plastic cup, she unscrews the cap on the mini vodka bottle and tips in a hefty mouthful. "Lucy knows." Next she reaches for a juice bottle. The attendant must have been completely over us because she only provided orange. Mac makes a face as she pries off the lid. "I don't like orange juice."

Lucy is Quinn's best friend, so I figured she would know. "Who else?"

Mac's cheeks burn red as she puts her muscle into removing the bottle cap. I snatch it before I cop an elbow in the face. It pops off with minimal effort, and Mac's lips pinch. "I already loosened it for you."

"Clearly."

She takes the opened bottle and begins pouring.

"You're welcome."

"Thank you," she replies primly. Setting the juice bottle down, she picks up her mixed drink and takes a sip. "Evie."

"Evie knows too?"

"Mmm hmm."

Mac unwraps a cookie.

Christ. It's like pulling teeth. "Who else, Mac?"

"No one else."

Anger tightens my jaw. When I speak it's between clenched teeth. "So you girls all got together and came up with this little plan of just telling them, *when they approach Quinn again,* that you just don't have the money?"

Mac nibbles her cookie before taking another sip of vodka. "That's correct."

"No."

Her brows rise. "No?"

"Just no."

Fire lights her eyes. "What, because we have vaginas we can't handle our own shit?" I pinch the bridge of my nose with my thumb and forefinger and count to ten. I reach five when she adds in a snide tone, "Do you think our plan requires a penis, Jake?"

That question is clearly a trap. I change my approach. "Is Quinn doing okay?"

It works. The fire fades as she nibbles on her cookie again. "She's stressed, but she'll be okay."

"Did these guys give a deadline for the money?"

"She has three days."

It's not ideal, but it's better than three hours. And it's time enough to get to the bottom of the situation.

Chapter Twenty-Three

Jake

It turns out there's no time to get to the bottom of *any* situation. Clearly these guys lied when they told Quinn she had three days to pull the money together. It's hardly a surprise for two reasons: The first is that we're dealing with criminals; relying on their word is the equivalent of making a fist and using it to punch your own face. The second reason I know they lied is because after our band finishes playing at the festival, we return to the hotel and see the evidence: a trashed hotel room shared by Mac and Quinn.

It looks nothing like it did when we left for the venue earlier in the afternoon. Bullet holes litter the wall. Smashed glassware and furniture cover the plush carpet. Picture frames hang crooked. Empty bottles of alcohol lie tipped over across the bar. And the worst of it, Mac's gun, *Polly*, is calmly resting on the dining table.

Mac is seated in one of the remaining chairs, hair a little wild, calmly chugging a shot like it's just another day in paradise. I scan her for injuries. When I find none, I survey the damage a second time. "What the fuck?"

She lets out a breath. "You know the guys who want that money from Quinn?"

I step inside the room, my shoes crunching over broken glass. "Uh huh."

"Well they sent a guy to collect it a little early."

"I see that," I growl, even though I don't see at all because my eyes are blinded by anger. "And you thought a gun fight and hand-to-hand combat would be the best way to inform this guy that Quinn doesn't have the money?"

Mac's lips purse in a pissy expression. It doesn't make sense. If anyone has the right to be pissy, it's me. "I took care of the situation."

"Would you care to explain *how* you took care of the situation?"

"Well …" She draws in a breath. I'm expecting the explanation of a lifetime and know I need to brace accordingly, so I walk over to the table, pick up the vodka bottle, pour a shot, and down it fast. "It started when we got to our room and found three drunk guys partying by the corner bar."

"Three drunk guys were …" I need another shot. I pour it. "How the hell did they get in your hotel room?"

"Jared is downstairs dealing with that particular issue right now."

"Okay." Good. I down the second shot. "And?"

"They were trying to meet the band. Mostly Evie. So we yelled at them to get out, but they wouldn't go. Quinn threw a chair because in the self-defence training Travis gave us last month, he said to use whatever weapon we happened to have handy. They reciprocated and started throwing bottles of rum."

"Just …" I take a deep breath and let it out slowly. "Where was Sean? Didn't he check your room before letting you go in?"

Sean is the newly hired security with Jamieson and Valentine Consulting. He comes with high credentials, having been a bouncer at the Florence Bar for three years. It's one of the best and most high profile venues in the city of Sydney.

"No, he didn't check our room."

My eyes flatten. "He's fired."

"Would you …" Mac sighs, clearly exasperated. "That's not your call."

"It seems you've forgotten, but I'm a part of this band too, Princess. That means I get a say in who handles our security, and I'm saying that Sean is no longer welcome."

"Fine." She pours another shot and lifts it to her lips. I snatch it from her hand and swallow it down. The burn of alcohol spreads swiftly through my chest and leaves my legs weak. I pull out the last remaining chair beside Mac and sit. "What happened after that?"

"One of them managed to tackle Quinn to the floor when the sound of a gunshot ricocheted through the room. That's when we knew shit just got real." *Right,* I think to myself irritably. *Because drunk guys trashing your room and tackling you to the ground isn't real enough.* "There was this guy in the doorway wearing a hoodie and baseball cap with sunglasses covering his eyes. He had a gun and was demanding that Quinn leave with him. Well, I wasn't having any of that, and I told him so. He pointed the gun at me, threatening to shoot me if Quinn didn't go with him right that very second."

"He pointed a gun at you?" Rage blinds me. I want to find this guy and throw his bloodied body into a cage of lions.

There's no mistaking my fury and Mac nods, indignant. "He did." She pours another vodka shot, and I notice the bottle shakes in her hand. My rage recedes. I take the bottle and set it on the table. Then I take both her hands in mine. They're ice cold. "Are you okay?"

"No! I'm angry! All I could remember was Jimmy shooting Evie and seeing her bleed out on the floor. There was no way in hell I was letting something like that happen again. Not on my watch."

Mac

"So I grabbed my gun and threatened to shoot *him* if he took one more step toward Quinn."

"You *what?*"

Jake's high tone makes me wince, and his hands squeeze mine so hard they turn purple. It's exactly like I told him before. I *took care of the situation.* "Was I supposed to dither about a bit before calling in the people with penises to handle the crazy gunman?"

"Jesus, Mac, will you let it go?" He drops my hands, eyeing me with aggravation. "It's not because I thought you couldn't take care of yourself. I'm freaked out because it's *you*, and I happen to care about you a lot."

It's possible I believe him. Slightly. "Well, anyway, Sean must have heard the noise, and he came in from behind and tackled the guy to the floor. There was a scuffle and he ran."

Jake rubs at the stubble on his chin. He looks weary, but it's better than looking on the verge of a heart attack like he did earlier. I nudge the full shot glass along the table, pushing it in his line of sight. He takes it and tosses it back.

"There *is* good news."

"Oh yeah?"

"Travis knows now," I tell him. "So you don't need to worry about going behind my back to tell him."

"I wouldn't have done that. Believe me, Mac. I've learned my lesson. But I'll be honest and say I would've done everything to convince you to tell them. I know things are tense between all of you right now, but Quinn is in a dangerous situation, and evidenced by tonight, it's put everyone close to her in danger as well. Keeping your brothers out of the loop just leaves them unprepared and vulnerable too."

"I agree."

"Good," Jake says, sitting back in the chair. He's wearing a sleeveless tee shirt, biceps bared and arm veins popping from a demanding night of pounding the drums. His muscles ripple with the simple movement, and my adrenaline must still be surging in the aftermath because my body heats.

Jake stands and swipes the bottle of vodka from the table. Then he takes my hand and pulls me from my seat in one easy jerk. Standing an inch apart, he lets go to grasp my chin, his eyes searching mine. "You need me to take care of you?"

And just like that, he reads me like a book.

Just a simple nod is all it takes before I'm being led toward the bedroom.

Jake seats me on the edge of the mattress and pushes my thighs apart. He sinks to his knees between them and my breath quickens. He takes the hem of my Jamieson band tee shirt and tugs the soft cotton upward. I raise my arms and his calloused hands skim up along my rib cage, leaving goose bumps in their wake.

A light chuckle escapes me. He knows I'm ticklish there. I see his answering grin before it's hidden when the shirt comes over my head.

Jake tosses it behind him and his hands return to my hips. He leans in and presses a kiss to my bare belly, and I shiver. His fingers trace lazy, maddening circles along my skin. The touch is featherlike and reverent, as if I'm going to break. It turns what I thought would be something rough and fast into something delicious and sweet.

"Jake," I say on a long moan when he unclasps my bra and takes a nipple inside his mouth. He sucks sharply and the deep pinch leaves an answering throb between my legs. My hips shift forward involuntarily and my fingers grasp his rounded shoulders tightly.

Jake sinks down, seated on his knees, as he reaches for the button on my jeans. He expels a short puff of air when it releases and the zipper slides slowly down. I lift my hips as he tugs them out from underneath me and down my legs, dragging my panties along with them. The action has drawn my legs back together. His large palms slide along my upper thighs until he's nudging them apart again, leaving me bare to his gaze.

"Roll over," he says in a low, gruff voice, surprising me, but I do it.

My boobs and belly are pushed into the mattress with my legs off the bed. He spreads them a little wider then his fingers find me. They slide through wet, slippery heat before rubbing over my clit and back. He repeats the action, over and over, until my ass rises instinctively in the air.

"Oh god," I gasp when his mouth latches on to my clit and a thick finger slides inside me. In and out, in and out. And then another finger.

Jake groans when I push back against his face, my entire body pulsing with the need to come—and come *hard*.

Then his fingers pull out. It leaves me achingly empty, but they don't disappear. Instead, he glides a slick finger upward until he reaches the tight ring of my ass. He brushes over it gently, once, twice, and *oh my god*.

"Jake!" His name bursts from my lips when the illicit touch disappears.

"You like it?"

"More," I beg, reduced to one-syllable words. "Please."

"Give me one second," he says, his voice gravelly.

I turn my head. Jake is bent over, searching through the toiletry bag in my suitcase, his jeans pulling tight against his rounded, muscular backside. When he finds what it is he's searching for, he straightens and rips off his jeans.

My head sinks into the bed, and I'm gasping when he returns with his finger slicker and more insistent. Jake's mouth finds my clit again, and he sucks hard as that thick digit slides over my ass, pressing more firmly each time, until it eventually breeches inside. The invasion feels wicked and delicious.

"Is that good?" he asks, drawing back.

"Just ..."

It's the only word I can manage. *Just keep going,* I beg silently, lifting up on my knees and pushing my ass back toward him.

Jake hears my silent plea and that thick finger returns, rubbing firm along my ass until it pops back inside.

It's sensory overload. My eyes screw shut, white spots dot my eyelids, and I cry out—almost a scream—as I come so hard I fear I'll break apart.

I barely catch a breath when my hips are seized in a vicelike grip and lifted. His cock slides inside me. "Mac," he breathes, his voice tight like he's barely holding on.

He draws out and my ass cheeks slam against his hips when he pulls me toward him at the same time he rams his cock in me. The force and the intensity steal my breath.

Jake doesn't stop. His body heaves and his breath punches the air with every thrust. I'm gasping when he comes, my name on his lips and his cock pushing so hard inside me I collapse against the bed. He lands on top of me with a groan, his chest hot and slick with sweat.

Three weeks pass after the Melbourne incident and nothing has been resolved with Quinn's situation. Travis keeps muttering things like, "It's in the hands of the proper authorities," and "Stay out of it, sweetheart." The exclusion has my frustration levels at an all-time high. At least they arrange round-the-clock protection for Quinn, so wherever she goes she has either Casey or Travis attached to her side like Velcro.

Regardless, life has to go on and Evie's birthday arrives. My miraculous assistant has managed to pull off an amazing birthday party. We're at the Florence Bar with the private function room decorated in the theme of vintage glamour. Both Travis and Casey haven't left Quinn for even a second, so we choose to forget the dark cloud hanging over us for the night. Drinks flow freely, laughter rings out, and my brother Jared takes to the stage, stealing the microphone to give Evie a birthday speech.

It turns out to be more than a speech. It's a marriage proposal. He's holding Evie's hand, his eyes radiating love and hope. My vision blurs. I hate that I'm happy for him. I want to hold on to my anger but they make it so hard.

"... and it was then that I knew ..."

I tune out Jared's words as my eyes seek Jake across the room. He's standing near the curved stage opposite me, his body encased in a tuxedo. You can see the hint of a tattoo peeking above the collar of his stiff, white shirt. I know the ink intimately. It reads *Jamieson* in beautiful cursive and underneath in small print says, *"Family is more than blood."* It encapsulates everything we stand for. Whether right or wrong, we stand for each other.

My gaze lifts from the tattoo to his face. Jake is watching me so intensely my lungs constrict. My fingers tighten around the champagne glass in my left hand when he nods toward the exit. I don't even need a moment to think about it. I hold up my right hand, mouthing, "Five minutes."

His lips curve, a mixture of male satisfaction and heated anticipation.

"Be still my beating heart," my mother mutters from beside me as I down the last mouthful of my champagne. I give her a quick glance. Her eyes have shifted from Jared and Evie. They're now focused on Jake and the way he's looking at me, as if I'm ice cream on a blistery hot day.

If I was the type to melt in a dreamy puddle, I'd be covering the entire dance floor. Instead, I clear my throat and offer an "excuse me" to my mother before heading for the coatroom. The champagne has made me lightheaded.

Jake stands waiting for me just outside the exit. He's holding a white glossy box in his hand. After a quick glance behind me, we begin the walk to the parking lot. I nod at the package. "What's that?"

He lifts the lid. It's an enormous slice of birthday cake. The soft, fluffy sponge is layered with thick white cream. Rivers of salted caramel ooze from the sides. *"That* is dessert."

I arch a brow as Jake unlocks his car—a piece of junk dodge-something-or-other that he's slowly restoring with Casey. "I thought *I* was dessert."

He opens the passenger door. His eyes travel over me as I slide inside. My hair had been set in rollers and then pinned to create glossy 1920's waves. My body is encased in a strapless, floor-length gold gown that glitters with every step I take, and my bared shoulders sparkle with shimmery, gold dust. I'm basically a walking Oscar award.

He shuts the car door behind me and climbs in the driver's side, placing the cake box on my lap. "Princess, you *are* dessert. Ever since I saw that cake, all I've wanted to do is lick cream and caramel from those golden tits of yours."

Heat floods my body and a powerful sense of urgency hits like a tsunami. "Plant your foot, Romero," I bark. "Otherwise, I'm going to start without you."

Jake floors it. We squeal out of the parking lot as if the hounds of Hell are chasing us, the back end of the car fishtailing wildly.

His mouth fuses to mine the second we step inside the empty duplex. The cake box I'm holding crumples between us. Jake puts his hands on my hips and walks backward, pulling me toward the kitchen as he kisses me.

It's not until I'm lifted and set on the counter that he breaks his lips from mine. I glance down and find the cake has oozed from the crumpled box and now decorates my dress. I squawk a loud curse that has Jake laughing.

"Fuck you," I mutter and lift the broken lid. I scoop out a fistful of cake, and before he gets a chance to escape, I smush it in his face.

Jake gasps, his mouth dropping open. Bits of cake and cream fall from his face and splatter the floor. I erupt with laughter. His eyes flatten with serious intent and my merriment dies clean away.

"Oh no, Princess," Jake growls. "Fuck *you.*"

He grabs the edges of my strapless dress and yanks down, baring me to the waist. He loads his finger with cream and covers my nipples with it. It clings in thick, cold clumps as he tosses the ruined cake box to the side.

He's not done. Jake grabs the hem of my dress and tugs it upward, leaving it to bunch around my hips. My lacy red panties are grabbed too. Jake wrenches them down my legs and shoves them inside the pocket of his pants.

Then he spreads my legs and steps back to stare. "Jesus Christ," he mutters. "That is the sexiest goddamn thing I have ever seen."

"Jake," I breathe.

His steps back between my open legs. My breath catches as love wells inside me, the emotion so strong I feel it will literally break me apart.

Then Jake ducks his head and takes a nipple deep in his mouth. He sucks fiercely, forcing a painful jolt of pleasure to spike through me. My hands grasp his head as my own tips back. A deep moan leaves my throat.

"Everyone's eyes were on you tonight." Jake's voice is rough as his mouth shifts to my other nipple. "But they don't get to see this." His hand gropes the abandoned breast, his fingers curling and digging in with a strong grip. "No one gets to see you the way I do."

Jake speaks the truth. There's no one who sees me the way he does. There's no one who touches me the way he does. There's no one who exists for me the way he does.

He's the only person who taught me how to let go. Who *allowed* me to let go. He's the only man who makes me ache with just a single glance. His is the only smile that will stay with me until the earth is nothing but dust.

Jake is the man who rages for me. And at me. The man who gives me everything that he is and demands everything in return.

And he's mine.

Chapter Twenty-four

Mac

"Earth to Mac."

My head is lost in Jake. I shake him free and focus on Evie. Her forehead is wrinkled with bewilderment. "You've been so scatter-brained this morning."

"I'm just tired," I reply as we put our bags in the back of her Toyota Hilux. It's the Sunday morning after Evie's birthday party and neither of us seemed to have slept much at all. It hasn't stopped us from getting up and out the door early today; our plan is to take advantage of mid-season sales before they end.

Evie's phone rings, saving me from further inquisition. She digs through her handbag. Her eyes sparkle when she pulls it out and checks the screen. "It's my fiancé," she says with glee.

Evie's been throwing the word around like confetti today as she talks wedding plans. It's exciting but I'm struggling to find enthusiasm. My body aches in too many places and my inner thighs are chafed like they've been attacked with sandpaper. Jake's three-day growth has left the area tender, and every step has my panties rubbing me raw.

I steal the car keys while she talks and climb inside the car, choosing to drive us home. The outside noise mutes as I shut the door and turn the key. The engine rumbles to life beneath me. The blessed relief of sitting down has me exhaling in ecstasy as I wait. A few minutes later, Evie opens the passenger door, her brown eyes wild with panic.

"What?" I bark when she fails to open her mouth.

"It's Quinn," she says and my stomach knots in an instant. "She's in the hospital."

Oh no. "What happened?"

"I don't even know. Jared was vague. Why is everyone so damn vague this morning?" she snaps.

"Well what did he say?"

"Something about shit going down, and that Quinn is in the hospital but okay."

"Define okay."

"Scrapes and bruises but mostly she's in shock. I think he said they would release her soon?"

"Well, don't just stand there," I boom. "Let's move."

Evie climbs in the car and we take off, making our way out of the rabbit warren that Sydney Westfield shopping complex has the nerve to call a *parking lot.*

"Why did Jared ring you and not me?"

"I don't know." Her brows rise. "Maybe it's because you've been looking at him lately like he single-handedly wrung the neck of every puppy on the planet?"

"I don't look at him like that." It's a lie because I do. My brothers' betrayal runs deep. I might be happy over his engagement, but he still lied to me. They all did. The apology Mitch gave helped lessen the intensity, but it still sits there between all of us, throbbing like it has its own pulse.

"You do."

"Well ... That's because Jared is a jerk."

Evie's nostrils flare from the passenger seat, causing her indignant response to come out sounding like she has a goober stuck in her throat. "Yes, but he's the jerk I love."

I snort. "More fool you."

Evie's fist connects with my arm.

The offending thump sends a sick lurch to my belly. I take my hand from the steering wheel and rub the pained area. "Ow! Bitch."

Without taking my eyes from the road, my fist shoots out. I can't see where my punch lands, but the impact zone feels soft.

Evie sucks in a wheezy gasp of outrage. "You just punched me in the tit!"

"Hahahahah— Oomph!" Her fist connects with my boob. The pain folds me in half. My chin hits the steering wheel and the car swerves. "Evie!" I yell.

Evie grabs the wheel and corrects our course while I pull myself together. She apologises but amusement coats her words, rendering it ineffective.

"I'm driving here," I hiss as I retake the wheel.

She folds her arms. "You punched me in the tit."

"You started it."

"Did not," she retorts.

"Did too."

"Did not."

"Did too."

"Did— Oh my GOD! Pull over up ahead!" Evie yells.

My eyes scan the distance ahead and land on Mary's. We're driving through the city fringe in Newtown, and this place has *the* best burgers in the southern hemisphere. Other envious burgers aspire to be like these. They ooze with a special Mary's sauce that none of us have been able to replicate.

The universe is with us today because I find a parking spot. I reach for my purse, and Evie and I both pause to share a mutual glance of guilt. Quinn is in the hospital and we're stopping for burgers.

I clear my throat. "Jared said she was okay, right? Her life isn't hanging in the balance."

"This is true." Her smoky brown eyes turn to Mary's with longing. "I mean, hospitals serve shitty food, don't they? Stopping to pick up a burger for Quinn is the right thing to do. We're basically doing this for her."

The rest of the drive to the hospital is a non-violent affair as we stuff our faces with food. After parking, we find our way to Quinn's room. The door is closed but privacy be damned. If that was what Quinn wanted, she would have run from us long ago. I plant my palm on the door and shove it open. It flings back with force and bangs into the doorstop behind it with a loud *clunk*.

"Mac, for god's sake," comes Evie's exasperated voice from behind me. "Can you just try for a little less force next time?"

"Shut up, Sandwich," I snap then throw her under a bus. "If you didn't decide to make a food stop on the way here, then I wouldn't have had to rush."

We both stop and look at Quinn. She's a mess. Her best friend Lucy messaged us on the drive here telling us Quinn looked like she'd gone ten rounds with Mike Tyson and lost. It's the truth, and the visual evidence has my eyes narrowing to slits.

Evie gives her the burger. Quinn turns green and nudges it furtively away as she fills us in on what happened. It all started with a scuffle, which is how the best kinds of stories start, but it involves David, which makes it shitty. Quinn wraps it up by telling us Travis has been arrested for manslaughter.

My mouth falls open. "What?"

"David's dead," Quinn states. "He was shot, and they think Travis did it."

What. The. Hell.

Last night we were having a party, Quinn's situation put on hold so we could celebrate Evie's birthday. Less than a day later, David is dead, Quinn is in the hospital, and Travis is behind bars. Who's running this damn show? The Thunderbirds? My brothers have clearly fucked up somewhere along the line for this to happen.

"Well, did he do it?" I ask, because I can't blame Travis if he did. The only way to stop a man like David is to put him in the ground. It's a harsh way of thinking, but that's the cold reality.

"No!"

Quinn explains that she's yet to give her statement. Travis is stuck behind bars until they're given the full background of the situation. It leads us to the question of the hour—who shot David?

First we need to arrange for my brother's release. That means springing Quinn from the hospital and taking her to where he's being held. After handling the paperwork, we're outside within the hour. Quinn and I wait by the entrance while Evie gets the car and brings it around.

"Mac," Quinn croaks and clears her throat. "I've just realised I left my phone on the counter where we signed the release papers. Would you mind ducking in to get it for me?"

I roll my eyes at her forgetfulness. After commanding her to stay put, I go inside to look for it, but it's nowhere to be found.

When I walk back outside, Quinn is nowhere to be found either. Evie is standing alone by the car waiting for us. "Where's Quinn?"

"I don't know," she replies. "I thought she was with you?"

"Did you see her at all?"

Evie shakes her head. "No?"

My gut twists. Something isn't right. I jog away from the entrance and scan the parking lot that stretches out in front of us. "Quinn?" I yell, looking left and right. Oh my god, she's vanished right beneath our noses. My brothers will have my head on a platter. My lips pinch tight as I pull out my phone and scroll through my contacts. I start with Travis. It's possible Quinn's information about his incarceration is faulty, and if she's gone, he should be the first to know.

Travis answers. "Yeah?"

Relief hits me. "Trav, thank god. Quinn said you'd been arrested."

His chuckle is low and amused. "Christ, she isn't worried is she? It's all been sorted out. I'm on my way to the hospital now. Are you there?"

My brother's response has fear snaking up my spine. If Quinn isn't with him, and David is bound for the morgue, then something very, very bad is at play. "I am, but there's a problem. A really big, horrible problem."

"What?" he barks.

My eyes do another scan of the hospital entrance and front parking lot. It gives me nothing. "Quinn's gone."

There's a pause then, "What the fuck, Mac?"

"Don't shout at me!" I shout as I jog back to Evie. I left her alone for one minute, but apparently that minute was enough for all holy hell to break loose. "I already know I fucked up. Oh god."

Travis orders us home to the duplex and hangs up on me. Frustration rattles my bones as we park in the driveway. They expect me to keep them in the loop when shit goes down yet I'm always kept out of it. Are we supposed to just sit on our hands and wait now? Balls to that.

It grates me to ring Jared, but I do. He doesn't answer. I try Mitch. He doesn't answer either. Evie sinks to the edge of the couch, biting her nails as I pace back and forth along the living room rug. "You'll wear a hole in it," she says.

I couldn't care less. I'm too busy working out our next plan of attack. I pause and look at her. "Those guys who want the money have to be the ones who have Quinn, but who the fuck are they?"

She gives me a blank look.

"Did Quinn mention anything to you?"

Evie shakes her head.

"Okay." I put my hands on my hips, my brain working overtime. "Well, David owed shitloads and considering the way they're trying to collect their money, they can't be good guys, right?"

"I guess."

I begin to pace again. "So the loaned money can only come from some kind of criminal activity, like a crime group. Probably one that traffics drugs. I mean, that's where the big money is, isn't it?"

Evie shrugs like she doesn't have a clue.

"Great sounding board you are," I snap, pausing to face her.

"Don't get pissy, Macface," she snaps back. "I'm just as upset as you about this situation, but what are we supposed to do?"

"I don't know!" I throw my hands up in the air. "But I do know that sitting around doing nothing isn't going to help anyone."

Evie huffs.

I crack my knuckles in annoyance. "If I had access to resources, I'd have this situation dealt with before you could blink."

"What kind of resources? You mean like Google?"

An idea hits. "Yes!" I point a finger at her. "Now you're starting to think like a badass consultant."

"I am?"

"Yes. Now go get me a packet of salt and vinegar chips from the pantry. I can't think on an empty stomach."

Her mouth falls open. "How can you be hungry at a time like this? Especially considering we just had burgers not long ago."

"Don't give me smack talk, Sandwich," I bark as I head for the study at the back of the house. After taking a seat at my desk, I roll my chair toward my laptop and flip open the lid. It would be handy if Google gave me a detailed list of organised crime groups in Sydney that run drug trafficking rings, along with their address and contact information, but that's not going to happen.

It's entirely possible that my brother's firm has a list though. All I need to do is hack into their system.

Evie wanders in with my packet of chips. The bag is open and she's stuffing them in her mouth.

"I thought you weren't hungry after burgers."

She shrugs. "I could still eat."

I snatch the packet. Reaching in, I pull out a chip and crunch, chewing slowly, as I stare at the blank screen of my laptop.

"What are you doing?"

"Trying to work out how to hack Jamieson and Valentine Consulting's computer system."

She snatches the chip packet back. "Why don't you just ring Tim?"

Tim is their receptionist slash assistant. He's short with a slim stature, dark hair, and rich brown eyes fringed by thick, sooty lashes. He's also the office gossip. He knows everything that happens in that office before it even happens. I've made it my business to become his friend accordingly, but it's an antagonistically mutual relationship.

I pick up the phone and dial. Tim answers on the third ring and rattles off his long greeting.

"It's me," I reply.

"Who's me?"

"Fuck off, Tim. Shit's going down and I need information."

"I'm sorry," he sing-songs. "I think you have the wrong number."

"Tim," I growl, knowing he's swinging around in his fancy office chair at this very moment, playing with the styling of his hair to make sure each strand sits just so. It's how Tim conducts all his phone chats.

He sighs a long lilting sigh that still manages to sound peeved. "Mac, if I give you any information, I'll get fired."

"Come on, Tim. Don't be a little bitch."

"Screw you, Mac," he hisses into the phone.

The line goes dead.

I re-dial.

Tim answers, once again rattling off his long greeting.

"Quinn's life is hanging in the balance," I bark into the phone. "What if something horrible happens because you didn't pass on the information we needed? What then, Tim? Huh?"

His tone is incredulous. "You think *you're* the one that's going to save the day?"

"Well, I can't sit around twiddling my goddamn fingers."

Tim huffs. "Let me see what I can find out."

He hangs up before I can ask for the list of Sydney crime syndicates. "Mac?"

Our heads swivel to the door. Jake is standing there shirtless, wearing worn, faded jeans. "Did you just say something about Quinn's life hanging in the balance? What's going on?"

Evie's expression is grim when she answers for me. "Quinn's been kidnapped."

"What the hell?" he bursts out angrily. "When?"

She fills him in, starting from the beginning and ending with the now. Her loose lips give him every detail of my involvement.

Jake turns an accusatory glare my way, and I lift my chin, defiant in the face of his anger. "Evie, sweetheart," he utters softly, never taking his eyes from mine, "I think I hear your phone ringing out in the kitchen."

She cocks an ear. "No. I don't think it's—"

"It must have just stopped."

"I'll go check. It might be Jared," Evie says, hope colouring her words despite the release of a tired sigh. She pushes up off the chair from the other desk in our study. *Quinn's* desk. My heart thuds with fear, each beat more powerful with every minute that ticks by without word. I've been able to lock it down until now, focused solely on what I can do to help, which keeps me determined and calm, but Jake is here now and that's all it takes for my control to flounder.

He speaks, his voice gritty like sandpaper. "Every time."

"Every time?"

He walks over to my desk and leans his backside against the edge. "Every time something like this happens, you just shut me out. I know we're trying to find our way back to the way we used to be, but it's not working. We're not the same people we used to be. You used to be tough, Mac, but you were also sweet. But I don't know where the sweetness went. You're harder now. More driven, maybe, and more reckless. Your constant need to get caught up in any dangerous situation that comes your way is relentless. I know your brothers are out there doing what they can for Quinn, but so are the authorities. Let them do their job, Princess," he pleads softly. "Please?"

I stare hard into Jake's eyes, my chest burning with anger. Does he not know me at all? "I can't sit here and do nothing," I snap. "I'm a Valentine. It's not in my nature."

My phone rings. A quick glance shows Tim's name on the screen. Jake gives me a look when I go to answer.

"I have to get this."

He pushes away from the desk. His fists curl and the veins in his arms bulge as he steps away. A few deep breaths later, he turns. "Forget it," he says over the sound of my ringing phone. "This is not the time for that particular conversation anyway."

My heart feels heavy. For the first time I begin to question myself and the future I've mapped out in my head. Is it going to cost me in the long run? Are marriage and kids really so bad? Sometimes I let myself picture our tiny baby lying naked in Jake's big, tattooed arms, just to see how it makes me feel. If I'm honest with myself, the image makes me melt faster than butter on toast. So why do I deny myself? Why do I have this need to prove myself *all the damn time*?

The questions flit through my mind in the span of seconds, and in half that time I push them away without answers. We're all feeling vulnerable right now, worried sick for Quinn's safety. Now is not the time to question my life choices.

So instead of going after Jake, I choose the easier option. I pick up my phone and answer Tim's call.

Chapter Twenty-Five

Mac

The scent of flowers is strong as I drag my feet down the aisle, bouquet in hand. My dress is pale pink with a strapless bodice, but the flowing skirt is made with a shit tonne of layers and ruffles. The weight is the equivalent of an elephant. I'm literally wearing an elephant. At least, that's how it feels.

I lift my chin and smile at all in attendance. Sweat breaks across my brow with each determined step. Did I mention the dress is also hot? The fires of Hell rage beneath these skirts. I have to give Evie credit for the selection. The contraption is incredibly beautiful, but I can't wait to get it off. Preferably with scissors.

Gritting my teeth, I shift my gaze to Jared. He's faring no better. His face is green, and he looks ready to puke. I'm not sure why. Nerves? Cold feet? Either way, if I'm suffering, it's good to know he is too. Beside him stands Travis and Mitch, both looking more handsome than they have a right to and far more relaxed than their younger sibling.

My mother dashes away a tear as I sweep past her. She'd been with us just moments earlier, rushing to her seat last minute. These past eight months have kept her caught up in wedding preparations. There's nothing she won't do and no lengths she won't go to ensure her baby boy receives the wedding of a lifetime.

Sweeping off to the left, my eyes shift to Quinn. She's glowing today. It's definitely a post-sex glow. She thought sharing the details while we were having our makeup applied this morning would be entertaining. She *actually* thought that. Evie couldn't be left out, of course, and included comments about Jared in comparison. It was all I could do to keep my breakfast down. Hearing about my brothers' sexual shenanigans is up there with other such fun activities like setting my goddamn pubes on fire.

I have to remind myself that we're lucky she's here at all. Tim's phone call confirmed what I'd already determined. Quinn had been taken by the Zampetti crime group, a human trafficking operation so slick no one can get near them. These were the people David owed money to, but they hadn't kidnapped Quinn for the reason we'd all assumed.

The Zampettis had a mole in their midst. A federal agent with the Australian Police. And they knew it. What they'd so brilliantly deduced before any of us could was that the undercover agent had a daughter and her name was Quinn. This was big news, even to Quinn, who'd never known her father.

His name is Seth McKinnon, and it turns out he knows a lot. So much, in fact, that the Zampettis' plan was to use Quinn to extract all of it.

Tim barely paused for breath during the entire recount. He ended the conversation by informing me that when the Zampettis transferred her and Seth from the house they were stashed in, Quinn had managed to run the car off the road and slam it into a tree, thus making her own escape.

Quinn hadn't needed my help. She hadn't needed anyone's help. She'd saved herself. Travis could've done with some help, though. Not trusting that Seth was who he said he was—an undercover agent—my brother had punched him in the face. It wasn't until *after* Seth lay unconscious on the ground that Travis found out the family connection. My brother had literally punched his girlfriend's father. In. The. Face.

If it's possible to die from laughing too hard, I wouldn't be standing here today, yet here I am with my face turned toward the end of the aisle as we wait for the maid of honour to make an appearance.

Travis drank a lot that night. I had too, because in the aftermath of that day, Jake left. Whatever particular conversation he wanted to have hadn't happened. I cancelled the band's commitments for two weeks because we needed a break, and he'd subsequently packed a bag and disappeared. Where he went, I don't know. Jake never answered my calls or returned my messages. He simply reappeared two weeks later and that was that.

His actions have made it clear he's done. So I let it go. I let *us* go. And it *hurts*. But I have no choice. Jake wants too much. For him it's all or nothing. I can't give him my all right now, so it has to be nothing.

My eyes shift to where he sits with the band, dressed in a black suit, his black tie secured in an impeccable Windsor knot. They're positioned in the front row, representing the bride's side of the family. His is the only head that isn't turned toward the church entrance. He's watching me instead. His eyes lower, lingering on my tits, before rising again.

The heat level beneath my skirts soar higher. We've been snapping at each other for months, and my nerves are frayed. I don't know how to be *nothing* around Jake. Clearly, he doesn't know how to be nothing around me either.

Thankfully, there's a commotion at the entrance. The maid of honour has arrived. Wearing a suit similar to my brothers, except with a pink tie to match the colour of the bridesmaid dresses, Henry makes his way up the aisle. Evie has forced him to carry a bouquet. There had been a huge fight over that, but to Henry's credit, he appears unfazed as he walks toward us, managing to move a lot quicker than we'd done in our ridiculous dresses. Still, he's moving *too* quickly. His pace is out of step to the music.

"It's hot in here," he mutters when he reaches his place by my side.

"Hot?" I snort. "Be thankful Evie didn't put you in this dress. Being strapped to the roof of a burning building would be cooler than this."

Henry rolls his eyes at my complaint. "At least you don't have to wear a tie. Feels like I'm slowly being choked to death."

"I'd rather choke to death than burn alive," I retort.

"I'd rather—"

"Shush," I hiss. Evie has made her appearance, her arm tucked inside Coby's. Their father is an absent one. Never having liked the responsibility of children, he left when Evie was young. She has us now so there's no looking back.

My hands rest on Elijah's shoulders. His rest lightly on my hips. We're at the wedding reception and moving about the dance floor to Ella Henderson singing "Yours." He's talking to me, but I'm not paying attention to a single word he says. My gaze is busy searching the room for Jake. I don't have to look too hard. He's making his way between twirling couples, shoulders tense as he heads straight for us.

Elijah pauses when he reaches us, forcing me to stop alongside him.

"May I cut in?" he asks Elijah, his eyes on me.

My dance partner takes a gracious step back and my hands fall from his shoulders. "She's all yours, Romero," he says with a light clap on Jake's back before striding away.

Jake picks up where Elijah left off and once again I'm being spun about the room. He moves stiffly at first, holding himself like a tightly wound coil. I rack my brain, and for the life of me I can't recall what I've done this time to rile his temper. "What's up your ass?" I snap.

He doesn't hesitate with his answer. "You."

My nostrils flare. "Why?"

We twirl past my dancing parents, and I scowl at them. Why are they doing the electric boogaloo to a slow dance song? I make a mental note to question Jared about them doing weed in the bathroom. I saw Meryl Streep in *It's Complicated.* Parents get up to some crazy shit when they think their kids aren't watching.

"Why?" Jake repeats. "Because you're beautiful."

The compliment is delivered with a furrowed brow and a growly tone. I don't know whether to accept it with grace or abandon him on the dance floor. "And that pisses you off?"

"Yes. Every male in this room has monopolised your dance card. The only one you haven't danced with yet is me."

"Well, we're dancing now."

Jake's palms move lower on my hips pulling me closer. "And I like it."

Without warning, he pushes me outward and twirls me under his arm. Jake has moves and this particular one, he executes effortlessly. Unfortunately, I'm wearing my elephant dress and stumble; the heel catches inside the hem halfway through the turn. I hear a *rip* as it snags the delicate fabric. There's nothing I can do to halt my momentum. I'm going down. *Damn dress,* is all I can think as I begin a slow-motion descent to the floor. *It's not designed for physical activity.*

Jake recovers and jerks me upright before I take a header across the dance floor. My chest slams into his and the breath leaves my lungs.

"My bad," he says, a grin crinkling the corners of his eyes as he takes the blame for what is so clearly my fault. With our bodies now mashed together, there's no mistaking the press of something incredibly hard against my belly. Frankly, it's a surprise I can feel anything at all, what with all the layers, but this ... *this* is unmistakeable. Jake is hard and he's not even trying to hide it.

Jake crouches down to help de-snag my heel. His hands find their way beneath my dress. A warm palm wraps around my ankle. Jake lifts it and my hands fall on his shoulders to steady myself.

I'm dumbfounded and stare at the top of his bent head as he carefully unhooks the torn ruffle from the sharp heel of my shoe.

What new kind of fuckery is this? Sweet, gentlemanly behaviour isn't Jake's usual arsenal of choice. It has my heart thumping against my ribs and my defences scrambling.

Jake re-settles the skirts and stands. Taking note of my stunned expression, he tucks a hand underneath my chin and tilts my head until our eyes meet. "You okay, Princess?"

"I'm okay," I reply, smoothing a rogue curl that escaped my whimsical up-do. "Though you're a shit dancer, Romero," I advise, my lips twitching as we once again begin to dance. "Maybe you might benefit from some lessons."

His laughter rings out and draws the attention of every breathing female in the room. "Thanks, sweetheart. I'll take that under advisement."

"You do that," I murmur, my pulse rate increasing at the endearment.

"So ..."

"So?" I prompt.

"I have a plan."

I nod. "Well, good for you."

Jake rolls his eyes. "And I need your help."

My interest is piqued. He knows it too. "Oh?"

Thirty minutes later we're in the back parking lot. Jake holds my hand tightly in his. He's holding a suitcase in the other as we run toward a white vintage car. It's a dark night and the outside lights are dim, but there's no mistaking it as the wedding car. It's decorated in shaving cream, condoms, and streamers. It's downright tacky and screams of Frog and Cooper's handiwork. Clearly they were out here earlier, up to their own brand of mischief.

Hair comes loose from my pins as we run. I hold the back of it and spare a quick glance behind me. There's no one around to see what we're up to.

"Have you got the keys?"

"In my pocket," Jake replies.

We arrive at the car. He lets go of my hand and slides the key in, popping open the boot. It lifts with ease and reveals Jared and Evie's suitcases. They're packed and ready to leave, heading to the airport direct from the reception for their honeymoon destination.

Jake pulls Jared's suitcase out and replaces it with the identical one he's carrying with him.

"This is so bad," I say with more than a little glee.

"Too much you think?" Jake asks, amusement glittering in his eyes.

"There's no such thing as *too much* when it comes to my brothers." My gaze falls to the replacement suitcase inside the boot. "Show me."

Jake chuckles as he reaches in and unzips his way around the bag. He lifts the flap, and I burst out laughing.

"Shush," he says with force and takes a furtive glance left and right.

"Whose idea was this?" I ask, eyeing the contents inside the suitcase. My brother is heading to Thailand for an entire week with nothing but G-strings. They're bright and come in all the colours of the rainbow. Some have images—pineapples, bananas, jellybeans— and some have animal print. There's even one with the words *Badass Brigade* printed on the front.

"It was my idea," he replies.

"You're evil."

Jake cocks a brow, his expression downright devilish. "I know."

"I like it."

"I know that too," he says with a smirk as he locks the boot and pockets the keys. It's a simple matter of placing Jared's real suitcase in the boot of the Subaru that Travis owns. All we have left to do now is replace the stolen car keys before anyone notices them missing.

"Jared is going to kill us," I announce as we stroll back to the reception, taking our time now that the mischievous deed is done.

Jake takes my hand in his and threads our fingers together. He shrugs. "Probably."

"You don't seem scared."

He squeezes my hand and grins in the dark. "I can take him."

I return his grin. "I have no doubt."

"Do you think he'll realise it's us who did it anyway?"

"Of course," I reply, pointing at the security camera trained on the back parking lot. It's likely tracking our every move. I blow it a kiss and give a little wave. "The first thing my brother will do when he returns is check the security footage. Be prepared for payback, Jake. When it comes, and it *will* come, it's going to be big."

"Unless we delete the tapes before he sees them."

I arch a brow. "Where's the fun in that?"

"You *want* him to know it was us?"

"Of course. That was an epic prank. We should get credit for it."

Jake lets go of my hand when we step inside. The loss of contact leaves me bereft. His glance at me is wistful. Does he feel the loss like I do?

There's a gathering around the cake table. As we make our way toward it, Henry materialises at my side and looks between the both of us. "Where were you two?"

I widen my eyes and give Henry the speech we rehearsed when we plotted the execution of our prank. "We were in the kitchen making sure there was enough champagne for the toasts."

Henry's gaze narrows with suspicion. "That's funny, because I looked for you both in the kitchen, Mac, and neither you nor Jake were in there."

"You were looking for us?"

"Evie wanted the both of you here for the cutting of the cake."

"You must have just missed us," Jake interjects smoothly and as if on cue, waiters emerge en masse from the kitchen bearing trays of freshly poured champagne.

"Must have," Henry mutters, not sounding like he believes us in the least.

A waiter passes by and Jake plucks two glasses from the tray then hands one to me. "Thanks, Romero."

"Anytime, Valentine."

I hide the twitching of my lips by taking a sip of champagne, and we turn to face the bridal couple. Evie and Jared have the knife to the cake and slide it downward. Camera's flash from all directions and they look up, smiling. My brother is definitely happier than he has been in a long time. "Oh yeah," I mutter to Jake. "He's definitely going to kill us."

"You worried, Princess?"

"Not at all. We'll go down fighting."

Jake nudges my shoulder and gives me a wink. "Together."

The smile I gave him is puny at best because there *is* no *together*. Hell will freeze over before Jake puts his pride aside and agrees to me working in any type of dangerous situation with Jamieson & Valentine Consulting.

I can't see my brothers agreeing either, but it's not about agreement. If it were, I'd have asked to join the team already and been given a flat 'no.' It's why I have to show them instead. Actions speak louder than words.

So I've decided I need a case of my own. One I can work on without interference. My plan is to visit Tim at the office. There's a tray on his desk that contains files of new casework. Unless it's marked urgent, they're handed out on Tuesday mornings at the weekly staff meetings. I'll need to visit on a Monday.

"What are you up to, Mackenzie?"

I jump a mile in the air. When my heart rate recovers, I turn and face my father. The wedding is a black tie affair, and he looks like a distinguished Robert Redford in his sharp suit and glass of scotch in hand.

Dad takes my empty glass. He places it on the tray of a passing waiter and picks up a full one.

"What am I up to?" I repeat as I take the offered champagne. "Nothing, why?"

"You think I don't recognise the look on your face? You're my little girl. You've been scheming and hatching plots since the dawn of time. And here you are, up to mischief at your brother's wedding no less." He turns to Jake. "Romero. Good to see you as always."

Dad's tone indicates it isn't good to see him at all. Their relationship is a strained one. My father likes to blame Jake for my failure to attend FDH. Jake likes to act as though it doesn't bother him. He straightens his shoulders beneath the weight of my father's stare. "You too, sir."

"Are you keeping my daughter out of trouble?"

My fingers tighten on the stem of my glass.

"No offense, sir, but it's not up to me to keep Mac out of trouble. Though, I guarantee if she was, I'd be right there doing whatever I could to help."

My father takes a sip of scotch and contemplates Jake over the rim of his glass. "If she *was* in any trouble, the first thing I'd hope you do is tell me."

"I'm standing right here," I snap. "And I'm not in any trouble."

"Sir, she's not in any trouble."

"But she always manages to find herself in the thick of it..." Dad looks at me "...don't you, sweetheart?"

The words are delivered as if I'm the family joke. My skin prickles with anger. My brothers are trusted to take care of themselves. Why does he never trust me? I lift my chin, hiding the hurt. "Thanks for the vote of confidence, Dad."

I shove my glass at him. He takes it, his expression one of surprise as I stride off.

Chapter Twenty-Six

Mac

The hurt still smarts weeks later, but I have to push it aside. On top of our current hectic schedule, we've been in final preparations for an awards ceremony. *Jamieson* has been invited to play. We accepted, but of course the path to true success never runs smoothly. Life always manages to plant a hurdle the size of Mt. Everest in your path just to piss you off and make everything difficult.

In this instance, my hurdle is Frog.

"Please tell me you're joking," I say into the phone. Panic tinges the edges of my voice.

"I'm not," my doped-up sounding bassist replies.

I'm at Evie's house for a barbeque. It's supposed to be a relaxed affair with the band and my family. A celebration of Jared and Evie finally finishing up renovations on their money pit. The pool has been installed. The gardens are done. Life is supposed to be good. And Frog and Cooper are supposed to be here. But they aren't. Frog has just finished informing me he's managed to break his arm and is now at the hospital with Cooper.

"Are you okay?"

"I am *so* fiiiiiiiiine," he slurs.

"And your arm?"

"My arm is *so* fiiiiiiiiine."

My lips pinch. Frog is currently high on heavy pain medication and now we're short a bassist. The awards are *tonight*. "How could you do this?"

"Don't be mean, Macky Wacky," he says, sounding hurt.

"I'm not being mean," I hiss into the phone as my mind runs at a million miles an hour. The exposure for Jamieson tonight is huge. It's going to be televised to millions of people. We can't back out, which means we need a replacement bassist. We need—

"Give me that," Jake says, cutting off my scrambling thoughts. He snatches my phone and takes control of the call, leaving me to pace the carpeted floor of Evie's bedroom.

It's a beautiful room decorated in Hampton's style with lots of white. It's my favourite space in their entire house, but it fails to soothe me right now, especially when my eyes fall on Evie. She's just emerged from the ensuite bathroom. Her face is green and her long, voluminous locks hang lank around her face. She looks like a bedraggled kitten emerging indoors after being caught in a thunderstorm.

I pause my pacing and point at her. "No. Just ... no."

"I'm sorry." Her voice is a rasp.

"Oh my god, why does everyone have to be an asshole today?" I cry. "I don't have time for this."

Evie lips press flat as if she's trying to hide a smile. I'm gobsmacked at her nerve. My brilliant bassist is in the hospital with a broken arm, and my lead singer has a voice like sandpaper. How can she find this amusing? My temper steps up a notch. "This is funny to you?"

"No!" Her smile blooms, and she places a palm against her belly. "I think ... I'm pregnant."

I stop breathing. My feet freeze to the floor, and my heart begins thumping a wild, jagged beat. This is what I wanted. What I've been hoping for. So why does it *hurt?*

Jake ends the call with Frog and hangs up my phone. His body is stiff as he carefully sets it on the bedside table. Does it feel like this for him too? This stabbing pain of loss?

"You …" I try to form words. To say something. Anything.

Evie's lips curve. "Aunty Mac."

I force my legs to move. One step in front of the other, they walk me toward my best friend. My arms wrap around her, and I pull her in for a hug. "Congratulations, Sandwich. I'm so happy for you."

"I'm happy too." She squeezes me tightly in return, whispering, "But I'm scared."

Her words send a pang directly to my heart. I'd been scared once too. "Don't be scared. You've got this, okay? And you've got us."

"Good, because I can't do this without you."

My phone rings again. I squeeze her back and step away.

"It's the venue," Henry says, handing me the phone as he steps in to give Evie a hug.

"Excuse me," I mutter and leave the room, jogging down the stairs with the ringing phone. Jared is walking out of the kitchen as I reach the bottom step. My brother is going to be a daddy. I want to be happy for him. But not right now. Jared needs to get away from me before I fall apart.

"Mac, can you—"

"Not now," I snap as I charge toward the downstairs bathroom.

I press the red button on my phone, ending the call without answering it as I slam the door behind me. Setting the device on the vanity counter, I stare at myself in the mirror and touch a hand to my cheek. My makeup is immaculate and my straightened hair hangs in a perfect sheet down my back. The surface shows no scars, but the hurt is bubbling up inside like a throbbing volcano. I feel it rising, hot and thick. I keep swallowing it down but it won't be stopped.

The door opens swiftly.

I spin around.

Jake stands there, jaw trembling, silent. He knows the scars are there. He sees the pain. He feels it too.

My eyes fill as he steps inside the room and shuts the door behind him. The next minute I'm folded in his arms and the last of my control, having held strong for too many years, finally snaps. A sob rips from my chest. The broken sound echoes through the small space. My entire body trembles and his arms lock tighter, holding me against his chest as we sink to the floor.

"Jake," I sob.

Jake

A sick feeling lodges in my gut when Evie gives the news. Our friend has something we both lost and the pain of it is raw. A wave of it crosses Mac's face as she stands frozen to the ground. It's overwhelming and unexpected, and she can't hide it.

Oh, baby.

My heart breaks when she rushes from the room. I follow behind, knowing I can congratulate my friend later. Right now, it's Mac who has my attention. Mac who needs me.

"I'm here. It's okay," I whisper, my arms holding her close inside the quiet of the bathroom. My hands rub up and down her back as we sit in a huddle on the floor.

"It's not," she sobs, her fingers digging into my skin.

"It *is* okay. It's okay to be upset."

"It's not okay to be upset. My best friend is up there, and I should be up there with her, celebrating, but I'm down here crying like a stupid girl."

"I hate to break it to you, but you *are* a girl."

A laugh escapes through the tears, and Mac pulls back a little, wiping at her face. It turns out my girl is not a pretty crier. Her eyes are swollen and red, and a river of mascara tracks down her cheeks, but there's honest emotion on her face and it's beautiful. Even like this, my heart bleeds for her and swells with love, all at once. Her strength floors me, but her vulnerability is something I would kill to protect.

"Lucky for you, then. If I was a guy you wouldn't be able to fuck me, would you?"

I shrug. "I don't know. I think if you were a guy, I'd turn for you."

Laughter bubbles from Mac's throat. "Stop trying to make me feel better."

Cupping her cheeks in my palms, I wipe away her tears with my thumbs. "I can't help it. I'm the man who loves you. I'll never stop."

"I love you too." Mac's eyes fill with fresh tears. "But what does that even matter? I can't be the woman you want me to be. I can't give you what you want."

"What do I want?"

"You want the happy ending, Jake. You want marriage and family. You want our lives to keep going on how they are, and they can't."

"What's wrong with wanting all that?"

"Because I can't give it to you."

"You can't? Or you won't?"

Mac swallows, regret etched all over her face. "Both."

"Then I'll take whatever you're willing to give."

I cringe, knowing I sound like a pathetic asshole.

"Jake ..." Mac scrambles to her feet, and I rise with her. Taking a washcloth from the towel rack, she gives me her back and flicks the tap on, wetting it. I watch her in the mirror. Each dab of the cloth against her cheeks wipes the hurt from her face. She looks at my reflection and meets my eyes. "I can't do this."

A hard rap comes at the door. "Mac?" Henry calls out. "Are you in there? I have an idea about the replacement bassist."

"Be right out," she calls back. Then she turns around and speaks softly. "I need to go sort this out."

"Mac ..."

She breathes in deep as though drawing in all her strength, because when she lets it out there's no trace of emotion left. None. "You deserve better than whatever I can give."

I give her a stony stare. "Am I getting the *'it's not you, it's me'* speech?"

"Jake, you started with nothing and now look at you. You're living your dream. You have everything you ever wanted."

"Except you."

"You don't need me."

My voice cracks. "Of course I *need* you. It's always been you and me. Right from the beginning, remember?"

"We were just kids in the beginning," Mac says. "And kids grow up. They change. They grow apart."

"You don't get it, do you?" I say, pushing her back against the bathroom counter, my body pressing against hers. I put both hands on either side of the vanity, locking her in place.

"Get what?"

"That in this one universe, there are nine planets. Of those planets, there's just one that holds two hundred and four countries, seven seas, and seven billion people. Of those seven billion people, I had the privilege of meeting just one girl. And that one girl not only stole my heart, she set my world on fire."

"Jake," she whispers, her emotionless façade slipping.

"When I said I belonged to you, Mackenzie Valentine, I didn't mean in just that moment. I meant across time. Across planets. Galaxies. Hell, the goddamn universe. Princess," I take her chin in my hand, staring hard into her brilliant green eyes. "I meant forever."

Chapter Twenty-Seven

Mac

We stare at each other for a pulse-pounding moment. Then I clear my throat. "Well … Okay then."

I wince at my response. *Really, asshead? Jake says he belongs to you across space and time and you give him an 'okay then'?* Can I be any more emotionally stunted?

Henry's knock comes at the bathroom door a second time. "Shit," I mumble.

Jake lets out a deep, weary sigh. Standing off to the side, he says, "Go," as he opens the door to let me walk through. "But this isn't over."

I stride passed him, and because I can never give a single inch, I say coolly, "It never is."

"Fuck it," he mutters and in the next second the back of my sleeveless floral blouse is grabbed in a fist and I'm being dragged backward.

Henry, standing with my phone in hand waiting for my direction, stares bewildered as I flail on my heels.

"I'll be out in a moment," I tell him in an authoritative tone, ignoring his wide eyes. "Go find out where Quinn is. She and Travis were supposed to be here over an hour ago and—"

Jake slams the door shut in Henry's face.

"What the hell was that?" I spin to look at him. The hard glare on his face warns me he's not in the mood to argue. Too bad. "We have an emergency on our hands and you want to play hide and seek inside my brother's bathroom?"

"I give you the fucking universe," Jake growls, "and you give me '*well okay then*'?" That was exactly my thinking, but clearly I'm suffering the effects of an emotional overload during the middle of a work crisis.

"I'm sorry," I bite out, "but I can't compete with that right now."

"Compete? This isn't a damn competition, Mac, but if it was, it's obvious there's no winner here. All I see are two losers who can't get their shit together."

"Speak for yourself," I retort.

Jake is fed up. He grabs the front of my blouse and shoves me around until my backside hits the bathroom counter. "I spilled my fucking heart out to you, you cold-hearted bitch."

I jab a finger in his face. "Don't you ever call me a bitch."

His brown eyes narrow. "Bitch, bitch, bitch."

My slap is a loud crack in the room.

Jake's head slams sideways from the blow. He stands there for a moment, breathing heavy, shoulders tense. He's struggling for control. *Fuck that.* Jake is always on at me to *let go.* Let's see what happens when he does.

I bare my teeth. "Fuck you."

"No," Jake replies, his tone harder than steel. "Fuck *you.*"

He reaches for my pants. Not bothering to undo the pretty yellow button, he rips it open. My eyes watch as it pings across the room and hits the tiled wall before dropping to the floor. My gaze cuts back to his. The heat in his eyes is unmistakable, causing my breath to hitch. "Jake, you can't—"

"I can. So shut your fucking mouth, Mackenzie."

My pants are yanked down. The zipper unfastens on its own accord from the force. My panties are shoved down next. Jake leaves them bunched around my calves as he lifts me and sets my bare ass on the counter.

He spreads my legs, pushes his way between them, and unzips his jeans. "What are you doing?"

Jake slips a hand between my legs. The rough pad of his finger finds my clit and he rubs, finding me wet. "What am I doing?" The next moment his hand is gone and his thick cock is pushing inside me. The intrusion is unexpected yet my body pulses around him, welcoming it. I bite down on my bottom lip, unable to stop the moan from escaping. "You're a smart girl," he states. "You work it out."

"Jake," I gasp, my hands sliding around his neck when he fully seats himself inside of me. I bury my head in his neck and breathe in the familiar scent of his warm, male skin.

"Look at me," he demands, his shoulders bunching with muscle as he grabs the naked cheeks of my ass in his big hands.

I draw back and look him in his eyes. They're dark and burning with anger. "Look me in the eye while I'm fucking you, Mac, and tell me you don't need me. Tell me you could walk away from me tomorrow and never look back."

Jake

My chest burns with fury and my body aches with the animalistic urge to thrust. The crumbs Mac offers me aren't enough. It's never enough. She takes too much and gives too little, and it's ripping me apart. There's no backing down now. Not anymore. Not even with me buried inside her, the heat of her body pulsing around my cock.

When Mac doesn't answer, I pull out and drive back in, ignoring the sharp bolt of pleasure that spikes through me. "Tell me!" I roar, desperate, because if she walks away, all the light in the world will die. *Don't leave me in the dark.*

Her jaw locks tight but a fat tear spills over and falls down her cheek. "I'm not walking away," she whispers, her voice thick. "I need you." Emotion clogs my throat as I watch another tear fall following the trail of the one before it. "If I had to live without you, I wouldn't survive it."

And I realise it in that moment. She's not the one who's always walking away. It's me. Goddammit, *it's me.* I grab her head in my hands, her hair like golden silk beneath my fingertips as I drag her forehead to mine.

Another rap comes at the bathroom door. My mouth presses in a thin line and her lips curve at the frustration in my expression. She cups my jaw, her fingers sliding along the stubbled skin in a soothing gesture. "I've got this." Turning her head toward the door, she calls out, "Get lost, Henry."

Goddamn, Mac is sexy. My cock pulses inside the heat of her body, and I draw out nice and slow, the pace a delicious torment.

The sound of a throat being cleared floats gently toward us as I sink slowly back inside. "It's ahh Quinn."

Mac lets loose a long, slow hiss, and it's my turn to grin. "Relax, Princess, I'll get this one," I tell her, and over my shoulder call out, "Get lost, Quinn."

Quinn's intake of breath is sharp and clearly audible.

Mac snickers. Her laughter tickles my skin as she buries her head in my neck.

"Well holy shit," we hear Quinn mutter, her voice fading as she walks away. When we're both sure she's gone, we don't waste any more time. Mac's mouth falls on mine, and I yank up her shirt. My hands grope at her lace-covered tits. Her nipples are peaked, and she kisses me as I pinch them both. *Hard.* Mac breaks away, her back arching.

I thrust again and she gasps a soft keening sound that sends hot shivers down my spine. "Harder," she orders, even though she knows she doesn't get to dictate terms when it comes to this.

My pace slows further, and her frantic hands find the globes of my ass. Her fingernails dig in deep. My voice is forceful. "Ask me nicely."

"Please," she begs, heat stealing over her cheeks.

The word is pretty on her lips, but I want more. I want her to see it too. I pull out and turn her around so she faces the mirror. Planting a hand in her back, I nudge her downward, forcing her ass to rise in the air. The cheeks are smooth, round, and bare to my gaze. Taking the root of my cock in hand, I push the fat tip just an inch inside as she grips the edges of the vanity.

I find her eyes in the mirror. "Say it again."

"Please," she whispers.

I thrust back in at the same time my palm comes down. The sound of a slap renders the air. Mac hisses and moans as I massage the reddened skin of her ass cheek.

"Jake," she rasps. "They'll hear us."

"No they won't," I soothe. "Everyone is outside."

But there's no time to play like I want, so I abandon my restraint. Hard, aggressive thrusts push Mac again and again into the counter. Her teeth dig into her bottom lip and her lids close as she hangs her head.

Mac

Jake fists my hair and yanks my head back so all I can see in the mirror is him driving inside me, messy and hard as my orgasm builds.

His muscles are bunched tight, straining, and his breath comes in fierce pants.

"Jake," I say on a long moan. His wicked gaze watches as pleasure burns through me like a raging inferno.

He groans and bows over my back, wrapping both arms around my middle like a manacle. "Baby," he grunts as he bucks against me, coming with an unleashed power that shakes his entire body.

Jake holds me to him for a long moment. The side of his face is pressed against my back. The beat of his heart is frantic against my skin. I surrender to the sound and let it lull me for a minute. Then his head lifts. His dark eyes find mine as his lips touch my shoulder in a tender kiss.

Jake is two sides of a coin: wickedly formidable on one when he lets his rough side out to play, and irresistibly sweet on the other. When both sides combine like they've done today, it becomes a powerful force of nature I can't withstand.

Amusement glitters in my expression. I like seeing him spent because of me. "Are we done here? Because I've got shit to do."

Jake unlocks his arms from my middle and slowly straightens. "You're so sweet."

"If you want sweet," I say to him in the mirror, "then you've picked the wrong girl."

"My bad." He pulls out and reaches for the washcloth that's folded neatly by the sink. "I guess I'll go find some other girl to poke my cock into. I'm sure there are plenty of girls out there sweeter than you."

I grab said cock in my palm and squeeze gently. "You could, but there's a slight problem with your plan."

Jake looks down at his dick in my grip before his gaze lifts to mine. He arches a brow. "Oh?"

"You don't like them sweet."

He gives me a cheeky grin and holds up both palms. "You got me."

"I do," I say, offering a grin of my own in return. "Literally."

Jake shakes his head with amusement and unpeels my palm from his cock, replacing it with the washcloth. "Clean yourself up, Princess. You look like you just got royally fucked."

My eyes are quick enough to spy Henry stuffing a fifty-dollar note in his pocket as I stalk inside the back study where he, Evie, and Quinn have congregated to resolve our current crisis.

"What's going on?" I bark.

I take satisfaction in seeing the three of them jump. I know what they're doing. Sneaky assholes. They know about me and Jake and are placing bets on our relationship. If they think I'm oblivious to what goes on in our little group, then I'm the Second Coming. Sometimes I think they forgot who they're dealing with.

Resolving to corner Travis and find out the exact bet—because there's no doubt it's more than just the three of them involved—he can ante up a wad of cash on my behalf. Secretly.

Schooling the smirk that rises on my lips, I take the office chair Quinn just vacated and sit, giving them all an eyeball in turn.

"What about Grace?" Henry asks, referring to his younger sister.

I swivel my chair in his direction. "What about her?"

"She can play bass. I could give her a call?"

I've met Grace on occasion when she's flown into Melbourne, returning from her modelling assignments. Her visits are rare yet she always takes the time to send us care packages filled with makeup and clothes from photoshoots. She's spirited, fun, and my kind of girl.

She's also Casey's kind of girl. I know that cocky charmer's type. He likes them feisty, and his head always turns for a second look whenever a redhead passes him. Having her here will fit well with my matchmaking plans. Putting Grace in his line of sight will be a challenge impossible for him to ignore.

"Where is she right now?" I ask Henry.

"Melbourne."

Just an hour's flight away. "Set it up," I tell him, steepling my fingers together.

He tugs his phone from his pocket, dials Grace, and leaves the room as he speaks.

Evie, unusually quiet since my arrival in the room, begins to heave in silence. Her brow is lined with a light sheen of sweat. The glare I send her way is edged with anxiety. "Stop it, Sandwich. There will be no heaving, no sweating, and definitely no puking today. Vomit on the inside, like a winner."

Evie swallows a few times before her eyes goes wide. I know that look. She's about to gush like an overturned fire hydrant.

I point to the door. "Go."

"Sorry," she gasps. With a hand flying to her mouth, Evie stands and flees the room.

My hard stare turns on Quinn.

"What can I do?" she asks.

I check my watch. It's eleven a.m. "Arrange flights for Grace. We need her here yesterday."

She nods, stands, and leaves the room to get the iPad she works from.

"Oh, and Quinn?"

She turns at the doorway.

"Find out where Casey is too, will you?" There's no supressing the grin. "He can pick her up from the airport."

Quinn cocks her head. "What's so amusing?"

"Nothing." I wipe the expression from my face. "Stop wasting time, asshead, and do what I asked."

"And what will *you* be doing? Spending another inordinately excessive amount of time in the bathroom with Jake?"

"You can shove your big words where the sun don't shine, Quinn, because I'll be right here taking care of business. I have to consult with the stylist now that Frog is out and Grace is in. Her security also needs to be arranged..." because Grace is a big deal "...along with an extra rehearsal for this afternoon. The event organisers need to be contacted so we can add her to the list. Then there's the—"

Quinn waves a hand cutting me off. "Okay, okay." She begins to walk away, saying over her shoulder, "I get it. Now that you've done Jake, you have other shit to do."

"Quinn," I snap.

She stops and turns around.

"What I do with Jake is none of your business. Or anyone else's for that matter."

Quinn strolls back to the study and leans against the doorframe folding her arms. "Oh? Like you made me and Travis your business?"

"This is different. There's history there that you have no idea about."

With a shrug, she pushes off from the side of the door and says, "Well … maybe it's time you shared that history with the rest of us," before leaving.

I sit back in my chair with a huff, head tilted to the ceiling, as I close my eyes for a brief moment. The time for sharing has long passed.

Hasn't it?

"I see your minions have scattered."

I open my eyes. Jared stands in front of the desk, a beer in one hand and a champagne cocktail in the other. I know why he's here, and I also know it's best to just get it over with rather than brush him off the way I want to.

Like ripping off a Band-Aid, Mac. The sting will be sharp and it'll throb for a little while after, but then the pain will eventually go away.

"It's a little early for drinking, isn't it?" I ask, which is a ridiculous question because if there's ever a time for alcohol …

Jared snorts. "Tell me you didn't just ask me that," he says, extending the crystal flute toward me. The glasses were a housewarming gift from our parents. They were very astute with their present, no doubt foreseeing many occasions that would be cause for future celebration.

I take the champagne while he takes a seat opposite me. "I didn't just ask you that."

"Good," he replies as I bring the glass to my lips. "Because I figured you'd need the drink after having an epic bout of sex in my downstairs bathroom."

Fizzy alcohol sprays from my mouth. It showers the desk and my rumpled blouse. I set my flute on the desk and grab for a tissue to dab at the mess. "Jake and I were merely taking some time to resolve an issue."

His brows soar sky high. "Well, clearly you resolved the shit out of it."

There's only one thing I can do and that's to roll with it, so I give my brother a cool stare. "I'm a Valentine. I do what it takes to get the job done."

Laughter explodes from my brother. Loud and infectious, it rings out across the room. My lips twitch, and I can't help the responding chuckle.

When his amusement dies down, he shakes his head and looks at me.

"What?" I ask.

"I should've known there was no embarrassing you with that statement. You're tough as nails, Mac." Jared looks at me with a mixture of pride and admiration. "Nobody pulls one over on you."

"Like you were just trying to do now? What was your plan? Blackmail me into forgiving you?"

"Blackmail?"

"You know what Jake and I did. What were you going to do, use it as leverage?"

Jared sets his beer on the desk and lets out a breath. "What, like running to Mum and Dad?"

He's done it before. "It's not beneath you."

Jared shrugs. "Like you said, we're Valentines. We do what it takes to get the job done."

"Touché," I reply over the rim of my glass. "But I think we're a little old now to go running to our parents and tittle-tattle."

"Oh, I don't know. I don't think we'll ever be too old for that." Jared picks his beer up with a wry grin and takes a sip. Then he leans forward and rests his elbows on his knees, staring at the bottle as though it holds all the answers to the universe. "You're my sister, Mackenzie. And I love you. I can't have you angry with me anymore."

I nod, rubbing my lips together. "Well, you're my brother, Jared, and I love you too. The truth is I'm not angry. Not anymore."

Jared exhales. It's a deep sound of relief. When he looks up, his eyes are sad and heavy with guilt, and I realise what's going through his head. It's not just the betrayal. It's the car accident. He was the driver and blames himself for my miscarriage. "I'm still hurt over what you all did, but the car accident was exactly that," I tell him. "An accident. Maybe you should try forgiving yourself."

"I'm not sure I can. The truth is..." he begins and pauses, swiping a hand across his jaw "...the truth is that ..."

I say what he can't say himself. "You and Evie are having a baby."

His eyes search mine. "You know."

"Of course." My heart gives a painful thump, but I force my lips to curve. "I'm a Valentine, remember? It's my job to know everything."

Jared gives a shaky laugh, taking my teasing tone as a sign that his news hasn't caused me any hurt. "Sometimes you scare me, Mac."

I hold my champagne cocktail toward him for a toast. He clinks it with his beer bottle and after we both take a sip, I say, "Sometimes I scare myself."

Chapter Twenty-Eight

Mac

We have too many live commitments to cancel after Frog's injury. Thankfully Grace has agreed to stay for a full eight weeks. She's going to cover his place with *Jamieson* until he's healed and able to play again.

Three weeks into her stay, I make the time to visit Jamieson & Valentine Consulting. I dress carefully for the occasion. Of course, I'm only lifting a file, but I'm doing it inside an *office environment* so I feel compelled to look the part. Dressed in a sharp black suit, deep red lipstick, and matching Louboutins that bear a stiletto so sharp it can stab a troublemaker in the heart at fifty paces, I step out of my brother's vintage Porsche. Jared isn't working today and because he's playing nice lately, I've taken advantage and asked for the use of his car. I need to buy my own, but the last thing I ever feel like doing during what little down time I have is stroll through car yards trying to find a car that's the perfect fit for me.

I reach inside the car and collect the box from the passenger seat before carefully locking the borrowed Porsche. After dropping the keys in my Mimco tote bag, I stride along the cement path leading toward the building.

The *drilling, clanging,* and *whizzing* sounds of various electrical tools render the air from the construction site across the street. A sharp wolf whistle rings out, cutting clear through the noise and busy street traffic. My nostrils flare. "Pervy assholes," I mutter beneath my breath, ignoring the insult.

With my hair pulled into a sleek bun at the nape of my neck and my game face on, I stride up the steps and press a palm flat on the entrance door to my brothers' offices, ready to push it open.

"Hey, Mac Attack!"

I know then that it's Casey Daniels who wolf-whistled. It's his special nickname for me. I turn and literally choke on air.

Both Casey and Jake stand on the opposite street corner. They're waiting at the traffic lights, holding matching takeout coffee cups. They both wear sleek pants and sharp-collared shirts—Casey's is deep purple and Jake's a rich navy blue with dark grey pinstripes. The only difference is that Casey wears a tie.

The light turns green and the vision of them walking toward me is a figurative punch to the eyeballs. For a brief second I imagine being in a naked sandwich between the two of them. *Stand down, you dirty whore,* I order myself, but it's an effort because *Jesus Christ,* the thought of them naked and all for me is enough to make me weep.

Grace is one lucky bitch but when my eyes cut to Jake, I know that I'm luckier. His collar is open and shirtsleeves rolled up exposing tanned, tattooed forearms and thick veins. Today he's clean-shaven and the short buzzed hair has grown a fraction. He's forgotten about his weekly cut. The ends are a rich sun-kissed gold and silky to the touch. His stride isn't smooth like Casey's. It's powerful, giving him a dangerous edge. He's the epitome of the Big Bad Wolf when he chooses to let it out, and there's nothing sexier than when he lets it out with me.

When my haze of lust lowers a notch, it hits me that Jake is *here* when I'm about to instigate my plan. Hell. Just weeks ago I was telling Quinn she needed to rein in her man, and I can't even keep track of my own.

I'm slipping. But it's not really like he's my man, is he? Or is he? I don't know what we are anymore. It changes day to day.

"Princess," Jake mutters when they reach me. Touching a hand to my side, he leans in and kisses my cheek. "You look dressed to kill."

"Funny you should mention that. I happen to have a list handy of people who need to die today."

I don't but it sounds good, and it's advantageous to keep people on their toes, regardless of whether they're friend or foe.

Casey grins and gives my cheek a quick peck too. "I hope I'm not on it," he quips.

"Neither of you are on it," I tell them. "But that could change at a moment's notice, so watch your backs."

Jake's eyes crinkle. "You think you could take us?" he asks, putting an arm around my shoulders and drawing me closer.

My girl parts tingle. I have to school the amusement because I know he means his comment in a completely different context to the one in my head. Still, I answer honestly. "I know I can."

Casey nods, mockingly impressed as he takes a sip of coffee. "Then we'll be sure to watch our backs."

My expression turns scathing. "Don't patronise me, hotdog." The nickname had been bestowed on Casey by Evie because of his hotdogging moves on a surfboard. I like it and use it liberally. Casey is a cocky bastard. The nickname knocks him down a peg or two. My eyes shift to the disposable cup in his hand. "Having trouble controlling your office boy? Times must be tough when you have to get your own coffee rather than send Tim out to get it for you."

It's common knowledge that Tim has an ongoing dispute with the barista across the road. Because of it, Tim refuses to tip his services. So now every time he orders a coffee, the barista makes it weaker than piss. Casey seems to be the one suffering the consequences what with Tim delivering him the bought coffee each morning. By the looks of it, Tim has no plans on ending the feud anytime soon.

"Tim's not in today," Casey tells me as the three of us walk up the steps to the office.

"He's not in?" Good. That will make lifting a minor little file that much easier to do.

"Nope," he says, holding the door open to let Jake and me through. "It's his birthday."

"I know. That's why I'm here. But I didn't realise he was having the day off."

Tim's birthday is the ruse I'm using to explain my appearance in the office. I glance sideways at Jake as the three of us walk around the sleek wood-grain reception desk and toward Casey's office. "So what are you doing here?"

Jake and Casey share a mutual look as we step inside the spacious corner room where he works. "You didn't tell her?"

"Tell me what?"

"No I didn't tell her," Jake says to Casey. "I was waiting until after our meeting with the bank."

"The bank?" I echo.

Jake turns to face me. "Casey and I are investing in a car restoration business."

My brow furrows. "Why are you investing in a restoration business? There can't be any value in that. They're just cars. They *depreciate*," I point out helpfully.

Casey gives me a withering look as he sits down in the seat behind his desk. "They aren't just *cars*."

"Is that so?" I return his withering look with one of my own. "I'm sorry. I didn't realise you were investing in mechanical unicorns that fly you to outer space."

Jake's eyebrows rise at Casey as if to say *and you asked me why I hadn't told her*. "They're better than any kind of mechanical unicorn, Mac. These are exceptional pieces of machinery—either bought as original collectibles or vintage muscle cars that get restored to mint condition."

"And they make a lot of money?" I ask.

"Some do, some don't," Jake concedes. "It's more a labour of love that will probably take up a fair amount of spare time. Are you going to be okay with that?"

Jake and Casey both have a passion for restoring cars. It makes sense for them to share it with an investment like this. That they're also able to get their hands dirty on the machinery is likely the bonus that has them signing on. Not to mention if Jake is talking cars with Casey, it means he isn't talking cars with me. Don't get me wrong, I appreciate cars. They move fast and get you where you need to go, but my knowledge only extends to changing a tyre and filling the water for my windscreen wipers. That's where I like to keep it. "Of course I'm okay with that."

His eyes soften. Tucking a hand beneath my chin, Jake leans forward and presses a tender kiss to my lips. "You're a sweetheart."

"I thought we decided I wasn't sweet," I whisper, my heart doing flutters from his loving gesture. It's seems today is a good day for us. A rare one that offers a glimpse of what we'd be like if we actually got our shit together.

"You are where it counts." Jake drops his hand and glances meaningfully toward the juncture of my thighs. His dark eyes lift. "I've never tasted anything sweeter."

My breath hitches. Wild thoughts of where we might find some private space so he can taste that sweetness right now run riot through my head.

The loud clearing of Casey's throat cuts through my fog and reminds me we aren't alone. Even Jake appears startled at his interruption. "If you two are finished having sex in my office, I'd like to get some work done."

"If you think that's sex, then you're doing it wrong," Jake quips.

"Har har," Casey mutters as he lifts the lid of his laptop.

"Need to use the bathroom," Jake says, already walking toward the office door. "If you aren't going to be here long, I'll take you out for lunch," he calls to me over his shoulder before disappearing.

I turn to look at Casey. He's tapping at his keyboard, his two fingers moving at a glacial pace. It's like watching a chicken peck at the ground on a lazy Sunday afternoon. "Whatever you're typing, it's going to take all day."

His blue eyes flick to mine before returning to the screen. "Well, you can either stand there and watch or do it for me."

"Why would I do it for you? It's likely something Tim should've done for you last week. That would mean doing him a favour."

"And you know what that means?"

I arch a brow. "What?"

"Tim would then owe *you* one."

"I like how you think." I walk around his desk to where he sits. "Move."

Casey doesn't waste time vacating his fancy office chair. He stands and picks up a file from his in-tray as I set my box beside the computer and take his seat. My gaze goes to the screen as I unpin the button on my suit jacket. The man is apparently trying to transcribe his own handwritten notes into an email, and all that tapping has only gotten him so far as the salutation. I poise my hands over the keyboard before I tackle the correspondence. "You know what else this means?"

"What?" Casey asks, leaning against the side of his desk as he flicks through the loose papers in the file.

"You'll owe me one too."

Casey's answer is a deep chuckle. "You're a smart girl, Mac," he says as I start typing. My fingers flash over the keyboard because I'm *just that good.* "Quick on the uptake too. If Jamieson doesn't watch its back, I might just lure you over here to work for us."

My fingers freeze, the words blurring in front of my eyes. Then I realise what he means and force myself to keep typing. "There's not enough money in the world for me to consider becoming a secretary for my brothers."

Casey bonks me on the head with his file before tossing it back in his in-tray. "I wasn't talking about secretarial duties."

I stop typing all together and swivel the tall leather chair to face him. "What *were* you talking about?"

"If you have to ask, then you're not as smart as I just gave you credit for."

That's true. "Well, I have an idea," I concede and fold my arms before saying coolly, "but what makes you think I want to become a member of the Badass Brigade?"

Casey winces. "You know we don't actually call ourselves that, right?"

I shrug. "The moniker fits."

With an exasperated sigh, Casey takes a seat on the opposite side of his desk. "There's no stopping any of you with those ridiculous names you throw around is there?"

"Why would we stop? Besides, I heard Grace calling you Batman the other day. Granted, she probably didn't mean it in a nice way considering how you accused her of trafficking drugs and smashed her phone against a wall, but still ... you should be on board with that. It's cool."

His fingers tap irritably against the armrests of his chair. I chortle gleefully to myself. Any mention of Grace winds Casey up tighter than a spring. Their initial meeting got off to such a rocky start. When he collected her from the airport, he saw her hunted down by airport security and assumed the worst. The whole situation had me doubting my instincts until I saw the two of them together. Casey is the kindling to Grace's spark. All that's left to do is sit back and watch the fireworks.

"It's better than *hotdog*," I add.

"That's true."

"And we're getting off topic."

"True again." Casey eyes me speculatively. "The thing is, Mac, you have a flair for this kind of work. You're a Valentine. It's in your blood." My lips quiver beneath the minor praise. "But the issue is that you have a tendency to go rogue. You're like Maverick from Top Gun. You put yourself in danger unnecessarily to get the job done. That needs to stop."

My expression pinches. "I'm not a maverick," I snap.

His brows rise, and he nods as if to say *you sure as hell are.* "You're also quick to temper."

"I'm not perfect," I counter.

"Anyone who claims to be perfect is a fraud. You're the opposite of a fraud, Mac. You're honest and direct, and you have an exceptional ability to read people and situations in a way that no one else can. So if you ever decide you want to join the team, I'll put in a good word for you."

My mouth falls open. "You would do that for me?"

"I would, because there's something else I also happen to know about you ..."

I give up the farce of typing Casey's email. Reaching forward, I close the lid of the laptop that rests between us. "What?"

Casey leans forward in his seat and looks me dead in the eye. "I happen to think you're worth it."

Elation has me wanting to leap up and dance the boogie. I settle back in my chair with exaggerated casualness. "Oh, I know I am."

Casey rolls his eyes. "Sure you do. Now tell me ..." His eyes shift to the box I set down on his desk earlier. "What's in the box?"

"Tim's birthday present."

His face pales.

"You didn't get him a present, did you?"

Casey gives me a blank look.

"Dammit, hotdog. Tim is your assistant. How could you forget to buy him a gift? No wait." I hold up a hand. "I know why."

Grace. My machinations have a part in him losing his mind over her. Standing, I pick the box up and peel away the envelope that holds the card, tucking it inside my handbag. I walk around the side of the desk and place the box on Casey's lap. "It's Prada, but you'll need to get him a birthday card."

"Thanks, Mac." His expression is all gratitude. "He doesn't need a card though. Cards are for girls."

"Tim *is* a girl." I redo the button on my suit jacket and smooth a hand over the sleek fabric of my pants. "Now, if you'll excuse me, I need to go find Jake. He promised me lunch, and I'm ready to collect."

Leaving Casey's office, I look over my shoulder. He's moving around to his side of the desk. His brows are drawn when he takes a seat and lifts the lid of his laptop.

Satisfied his focus is on his work and not me, I walk past Tim's desk and lift a file from the new case tray without breaking stride and without having a clue of the contents. Casey might be willing to put in a good word for me, but that doesn't mean Travis and Jared will listen. I still need to prove myself.

I slip the file inside my tote and head off to find Jake.

Chapter Twenty-Nine

Mac

Later that night I'm at the Florence Bar where Jamieson is playing. The venue is booked to capacity to see them live. I switch my sharp office suit for skinny black jeans and a fitted *I'm with the band* tee shirt. When I arrive at the venue to oversee the setup, I put the stolen file to the back of my mind. It's resting in the locked drawer of my desk at home. There hasn't been time to look inside it yet, but I'm eager to get started. This will be my first case for Jamieson & Valentine Consulting. Granted, it's unofficial, but that only makes it all the more challenging. I'll have to utilise all my skills to pull it off without relying on anyone else.

"Where do you want this to go?" a burly man asks as he climbs the stairs off the side of the stage. A massive amplifier is wedged high on his shoulder.

"Just over there," I tell him, pointing to the right-hand corner.

We have a crew do our hard labour now, but they still need direction. The band sits backstage, chilling and getting ready, basically acting like big deals. They deserve to, though, because they are. It's their hard work that got them to this point so rather than take their egos down a notch, I let it slide. Mostly.

The venue is already hopping, the dance floor a complete crush as revellers dance and drink their Friday night away, waiting for Jamieson to take the stage. A DJ sits in the booth, pumping "Do

I Wanna Know," by the Arctic Monkeys when an argument in the crowd catches my eye. Normally I'd ignore it. Despite us having our own personal security, the Florence Bar employs the best bouncers in the city. They can handle anything. But this argument happens to be *with* our own personal security—Casey and a brunette in a red dress. It takes a lot to ruffle his smooth feathers, but right now they're standing on end. His eyes are hard and every muscle tense. Casey is *riled.*

"If Jake keeps looking at you the way he does, I'm going to have to punch him," Jared—the other half of our personal security for tonight—grumbles from beside me.

My eyes shift from Casey to Jake. He's the only one in the band who helps with the setup, mostly because he doesn't trust anyone else with his equipment. If a single drum is placed even an inch out of the alignment Jake prefers, he throws a tantrum of the likes you've never seen.

Right now he's seated at his drum kit, sticks in hand and eyes on me—just like my brother said. I want to tell Jared that if he so much as touches a hair on Jake's head, I'll shave his eyebrows off while he slept. It wouldn't be an idle threat either, because I've done it before. The night before Jared's school formal. The best part of the entire retribution was seeing my eighteen-year-old brother in a suit, minus two eyebrows, while our mother asked him if he wanted her to draw a pair on his face for him.

Jake doesn't need me defending him, though, so I bite the threat back. Instead, I give my brother a steely-eyed stare. "After everything that's happened, you think Jake would tolerate you even looking at him crossways? If you so much as tried punching him, he would put you in the ground."

"He would not," Jared mutters.

"Would too."

"Would not."

"Oh my god." I give him a withering look. "You're going to be a father and you're still ten years old. Your future kids are lucky they'll have an Aunty Mac in their lives to teach them how to kick your sorry ass."

Jared folds his arms, turning his glare at Jake toward the bopping crowd instead. "You wouldn't dare."

I snort. "This is me you're talking to."

He sighs, his eyes moving over the mass of dancers. "I know."

With the setup under control, I motion to Jake, silently asking him if he wants a drink. His answer is a cute grin and wink that has me sighing.

"Be right back," I tell my brother.

My heels click as I make my way down the stairs. I skirt the pulsating dancers as I move toward the bar. I'm halfway there when I notice Casey still arguing with the brunette. Now that I'm closer, I realise she looks familiar. I veer toward them. They're so caught up in their disagreement, they don't notice me.

"You're wrong, Morgan," I hear Casey saying, and it hits me. She's the new detective in Sydney's Cybercrime division. I've not only seen her in this very bar once or twice before, I've heard Travis bitching about her involvement with Casey before Grace arrived on the scene. "Grace isn't leaving."

Leaving? Like hell. Even if Grace *had* planned on leaving, I'm hedging my bets on Casey not letting her go anywhere.

"Oh, but I'm not," I hear Morgan reply. "You see, her return flight is already arranged. She booked the ticket yesterday morning."

Goddammit, Grace, what are you doing?

"Don't you see?" she continues, leaning close and putting a hand on his crotch. "Grace doesn't want you. But I do."

If Casey's expression is anything to go by, Morgan is about as wanted as a shit sandwich. When her tongue goes for his neck, he grabs a fistful of hair and yanks her off him.

"Don't touch me again," he growls, shoving her away. Her shoulder smacks against the man behind her, and he throws Casey a filthy look as he helps right her.

Morgan clearly deserves a fist to the throat, but it goes against the man code to punch her. Luckily, I'm female and not confined to those rules. I'm quite happy to enact violence on Casey's behalf, but the silly twat doesn't seem quite done with her diatribe. Eyes wide with amazement, I watch as she continues to antagonize one of the few people who has ever had my back.

She even has the gall to sneer at him. "The apple doesn't fall far from the tree, does it?"

"What's that supposed to mean?"

"That you're just like your loser father."

Casey doesn't talk much about his past. He had a shitty childhood and lost his family, including his violent drunk of a father, in a shooting. That she dared say such a thing would cut him to the bone.

"What do you know about my father?"

Her brows rise coolly, her expression triumphant as if she holds the ace card in her back pocket. "It's all in the report."

A loud disagreement erupts between two buffoons behind me and I miss Casey's reply, but I don't miss the spark of fire in Morgan's expression. "Believe me, you'll be sorry," she says with a hiss.

My eyes narrow.

"Is that a threat?" Casey growls.

"You can take it any way you want to."

He jabs a furious finger toward the exit. "Leave. Right now. I'll get the damn report some other way."

So that's what she's holding over Casey's head. A report relating to his family. Clearly it's important to him. I don't know why Morgan has it, or why it's important, and unless he wants to share it's not my place to know, but damned if I'm going to let that bitch hold it over him.

If she isn't going to hand it over, then I'm going to get it.

Unfortunately I'm waylaid from retrieving the report after Jamieson's show. Casey and Grace have one hell of an altercation in the back room when the band finishes their final set. It seems Grace saw Casey and Morgan together, and it hasn't gone down well. Her reaction isn't irrational. Her ex-boyfriend is a philanderer, and she has issues with trust. But I was there. I know what really went down. And although Grace deserves an explanation, she has nothing to fear. But instead of Casey getting the chance to explain, everything gets heated. Henry is furious. Grace is his little sister and it's only now that their relationship is coming to light for him.

Poor Henry. He's always the last to know anything. He cocks back a fist, ready to smash Casey into the wall, when Jared gets in the way. To Jake's (probable) delight, Jared takes the punch and almost goes down. In the fracas, Grace steals the keys to Casey's beloved Marjorie, his beautifully restored Corvette Stingray, and takes off. He chases after her, naturally. And that's the last we see of them.

I have faith in Casey, so I leave the back room to direct the packdown. Thirty minutes later, Jake finds me on the stage. His face is pale. I'm almost scared to ask. "What is it?"

"Henry just got a call from Travis, and ..." He takes a deep breath.

"Spit it out, Romero," I snap, my chest beginning to tighten with dread.

"Casey and Grace have been in a car accident."

"You're wrong." It can't be happening again. "They were just here and ... and ..." I was about to say everything was fine but their actions when leaving were volatile.

"Mac ... I'm sorry, but it's true."

I close my eyes. My legs feel ready to give out as I relive my own nightmare. The grinding of metal. The shattering of glass. The absolute fear. It's something that stays with you forever. I sink down on the amplifier that the stagehand is trying to take away. He gives up and goes to find something else he can do. I open my eyes and look up at him. "Are they okay?"

"Casey's in an ambulance. They're cutting Grace from the car."

"Jake," I swallow, my hand reaching blindly for him.

He takes it and holds tight, his huge palm offering warmth and comfort.

"We need to get to the hospital," I say.

"I'll take you. Everyone else has gone ahead."

I nod, letting him lead me off the stage so I can collect my bag. We reach the back room and Jake folds me up, securing me in his arms. "Are you okay?"

"I'm fine," I croak.

"Don't lie, Princess. Not to me."

"It's just thrown me, that's all. Car accidents aren't fun, you know?" I say, trying to be glib while I pull myself together. I step back from his embrace. "We should get to the hospital."

Jake

Mac steps away, not willing to open up. I let it go until we're both in the car and on our way. Her car accident is not something she's spoken to me about, yet it's clearly still affecting her. "Tell me about your accident, Mac. Please? I need to know."

"No you don't, Jake," she says, turning her head out the window. "It's in the past where it belongs."

"Where I belong?" I ask, my voice bitter as I slow the car to a stop at a red light.

"Don't be dramatic," she snaps, her quills rising. "I'm just saying there's no point in rehashing past hurt."

"How is it rehashing if we haven't talked about it before?" I argue. The light turns green and I accelerate.

Mac swallows, a flush appearing high on her cheeks. "It's just ... hard to talk about."

I reach across and squeeze her knee. "But if you can't talk about it with me, then who *can* you talk about it with?"

"What's the point in talking about it at all?"

Frustration rises and I suppress the emotion. "To share the burden." I shift my hand and take hold of hers, linking our fingers in her lap while I drive with one hand on the steering wheel. "With me."

There's a long pause. It stretches into a minute, then two, and just when I'm beginning to think she's not going to say anything at all, she speaks. "My brothers were lecturing me. Again," she says, her voice sad and distant. "We were on the Motorway, and I remember being angry. So angry with you I couldn't think straight. They were relentless and wouldn't stop, even Jared who was speeding along the road. So I told them the one thing guaranteed to shut them up."

"Which was what?" I ask.

Her breath hitches with a choppy sound. "That I was pregnant."

The road blurs in front of my eyes, and I squeeze her hand in mine.

"It shocked Jared the most. He veered right off the road and before he could recover control, the car hit loose gravel and that was it. I remember the car flipping like it was in slow motion. Travis and Eli were in the back with me and even though I had my seatbelt on, Trav still reached out to pin me back in the seat."

Her head bows and the sight is a knife to my heart. We reach our destination and I indicate, turning in to the hospital parking lot. It's late at night and there are plenty of spots available. I find one and ease to a stop. After turning off the ignition, the car settles into silence. All either of us can hear is the quiet ticking of the heated engine.

"When I woke in the hospital, our baby was gone like it was never even there."

I turn in my seat and look at her. She's staring out the front windscreen, remembering.

"I'm sorry," I say. The words feel trite, but they need to be said regardless. "I'm sorry you went through it alone. I would have been there in a heartbeat had I known."

Mac nods. "I know. I should have known all along, but I was young enough to still have faith in my brothers. I trusted them."

"I would have held you through every minute and never let go."

But she never got to have that. She was robbed of that comfort and her emotional wounds never healed as a consequence.

"I appreciate hearing that, Jake, but like I said, it's in the past and we should leave it there, ok?"

I nod. It's a touchy subject. That I got this far at all is an achievement.

Mac fumbles with the door handle. When it opens she snatches up her bag. "I'll see you inside," she says and takes off, clearly needing space.

I huff and tip my head back against the seat. "Shit," I say with a heavy heart, letting the stillness settle over me as I contemplate my next move.

My mind is perplexed. On one hand it would be easier for all of us if I walked away. I'm a daily reminder of what she lost and a contributing factor in how she lost it, which is likely making me a hindrance to the healing process. On the other hand, I love her. Not being around her feels entirely impossible. Does that make me selfish?

A rap comes at the driver's side window of my car, startling me from my internal contemplation. I tuck away my thoughts for another day and turn my head. My eyes widen in shock. It's Luke Fox. He's wearing a paramedic's uniform. His blond hair is longer and tied in a stubby ponytail at the base of his neck. He gives me a brief wave and steps back, allowing me room to open the car door.

"Jesus Christ!" I exclaim as I get out, shutting it behind me.

Luke grabs me in a bear hug. We slap each other's back before stepping away, both of us grinning. "Romero." He shakes his head as if he can't believe I'm standing here.

I do the same. "Little Fox."

We both speak. "What are you—"

"How are—"

Then we both stop and my face sobers. "My friend was in a car accident," I explain, waving to the hospital entrance. "Walk in with me?"

"Shit, mate," he says, falling in to step beside me. "He okay?"

"I just got here so I don't know." I pocket my car keys and shrug. "Last I heard he was brought in by ambulance."

"Oh geez. The Corvette Stingray guy?"

"That's the one."

"I'm the one who brought him in."

I stop Luke with my hand and search his face. "And?"

"And he and the girl are both going to be fine, but ..."

Luke trails off and his heart looks ready to bleed out. My stomach drops. "But what?"

"His car, man. It's gone. Never seen anything break my heart so bad as seeing that beautiful piece of machinery crumpled across the road."

I feel sick. Not Marjorie. Casey will never recover from the loss. Luke pats my shoulder in sympathy. "You need a barf bag?"

I take a few deep breaths. "No. Your shoes will work just fine."

"Ha. Get stuffed, Romero."

I chuckle, suddenly realising how much I've missed my old friend.

"What?" he asks, putting hands on his hips. Luke is so grown up now. Still his old self, yet appearing capable in a way he never was before. And confident.

"You're a paramedic now? And in Sydney? Seems a profession that's too respectable for your sorry ass. How did this come about?"

His eyes harden. "Well, I'd tell you, but one day a few years back I woke to find my best friend had left in the middle of the night without a word, so it seems like what I've done since then is none of his business."

I nod slowly. Luke has every right to be angry. "That's fair. You don't owe me anything. Leaving the way I did wasn't right. You deserve an explanation and maybe one day you'll be ready to hear it. When that day comes, look me up, ok?"

There's nothing more I can say, so I turn and walk toward the emergency entrance. The automatic doors whoosh open and cool air escapes.

"Ah hell," I hear Luke mutter. "Romero?" he calls out.

I turn. Luke is jogging toward me, his heavy black boots slapping against the pavement.

"You know I can't hold a grudge," he complains as if he really wants to be mad at me but finds it impossible. "And I know why you did it. I was proud of you for getting out. For a second I was just pissed because..." he clears his throat "...I didn't realise until now how much I missed you, ok?"

I nod, my eyes looking everywhere but at him because showing emotion with your mates is painfully awkward. "I missed you too."

Luke brandishes his phone. "Give me your number. We'll do beers this Sunday arvo, yeah?"

Chapter Thirty

Mac

After hearing the news last night that both our friends were going to be okay, we vacated the waiting room and went home to get some sleep. I've come back this morning alone, wanting to check on Grace myself. I know what she's just been through, and I know how important it is to have those you love surrounding you. So when I step inside Grace's hospital room it gives me satisfaction to see Casey by her bedside.

Grace's head is tipped back at an odd angle on her pillow and her mouth is open, emitting a light snore. Her arm is wrapped up and she's covered in bruises.

"How is she?" I ask softly.

"Her arm is broken," he replies, watching for my reaction. Frog is out of action as our bass guitarist because he broke his arm. Now our replacement bass guitarist is out of action because *she* broke *her* arm.

My right eye begins to twitch. "Step aside, Hotdog," I command. "I'm going to break her other arm."

I expect Casey to chuckle at my threat. I don't mean it. Clearly. Yet Casey's body goes tense and his eyes harden. "Not in this lifetime. Or any other for that matter."

My lips curve. "You're in love with her."

"That's for Grace and I to discuss."

"I agree."

My expression turns grave. "Make sure you don't leave her side, Casey."

After a group discussion last night in the hospital, we discovered there were witness reports stating the car that hit them sped up rather than slowed down. There were no skid marks on the road and the offender fled the scene. That's all that's known so far, but it's enough cause for concern. Especially after the words Casey had with Morgan last night. She may be a detective, but it doesn't necessarily mean she's a good person. I have every reason to believe she's involved.

"That's why you're here, isn't it?" he asks.

"I'm here to check on my friend."

His eyes soften on mine. "You're here to make sure she isn't alone. That she has the one person she needs most by her side."

I absorb Casey's comment, coming to the slow realisation that he knows about my past and my own accident. I can only conclude that Travis, being his best friend, must have told him. "She needs you," I say, for some reason not seeming to mind that he knows. It's easier than having to explain myself.

He nods his agreement. "She does. And for what it's worth, I won't leave her side. Not for a second."

"Good." I need to leave now before I make a fool of myself and say something nice. "I have to get going. Make sure to tell Grace when she wakes that I'll be stopping by later to make good on my threat."

He chuckles lightly. "I'll be sure to tell her."

The following night I make the time to issue a search for the report Casey is looking for. I figure Morgan's house is the best place to start. Granted, it's probably considered breaking and entering—of a detective's house no less—but that woman is due some retribution, and who better to give it to her than me? Besides, it's not really theft if the report belongs to Casey, right? I *owe* him this. And I'm not apprehensive in the least. I give zero fucks for the law I'm about to break. Sometimes you have to do something a little bad to achieve something good.

Dressed all in black, with black combat pants and boots that keep my footsteps silent, I drive to the address I found on public record for Morgan. I do a slow drive by first. It's late and dark out, and all the lights in her house are off, but it's not late enough for her to be home and tucked up in bed. At least I hope. There's no way to be one hundred percent sure.

I park a few houses down. When I get out of the car I slide the keys inside the tight pocket of my pants. It's a small pocket situated on the side of my knee, secured with a zip that keeps them from jingling noisily. It's where I keep my bobby pins. Four of them. Two for the lock and two for spare. They're already twisted and bent into position, ready for their infiltrating task.

I learned lock-picking at the tender age of ten. Funnily enough, it's a skill my father taught me. His reasoning? *I don't want my little girl ever being put in a position she can't get out of.*

"Well, sorry, Dad," I mutter under my breath as I jog toward the lowset red brick house. "This doesn't really qualify as a position I can't get out of, but I promise I'm using my powers for good and not for evil."

There's a standard timber fence that sections the backyard from the front. When I find the gate, I turn and give the neighbourhood a quick scan as I slide on a pair of black leather gloves. Satisfied I haven't been seen, I put my hand through the large hole that serves as a handle and check the latch. It's padlocked, but tonight is my lucky night because it isn't secured. It's left hanging off the sliding bolt, seemingly forgotten. I unhook it quietly and glide the bolt across in one smooth motion, opening the gate. I wince when I close it behind me and it creaks.

I can't help but notice her yard, even in the dark. It can do with some work. The grass is overgrown and brown, and the untrimmed trees are in desperate need of love, but I'm not here to perform landscaping miracles. I need to get in and get out.

My breath comes in short pants as I jog lightly to the back of the house. *Christ, I'm a bit unfit,* I realise. I take a moment to compose myself while I check the back door. It shows a simple pin and tumbler lock. Sticking one bobby pin in the lock to apply pressure on the barrel, I insert the one I've bent into a pick and spend five long damn minutes finding the internal seized pin. After hearing an audible *click,* I move on to the next pin, and the next, until all five internal pins are released and the lock turns.

I grin as the door opens. "Come to Momma."

The next morning I wake successful, and still dressed in my 'robbers' outfit, having crawled into bed and fallen asleep in the early hours. I'd started off the search in Morgan's bedroom and it hadn't lasted long. After rifling through a few drawers, and flicking through some books and papers on her desk, I moved to her bed, lifted the mattress, and there it was. Scanning the pages quickly, a few words popped out at me: *autopsy* and *Daniels.* Knowing I had the reports Casey needed, a grin of satisfaction spread across my face as I fled the scene.

With a low chuckle, I roll over on my bed to eyeball the stolen file that I'd slapped on my bedside table last night before crashing.

I'm feeling rather pleased with myself until my gaze encounters Jake. My gleeful chortle dies a quick death.

He's leaning against my bedroom wall, bare-chested, arms folded, and wearing nothing but a pair of black boxer-briefs and a furious glare.

My gaze drops to the bed where Jake has laid out the black beanie used to cover my pale hair and the black leather gloves that kept my fingerprints from any surface I came in contact with.

Fuck. The sun is streaming in through the blinds, and I know it must be late morning already. Clearly I'd forgotten to set the morning alarm. A rookie mistake. And now I need to get past the gauntlet that is Jake and somehow get the file to Casey before he enacts his own plan to retrieve it.

My eyes flick up, meeting his. "Morning," I say coolly.

His jaw ticks. "Care to explain?"

Jake's car keys rest on top of the report file, and I know he's seen them. Not only had I performed a *break and enter* last night, I had also added *car theft* to my criminal repertoire. Explaining *that* will likely cause my untimely death. I pretend to consider his question for a moment. "Not really."

Jake pushes off from the wall and moves toward the bed, bringing him closer. "Well you're going to."

"No," I say, casually sliding across the mattress and away from Jake. "Not today. I have things to—"

Putting one knee on the bed, Jake leans across and grabs the back of my long-sleeved shirt in his fist. He yanks and I hear the distinct sound of a *riiipppppp.*

"My shirt," I gasp as I fly through the air and land on my back on the mattress with a hard bounce.

"I don't give a rat's ass about your shirt," he growls, climbing on the bed and straddling my body.

His hard thighs trap me in place, and his hands pin mine to the bed. Moving will likely end with a cracked rib.

Jake leans his face down until I can't look anywhere but in his eyes. "You can start with why you're dressed like a thieving little bandit."

"Because I stole your car."

"Why did you steal my car?"

"Because I couldn't get a cab."

I actually considered calling for a taxi, but then my movements would be on public record, easily placing me at the scene. I'd had to rule it out.

"Stop leading me in circles, Princess, and spit it out. What *did you do?*"

I huff deeply, letting my frustration out. Jake isn't going to just drop this. It leaves me with two choices: lie or be honest. I chose door number two, because while I sometimes keep things from Jake, he doesn't deserve outright deceit.

I spill out my early hours' adventure, rethinking my choice of honesty as he sits back on the bed, his fury a slow-building thunderstorm.

There's silence for a tense moment when I finish speaking.

"You committed a felony," he says in a soft voice. I'm not fooled by the tone. His anger is a barely leashed lion. "And you used my car to do it."

My lips press into a thin line. I hadn't thought that particular implication through, and now I'm angry at myself. "I'm sorry."

His expression narrows to one of vengeful retribution. "Oh, you'll be sorry."

"I will?"

"When I paddle your ass."

"Jake—"

"Shut it," he growls, his voice rising. "You broke into a detective's house. You stole her property. You—"

"Casey's property," I mutter.

"Don't interrupt me when I'm explaining your stupidity to you."

That gets my back up. "Stupidity? I parked down the street. I had that lock picked in three minutes." It was actually over five, but if there's ever a time for exaggeration ... "I was in and out of that house, *with the file*, in under eight minutes." It was really ten minutes, maybe a bit more. "I left that room exactly as I found it. *And I didn't get caught.*"

"Yes you did," Jake corrects. "By me."

"Rookie mistake," I mumble under my breath, because I seem to have made a few of those. Perhaps I still have a little left to learn.

Disappointment darkens his eyes. "Why didn't you tell me what you were going to do?"

"So you could stop me?"

Jake shakes his head, mirthless laughter escaping his lips. "If I've learned one thing, there's no stopping you from doing anything once you have a mind to do it. At the least, I would've gone with you."

"You would've ..." I trail off.

He holds out a hand, palm up. "Let's go."

I take it. "Go?"

"To deliver the file to Casey at the hospital," Jake explains, leading me off the bed. "The sooner he has it, the better right?"

My thoughts exactly, but it turns out that talking about delivering the file and actually doing it are two different things. Deciding not to waste time getting changed, we drive to the hospital, Jake's jaw grinding over the numerous times he has to adjust his seat to get it right.

When we arrive, Jake peels off toward the cafeteria to get coffee, and I go in the other direction, cradling the report—now placed inside an A4 sized yellow envelope—in my right arm.

"Excuse me," booms the voice of hellfire itself.

I pretend not to hear and quicken my pace along the corridor of Casey's ward. Houlihan is bearing down. The nurse runs her ward like a prison. Getting inside a patient's room involves triplicate forms, the third degree, and potentially a pack of cigarettes as a bribe, if I had the nerve to try. I don't. She'd probably crush them in her meaty fist.

"You there!" she booms, her voice closing in.

I begin to jog, turning to see where she's situated. My glance encounters no one. Turning back around, I find Houlihan standing right in front of me. I come to an abrupt halt before smacking into her.

"He's resting," she growls.

I wave the envelope, my evidence, and force a polite smile. "I just need to deliver this."

"This is not a mailroom. It's a hospital. Take your envelope and deliver it during visitation hours."

Okay, *now* she's beginning to piss me off. I tried nice, even when she came out swinging. All gloves are off now. "Step aside," I command, my eyes narrowing. "This matter is urgent."

"I don't care if your *matter* is from the Prime Minister himself. You can wait until visiting hours or I can call security."

"And visiting hours are when?"

Her lips purse. "Ten through to twelve and two 'til four."

I glance at my watch. The display shows *9:55am*. Is Houlihan kidding me? When I look back up, her squiggly eyebrows have snapped together and are focused on a man in scrubs entering her nurse's station. According to his tags and the stethoscope around his neck, he's clearly a doctor. Apparently even those lofty credentials aren't going to save him from breaching her domain.

"Goddammit," she mutters in her gravelly tone. "Don't move."

Houlihan marches toward the intruder and with her back turned, I grab the handle of the door she was guarding and bolt inside, forgetting my plan to slip the envelope underneath it. Hell, I forgot about the damn envelope itself after that altercation.

Casey is fully dressed and standing by his bed.

"Christ you were right, Casey," I mutter, rolling the tension from my neck. "Houlihan is hardcore."

Then my gaze takes in the entire private room. Jared and Travis are standing by the other side of the door, and here I am waving the evidence of my thievery in their faces. I tuck it quickly behind my back. It's not my smoothest move. I'm beginning to realise that stealing the file had been the easy part. Actually getting it to Casey is the part requiring finesse, and I'm failing miserably. It doesn't help that they always think the worst when it comes to me.

Casey narrows his eyes. "What's that?"

"What ... this?" I bring the envelope back out looking at it as though it miraculously just appeared in my hand.

"Yes. That."

"I'm not sure," I tell him, widening my eyes in an attempt to portray a baffled expression. "I found it on the floor outside your room just now."

"Jared," Casey says, not taking his gazing from mine. "Was that envelope on the floor outside when you walked in five minutes ago?"

I look everywhere but at any of them, knowing I'm about to get caught.

"No," Jared growls.

Tension crackles in the room.

"Well, fun chat," I tell them in a casual tone, knowing it's best to leave now rather than die for my efforts. I can't imagine there ever being a good time to deliver stolen goods, but here and now, with my brothers in attendance, is clearly the worst time in the history of the world. "But I've got shit to do."

I turn.

Jared bars the door.

"Out of my way," I bark, panic clawing its way up my throat.

Travis snatches the envelope from my hand and gives it to Casey. *Shit.* I turn back to Jared. "Move, asshead!" I boom.

But he doesn't budge. There's nothing I can do, so I stand back and watch hell break loose before my very eyes.

It starts with Casey checking the contents of the envelope. He flicks through the papers, his hands beginning to shake. "Mac," he breathes. "How did you …"

Travis eyeballs the report and visibly jerks. When Jared asks what it is and Casey tells him, they turn and look at me, all three taking in my uncharacteristic outfit with dawning comprehension.

What ensues is a lot of yelling, bulging veins, and sweeping arm gestures.

"I only did what you guys were going to do anyway," I say, using a cool tone in an attempt to diffuse the anger. It's a bad choice because it only fuels the escalating situation.

"After we finished her background check and knew what we were dealing with!" Casey roars then flings words at me like *"danger"* and *"putting your life on the line."*

My own rage builds. That report is a gift. It's supposed to *help* and a little appreciation won't go astray. Maybe even a little admiration at my expertise and aptitude for completing such a daring mission. "And what if Morgan destroyed it while you were all dithering around with background checks?"

"Then it would have been too damn bad!" Casey yells back, going nose to nose with me, his fury far exceeding mine. "What you did was stupid and dangerous and not worth risking your life!"

My expression softens, and I throw his words back in his face. "I happen to think you're worth it, Casey."

He sags like a whipped puppy.

I know then that I have him and that I'll live to see another day, at least until Jared and Travis start in. Before I can defend myself, Travis has my bicep in a painful grip and starts marching me out the door, saying, "We're going to have a conversation, Mackenzie 'Lone Wolf' Valentine, and by *conversation* I mean I'm going to talk and *you* are going to keep your piehole shut and *listen.*"

Jake is walking up the corridor when we emerge, takeout coffee cup in hand. I jerk free of my brother. "Enough, Trav."

"Enough?" His brows shoot up. "I haven't even started with you yet."

"And you're not going to," Jake says mildly, reaching my side.

"Jake—" he begins.

"Mac did what any of you would have done yourself had you known about it, so let her be, okay?"

Travis flares his nostrils. "But she's—"

"What? Your sister? Yeah, she is. And you should be proud she has the courage and loyalty to stand up for her friends and family the way she does. Would you rather she turn her back on them when they're in need?"

"I would rather she didn't break the law," Travis growls.

"So would I, but like she told me this morning, sometimes you have to do something bad in order to achieve something good, and I happen to agree with her." I stand watching their exchange. My heart warms from Jake's defence. He hands me the coffee and folds his arms. "Are you done now?" he asks my brother with narrowed eyes, appearing ready to take Travis out at the slightest provocation.

"This is not Command Central," barks a voice from our left.

We all turn. Houlihan is moving in on our huddle.

"Yeah we're done," Travis mutters quickly, already preparing to flee.

"Good," Jake mutters back just as quickly. "Then we should go."

"Now," I hiss, leaving them behind in my rush. Houlihan is a shark. Those who get left behind in deeper waters will get eaten first. I've already enacted a break and enter early this morning *and* survived two attempts on my life today, the first with Jake and then with Casey and my brothers. I'm not planning on a third.

Chapter Thirty-One

Mac

Weeks after Casey and Grace's accident, I find myself back at the Florence Bar, this time inside their private function room. I'm hosting a surprise retirement celebration for my father. It's due to kick off in fifteen minutes, but my mind is still on my two friends.

We received the news weeks ago that Grace has cancer. She was supposed to be undergoing treatment but instead she chose to be here with us, and with Henry, spending time with family. The news was a huge blow to all of us, a reminder that there are some things we can't protect those we love from, and that life can be utterly, sadistically cruel.

Henry is suffering. Their mother died from breast cancer, and now Grace has the same disease. She didn't want him to know. Her plan was to battle through on her own, but that's not how we work.

The news came at the same time Casey's brother, Kelly, came to light. Kelly is a member of the Sentinels biker gang, and the brother that Casey had feared dead for many, many years. It turns out Morgan is a member too, the very detective that had been giving Casey such a hard time. They ended up arresting her for attempted murder. She was the one causing trouble for the both of them all along. When Kelly found out her plan to remove Grace, he kept Grace safe, though he could have gone about it in a better way.

At least there were no casualties in his plan, apart from Grace giving Morgan a bloodied nose. Thoroughly justified. But now Casey has another battle on his hands, and it's one he can't fight with fists or guns. There's no weapon in the war against cancer.

My heart heavy, I walk to the bar to arrange a congratulatory scotch whiskey for Eli, having spied him making an early entrance to the party. My dad, Chief Inspector Valentine, stepped down a week ago leaving the safety of Sydney's population in the hands of Elijah Rossiter. Eli will be the youngest Chief Inspector our city has ever seen.

It makes him a big hairy deal in the policing world, and he smiles warmly as I take the drink and stride toward him in my gold Jimmy Choo's and a strapless dress that clings to every inch of skin.

"Inspector Rossiter," I say teasingly when I reach his side, holding out my right hand. His hair is slicked back, his tuxedo sleek, and his confident presence fills the room. "Congratulations."

"Ms. Mackenzie Valentine," Eli replies, his light blue eyes crinkling at the corners. He takes my hand and leans in, kissing my cheek. "Thank you for inviting me."

"You don't need to thank me," I say, handing him the glass. It's Glengoyne, aged seventy-five years apparently. It cost me my left tit, so I'm hoping he appreciates it. "You're practically family, Eli. And you know how Dad loves to talk business at these parties. You're the best at deflecting him."

"True," he replies ruefully and scans the party, noting the slow-filling room. "Am I early?"

"Of course not. Everyone else is simply late. As usual."

"Rude of them." His chuckle is slow, eyes lifting to mine as he takes a sip. Eli sighs deep with appreciation after swallowing and gives me a wink. "But then I wouldn't get you to myself if they weren't."

I dismiss his comment, used to Eli's teasing. "As host of the party, I'm afraid you won't have me for long."

"Well, I'm afraid I can't stay long either, but ..." he reaches inside the pocket of his perfectly cut jacket and pulls out a business card, offering it toward me between two fingers "...here's my new business card. I have a new private number. If you ever need anything, *anything at all*," he stresses, "use it. Okay?"

There's the brotherly attitude I know. I laugh as I look at the white card and turn it over in my fingers. It's thick and matte, the font in perfect, simple lettering. It suits him. "Sure. Next time I find myself in lockup and need bailing out, I'll call you."

His brow furrows in an expression of severity. "I don't want to hear about you doing anything that requires being arrested. If you do, I'll leave you in there until you learn your lesson."

Eli's tone is utterly serious. I cock my head. "You would?"

"You're a Valentine, Mackenzie. And the Valentines are held in high regard in this city, including you. And I know you would never do anything to besmirch the family name, especially not get arrested."

"Eli ..." I trail off, taken aback as I think of every reckless thing me and my brothers have done over the years. We've literally dragged the Valentine name through the mud so many times I'm pretty sure it's entombed there for all eternity.

Elijah's booming laugh fills the room.

"Oh my god!" I flick him on the arm with the business card in my hand. "Eli! For a minute I thought you were serious."

His grin disappears. "I am serious."

I laugh and shake my head. "You are not."

Mitch arrives through the back entry in his own tuxedo and catches my attention. His appearance is remarkable, though I'm sure he knows it. My eldest brother has a presence that commands the room and sharp eyes that stick you like a pin, but tonight they're dark and weary and his movements are sluggish. Mitch is tired from working overtime. I've hardly seen him in months. I point his way, knowing he could use his best friend right now. "Go and harass my brother. He's the one who deserves it, not me."

Eli gives me a casual salute with the hand that holds his scotch and turns to leave, saying, "Thanks for the drink."

"Wait." I grab his arm, halting him as an idea hits me.

His brows rise in question.

"I do need something." And it's a risk bringing it to the attention of the newly appointed Chief Inspector, but it's a risk I feel will pay off. I can trust Eli. I know it just as I know the sun will rise tomorrow, so I speak my mind, and the truth. "I have a case."

He blinks. "You have a case."

I nod firmly. Convincingly. "Yes. With Jamieson and Valentine Consulting."

This time his brows don't just rise, they shoot up so fast they almost fly off his face. Eli doesn't usually give much away, but it seems he can't contain the surprise this particular news has on him. "You're working for them now?"

"Unofficially. But you have to keep this between us for now, okay? I can trust you right?"

He huffs and rolls his eyes as if my question insults him. "Of course you can trust me." He leans in a little and I relax. Already, he understands my need for discretion. "Tell me about this case."

"It's drug related." Eli, having graduated alongside Mitch from Charles Sturt University, climbed the ranks of the narcotics division while my eldest brother busied himself with homicide. If anyone can help me with this case, it's Inspector Elijah Rossiter.

"Drug related, you say?" He looks at me closely, his interest piqued.

"Yes." I've managed to skim-read the file I lifted from the office. The contents include background information on four criminals and their potential ties to a high-threat drug syndicate. The request memorandum was simply to pad the file with further information for Operation Strike, a multi-pronged investigation that's working to tackle the effects of ICE in Australia.

Already, I'm in over my head. What kind of padding do they need? Is the firm simply required to hand over any and all information pertaining to the four criminals that they already have on file, or perform some kind of surveillance?

"What do they need?"

After a quick glance around to ensure privacy, I lower my voice. "Something to do with Operation Strike."

"Mac." Eli's jaw hardens. "That's a dangerous and extremely covert operation. I don't think—"

"Eli," I hiss as he downs a mouthful of expensive scotch. "I can handle dangerous. I just need some direction. And you said you'd help me with *anything at all*," I remind him.

I expect anger for putting him in this position, but instead he smiles tightly as though he knows arguing with me is useless. Which it is. "Okay. I'll help you. On one condition."

I'm so grateful at this point, I'm willing to offer him whatever he wants. "Anything."

"Lunch," he says. "It's been so long since we caught up with each other. I want to know what's going on with you. And there's something I want to talk to you about."

I nod. I can do lunch. Easy. "Lunch sounds perfect. I'll bring the file?"

"Please," he replies, then looks toward Mitch. Jared has since joined him and they're both deep in conversation as they walk away from the bar, drinks in hand. "Can I go now?"

"You can go," I say imperiously.

He grins and shakes his head, walking away.

I make my own way to the bar. After handling a few issues, I phone Travis when I notice he's yet to arrive. My other brother is late. Again. It's unacceptable. I place a call. He's driving and I'm placed on speaker while Quinn convinces me they're only five minutes away (which likely means they only just left). I end the call and return my phone to my clutch then tuck it on the bottom shelf behind the bar. I won't need it for the rest of the night.

When I straighten, Jake is behind the bar with me, appearing like a sexy magician. "You look beautiful," he tells me, inspecting me thoroughly.

"Thank you. You look..." my eyes run over his black collared shirt with rolled-up sleeves and black pants "...good enough to eat."

His lips curve. "Then what are you waiting for?"

Jake's question makes me pause. That's it. That's all it takes. One suggestive comment and I've lost my mind. But I'm the host. I can't just run off like we usually do for a random sex session.

You can! my vagina cries recklessly. *Don't leave me hanging here!*

I compromise because I find saying no impossible. "Give me an hour."

Jake

I give her the hour. Right down to the second. Then I have her arm in mine and I'm leading her out the back door. You have to be forceful and decisive when it comes to Mac. She responds to it, like I'm the sun and she's a flower unfurling beneath it. That analogy makes me sound like a dick, but it's how I feel. How *she* makes me feel.

The time for contemplating my next move is over. Now it's time to implement it. Grace and Casey's accident helped make my decision. Life is too short. And I'm a selfish bastard. Impatient too. The emotion burns hot enough that some days I fear I'll choke on it. If Mac needs time to heal, she can spend that time healing with me.

"Where are we going?" she asks as I rush her outside. She's trotting beside me in her high heels and slinky dress. Good. Her struggle to keep up will give her no time to think. "And where's the fire?"

"You'll have to wait and see," is my brief reply. I pull the car keys from my pocket and lead her to my Dodge Charger. "Get in," I command after unlocking the car and opening her door. She slides in, pulling the sleek material of her long dress around her ankles so it doesn't catch when I close the door behind her.

I walk around the car and hop in the driver's side. We leave the venue behind as I pull out into evening traffic. It's not until I turn down the street of her family home that she speaks. "Why are we going to my parents' house?"

"I told you to wait and see."

"I'm not a wait and see kind of person." She folds her arms. "I like to know where I'm going and who's going to be there and what we're doing," Mac says as I park in the driveway. "And why," she adds.

I turn off the ignition and look at her, my grin wry. Of course she does. That's my girl, and I wouldn't change her for anything. "Do you trust me?"

Her eyebrows pull inward, like I've presented her with a Rubik's cube. "I used to once. A long time ago," Mac says with darkened eyes. "I trusted you with my life."

I'm careful to keep my voice steady. "And now?"

"Jake, I ..." Mac's gaze drops to her lap as if it holds all the answers.

"Look at me," I demand.

Her eyes rise. We stare at each other, the space between us heavy. "I do," she says with some surprise. "I trust you."

Her declaration is all I need to hear. I get out of the car and walk around to open her door. Mac steps out, taking my hand. I shut the door and rather than lead her toward the house, I lead her down the street. We walk along the road heading toward Mort Bay Park by the harbour.

When I find the right spot, I stop, and she stops with me.

"The last time we stood here together," I begin.

"Was the day I asked you to stay." Mac's chin rises. "And yet you left anyway."

I breathe deep and take both her hands in mine. "Are you bitter?"

Of course she is. Mac's eyes hold pain and regret beneath the glow of the streetlight. They answer my question better than any words can.

"If I could go back and change it I would, but I can't," I say. "Neither of us can." The air gusting between us stills and makes the thumping of my heart feel louder and stronger. "Are your memories of that day really that bad?"

Her cheeks warm, and I know she's remembering our first kiss. Nothing had ever felt more awkward or beautiful. It was the start of a love affair so turbulent and wild, there are days where I'm not sure I'll survive it. But I don't care. I'll go down loving Mackenzie Valentine until the day I die.

"No, Jake, they're not bad. My memories of that day are bittersweet. I look back and see two young kids on a collision course, and I want to yell at them and tell them to … to …"

My chest tightens with anticipation. Mac is opening up her heart. It's rare and I find myself hanging on her words like each is a precious gem. "To what?"

"To never let go." Her breath catches and her eyes fill. "To stay in that moment forever because it's the most perfect one you will ever have."

"That's why we're here," I say with a galloping heart. I release her right hand and tug the small box from my pocket. With it clutched in my fist, I drop to one knee.

A harsh sob escapes Mac's chest and her hand quivers in mine. When I'm steady, I look up. Emotion is rich in her wide eyes.

"Because it's time we let go of the past and move forward together. We can create a new perfect moment, right here, where we made our first. You know I love you, Mac. You've always been mine. Does that make me a selfish bastard for wanting the world to know?" I fumble a little as I open the ring box. We're in the perfect spot because illumination from the streetlight sets the square-cut diamond beaming brighter than the sun. "Marry me, Princess."

She blinks and stares. Mac is speechless. It gives me the urge to whip out my phone and snap a photo for the future. I could show everyone the one time where Mac didn't have a witty comeback. But I don't because it will ruin the moment.

"Say yes," I instruct, squeezing her hand, "and I'll let you have the last word."

"I always get the last word anyway." Mac is trying for flippant, but she doesn't pull it off. Her voice is choked with too much emotion.

Mac

I want to say yes. More than my next breath. But I'm not ready. I'm not ready to create a new perfect moment only to sit back and watch us fall apart all over again. It destroyed me once. Next time it will put me in the ground. And there *will* be a next time. Of course there will be. I feel it deep in my bones. This is me and Jake we're talking about. The two of us were destined for disaster the moment I splattered spaghetti sauce down the front of his shirt and stomped up the stairs in a childish girly tantrum.

"Mac." Jake's voice cracks, and he squeezes my hand a second time.

I'm giving him nothing. It's unfair. It makes me feel like the bitch I'm touted to be.

"Please," he begs.

"Yes," I blurt out, because I'm hurting him and hurting him hurts me. "Yes."

Jake exhales a breath of relief. He rises to his feet and looks at me, his eyes alight. Then they drop to the task of pulling the ring from the box. He does it with trembling fingers, and the sight makes my heart squeeze. When it's free, he takes my ring finger and slides it on, his gaze on me and his grin boyish.

I love him. I love Jake Romero from the base of my toes to the very tips of my fingers. He deserves all of me, but I can't give it. And I hate myself for it.

The ring feels snug. I look down, spreading my fingers as I stare. The diamond is huge. I adore it. It rests there like a weapon. A primed fist with this baby on the end of it would cause more damage than Superman on steroids. But it's supposed to represent so much more. A future. Is that even possible for us?

"What do you think?"

My eyes shift from the ring to Jake. His expression is hopeful, and he's biting his bottom lip. "I think it's incredibly beautiful."

His boyish grin morphs into a blinding laugh. He hugs me and picks me up swirling me around in his big, powerful arms. Jake's enthusiasm is infectious. I've never seen him happier and it lifts my soul. An enormous smile overtakes my face.

"I want to make a toast!" he shouts, loud enough for anyone in the nearby houses to hear.

"Jake!" I shake my head, looking down on him as he holds me up with no apparent effort. "We have no champagne."

His expression sobers and his eyes deepen into pools of dark whiskey. "To the future Mrs. Romero. She burns hotter than the sun and fights harder than a warrior in battle, and I'm the lucky man that gets to wake beside her every morning until the day I die."

Oh god. "Jake," I whisper and cup his cheeks in my hands, the ring feeling foreign and cumbersome on my finger, and yet so very, very real. "I …" Fuck. Why is this so *hard*? "You know I'm a grouch in the mornings."

Jake chuckles and touches his nose to mine. "I love a woman who can admit her faults."

Chapter Thirty-Two

Mac

We return to the party. Jake once again opens my car door and I slide out. "How are we going to explain the giant rock on my finger?" I ask, re-settling the skirt of my dress so it doesn't catch in my heels. The fabric remains unscathed. It's unusual, but we were careful this time. For some unfathomable reason, Jake decided I was fragile glass and his touch was slow and whisper soft. It was something new for us, and I found it drove me mad in the most delicious of ways. The added plus was sneaking in to my parents' house and making use of my old room.

"Leave it to me," Jake says smoothly and links his arm with mine.

"I don't think so." We stride toward the back entrance. "You'll bungle it."

He snorts. "Hardly."

I fiddle with the ring, looking down at it. "Perhaps I should take it off," I say, expecting an immediate protest. "It might be easier to explain tomorrow."

"Now is the absolute best time to explain. Everyone is drunk."

Jake has a point, but there's been no time to prepare. There's a lot of back story involved. We need to work out what to share and what remains better left unsaid. Perhaps we should tell them next weekend. We can plan a barbecue and get everyone drunk all over again. "How about—"

"You're right," Jake says in a rush. "Take the ring off. Now." His voice is sharp and low as he pulls us both to a halt.

I stumble. Jake doesn't help right me. He basically shoves me away until I'm situated half behind him. "What the ..." I trail off, looking up. Elijah Rossiter and another man are walking toward the parking lot. It puts them directly in our path. It seems Eli stayed longer at the party than he was expecting to. It's highly possible my father cornered him with scotch whiskey and World News conversation.

"Son of a bitch," Jake mutters, standing tense in front of me as he stares at them. "Take it off," he hisses through gritted teeth.

"Have you lost your mind?" My brows snap together. I'm thoroughly confused. "Why? And put it where? Up my butthole?"

"Give it to me. Discreetly. This is one of those times you need to trust me. Please."

I do as he asks, knowing he better explain this later. I feel oddly bereft as I slide it from my finger, like I'm a cop on suspension handing in my piece.

Jake takes the bit of jewellery and slides it in his pocket imperceptibly. "Let's go," he commands and starts for the door, hands in his pockets and head down. He's moving fast. I trot a little behind him to keep up.

"Fuck," Jake mutters. Eli has spotted us. "He saw us."

"So what if he did?" I say to his back as he keeps up his hurried pace. "What is *with* you, Jake Romero?"

Eli appears indecisive until the man beside him says something that leaves him oddly pale. Then they start toward us, leaving no option but to stop or appear rude. Jake's expression is hard, yet he gives nothing away. He just stands there, stiff as a board, blocking me from both of them.

"A lovely party," Eli says as I step around Jake and smile at my brother's best friend. "I'm sorry I have to leave."

"Thanks for coming."

"Anytime," he says in a soft tone. "You know that."

Jake stiffens further.

"This is my little brother, Adam Rossiter," he tells us, nodding to the man beside him, and I jolt with surprise. Eli has a brother? A *not so little* one. Adam has a tattooed neck, bulky shoulders, and a buzzed head. He looks like a thug. Not a sexy one like Jake. More like a scary one that would slit your throat in the night for a measly fifty dollars. His eyes aren't just cold. They're *cold*. Like ice. "But we just call him Ross."

Ross makes no move to shake either of our hands. He simply stares at the both of us in turn, not speaking. Oddly enough, Jake doesn't say a word either. The tension feels thicker than my homemade pasta, which no one even pretends to eat.

"Ross, this is Mackenzie Valentine and Jake Romero, the drummer in Jamieson. And if you haven't heard of Jamieson, then you must be living under a rock. They're probably the hottest band in the country right now."

Eli's jovial tone falls flat under the unexpected tension. I repress an instinctive need to roll my shoulders and instead I give Eli's *little* brother a polite smile. "Well, it's nice to meet you, Ross."

His response is silence.

The tension heightens to impossible levels.

"Well, we should get back inside."

"Of course," Eli replies. "I'll see you soon," he says to me, referring to our lunch plans.

The comment doesn't go unnoticed. Jake's eyes narrow. We turn from them and resume our path to the back entrance of the bar. Rather than taking my arm like he usually would, Jake pushes me ahead of him. I stumble. Again. "What is *wrong* with you?" I hiss as we walk away.

Jake

Everything. Everything is wrong with me. My entire body pulses with dread. Adam Rossiter is Ross. How is it possible that this notorious gang leader is the son of the Deputy Commissioner *and* Eli's brother? Do the Valentines know? Because judging from Eli's body language, he wasn't happy to see us stumble across them.

Ross knows my true identity now. I'm not just 'Jonah' anymore, the alias I used years ago in Melbourne. He knows where to find me. And the worst? In one single moment of bad timing, he knows the person I love above all others.

I turn my head, looking behind me as we reach the back door and Mac steps inside. Ross is watching us. He holds up two fingers and a thumb, mimicking a gun. He aims it at Mac, and with a slow grin, he pulls the trigger.

My glare is hard and cold, but my insides are screaming with fear. Ross isn't an honourable man. He fights dirty. And he hoards grudges like a squirrel hoards nuts. The only people who leave his gang are the dead kind and here I am, alive and breathing, and he hates it. I'm a marked man.

I turn back. Waves of tension roll through me as I step inside behind Mac and shut the door. I need to find Mitch and I need to find him *right now.*

Mac stops me in the coatroom with a hand to the chest. "What was that?"

I open my mouth and snap it closed. *Jesus Christ.* I want to tell her. There have already been enough secrets kept between us, but I can't. She'll get herself caught right in the thick of it. And the thought of Ross getting his hands on her is unthinkable. It chills my blood. "It was nothing. I initially thought Adam Rossiter was someone I used to know. Someone who's not a good person."

Her nostrils flare and her tone is an accusation. "The Rossiters are close friends of the family," she hisses. I'd bet all my earnings on the fact that Adam Rossiter is the black sheep she's never met. "They're the good kind of people. And you were rude."

"You're right. I was," I concede. "I'm sorry."

Mac presses her lips together, annoyed. She was gearing up for an argument and my hasty apology has shut her down.

"Go find Evie and Quinn, Princess. They're probably looking for you to do the toasts by now."

She nods and moves away. "Wait," I call. Mac stops and turns her head. Green eyes search mine. God, she's so precious, not at all invincible like she believes herself to be. She joked to me once when she was young about being Teflon. I believed it then and I believe it now, but Teflon only covers the surface. Beneath the protective layers, Mac is just as vulnerable as the rest of us. I know that better than anyone. "Don't leave the party without me, okay?"

Mac cocks her head but she doesn't argue. We never leave together. But that was before Ross. Everything is different now. "Okay."

"Good." I make my way through low murmuring guests toward Mitch and Henry. Mac's brother has his hand on Henry's shoulder, and he's handing him a full glass of scotch. "What's happened?" I ask, reaching the two.

Mitch looks up. "Henry and Casey had an altercation."

"And I'm going to kick his ass," snarls my normally easy-going best friend. I don't think he'll ever come to grips with the fact that Casey is seeing his little sister.

"What did he do?"

"Breathed," Henry fumes.

"That's unfortunate," I sympathise, "but we have a bigger situation to deal with right now than a little tiff."

Henry is too caught up in his anger to heed my warning but my comment catches Mitch's attention. "What?" he asks, eyes wary.

Before answering his question, I allow myself a brief moment to seek Mac in the crowd. My shoulders relax when I find her deep in talk with friends, though her expression is etched with concern. Something has her troubled. I make a note to ask her about it later before I focus back on Mitch. "We just encountered Ross in the parking lot. Adam Rossiter," I stress. "He was there with Eli. His older brother," I further clarify for Henry's sake.

"Who's *we*?" Mitch asks, seemingly unsurprised at my announcement.

It leads me to the conclusion that he's long since known the familial connection. Frankly, how could he not considering he and Eli are close friends? But *thanks for sharing that information, mate.* My arms fold in a tense knot. "Mac and me."

"Who's Ross?" Henry asks, joining the conversation.

"The leader of the King Street Boys," I remind him. Henry knows of my past. He always has. When I met him at university, I needed a friend. I took a risk by opening up to Henry. He's kept my past private, but I never included Mac in that history. It was too painful, and then time passed and it got easier not to mention her at all.

"Oh shit," he mumbles.

Mitch rubs his jaw, his response even less helpful. "I heard he was in town."

"You heard?" I growl and blink slowly, trying to get a hold on my rising temper. "You fucking *heard*?"

"Relax." He places a hand on my shoulder. The placating gesture makes me want to punch him in the face. "He can't touch you."

A grunt of frustration leaves my throat. "You never told me he was Adam Rossiter, son of the Deputy Commissioner and Elijah's goddamn brother."

"There was never any need," he says in a low voice, his eyes skimming the party to check who's in hearing distance. "Let's take this conversation to the bar."

"Yes," I say through gritted teeth. "Let's."

We weave through clusters of guests and reach the bar. Henry trails behind us. Vince, the barman, takes our drink order, and I waste no time picking up where we left off. "So? Care to tell me why I've been kept in the dark?"

"It wasn't that we kept you in the dark," he says. I listen with one ear as I seek out Mac again. She's standing with her father now. He has an indulgent smile on his face as he chats with her. Mac is clearly not feeling the conversation. Her lips are pinched in an irritated line. "The Rossiters are an important family in Sydney," Mitch continues, "but Mrs. Rossiter, Leanne, is his second wife. The first lives in Melbourne. They divorced at least twenty years ago, from what I know. Apparently she returned there to be close to her family and took Adam, who was only six at the time, with her."

"What about Elijah?" I ask, my gaze returning to Mitch. My shoulders are tense as I focus on the story they should have told me years ago.

"There's a five year age gap between the brothers. He stayed behind to attend the Academy. They aren't close. They never have been, for obvious reasons." Vince sets our drinks on the bar. Mitch twists to collect them and hands a schooner of beer each to Henry and me before taking one for himself. He sips it and frowns. "You say they were in the parking lot together?"

"Yes," I confirm.

"What were you and Mac doing out there in the first place?" Henry chimes in, standing there slightly smug with his beer in hand.

Really, asshole, my eyes convey in a singular glare. *This is the topic you wish to address right now?*

He shrugs as if hearing me.

"None of your damn business."

They both smirk and it riles me further. We're in the middle of a volatile situation here and it seems I'm the only one taking it seriously.

"Now is probably a good time for you to share how you got me out of the gang, Mitch." I never pushed the issue before when I should have. I was just grateful being free to live my life. And when you have a past like mine, putting it behind you is the smartest course of action. Unless said past returns to bite you in the ass.

"It's sensitive information, Romero."

My voice is tight. "Don't make me strangle you right here in this bar."

His lips press together. "Maybe tomorrow—"

"Now."

"Romero, I think—"

"Now."

Mitch clears his lungs in a long, audible whoosh. He knows I'm not going to let this go. "Can we trust you with it?"

My mouth curls in a sneer.

Mitch and looks pointedly at Henry.

"Henry stays," I tell him.

"Okay." He nods slowly. "The Rossiters come from a long line of wealth and a long line of gambling. Their bloodline includes an extensive history of throwing their money away. Alan, the grandson of George Adam Rossiter III, was the only brother of four that went to college rather than indulge in the playboy life style like the rest. So in his will, George gave Alan control of the entire Rossiter estate. Worried about his own sons following the same legacy, Alan subsequently changed the inheritance for Elijah and Adam. Rather than receiving a huge sum when they turn twenty-one like their predecessors, he changed it to thirty-three. Elijah comes into his funds in just three months. Adam has another five years."

"And what does any of that have to do with getting me out?" I ask as Mitch finishes the rest of his beer.

"Everything," he says, setting his empty glass on the bar behind us. "Alan and my father went through the Academy together. They used to be partners in the Intelligence Division. But during an investigation into the missing daughter of the Mayor's cousin, they went out to question a lead and got caught in gunfire. Dad pushed Alan behind their car just before bullets rained down in the street. He took the hit instead and saved Alan's life. Alan always said he owed him ever since. He kept on at Dad to cash in his marker. It was a running joke between the two. Alan kept trying to find ways to give him money that he would never accept. Dad kept calling him a pain in his ass, saying he should've let *him* take the hit so he didn't have to put up with his sorry ass."

"Everything okay here?"

We all jolt at the booming voice. Caught up in the tale, the three of us didn't notice Steve Valentine himself walk over to our huddle. He signals to the barman and calls for a whiskey.

"Everything's fine," Mitch assures him.

Except it's a lie—one in a long line of many—and I'm tired of it. "Everything is not fine."

"Oh?" He looks at me, his brow arching and tension gathering in his big frame. It fills him until his entire body appears to increase in size. "Care to explain?"

"Mitch was doing just that. He was telling us the history of the Rossiters and how you saved Alan's life."

"Was he now?" Steve takes his drink from the barman, rumbling a thank you before turning hard eyes on his son. "And why would he do that?"

Mitch lets out a huff. "Because Jake just encountered Adam Rossiter in the parking lot."

Of course Steve knows of my involvement in the King Street Boys. Knowing the connection between him and the Rossiters, Mitch would have sought his counsel on the matter of my extraction. Not that Steve ever mentioned it, or even alluded to his knowledge. I've no doubt it's why he always looks at me as if I don't measure up to his high standards.

"That punk Ross is lurking around the party?" he asks.

"Apparently," Mitch replies. "So we thought it an appropriate time to explain some history."

"*We?*" I say, my voice loaded with sarcasm.

Steve ignores the friction in the way only a father of four dominant children can. "Adam Rossiter won't touch you," he tells me, his tone rich with authority and assurance.

Not if I have anything to do with it, but the image of Ross pointing a mock gun at Mac is in the forefront of my mind and it gives me chills. "It's not me I'm worried about."

Steve's gaze narrows in question. "Who *are* you worried about?"

"Mac."

"Why are you worried about him touching Mac?" His eyes seek his daughter across the room at the same time mine do. She's by the door of the kitchen now, talking with the staff. "Ross lives in Melbourne. Has done for most of his life. He likely has no idea who she even is."

I clear my throat, a flush heating the line of my cheekbones. Henry fidgets on the other side of me. "Can we talk in private, sir?"

The frown on his face deepens but he nods. We leave Mitch and Henry and move off to a quiet corner of the function room.

"Say what you need to say, Romero," he instructs and takes a sip of his whiskey.

"I'm worried about Mac because he saw us together in the parking lot."

Steve's eyes darken a fraction because it's obvious why we were in the parking lot together. Surely my relationship with his daughter is the worst kept secret in the history of the world.

"I see," he mutters.

He does. And the problem with him seeing is that our relationship has never been rightly addressed. I've always felt uncomfortable talking with Steve, knowing there's been no verbal acknowledgement of said relationship. I'm not sure he knows how much Mac means to me, but it's time he does. Right now seems a good a time as any to man up and clear the air.

"I'm sure you do," I reply. "I know I'm not the son-in-law you want for your little girl." My hands clench with nerves. Having Steve's hardened gaze directed on you is not easy to bear, but I press on. "I'm not a gentleman. I'm not refined. My choice of career is not distinguished or noble and my past is something I'm not proud of. My edges are rough, my tattoos are visible, and my language is colourful. I'm a drummer in a band, granted it's a successful one, but it's still a *band*. Our lifestyle is unstable. We're only as good as our last hit, and everything we've worked for could topple at any moment. I'm not good enough. You know that. I know that."

"Tell me something I don't know," he says in a prickly tone.

Shit. I'm an idiot. Rule number one in a relationship: never point out your faults to the father of the girl you love. I'm botching this up worse than a lost beat in an instrumental. "Okay, I will." My eyes find Mac for the millionth time that night. She's talking with Quinn now and though it appears she's paying attention to what her assistant manager is saying, her gaze is on us, watchful and inquisitive. "I'm a good person. I'm loyal. I have manners and respect. I'll do everything I can to make Mac happy, and I'll protect her with my own life. I love your daughter, sir. I always have." I pause before adding the final nail in my coffin. "And I asked her to marry me."

Steve's lips press in a thin line but his expression is resigned, as if he expected this all along. "And her response?"

"She said yes."

Silence reigns for a long moment. I grit my teeth, but I don't dare break it. I barely draw a breath if I'm honest. I've just laid it all out for him. God knows what he's thinking. Likely that he wants to put a bullet in me. Preferably at close range. If I had a daughter, it's what I'd be doing. It's to his credit that he's not reaching for a gun right now.

"It seems to me," he eventually begins, "that there's something *you* should probably know."

My shoulders draw tight, bracing. "And that is?"

"Mitch explained to you that Alan owes me a favour?"

I nod. "Yes."

"I called it in, son. For you."

Emotion blasts through me as if a bomb exploded in my chest. For a moment I can't see, I can only feel, and it's too much. It's the first time he's ever called me *son*. I've always just been Romero to him, the annoying young kid who broke his daughter's arm and stole her away. Instead of kicking me to the kerb, he's taken this valuable favour, a marker from the Deputy Commissioner—one of the most influential, powerful men in the State—that he's held on to for *years,* as if waiting for the moment where it's utterly necessary, important beyond all reason, to cash it in, *and he cashed it in on me.* "Sir," I choke out.

His voice is gruff. "Call me Steve."

"Thank you."

"I met your father once or twice, you know."

I startle with surprise. "You did?"

"What happened to him was a shit thing to happen, but he's still a good man, and I see glimpses of him in you. I know you did all the wrong things as a kid, but you were exactly that. A kid. One making adult decisions. They might have been bad ones, but you made them for all the right reasons. Since then you've been smart enough to ask for help. Smart enough to choose a better path. That shows strength of character and determination. It shows you're a man who does whatever he has to in order to take care of those he loves. You did what you had to do, Jake. Your father is lucky to have you." Steve takes my shoulder and gives it a squeeze. "And so are we."

I'm lost for words. I never realised how much his approval meant to me until now. It feels tangible, as if I'm literally holding it in both hands. Steve was always just there in the background, a hurdle I never quite figured out how to go over or under, or get around. Turns out I managed to go right through the middle. *Huh.* "That means a lot to hear, sir."

"Steve," he barks, letting go of my shoulder.

I nod and correct myself. "Steve."

"So tell me, if my daughter said yes..." a curious glint lights his eyes "...why is she not wearing your ring?"

"I made her take it off in the parking lot."

"Why?"

"That's the thing, Steve," I say, feeling odd using the familiar term. He's always been a *sir* to me. For years. "We ran into Adam Rossiter outside. I didn't want him to see the ring and put two and two together, so I've taken it back for now. But it seems he put two and two together anyway." I give him a rundown of our conversation outside (or lack thereof) and mention Ross pointing an imaginary gun at Mac before we re-joined the party indoors. "How are you so sure he won't touch either of us?"

"The only power Alan holds over that boy is his trust fund. He told Ross he would revoke the inheritance if you weren't left to walk free. It was the only course of action open to us and not an idle threat by Alan. Ross took him seriously, but there's something deeply evil in that child. He doesn't care who he hurts to get what he wants. And if he can't get at you ..." Steve breaks off, his face the colour of snow. "I need to talk to Alan."

Chapter Thirty-Three

Jake

Steam fills the bathroom as I check the water temperature in the shower. It's just short of blistering, which is perfect. I step inside and turn, holding out my hand. Mac takes it, letting me lead her. I pull her close until her naked chest is pressed to mine.

We have the duplex to ourselves, and we're taking advantage. My arms slide around Mac's silky skin. She relaxes into me and buries her head in my neck as the spray of water scalds our skin red. Lust spreads hot inside me, but I ignore it. We're both exhausted. I just want to hold Mac close and revel in this quiet moment.

It's been twenty-four hours since the party, but it feels like a lifetime when you're busy worrying every single minute of it. I'm still waiting to hear back from Steve. My body has been so tight with tension over the whole situation that I've been suffering a dull headache since I woke this morning. And Henry called earlier. He's spending time with Grace at the loft. His father arrived from Melbourne, and they're having a quiet family gathering tonight.

I absently stroke Mac's hair, my heart hurting for Grace, Henry, and Casey. They're my family. And it's so hard to know what to do or say. Sorry can be such a trite word. It doesn't convey the depth of emotion you're feeling as you watch the lives of those you love completely unravel.

Mac sighs. She's so quiet. "Are you okay?" I ask, my voice husky.

"I'm just tired," she mumbles into my neck. "So tired. I want to stand under this hot water with you for an eternity."

My lips kiss a soothing path along her brow. "Whatever you want, Princess."

Her lids flutter against my skin, soft as a butterfly. I like her this way. Her trust in me right now is strong, vital, and it tugs at my chest. If I've gained anything from our tumultuous past, it's the knowledge that this trust is fundamental to our future. We won't survive without it, but I can't explain about Ross.

I don't even want to think about him right now. I push all the worry to the back of my mind, though I know it will resurface later tonight leaving me sleepless for hours. Taking Mac's shoulders, I turn her so that her back faces me. Right now is just for us.

I pick up the soap. The suds are thick and creamy as I lather over her skin. I set the bar aside and massage her shoulders with firm hands, digging deep in the tense knots. She moans with pleasure, her head tipping back.

My eyes take in her beauty with wonder. That she agreed to marry me still hasn't sunk in. "Will you take my name?" I ask at random, because it rolls through my head. Mackenzie Romero. It doesn't have the same rolling lilt as Valentine does, but it gives me a sense of satisfaction. A sense of belonging. Of finding home. In her.

A furrow forms in her brow. "I haven't thought about it."

Disappointment wells. I push it aside. I proposed only yesterday. Mac needs time for it to sink in too. Time to think about the smaller details.

"Do you want me to?" she asks.

"Of course I want you to."

My hands fall away as Mac turns, and the shower beats down washing the thick suds away. "You don't think it's a little archaic?"

"Seriously?" I swipe drops of water from my face. "No. It's not archaic. It's a tradition that binds us, and our kids, as a family unit."

Mac steps back beneath the spray and the sudden distance feels more emotional than physical, as if a wall of hesitation has erected between us.

"I'm not going to force it on you, Mac. If you don't want to take my name, you don't have to."

"It's not that I don't want to," she protests. "It would just feel ... I don't know. I've always been a Valentine and I never imagined that changing. Do we have to decide now?" she asks, her chest rising and falling in agitation. "It's not like we're getting married tomorrow."

It's my first inkling that marriage is something she feels uneasy about, and my stomach drops. Did she say yes out of obligation? I want to ask and yet I supress the words. I'm a coward. I don't want to hear she's changed her mind, but I don't have to hear it when I'm beginning to sense it. Once again, our future feels hazy when just moments ago it was clearer than the green of her eyes.

"You're right," I say, reaching across to turn off the taps as hurt thumps deep beneath my ribcage. The bathroom settles into silence, save for the residual drips from the showerhead. "It's not like we're getting married tomorrow."

If at all ...

I step out and grab a fluffy white towel, handing it to Mac. She clutches it to her chest, watching me with tired eyes as water drips from her hair. "Are you okay?"

No. I'm not okay. My insides are bruised as if I've taken a punch to the gut. I want to stomp off and sulk, but I can't seem to tear myself from her side. Her hold over me is so strong the entire world could implode and it still won't break.

"I'm okay," I say, because above all else, I care most about what she wants. About her happiness. And I care about the limited time we have together. I don't want to ruin it with another in a long line of endless fights. "Come here."

Mac steps out onto the bathmat, her eyes shuttering, but not before I see the relief. That they shuttered at all just about kills me.

I take the towel she's clutching to her chest. She stands still as I use it to dry her off, letting me take care of her. "What do you want to do?" I ask, rubbing at her hair. She'd let it grow for a while but now it's back to its short, choppy style just above her shoulders. I love it this way. It's sexy. Sassy. It suits her perfectly.

"How about a movie?" Mac suggests. "I can make popcorn?"

"With butter?" I ask as she steals the towel from my hands.

"Uh huh," she murmurs, dabbing drops of water from my chest. Her eyes glaze a little, like they always do when she stares at it. I enjoy knowing my body gets her hot. A single glance and the rise in her blood pressure is entirely visible. But only to me. The crest of her cheekbones flush the palest of pinks. It gets my cock stirring eagerly. I flex a little and get treated to the corners of her lips tipping upward. "And a drizzle of golden syrup."

Mac knows my favourite.

An hour later we're settled on the couch, our bellies full. Mac is wearing a thin cotton tee shirt and panties. The most I bother with is a pair of boxer briefs, the colour a deep red.

I'm laid out on my back. Mac rests on top of me, but further down. The side of her face is pressed to my naked abdomen, her tits are squashed against my hips, and her fingertips flutter along my thighs. They trail upward, tickling lightly, absentmindedly, until I feel them tug a little at the red cotton. "I like these," she murmurs, her eyes on the television. We're watching a Dwayne Johnson action movie. Mac was agreeable because she thinks he's hot. Lucky for me she has a thing for the big, bulky dudes.

"That's because you bought them for me."

"I knew they'd be perfect on you. Red is your colour. It looks nice against all this tanned, tattooed skin," she says, her palm skimming up and over my abs. They contract slightly at the feathered touch. "Mmm."

Her touch lowers, leaving a trail of warmth in her wake. I snag her wrist before she reaches my rapidly hardening dick. "Uh uh," I rebuke, setting her hand to the side, though it pains me to do so. "Movie."

Mac huffs and my chuckle is deep, making her head wobble where it rests against my stomach.

My gaze returns to the screen of the television, but a scant five minutes later the flutter of her fingertips travel along my hip. Lust tingles down my spine.

"Mmm," she moans huskily when my cock jerks against her breastbone.

"What are you up to, hmm?"

"Nothing." Mac tilts her head and presses a kiss to my heated skin. "Nothing at all." Her tongue snakes out with a slow lick and a shiver racks my body. "Watch the movie, Romero," she orders.

Mac slithers downward. Her tongue trails a delicious path until it reaches the edge of my underwear. Then she hovers her mouth above my covered cock for a long moment. Her breath is light through the thin fabric, yet my cock feels it and gives another almighty jerk, knowing how close it is to receiving pleasure.

I grasp her chin with my thumb and forefinger, my grip harsh as I lift her head. Mac's green eyes are dark when they meet mine. "Somebody's hungry," I say, my voice gruff because having her like this, submissive and at groin level, steals my breath. "You want to suck it, Princess? You want it in your mouth? Or do you want it in your pussy?"

Mac licks her lips. "Jake ..."

"Tell me," I say, giving up all pretence of watching the movie. "What do you want?"

"Both," she croaks, her fingers tightening against my skin. I feel their pull, their need to touch, all the way down to my toes. "I want both."

My hand releases her chin in unspoken permission.

Free to do as she pleases, Mac tugs my underwear down. My hard dick surges upward, pulsing heavily. Without wasting a single second, her hot, wet mouth closes over the head. I watch as she slides down and sucks upward and my head tips back against the arm of the sofa. A hoarse groan breaks free of my throat.

Just like that I'm ready to come. My cock surges further inside the wet heat, desperate for more. I fist my hands at my side to stop them yanking on her hair to shove her mouth further down.

I let myself surrender to her mouth and tongue for an entire minute. Then I sit forward and grasp underneath her armpits, pulling her off and dragging her upward. Anymore and I'll shoot through the roof.

"I'm not finished," Mac snaps before my lips cover hers and smother her complaint as she straddles my hips.

She sinks into my body with a moan of surrender. The sound sets me on fire. My blood burns as I grab her thighs. My fingers dig into flesh as I stand from the couch and lift her with me.

I take the stairs one at a time as Mac kisses me, her lips soft, wet, and relentless. We reach her room and I toss her gently on the bed. She bounces backward, her breath hitching when I reach for her panties and inch them slowly down before tossing them behind me.

Leading with my left knee, I climb on the bed between her legs and spread them as I move upward. My calloused palms glide along her skin until I reach the crease of her thighs.

My finger skims along the golden skin just above her right hipbone. "You need a tattoo," I say, circling the area. "Right here."

"Oh?" Her body quivers when I lean down and lick my tongue flat across the spot. "What should I get?"

I bite down on my bottom lip, doing a bad job of halting the possessive grin. "Property of Jake Romero."

Mac gasps but her eyes light up with laughter. She rips the pillow out from behind her with a giggle and whacks me in the face with it. It's the equivalent of getting punched by a butterfly. "I'm not your possession!"

I laugh and cup her pussy with my palm. "Maybe not, but this is."

She tosses the pillow to the side and grabs for my cock where it still pokes out above my underwear. She holds it like a handle. "Then that makes this mine. Perhaps you should be getting a tattoo that says Property of Mackenzie Valentine."

I grin. "Gladly. He's proud to be all yours."

"Oh *he* is, is he?" My dick is still hard as stone, and she gives it a good squeeze. "And how do you know that? He's likely proud to be anyone's."

"Shhh," I whisper, putting a finger to my lips. "He has tender feelings, Princess. He'll be hurt to hear you think him so fickle."

Mac shakes her head, lets me go, and falls back on the bed with a giggle. "You're a total nut, Romero."

I grab both her knees before she can blink, lifting them up and spreading them wide. Holding them apart, I dip my head to where her pussy gleams pink and lick it in one long stroke. She hisses sharply and my eyes find hers, flashing with humour and lust. "But I'm your nut, Mackenzie Valentine."

"Yes," she agrees, breathless, her eyes rolling back when I find her clit and suck with relentless enthusiasm. "Mine."

Freeing my hands from her knees, I stroke my cock and ease the violent ache as I fuck her with my tongue and fingers.

"Please," Mac begs, her voice reedy and thin. I love hearing her lose control with me the way she does with no one else. She thinks I'm teasing, but if she came home with that tattoo I'd probably fuck her until my dick chafed raw and then blow my load all over the inked words. I can be a possessive, sordid bastard when I want to be.

"Because you asked so nicely," I answer, rising up and removing my boxer briefs before tossing them to the floor. I lift her hips and shift forward. Aligning my cock, I sink inside with one smooth thrust. Wet heat is a vice that sets my every nerve on fire.

"Hard and fast," she commands, so I rock against her with a painful, leisurely pace instead.

"Asshead." Mac's curse is muttered and slightly breathless, and it makes me laugh.

"If I told you to slow down, you'd probably go faster than a rabbit, wouldn't you?"

"Stop complaining," I say as I pull almost all the way out and punch back in with a hard thrust. She gasps with pleasure. "You like it any way I give it to you."

"What makes you think that?"

"Because you're always wet for me. All I have to do is look at you and you start dripping," I goad, increasing my pace.

"I do not!"

"You can protest all you like, Princess, but your body betrays you."

"You're so full of it."

I bury my head in her sweet-smelling neck, full on thrusting now and laughing at the same time. "Au contraire, my dear. It seems you're the one full of it right now."

"Oh good lord!" Mac snorts and then moans. "You're determined to have the last word tonight, aren't you?"

"Yes." I lift my head and look down into her eyes. "And if you have any sense, you'll let me," I say, slowing the drive of my hips. "Otherwise, I won't let you come."

"In that case." She cups my face in the warmth of her palms. "You're domineering and loyal and incredibly sexy, and I love you, Jake Romero."

My hips still completely. Her words soak deep beneath the layers of my skin until they reach my bruised heart. I lift a hand, brushing a wayward tendril of hair from her brow in a soft, gentle gesture. "I love you too."

There's your last word, her gleaming eyes say silently.

Ah hell. I surge forward, unable to play any longer. My thrusts become hard and fast, setting a frenetic pace, one she matches. Then the image of that mock gun pointed right at her flits through my head, and I falter.

The effort of suppressing the Ross situation all night has made my anxiety build, and now it's broken free from the restraints and surges through my head in a flood. I want to kill Ross for his sinister gesture. I want to hunt him down and tear each limb from his body until nothing remains but pieces. He wants to destroy what I love, a punishment, before he destroys me too. I can't live with this threat hanging over us. Ross hasn't let my exodus go like I'd hoped. He's held on to it all these years, letting it build into a need for retribution.

"Jake?"

I lift my head. The question in Mac's eyes makes me realise I've stopped completely. And worse, started going soft, even though she feels perfect.

Mac trails her hands down my back and grips my ass with needy fingers as she wriggles her hips.

"I'm sorry," I say around the lump in my throat, my insides heavy.

"What's going on?"

"Just stress," I mutter, grinding my hips, trying to recreate the easy pleasure of just moments ago. This is a first. My body is failing me and my stomach clenches with the frustration of it. I bite back a filthy curse.

"The tour?"

We leave for Spain in a week—the first leg of an international tour headlining for Sins of Descent, one of the biggest bands in the world. Mac has been in the throes of planning every detail for weeks. We'll be gone for weeks. I'm looking forward to it. Getting her out of the country. The timing of this tour couldn't be more opportune.

"I guess." Sweat breaks out across my shoulders. Her tight heat feels incredible, yet my erection is gone. Completely. "Christ," I mumble. I lift my body from hers and pull out with a jagged breath.

"Jake, it's okay," Mac soothes, seeing my aggravation.

"It's not." Drawing back, I sit kneeled on my backside, my stupid dick hanging like a useless lump between us.

"It is," she insists though her eyes are clouded.

Avoiding her confusion, I shuffle backward between her legs and dip my head, stroking her pussy with my tongue. At least I have this. She tastes sweet and musky, her texture sleek like velvet. It's more soothing to me than any of the verbal platitudes she's trying to offer.

"You don't have to ..." she pants, trailing off with a moan.

"Shut up," I order between licks. I do have to. Leaving her unsatisfied galls me. And I love this. Every stroke of my tongue, every thrust of my finger inside her, is a physical adoration. Whenever Mac snaps at me, or fights with me, I remember her like this. Her body agitated. Her moans breathless. Her skin hot as the sun.

"Don't stop," she gasps.

As if. It would be easier to stop a freight train with my bare hands.

Mac comes against my mouth, her back arching, hips leaving the bed. When she comes back down to earth, I lift my head. Her eyes are glazed, her body languid.

"You're amazing," she mumbles.

"I know."

"Come here." I flop down beside her and pull her against me. "Do you want me to—"

"No." I cut her off before she can finish the embarrassing question. "I'll be fine, babe." My lips press to the warmth of her brow. A quick kiss before I squeeze her body tight to mine. "Just give me an hour to nap and my trusty sword will be poking you before you can even blink."

"Do me a favour?"

"Mmm?" I mumble into the side of her face.

"Don't ever call it a sword."

"Why not?" I mock complain. "We can play pirate and busty wench. I can steal you away on my ship and tie you to the post in my cabin. I'll bend you over, lift your skirts, and fuck you silly with my heroic sword as the seas rage around us."

My cock twitches at the outlandish image and its heady relief. *Fuck.* We need to introduce some kind of role play into our lives.

Mac groans with exasperation. "I think you're forgetting something."

"What?"

"I'm not busty."

I reach over and grab a handful of tit, squeezing the delectable mound. "Damn, you're right. Maybe you should get a boob job."

Mac sucks in a sharp breath. *"Excuse me?"*

My greedy hand cops a slap and I retreat, laughing. She knows I'm teasing.

"Maybe you should try growing some muscle on that weedy frame of yours," she retorts.

I flex a bicep. Mac tries to wrap both hands around it but can't get her fingers to touch. "Not big enough, huh?"

"Not nearly," she jokes, letting go and settling into my side. "How are you supposed to give me my *Dirty Dancing* moment with those puny twigs?"

"Ha! You're a closet romantic!" I crow. Evie plays that movie so much my eyes will bleed if I have to suffer through it one more time. Who knew Mac was secretly watching it a thousand times too? "Should I start calling you baby now?"

"Fuck off, Romero." I can't see her face; it's buried in my neck, but I feel her grin against my skin.

"No?" I drag her body on top of mine. Mac sits up and straddles my hips. I take advantage and tickle my fingers down her sides. She hunches, giggling. "Nobody puts my Princess in a corner."

We tease and play for a few minutes before settling down. Mac eventually drifts off at my side as I trail gentle fingers through her hair. It's hard to imagine not having this every day. That she might not want this every day. Moments like these are heady for me. They heighten my love for her so much it hurts.

When I'm sure she's asleep, I climb slowly from the bed, careful not to wake her. After tugging on my underwear, I jog down the carpeted stairs and walk to the kitchen where my phone rests on the counter. I pick it up and dial. It's late but I don't care.

"Romero. Son," Steve Valentine answers in a groggy voice after three rings. "What's up?"

I lean over the kitchen bench as I reply, resting my elbows on the counter. "I want to know if you have any update on the Ross situation."

I've been told that father and son don't keep in touch. Alan has no contact information for Ross. And according to Elijah, Ross finding him in the parking lot of the Florence Bar was a random approach. Ross was trying to hit him up for money, which makes sense, considering Elijah is just three short months away from a considerable inheritance.

"I tried phoning Alan earlier," he tells me, "but I got voicemail. He's at the annual Governor's Ball, so I imagine he hasn't any new information. Hang on." A muffled clang comes through the phone. "Let me check my emails."

He taps at his keyboard for a few moments before he replies. "He's sent a quick message. Intel shows Ross returned to Melbourne yesterday. They located his flight details, and they have video confirmation of him exiting Melbourne airport."

My relief is so acute I sag against the counter.

He's gone, I repeat to myself. *He's gone.*

"You have nothing to worry about," Steve assures me. "We'll keep tabs on him. That gesture he made last night was probably nothing more than him trying to get to you. And it worked."

"You're right." I sigh deeply. "He got to me."

"Relax, son. He won't be coming back, but if he does, it won't be without us knowing about it first, okay? Get some rest. You have a tour soon. You're going to need it."

Chapter Thirty-four

Jake

The tour is a success. Every show sells out. Our debut LP skyrockets from the exposure and goes platinum. It's surreal, as though it's happening to some other band and I'm just watching on. The celebratory party is held on a tour bus as we drive through the night along a dark road from Pennsylvania to Michigan in the United States. Even Mac is screaming and jumping up and down at the news. Champagne sprays over us in a fizzy shower that soaks our clothes and swamps the floor.

It leaves us hungover for our last show of the tour and likely contributes to the meltdown Mac has after we finish up our final song. I should have seen it coming. She's been increasingly exhausted as our tour progressed. Quick to snap and generally irritable with faint bruising under the tender skin of her eyes. As our band manager, I can't imagine how intense and demanding it is for her to handle a tour of this magnitude, but I'm suggesting a holiday when we return. Somewhere tropical. White sands. Blue water. Pina coladas. Massages. It's the type of rejuvenation we both need.

I jog down the stairs by the side of the stage and head backstage after the show. Fans scream as I walk alongside the hip-high fence barrier that separates us from them, their arms outstretched, willing to touch any part of us they can get their hands on. Some hold pens and pictures, hoping for an autograph. Most hold phones up high and snap whatever photos or video they can.

Jared is with us, forming part of our personal security detail. He shields Evie heavily, his body a barrier as they lead the way. She's just over six months pregnant now, and while she's barely showing, Jared still protects her belly as if Satan himself is going to rise from the Underworld and snatch it away.

I'm last in our procession, trailed only by Mac. The threat of Ross seems a million miles away, but I can't shake it and glance behind to make sure she's close. Her eyes are glued to her clipboard, and she's talking into her headset. Ripped black jeans, a worn Jamieson tee shirt, and a purple lanyard around her neck complete her outfit. Her hair is in a messy side-braid with the back fastened in an untidy knot, and her expression is resolute.

She's been dealing with idiots and assholes for weeks, yet she's managed to bite her tongue. I fear it's coming to a head soon. Her pressure valve has reached critical levels. My princess is about to blow. *God help whoever gets in her path*, I pray silently.

It happens sooner than even *I* can predict when I'm grabbed from the side while distracted. For a moment I'm stunned, an exhausted kind that renders me ineffective for a fraction of a second. Apparently that's all it takes for an arm to snake around my chest, another to slither right into the front of my jeans and grope my junk, and last but definitely not least ... Mac to notice.

"Oh hey now," I say laughingly to whomever has me from behind. The hold isn't a strong one, and the arms and hands are slender and feminine.

I'm pulling myself free when Mac steps forward. Her eyes are flat. She's taking in the fanatical fan behind me like she's Muhammad Ali sizing up a lesser opponent. "Hold my clipboard," she barks and slaps it against my chest.

I grab it and watch, speechless, as Mac reaches the barrier and cocks back a fist with zero hesitation. *Oh shit.* I'm tossing the clipboard and grabbing for her, but I'm too late. Her white-knuckled hand punches forward in a blur. It connects with her target. Right in the bared midriff of the girl who had her hands on me. The girl folds instantly, hunching over the barricade but by no means down.

"Bitch!" she screams at Mac as she gasps for oxygen.

The violence stirs the crowd into a frenzy. They surge forward, a veritable human tsunami coming right for us. Mac appears oblivious, caught up in her anger as the girl rushes the barrier. Her hair is grabbed in two wrenching handfuls. Mac pushes her backward as the girl bares her teeth and bites at Mac's shoulder.

She makes contact and Mac shrieks as those furious fangs sink into her skin. Mac shoves her back and jabs another fist for good measure. Her punch lands in the girls face and she goes down. Security rushes forward as I grapple through people. My arms slide around Mac. I forcibly yank her backward.

"I'm going to sue you for assault, you ugly cow!" the girl screams from the ground, both hands covering her eye.

"You just try it, bitch," Mac growls, jabbing a finger at her as she wrestles against my hold. "I'll counter sue for sexual assault. They'll add you to the list of sexual offenders." Her finger jabs again. "I'll ruin your entire life, you fucking sexual predator!"

"Oh my god," the girl moans. "You're crazy."

"You better believe it!" Mac shouts, tugging free of my restraining grip. She jabs me with her finger. "This is my man!" The whole band surrounds us. They collectively still at her thunderous declaration as if we've reached the eye of a storm. Cooper is off to the side, phone high, capturing it all on video for later. "And that's *my* dick you had your hands all over!" Gasps and laughter break out around us and my eyes close. *Oh my fucking god.* Mac starts for the girl again, muttering, "I'll cut your goddamn fingers off." I grab her from behind again, my arms a manacle as they lock tight around her waist.

"Stay away from me, you psycho!" the girl screeches as security helps her upright.

Deep chuckles escape me. I turn my head and rest the side of my face against the back of Mac's head as I shudder, overwhelmed with hilarity.

"What are you laughing at, asshead?" she mutters at me in a low voice, turning her head so she can eye me sideways. "You were letting her do it. We are *so* done."

My mouth falls open. "But—"

Travis, the second half of our personal security duo, gets between her and the barricade. "Mac! What is wrong with you?"

"She needs to eat," calls Quinn, who's pushing her tiny body through everyone. Her expression is exasperated, as if she's spent an hour trekking the Sahara to reach us. Her outstretched hand holds a McDonald's cheeseburger.

Mac seems to sag, losing some of her fight as she reaches for it. Just as her fingertips touch the edge of the paper wrapping, Jared steps in and slaps it from Quinn's hand. It drops to the ground. "Are you kidding me?"

"Ouch," Quinn squeaks. His slap must have caught her on the fingers. She yanks her arm back like a naughty child caught in the cookie jar.

Travis vibrates with anger. He steps forward, eyes on his brother. *Uh oh.* "You just hit my wife, you fucking dipshit."

"I'm sorry. I didn't—"

That's all he gets out. One meaty fist flies out and in the blink of an eye, Jared is staggering backwards.

Holy mother of god. The Valentines are *all* out of control. Nothing explains Mac's temperament better than this. She's the only girl and learned the hard way in a house full of combative brothers.

Evie gasps when the punch connects. She's standing with Henry, on the fringes of the altercation. They've managed to collect the cheeseburger from the floor. It's ripped in half and they're both busy chewing. Evie's future baby daddy will lose his shit further if he sees that. And Cooper is still filming. Frog commentates from beside him as Jared straightens and returns the punch.

"Stop!" Quinn cries.

No one pays her any mind.

"Jake," Mac bleats, her voice feeble. She stumbles a little, heaving. Her skin is white as snow. "I think I'm going to be sick."

Her entire body turns away. Bending at the waist, Mac pushes free from my arms and vomits over the stage floor entrance.

Worry floods me in a weighty surge. Mac is never sick. I lean over and rub her lower back. Cooper is still filming, his camera now aimed in our direction. I shoot him an irritable glare. "Turn that shit off."

"And that was our tour," Cooper declares as he stands by the television in Casey's loft in Sydney, sharing his edited video. Our eyes are on the screen as Mac finishes her puke. It ends with Jared coming between her and the camera, his brows pulled tight as I lead Mac away. His hand comes toward us until it fills the screen and a curse renders the air. A long *beeeeeep* sounds and the screen goes black.

Rolling white credits follow as a Jamieson song begins to play. Dutiful clapping fills the room. Casey and Grace are seated on the couch. They stayed home during the tour so Grace could finish her chemotherapy. She's pale and thin now, her bones so fine they'll snap with the slightest pressure. It makes my chest tight. How does Casey stand it? I can barely breathe just looking at her.

There's a slight furrow in Casey's brow. He leans over, whispering something in Grace's ear. She shakes her head. He speaks again. She shakes her head again, rolling her eyes.

Seeming to give up, Casey leans forward and snatches a chip from the bowl that rests on the coffee table in front of him. He tosses it in his mouth with a loud crunch and manages a grin in Mac's direction. "So ... that was quite an outburst."

Mac *harumphs*. She's curled up in the recliner looking like she hasn't slept for forty-eight hours. She repeatedly insists she's fine and simply suffering exhaustion from the tour. My "incessant hovering" is making it worse. So I'm standing on the opposite side of the room, leaning against the kitchen counter behind me in an attempt to give her space.

Cooper folds his arms. "And we're still waiting to hear the full story."

All eyes in the room rise to me. Travis and Quinn are here sharing the opposite recliner to Mac. Jared is seated on the floor with his back resting against the couch Casey and Grace are seated on. Evie sits between his legs. His arms wrap around her, his hands rubbing over the lower rise of her belly. She has a packet of healthy baked vegetable chips resting on her chest, and she's munching them with a complete lack of enthusiasm. Cooper, Frog, and Henry are scattered about the living room floor, cross-legged and holding beers.

We've only been back in Australia two nights. Returning home was a flurry of activity, which was opportune because it left no time for either Mac or myself to explain the scene Cooper managed to capture on video for everyone to see.

Now there's no more dodging the issue, and I don't know how to start.

"There is no story," Mac says, taking the focus of attention from me. Eyes and ears swivel her way. They stare at her. And then they stare a little more, until she feels compelled to elaborate. "I met Jake when I was eleven, and he's been my best friend ever since. And that is all any of you ever need to know."

Her statement is brilliant. It's simple, succinct, and resolute, and despite the husky, sleep tone to her voice, it dares any person in the room to question her. Mac has managed to sum up our entire relationship in a single sentence. My arms are folded and my fingers dig into my biceps. It's all that stops me from walking over, collecting her from the chair, and carrying her straight out the door.

Questions burst forth, peppering the room like gunfire.

"But I don't get—"

"You're always fighting—"

"You told us you didn't know each—"

"How did you—"

"Why did you pretend—"

The only three who remain silent are Casey, Travis, and Jared … for obvious reasons.

"Everyone shut up!" I boom, my voice loud enough to bounce off the walls. Shock stirs the air and eyebrows rise. I never raise my voice. "Mac is tired, and you're all badgering her. If you want to know more than that …" I mash my lips together, pausing, thinking, before I speak. "We had a falling out when we were younger and it took some time for us to move past it. That's all."

Jared's expression is pained. "The falling out is my fault."

"And mine," Travis adds.

Eyes whip wildly about the room. Now everyone is wondering what Jared and Travis had to do with any of it.

"What was the falling out about?"

The question comes from Evie. Her voice is soft and wounded. We've hurt our friends by keeping our past a secret, but some things are best left in the past. And far too painful to rehash.

My eyes find Mac across the room. Her eyes are beginning to fill. She works so hard at keeping her emotions in check, yet it's clear how much the past still haunts her because a singular tear brims over and rolls down her cheek as she stares back at me. The hurt on her face is visible to the entire room. A surge of protectiveness wells up. "A private matter," I answer gruffly.

Mac stands. "Excuse me," she mutters to the room. She carries her stiff body away, only stopping to collect her handbag from the table by the front door. She opens it swiftly and exits in the blink of an eye.

I give chase, catching her in the hallway of the building. "Mac!"

She pauses as I jog toward her, but she doesn't turn. "I don't know what I was thinking," she whispers. The low, defeated tone in her voice is like nothing I've heard before. It sends dread snaking down my spine.

I take hold of her arm, turning her to face me. "What do you mean?"

Mac shakes her head. "Marriage. Babies. The white picket fence. You deserve it all. But I don't think I can do it, Jake. I'm sorry."

My mouth opens and closes. I don't know what to say. What to think. "Of course you can." I swallow past the dryness in my throat. "We were meant to be. This was how it was always supposed to happen. Us. Together. Why can't you see that?"

"I don't know why. It's like every time I think about our future, my mind clams up and blocks me from seeing anything at all."

My jaw tightens and my eyes lift to the ceiling as I blink at the sharp pain of her words. When I recover enough to look at her without yelling my frustration, I offer her an easy excuse. "You're just tired."

Mac doesn't take it like I hoped she would. "It's not that. It's not just now. It's always been that way. I've never been able to see it."

I take a step toward her and tuck a finger beneath her chin, lifting her face upward until she's looking at me. "Never?"

She closes her eyes as if my face is too much to bear. "Ever since the accident, it's just been a fog."

"Ever since I pushed you away."

"Yes."

Her affirmation is a soft whisper, and yet it packs enough meaning to hit like a tonne of bricks. Tears drip down her face as I take her shoulders in my hands and press my forehead to hers, closing my eyes too. We've tried *so* hard to make this work, but Mac has been like sand slipping right through my fingers. And now all the sand is gone, and my hands are left empty.

My eyes prickle with heat, and I tighten my jaw against the crippling wave of pain. "I'll always love you, Mackenzie Valentine."

"I'll always love you too, Jake Romero."

The silence stretches taut until I feel ready to break apart. "You need to go," I utter hoarsely.

Mac flinches.

I don't say anymore. I can't.

She draws away. Her soft footsteps are soundless as she walks down the hallway toward the exit. Yet I hear them. They're a heavy echo inside of my heart.

When I finally open my eyes, she's gone.

Chapter Thirty-five

Mac

I take a seat at the outdoor café table. It's noon and a beautiful day. Lush, leafy green trees line the full length of the busy street and flutter in the light breeze. The sun is out, bright and hot. People wander past the shop fronts, chattering, takeout coffee cups in hand and cute dogs on leashes. Christmas is only four weeks away and the atmosphere is festive. I want to appreciate it, but I feel like dog shit mashed into the bottom of someone's shoe.

My heart and my stomach are competing for the title of who can make me feel the worst. It's currently a tie.

I set my phone on the table. It lights up with a message.

Mitch: Where are you?

But it's not the message (which I ignore) that captures my attention. It's the background image that lights up along with it. Jake's face and mine are close to the screen. We're drunk and laughing uncontrollably while he gives the camera the finger.

You win this round, heart, I mutter to the offending organ when it squeezes so hard I lose my breath. Not to be outmanoeuvred, my stomach rolls over in a long, queasy thump. It feels as though I'm dying, my traitorous body attacking me from the inside out.

I haven't had time to Google in the four days we've been home from tour, but I'm thinking Lyme Disease or Dengue Fever. I'm utterly exhausted. My body is fighting whatever it is, but I'm losing the battle.

A waiter passes by with two coffees in hand. The delicious aroma reaches my nose and I heave. Usually the scent wakens me.

I take a deep breath. Realisation is a slow awareness in my thoughts, like I'm underwater and pushing my way to the surface. The answer touches at the corner of my mind. I recoil with horror and shove it away.

Thankfully, my dining partner arrives to distract me. I half-stand in my seat and the small motion leaves me dizzy.

"Sit, sit," he admonishes, waving a hand as if to shoo me back down.

I'm grateful for the small mercy and sink back in my seat. He leans across, all clean-shaven jaw, spicy aftershave and sharp suit, and kisses me on the cheek. Drawing away, he smiles, tugs off his jacket, and drapes it across the back of his seat before he sits opposite me.

"It's good to see you, Mac." He studies my face with care. "Though I've seen you looking better."

My outward appearance is clearly failing to hide my imminent death. "Thanks a bunch."

His eyebrows rise with genuine concern. "Are you okay?"

No. I told Jake I couldn't see our future together and it was a lie. A Big. Fat. Ugly. Lie. Because our future is amplified in my head until it's all I see. "We just came off tour," I explain, forcing blitheness to my voice that I'm not feeling. "I'm exhausted. And I haven't had any coffee yet today."

His brilliant blue eyes soften with sympathy, and he signals a passing waitress. "Let's rectify that."

He places an order for two coffees, an espresso for himself and a long black for me, requesting it darker and stronger than Satan himself. Does everyone know how I take my coffee?

The waitress leaves, and I'm gifted with a magnetic grin. "How was the tour, gorgeous?"

Gorgeous? A snort of disbelief escapes me. "Are you trying to make me feel better?"

He shrugs. "You're always gorgeous to me."

I sink back in my seat, surprised and yet unsurprised all at the same time. He's flirting. Elijah Rossiter is flirting with me. I thought I'd imagined it at the party and brushed it away. A frown creases my brow. "Eli—"

"Just accept a compliment and move on, sweetheart."

"Okay, okay."

"So ..." His face wrinkles in a wince as if what he's about to say next is going to hurt. "I heard about you and Jake."

"Ugh." My head tips back, and I draw in a long breath. The gossip network has been running hot. At times it can be convenient, but in this instance it's plain annoying. And embarrassing. My face flushes when I think of my outburst on Cooper's video.

"Are you sure you're okay?" he asks a second time.

The waitress returns with our coffee. The thick, pungent liquid is placed in front of me before she walks away. The scent rises inside my nostrils and sets my stomach into a deep clench. *Don't,* I bark silently. It ignores me, refusing to relax.

"I'm sure," I reply reflexively, a forced smile forming on my lips.

"Okay. Good." Eli expels a breath. "You're better off without him, you know."

"Whether I am or not, is not your call." My tone is defensive as I stir sugar into my mug. What am I doing? I don't drink my coffee with sugar. Eli frowns at my actions. He knows I don't either.

"You're right. It's not," he concedes with easy-going grace. "It's just ..."

"It's just what, Eli?" I ask, impatient when he trails off and goes silent.

Eli's cheekbones have sharpened over the years and there's a thin scar across his brow that I never noticed before. His lips are full and always quick to grin, but they're flat now. He's pressing them together. "He never deserved you."

His tone is accusatory and my body tightens with tension. "Has anyone stopped to think that maybe I never deserved him?"

I'm the one who can't let go of the hurt. *I'm* the one crippled by fear. It's *me* who holds tightly to the past despite numerous attempts from Jake to help me move on. He tried to keep me safe, even when I raged at him for letting me go. He's the one I fucked so coldly before walking out the door, acting like it meant nothing. Yet he still loved me. Jake told me I was his universe, and he held me on the bathroom floor at Evie's when I cried so hard I couldn't breathe. He held me so tight I felt maybe one day I would be okay as long as he kept holding me like that. I thought needing Jake made me weak, but I was wrong. He gave me strength. *And I gave him nothing.*

"Mac?" I tune back in. Eli is still talking. "Did you hear me?"

I blink, comprehension throbbing painfully at my temples. I pushed Jake away before he could do it to me a second time. I was convinced I had something to prove—to him, to my family, to myself— that I never needed anyone.

But I do.

I was convinced that nothing could break me.

But I'm already broken.

Jake was simply doing everything he could to piece me back together.

I stare blindly at the coffee before me, my eyes burning.

Eli reaches across the table and takes my hand. The contact is unfamiliar. I look down at our joined fingers. Eli's palm is cool and somewhat rough, whereas Jake's is always warm, his calluses thick and scratchy. I always thought them beautiful. Not just because of how they feel when he touches me, but because the hardened skin is a testament to the joy that drumming gives him.

I stand abruptly, breaking our contact. "I made a mistake."

Eli's voice is sharp. Confused. "You *what?*"

My legs wobble and my chest is tight. I grab the edge of the table as blackness edges my vision. Eli stands, reaching for me. The dizziness passes, and I bat his hand away.

His eyes harden as we stand across from each other. "You and Jake weren't a mistake. You were a fucking train wreck. You think it's been easy for me?"

My mouth drops open. "Think what's been easy?"

"Watching you love that asshole," Eli snaps, unleashing a burst of unexpected frustration all over me. His hands clench and thick veins pop over his wide knuckles. "Jake Romero took you from your family and then discarded you like trash. He broke you. And two years after you started getting your life back on track, he waltzes back in and fucks with you all over again. And we've all had to sit back and pretend we're okay with it!"

Eli has me blindsided, as if I were crossing the road and got struck by a car out of nowhere. My phone rings and I speak over the top of it, indignant. "He didn't *take* me from my family."

It rings out and moments later it *dings* with another message from Mitch, the text showing up on my locked screen.

Mitch: Mac, it's urgent. Call me.

"You should call your brother." I look up. Eli's gaze is on my phone, reading my message. "If he says it's urgent, it's urgent."

Palming the device, I search for Mitch's contact and dial.

"Mac," he answers.

"What is it, Mitch?"

"Will you be at the loft tonight for Casey and Grace's party?" He sounds breathless and his footsteps are loud thumps like he's jogging down a set of stairs.

"Yes, I'm helping host while Grace is sick. Why?"

"No reason. Gotta go."

He hangs up.

"What's going on?" Eli asks.

"I haven't the faintest idea," I reply and reach for my oversized bag where it rests on the ground between my chair and the table. "Either way, I don't have time for my brother's cryptic bullshit. I have to go."

"Mac, I'm sorry." Eli shakes his head and reaches for me. "Don't go."

I take a step back and his hand falls away. "It's not … I just realised that I have something I need to take care of."

"Mac!"

I'm already walking away, shouldering my bag. "We'll reschedule," I call out.

"Wait!" he calls back. "The file."

I pause, turning. "The file?"

Eli grabs his jacket from the back of his chair. He tugs his wallet from the inside pocket and tosses a twenty on the table with an impatient gesture before jogging after me.

"The *file*," he repeats with meaning when he reaches me. He looks around before leaning in. "Operation Strike, Mac. You wanted me to help you."

"Oh." I rummage through my bag and pull the sleek manila folder out. "Here." Eli flips it open and scans the first page quickly. "I have to go." I start walking backward, suddenly not caring about the file or being a Badass Brigade member in the least. I was *happy* with my life. I want it back the way it was. "Are you coming to the party at Casey's tonight?"

"No," he replies, a faint frown on his face as he looks up. "I have something I need to take care of."

Jake

Loud banging cuts through the quiet of the duplex. Someone is bashing their fist at the front door.

"Jake?"

It's Mac. I pause my packing, my stomach in knots.

"I know you're in there!"

Of course she knows. My car is parked out front, ready to load with my suitcase. Mac is a drug and I'm addicted. The only way I can be free is to leave.

But like any other junkie, I've promised myself one last hit. Just not right now. Not when I'm trying to be strong. Later tonight at the party. My final goodbye. To her. My final goodbye to everyone.

"Jake!"

I sink to the edge of my bed, a tee shirt scrunched in my balled-up fists.

Go away.

"Jake, please!"

Oh, Princess. Don't beg like that. With your voice all hoarse and desperate. It makes me weak.

I rise from the bed.

Don't, Jake. Fool.

My legs start moving toward the door. Toward Mac.

"Goddammit," she growls.

The front door judders as if she's just kicked it.

Mac

He doesn't answer me. He always does. But not this time. It's what I deserve. If you kick a puppy enough, he'll never come when you call.

My phone rings, the sound faint from inside my handbag. I ignore it and kick at the door from frustration. It rings again.

"Goddammit," I growl and reach for it, walking away.

Casey's name is on the screen, along with an image of him giving me the finger. My friends did that one night when I was sleeping. They hacked my phone and edited my contacts, adding an image to their individual profiles of them flipping the middle finger to the camera.

My brothers, Evie, Henry, and Quinn. Even the band, including Jake. I had to give them credit for that. It was funny, especially when I got a call from Dad and they'd managed to get him in on it too.

"Hotdog," I answer, putting the phone to my ear as I jog down the front steps.

"Mac Attack," he replies. "Need you."

I start toward our duplex on the other side. "What's up?"

"The party tonight. Grace won't sit down. She needs to rest and I can't do it all on my—"

"Say no more," I interrupt as I reach my own front door. "I'll be there in an hour."

"May God grant you a thousand of the best orgasms of your life," he replies and hangs up.

Using the key, I let myself inside. "Anyone home?"

No one calls back as I close the door behind me.

I shower quickly and plan my outfit as I massage a facial scrub over my cheeks and forehead. When I'm out, I dry off. After wrapping my hair up in my towel, I tug on the sexiest underwear I own. Black lace, demi cup bra and a thong so tiny I may as well be wearing dental floss on my butt crack.

After that, I slide on tight black pants. Horizontal zippers decorate the front and the back. My top is a fitted leather vest that zips upward into a low-cut V and pushes my breasts up and together to create some much-needed cleavage. I complete the look with sleek hair, heavy, dark eyes, nude lips, and strappy black stilettos. The whole process leaves me feeling battle ready.

With no one home, I call an uber and get assigned 'Louise.' She arrives in ten minutes. I open the car door to a driver who looks no older than ten. "Are you Louise? How old are you?" I ask as I slide inside the passenger seat.

I don't hear her answer because everything blacks out for a moment.

"Oh my gosh, are you okay?"

My breath comes with conscious effort as waves of nausea roll over me. "I'm fine," I say, buckling my seat belt.

We zoom off into the street but panic begins to creep in. *It's okay, I tell myself in a cool voice. You haven't eaten today. That's all it is.*

My breathing eases a little but the nausea does not.

I'm not pregnant. I'm just exhausted.

We're halfway to Casey's loft when I spot a pharmacy looming ahead. There's only one way to be sure. "Stop the car," I bark.

"What? Here?" Her tone is confused but she pulls over, parking by the kerb.

"I just need to—" My stomach heaves, and I gesture at the building we've stopped in front of. "Be right back."

Jake

Casey's loft is a crush of people by the time I arrive. My eyes seek Mac the moment I step through the door. She's standing in the kitchen, talking and laughing with Coby, Evie's brother. The craving sets in with a steady *thump thump thump*. Everyone is dressed in varying shades of colour, and she's all in black. The effect is dark and sexy, like Satan's blonde mistress. Her green eyes flicker my way as if she feels my stare.

You're so beautiful.

I draw air deep inside my lungs. They expand, my chest rising.

Be strong, asshole.

I force a distant expression, turn away, and exhale with care. Moving through the living area, I spy Henry in conversation with Cooper and Frog. I come up from behind and slap him on the back.

"Hey," he says, half turning.

I steal his beer and take a long pull before joining in their conversation. After about ten minutes, Henry leans in, speaking in a low voice. "Have you seen Mac tonight?"

"Yes." I look for her again and catch her watching me, her eyes pained. She knows I'm avoiding her. If she didn't get the hint at the duplex, she knows it now. I don't know what it was that brought her to my door this afternoon but pride will stop her from approaching me again. At least tonight. And after that it will be too late.

"Why?" I ask Henry.

"Because she doesn't look so good. I don't think I've ever seen Mac sick before. She's always seems so invincible, but tonight ..."

Mac turns away when someone steals her attention, and I study her face. Henry is right. Faint shadows line her eyes, and the golden hue to her skin appears faded. Her health doesn't appear to have improved since our return from tour. I abandon all sense of self-preservation and start toward her.

When I reach her in the kitchen, Mac is holding an arm across her belly, as if she's moments away from puking all over the timber floor. She watches my approach with wary eyes.

"Princess?"

The endearment slips out. *Dammit.*

"I'm not your princess," she snaps, tension gathering in her slight frame.

My jaw grinds. I get it. Mac humbled herself earlier today. Her desperate *"please"* still echoes in my head.

"You okay?"

"I'm fine."

She's not fine. Her movements are jerky as she twists the lid off a beer and thrusts it at me. I ignore it, instead studying her face. My eyes drop to her mouth when she bites down on her bottom lip. *Thump thump thump* goes my craving. I can't even be around her for even a minute without wanting to push her up against a wall and fuck her until the hunger eases. But it never does.

"Take the stupid beer," she growls, seeing the heat gathering in my eyes.

I huff and snatch it from her, setting it on the kitchen counter beside us.

"Mac, I ..." I look away, swallowing, and rub a hand over the short buzz of hair on my head. Am I making a mistake by leaving? My shoulders sag. What choice do I have? My voice hardens as I face her again. "We need to move on. Build some distance. I can't be around you ..."

Because it wears me down.

Her eyes close and the bitterness of heartache folds me up in its cold embrace. I cup her jaw before I can help myself. The touch is everything. For one brief moment we're connected and everything feels okay. But it's all an illusion.

My hand slides away and her eyes flicker open. "You're right. We need to move on."

Chapter Thirty-Six

Mac

Present Day...

I'm heaving into the porcelain bowl. My stomach cramps and purges but there's nothing left. I'm an empty husk of my former self.

The bathroom door opens quietly. I don't hear it, but I do hear, "Jesus, babe. You okay? How much did you have to drink?"

It's Kelly, come to see me brought low. He sits on the edge of the bathtub and rubs my back in slow circles that are oddly soothing. "Nothing," I moan, positive I'm about to die. How are women expected to survive this?

The door opens again and someone else steps in. This makes me happy because there's nothing I want more right now than a budding audience to witness my torture.

"Kelly. Come here often?" It's Grace. There's irony in her voice because she was sick earlier tonight, and Casey's brother found himself nursing her through it too.

There's a long pause.

"Shit," Kelly mutters.

"You're pregnant," Grace breathes in utter shock.

They've found the test resting on the bathroom vanity. The one I purchased on the Uber drive here.

Kelly snatches his hand from my back as if he just discovered I have leprosy. *Newsflash, biker dude, pregnancy is not contagious.* I want to voice the catty remark, but I simply can't. All I can do is hold tight to the porcelain bowl and pray my end will come swiftly.

"Who's the father?" he demands.

I lean back, using the backs of my hands to swipe at the ghastly mascara tracks on my cheeks. Kelly and Grace both stare and the weight of it is too much. "Jake," I rasp, my voice hoarse from puking. "It's Jake."

Of course it's him. It's always been him. Asshead.

I swallow as my revelation sinks in. For the first time in my life, I feel I've lost all direction. I'm having a *baby*.

"Are you okay?" Grace asks me softly.

"No," I choke out and then notice her face is as pale as the frosty paint on the walls. "Did I wake you?"

She shakes her head. "Your phone did." Grace plucks it from the pocket of her blue silk pyjama pants. Her brows furrow on the screen before she holds it out toward me. "Henry has rung you three times."

Kelly snatches the phone before I can reach for it. It rings immediately in his hand. He hits the green button and puts the device to his ear, using his other hand to bat away my feeble attempts to snatch it from him.

"This is Daniels," he answers.

I can hear Henry's voice but can't make out what he's saying.

"She's right here beside me," Kelly says into the phone.

He pauses as Henry speaks.

"No you can't talk to her. She's not well."

"Put her on," Henry roars loud enough for me to hear. And Henry never roars.

Kelly offers me the phone. "Your friend is a dick."

"I heard that," Henry says as I put the phone to my ear.

"All men are dicks, Hussy," I tell him, my voice rougher than sandpaper. "You know this."

"Well *your* man is the biggest dick of all."

"He's not *my* man," I retort, sagging into the side of the bathtub behind me. "And why is it you rang me a thousand times to tell me something I already know?"

Henry huffs sharply. "To tell you that he's gone."

"He's gone?" My fuddled mind tries to make sense of what he's saying. "Who's gone?"

"Jake."

"Gone where?"

"I don't know where!" A muffled *thunk* sounds through the phone as if Henry's kicked an empty box clear across the room. "He rang, saying he was quitting the band and leaving."

Denial shuts me down. "He's not leaving. He's just having a tantrum."

"He rang me from the road!" Henry shouts with frustration. "I checked next door. All his clothes are gone."

My stomach rebels with horror, and the phone slips from my fingers. "Mac?" Henry calls out. "Mac?"

I lean over the toilet bowl, blinded with fear. "Oh Jesus," I breathe. "Not again."

"Mac, are you okay?" Grace's soft palm lightly grasps my shoulder.

Kelly must have picked up my phone because I can hear him talking behind me.

"Jake's gone," I squeeze out as my belly heaves.

Not again.

Not.

Again.

He pushed me away once when I was pregnant. And now it's happening all over again. He's leaving again. I can't do this. I literally cannot do this again.

"Mac, breathe." My lungs expel a huge rush of air at Kelly's command. "Pull yourself together."

"Kelly," I hear Grace rebuke.

"She's spiralling."

He's right though. I *am* spiralling. This is not me. I don't *spiral.* When the going gets tough, the tough get going. I'm the tough. It doesn't get any tougher than me.

My eyes blink open as a sense of purpose fills me. I scramble to my feet in an awkward, clumsy motion. Hands reach out to steady me and I bat them away. A brief check in the mirror confirms I'm still a mess. My hair is tousled, my smoky eye-makeup is smudged and my face pale. But I don't care. All I care about right now is getting to Jake. I stare at my reflection, my mind racing. There's only one way to catch him before he disappears from my life completely, and only one way I can pull it off.

Gathering what little strength I have, I race from the bathroom.

"Mac!" Kelly shouts. I don't stop and turn. I also don't notice his older brother, Casey, emerging from his bedroom in wild, shirtless glory, asking, "What the hell is going on?" in a raspy voice.

I head straight for the bowl. The very one all partygoers had to put their keys into at the start of the party early last night. One set remains. The keys to Kelly's Harley.

What I'm about to do will likely get me killed, but I have no choice.

I grab them.

"Oh hell no!" Kelly bellows with a thunder so mighty the walls shake and windows rattle.

There's no time to look back. My legs move of their own accord, adrenaline giving me speed. I open the door of the loft and I'm out, running down the hallway toward the exit. Waiting for the elevator is suicide. I hit the stairs, somehow capable of flight despite moments earlier feeling weaker than cooked spaghetti. My breath comes fast and my hair flies out behind me as I leap to the bottom landing. My feet hit with a bone-jarring thud that causes my teeth to *clunk,* but I don't stop.

"Babe, stop or die!" Kelly shouts behind me, so close the threat feels like whiplash.

I'm out the door and hitting the pavement before he catches me. My bicep is grabbed with a mighty grip. I turn and swing on instinct with the same fist that holds his keys.

Kelly ducks. Then he straightens, eyeballing me as I stand white-knuckled and chest heaving. He's waiting for my next move. My eyes slide to the bike parked by the kerb. *Goddammit, it's so close!* They slide back.

Kelly's glare is hard enough to fracture the pavement. "Don't even."

My gaze narrows. "You don't understand."

"I don't need to." He jabs a thunderous finger at his motorcycle. "*That* is my baby. No one rides her but me. *No one.*"

"Then take me," I beg, the panic to reach Jake making me desperate.

Kelly shakes his head. "You're not thinking straight. Wait until you've had some sleep. We'll find out where he is tomorrow, and I'll take you then," he says, his voice taking on a soothing quality as if I'm a wild animal to be tamed. "Besides," he adds, eyes dropping to my belly with a dubious expression, "you're pregnant."

"No shit?" I hiss, ire rising.

Kelly huffs. "You can't ride a horse when you're pregnant. The same goes for bikes."

"What the hell do you know about pregnancy?" I shout, beyond frustrated.

"Clearly more than you," he points out like a big fucking know-it-all.

"Who do you think you are? The pregnancy police?"

He folds his arms. "When it comes to you, babe, looks like I have to be."

"I'm not your *babe*," I spit out, "and screw this." I start for the Harley, but Kelly grabs me and literally rips the keys from my hand. "Ouch!" I bellow. "That hurt, you fucking asshead!"

"Oh my god! You bitches are gonna send me fuckin' bat shit crazy."

Kelly stalks toward his bike. Swinging one powerful thigh over the seat, he settles. The machine lowers under his considerable weight. After turning the key, it rumbles to life. Then his head swivels to look at me and he huffs unhappily. "Well get the fuck on already."

"Stop swearing at me," I retort snidely as I walk to the bike and climb on behind him.

He shakes his head and honestly I can't blame him. My mood is up and down like a crazy, pregnant woman, which is ironic, considering that's exactly what I am.

Kelly hands me the one helmet he has with him. "Where are we going?"

"If I could be happy in only place for the rest of my life it would be here, at this very beach," Jake said. He was sitting on the bonnet of his car, feet resting on the metal bumper, and his gaze on the Melbourne beach in front of us. Waves rolled in, one after the other. It was hypnotic.

I sat beside him, his heavy arm wrapped around my back. My head tipped sideways to rest on his shoulder. "Why?"

"Because the ocean is the great unknown. It holds all the answers, yet it gives none of them up. You have to venture out through wild seas, risking your life just to seek them. It holds you at its mercy and yet you always come back to it. Over and over. Always searching. Always wanting more." Jake turned his head, looking down at me, his brown eyes dark and fathomless. "It reminds me of you."

I remember it clearly. We were so young and stupidly in love. He likened me to something so vast and intrinsically beautiful it left me feeling like I truly mattered to him.

"Why this very beach though?" I asked.

"Because it's here, with you, where I regained my faith."

"In what?"

His eyes left mine and returned to the sea. "Life, Mac. In life."

"Melbourne," I say to Kelly with conviction.

To his credit, my answer doesn't faze him. He simply nods and waits for me to pull the helmet over my head. When I'm done, I rest my hands on his waist and we pull out on to the street.

The air is cool on my bare arms. Dawn is coming. The dark horizon has begun to lighten, hinting at a clear blue day ahead. My mind is on Jake as we roll to a stop at a red light. I'm angry. Crazy angry. But I'm scared. The one thing I never wanted to happen has come to fruition.

Jake has left. And I'm having his baby.

The pain of the past twists my belly in a knot.

I'm not prepared to survive a loss like that again. I'm in this now. So deep there's no coming out. And damned if I'm going to do it alone.

Kelly and I are half an hour along the motorway to Melbourne when he begins to slow the bike. The rumbling engine cuts back. I look over his shoulder. "What's going on?"

Of course he can't hear me.

We pull over to the side of the motorway. Cars drive past sporadically as I tug the helmet from my head. "Why did you stop?"

"Because of that," he says, nodding ahead of him.

I'm running fingers through the snarls in my hair when I notice it. A 1979 Dodge Charger parked off the road ahead of us. The colour a candy apple red. The car unmistakeably belongs to Jake.

I climb off the bike, shove the helmet at Kelly, and run on unsteady legs toward the car. My senses are on high alert, my heart galloping in my chest. Something feels off and my fears are realised when I find no one inside. The Charger is empty. Jake would *never* abandon his car by the side of the motorway.

"Kelly," I gasp once, painfully, loudly.

He snatches my hand and pulls me to the far side of Jake's car, away from the oncoming traffic. We reach the large barrier that blocks the Motorway from suburban homes and local roads. Standing between the cement wall and the passenger side of Jake's car, Kelly takes my shoulders and glares. "You're letting your mind run away from you, Mac. It's likely just an empty tank and he's hitched a ride to get fuel."

My lungs ease a fraction at the sliver of hope Kelly offers. But when I look over his shoulder at the car, I see blood. A large smear of it decorates the headrest of the driver's seat. Panic surges. "Oh no." The words emerge as a breathy moan.

"What?" Kelly turns, following my line of sight. "Fuck."

The ground tilts. I fall against Kelly, and he grapples with my sudden weight. He turns me around and pushes me up against the passenger door of the car, propping me upright. "What kind of trouble is Jake in?"

My head is fuzzy as I sort through every dangerous altercation we've been involved in recently, which is a lot when I take the time to think about it.

"Mac!" Kelly barks.

I shake my head. "None. There's nothing I can think of."

"There has to be something."

"There isn't." Every situation we've been caught in hasn't directly involved either of us. "Not since, well, not since that one time at The Bar when we were being shot at."

"Who was shooting at you?"

"The King Street Boys."

Kelly steps back, my response a shock. "Babe, fuck. That's the biggest gang in Melbourne. What were they doin' shootin' at you?" Then his blue eyes flare with horror. "Oh shit."

"What?"

"Jonah," he breathes.

"Jonah?"

"Jake Romero is Jonah, isn't he? I fuckin' knew he looked familiar. He ran with Fox back in the day. He's a member of the King Street Boys."

"Was," I correct.

"*Is*," Kelly disputes with a harsh word. "Once you're in, you're never out. They *own* you."

"You're wrong. Jake got out. He's out."

Kelly shakes his head as he tugs his phone from his back pocket. "Babe, don't like repeatin' myself. Jake is *not out*," he says as he dials. "He might think he is, but the King Street Boys *never* forget."

Someone answers on the other end.

"Fox," Kelly barks into the phone. "Need you." He rattles off our approximate location without waiting for a response and hangs up.

"That's your big plan? Luke Fox to the rescue?" I huff and stalk around to the driver's side of Jake's Charger. "What, do you think—" I break off as I bend, looking again through the car window. The keys. They're right there, dangling in the ignition. I straighten quickly, looking at Kelly over the roof of the car. "You think Fox might have some idea of where Jake is?"

Kelly's massive hands come to rest on his hips. He has his mean face on, the kind designed to scare the big bad bogeyman in the dead of night. "Oh, he'll know."

"So why does he have to come all the way here? Ask him now." My voice rises from frustration when Kelly starts shaking his head. If I can just get an idea of where he is, I can get in Jake's car and drive there right now. "Just get Luke back on the phone and fucking ask him, you fucking asshead!"

"Cool it, Yosemite Sam," he says and my eyes narrow. "You do realise you're pregnant, don't you?" It's all I can do not to rip the side mirror from Jake's precious car and peg it at Kelly's head. "That thing can hear every word you say."

"Thing?" My voice is a shriek and his brow lifts. "Thing? I'm not giving birth to an alien!"

He has the audacity to appear dubious. "I'll guess we'll have to wait and see."

My hands curl around the side mirror. "Just call Fox," I command with gritted teeth. "Now."

"Babe," he begins.

My eyes narrow.

"Fuck's sake," he mutters with an eye roll. "Fox is going to tell me where Jake is and then he's going to take you home."

My instinct is to protest with a tantrum so wild you could see it from space, but I lock it down, eyes flicking to the dangling keys in the Charger. I look up quickly, meeting Kelly's piercing blue gaze as I find my calm. "You're right," I concede. "I'll go with Luke. I need to think of the baby."

He nods as if there's no doubt he was ever wrong. Conceited tool. If he knew me as well as everyone else did, he wouldn't believe a word I just said. But he doesn't. More fool him.

"Come stand over here," he orders, nodding beside him. Traffic is starting to build on the motorway but it's still light. It's Sunday. The usual early morning commuters are fast asleep, appreciating another day off, while I stand here on the roadside, tired, frustrated, scared, and about as pregnant as a girl can get.

It grates to do what Kelly says, but I do it. I might not know him all that well but if he's anything like Casey, he'll likely come over and drag me back where it's safer. And if he does that he'll see the keys and take them and that can't happen.

Kelly is leaning against the concrete barrier, eyes cold and focused toward the oncoming traffic. I can literally see his mind ticking over. I reach his side and follow suit, leaning against the same barrier beside him and fold my arms. "The King Street Boys have him."

It's more a statement than a question, yet he answers regardless. "Yes."

"What are they going to do to him?" I don't want to know the answer, but it's a question that needs to be asked. I need to be prepared. To know what I'll be walking into.

"If he refuses to go back? They'll kill him."

Jake won't go back. I know him better than anyone. He would rather die. "We're wasting time. Standing around waiting isn't helping him."

"Wrong. It's keeping you safe. And right now that's what Jake would want above all else."

Damn the man. He's just like his brother.

Ten minutes later, Luke comes thundering down the motorway. The rumble of his engine roars to a crescendo as he pulls over, directly behind Kelly's bike. He yanks out his keys, pockets them, and rips the helmet from his head, revealing mussed hair and grim eyes. "I already know," he says before either of us can say a word.

"Leander?"

Luke's answer is a harsh nod.

"Where is he?" Kelly barks.

With them both distracted, I start inching back to the Charger, my ears cocked for the location as my booted feet fall slowly on loose gravel.

"Somewhere along the Dockside Wharf," he answers as I reach the car door. *Almost there.*

"You need to take Mac—" Kelly breaks off. He's seen me. "What the fuck do you think you're doin'?"

"I'm—"

"No."

"You can't—"

His arms fold across a chest as vast and as rippled as the ocean. "I can."

"Screw you," I hiss and grab for the handle. I'm inside with the engine growling to life before he can get around the back of the car. The car tears off on to the road before I even pull the door shut. Gravel and dust flick out behind me. The back tyres spin under the wild acceleration and rubber burns, leaving behind a cloud of smoke that envelops both Kelly and Luke. It clears in a heartbeat as I slam the car door closed and risk a glance in the rearview mirror. They're not wasting time; both are already swinging legs over their Harleys.

I plant my foot, eyes searching for the next upcoming exit. The Dockside Wharf is back in Sydney. I need to get off this motorway and re-enter on the other side, heading north.

Chapter Thirty-Seven

Mitch Valentine

I tug the radio from the loop in my belt and speak into it with a low voice. "Is everyone in position?"

I'm crouched behind a rusted blue shipping container, a bullet-proof vest strapped tight to my torso and black Ray-Bans in place to cover my eyes from the early morning glare. The sun is beginning its ascent and casts a warm orange and pink glow across the horizon. I notice none of it as I scan the building layout in my hand one last time, mentally checking off each team's position as they report in.

Once done, I fold the sheet of paper and tuck it into the back pocket of my jeans. Nerves stretched taut with tension, I raise the radio to my lips, ready to give the go head when the growl of an engine rips through the eerie stillness. I cock my ears. The noise isn't that of passing traffic. Instead, it's getting closer until the thunderous roar is all I can hear.

"Goddammit," I bark tersely and get on the radio. "Hold position."

This sting is the biggest operation Sydney City Police have undertaken in years and one fool's inattention at the Dockside gates has the potential to bring the whole thing crashing down around our ears. I'll have their badge for this.

Leading this operation is a huge break for me. Teams from both the homicide and narcotics division have joined forces to put these criminals out of action for good, and I'm the one in charge. After almost two years of covert intelligence and undercover work to build evidence on every known member, this will be the biggest notch on my belt as detective for the Sydney LLC.

Fury grinds my jaw as I palm my gun and shift to the corner of the shipping container. I peer around the side and every drop of blood in my body turns to ice.

Dust kicks up as the Dodge Charger slides to a halt at the warehouse entrance, my goddamn little sister at the wheel. She looks like *Fright Night* dressed all in black with dark liner smeared beneath her eyes.

"Mitch," comes the voice of Tate Donavon from behind me. Tate is my partner, has been since the beginning, but I've got lead on this operation and despite him doing his best to keep his resentment under wraps, it emanates from his skin with tense body language and terse words. "I've got Kelly Daniels on the line."

I speak without taking my eyes from Mackenzie 'Death Wish' Valentine. "I don't have time for girly catch-ups right now."

"He says it's urgent. To do with Mac."

I snatch my phone from his hand. "Speak."

Kelly doesn't waste time. "Mac is coming your way."

How he knows Mac was headed this way, or that he even knows my current location, is beyond me right now, but there's no time for questions. "No shit, Sherlock," I snarl, my fingers tightening on the phone. "We're at Dockside Wharf and I'm staring right at her, so your warning can go suck a bag of dicks."

"Go get fucked, Valentine."

"I don't have time to trade petty insults. Casey was supposed to have her on lockdown at the party."

"He did but Grace was sick so he uh ..."

"He *uh* what?"

"He passed that particular duty to me before they went to bed so he could take care of his woman."

Fuck. My. Life. "Really?" My voice is so snide my eyes water. "Then you're fired."

"That slippery bitch was hell-bent on chasing down Jake and tried to steal my fuckin' Harley," Kelly cries into the phone as if his whole world had almost ended. "And that's not all of it. I have worse news and even shittier news," he goes on to mutter unhappily.

"What?"

"She knows the King Street Boys have him. That's why she's there."

My fist curls so tight around the phone I hear the device crack. "How does she know that?" I hiss, furious. We *know* they have him. He agreed to be bait in return for immunity against past crimes. We have the entire Dockside surrounded right this second, and my little sister is about to get caught in the crossfire.

This means Operation Strike is about to go down in a blaze of career-ending flames. "What's the shittier news?" I dare to ask, wondering how it can possibly get worse than this.

"Luke and Jake were tight. Like brothers," he says, imparting useless information that I already know. "Luke knows they have him because his older brother Leander knows. And you know what that means."

It takes less than a second to connect the dots. "Bingo," I mutter, referring to the leader of the Sentinels.

"Not just Bingo. The whole fuckin' MC is coming. They're armed and they're fuckin' riled."

My eyes drift close for one single, heart-pounding moment. I've got the King Street Boys on one side, the Sentinels bearing down on the other, and half of the Sydney police force bunkered down in wait. War is coming and it's going to be a bloody shit show.

My eyes fly open, lighting on Mac as she pushes open the driver's side door of the beautiful Dodge Charger. "Tell the Sentinels to stand down!"

Kelly's voice is grim. "It's too late for that."

There's nothing left to say. I hang up the phone and tuck it in my back pocket.

"Valentine," comes the voice of Tate from behind me again. I turn my head. He's holding out his radio. My own has been buzzing while on the phone. "It's Inspector Burns."

Inspector Keith Burns. My boss.

"I don't have time for another conversation. I need to get my sister out of there."

"That's the thing," he butts in urgently. "You can't."

"What do you mean *I can't,*" I bark, snatching the radio. I speak into it as Mac puts one booted foot on the ground. Then the other. She does it with purpose, her chest rising as she breathes in and stands. "Burns."

"You need to let her go," he orders me. "Snatching her out in the open will blow your cover and years' worth of work."

"Sir," I hiss, my voice low, my rage unleashing as Mac steps forward and swings the car door closed behind her. How in the hell did she get her hands on Jake's car? We knew the King Street Boys were following him. He was supposed to pull over, pocket the keys, and lift the hood as if suffering engine trouble. Intel told us they planned on snatching him last night, right before a huge shipment of drugs was due to arrive in the docks this morning. *Our* plan had been to give them the best opportunity possible to do so, helping us narrow down their exact location, and then lay in wait.

We have this operation fine-tuned to the minutest detail, including Plan B's for every possible scenario. Except we aren't prepared for Mackenzie Valentine and a goddamn war. "That is my little sister out there."

"It's too late, Mitch. You have to let her go. She can handle herself."

"Sir—"

"Let. Her. Go."

"I can't let her walk in there!"

"Goddammit, Valentine!" he shouts, setting my eardrums ringing. "I'm not asking you. That's a goddamn order, and if you defy me I'll demote you to traffic duty for rest of your godforsaken career!"

I ignore his threat. My sister's life is bigger than this. "The Sentinels are bearing down."

"What the!" he shouts. "How far out are they?"

Kelly Daniels

Mitch is beyond pissed, and I can't blame him. We know about their Operation Strike. We've known for *months*. And we honest to god planned to stay out of it. We've been wanting to put the King Street Boys out of action for years, but having the Sydney police do it for us is just the cherry on our cupcake. Except they got Jake involved. And now Mac. And that is *not* okay.

Mitch hangs up on me. I shove my phone into the pocket of my jeans and look sideways to Luke. We're stopped at a red light, both of us seated on our bikes and helmets in our laps. "She's already there."

His curse is loud and pained. "Fuck!"

The crescendo of what sounds like a thousand Harleys roar from behind us. We both turn. The Sentinels, my brothers in arms, are building. Bikes are coming in from the left and right to form a giant convoy of retribution as they thunder down the street toward us.

I get on the phone for one last, quick phone call.

Casey answers with "What the hell is going on?"

"War," I answer, my voice terse. "And Mac is caught right in the middle of it."

Travis Valentine

I wake to the buzzing ringtone of my phone, and our giant Rhodesian Ridgeback, Rufus, licking my face. "What the ..." I push him away with a sluggish hand. He returns. "Stop it."

"It's because you've got a chocolate handprint on your cheek," Quinn mumbles from beside me, her face smushed into the pillow.

"How the—"

"Sam," she answers before I can even finish the question, referring to our foster son. He should be tucked up in bed at this early hour but with consciousness now thrust upon me, I can hear cartoons from the living room. He's up and clearly has the blessed sense not to come in and wake us. God, I love that kid.

I swipe a hand across my cheek. It comes away with smears of chocolate and dog slobber. "Oh gross."

"Don't you dare," Quinn warns as I go to wipe my palm across the sheets. Her face remains smushed into the pillow.

"How did you even—"

"Because I'm a mother now. We see everything."

My phone blares on as Rufus comes at me again, tongue lolling and big eyes wounded because I'm repeatedly shoving him away. Chocolate is bad for dogs, right? But he's hardly going to drop dead at my feet after a few licks. I eye him carefully, holding his massive head back as that giant tongue comes for my face. He doesn't look ill.

Quinn rolls over, her big brown eyes blinking open, cheeks flushed a deep pink, and the imprint of our bedsheets lining half her face. Her white-blonde hair is a fluffy cloud of fairy floss around her head after she curled it for the party last night with something that resembled a giant stainless steel dildo.

"Are you gonna get that?" she mumbles.

"Ugh." My eyes slide to the mammoth clock on the wall. It's a round marble affair that required both Casey and I to lift in place. It's secured with serious bolts, but I still eye it every morning with trepidation. The little hand points to the five and the big hand is on the twelve. Who the hell is calling me at five a.m.? On a Sunday no less. My one sleep-in of the week.

"It's not going to fall."

How does she even know I'm glaring at the clock? "It will. One day it's going to come crashing down at the same time Sam walks past and it will crush every bone in his little body."

"It's not that heavy." She rolls over, used to my anxiety when it comes to our soon-to-be adopted son. I can't fathom how parents can remain calm when their kid is one step away from being snatched or falling down one of those giant sinkholes that Grace keeps talking about. They are just *that* vulnerable. Anything could happen. Parenting requires constant vigilance. Whenever I lose sight of Sam for a single moment, a freaky panic overtakes me. Does it ever get easier?

"It would only dent his head or something," Quinn adds.

My phone has not stopped its incessant ringing. I reach for it. "We should make him wear a helmet."

"You're being ridiculous."

The screen shows it's Casey Daniels, my best mate. "I'm not," I argue as I hit the answer key and put the phone to my ear. "What's up?" I ask him as Rufus comes at me again, undeterred. With only one hand free, I can't hold him off and he gets another lick in.

"Get in the car," Casey replies, his voice grim and leeching urgency. "I'll explain as you drive."

I don't hesitate.

Grace Paterson

I tug my legs through the pair of skinny jeans I left on the bedroom floor in the early hours of the morning. Last night's party had left me with only enough energy to slide them off and leave them crumpled in the corner before I crawled into bed. I do the zipper and snatch my phone from the bedside table. There's no time to lament on how the denim gapes at my butt cheeks. Cancer kicked me to the kerb. I beat it back and won, but there's still a long road ahead. And that includes food. So much food we're going to run out of room in Casey's loft to store it all. My former model management agency would love the look I'm rocking right now, which disgusts me. Emaciated is always the new black and it's not healthy. I'm longing to build some muscle on my frame and a nice round booty.

I scroll my phone contacts in a panicked motion. Names roll down the screen so fast I have to scroll back up. Who do I call first? There's no time to think about it. I pick and dial.

My brother Henry answers within seconds and my stomach drops with guilt. He's been like this ever since he heard about my diagnosis—hovering like a mother hen, accessible within a moment's notice, attending appointments, blending me kale smoothies that have me retching more than the chemotherapy does. After all those years of travelling for work, it warms me to have this close relationship with my brother again. It just sucks huge hairy nipples that I had to get sick for it to happen.

"Everything okay?" he asks, sounding equal parts anxious and husky with sleep.

I don't wish to cause him any alarm because I'm not an alarmist, but if there is ever a time to become one it's now. "Mac is pregnant," I blurt out, adding gossipmonger to my rapidly expanding repertoire of negative personality traits. "And you know that Jake is gone but Mac took off after him. Kelly called Casey and he was talking so loud I overheard the whole thing. Jake has been abducted and Mac is caught up in it somehow and something about Operation Strike and a shit show. I don't know!" I cry, throwing my free hand up in the hair with agitation as I pace. I should be looking for shoes to put on my feet, but I'm so frazzled I don't think I even know what shoes are. "Something is going down, Henry Bear. I don't know what it is, but I'm scared."

"Holy shit."

"Right?" I continue pacing on legs made of jelly. Mitsy snaps at my ankles and I do an abrupt turn to throw her off course. The psychotic white ball of fluff that barely resembles a dog wants breakfast, and I don't have time for her demands right now.

"Abducted by who?"

"The King Street Boys," I answer, having no idea who these assholes are.

"Holy shit," he mutters again, his voice all-knowing. Clearly he's well-informed on who they are. "Does Evie and Quinn know any of this?"

"I don't know!" I cry, throwing my hand up again before slapping it down on my thigh.

"Alright. I'll call them. Just sit tight and stay calm, Gracie Bean. I'm on my way, okay?"

Mitsy resumes snapping at my heels while I pace. Her jaw locks on the back of my ankle. I jerk my leg around to free it, but she must have a tooth snagged in the denim of my jeans. She skids across the sleek timber flooring, taking a long line of thread with her. The entire hem begins to unravel as she scrambles to her feet and runs off, panicked at being hooked. "Goddammit!" I shriek. I'm still attached and the thread pulls so tight around my angle it cuts off circulation.

"I said stay calm," Henry enunciates into the phone.

"I am calm," I growl as I reach down to yank the thread free.

"It's not good for your health to—"

"Just shut your face and get here."

Chapter Thirty-Eight

Jake

I sit on a chair inside a dark and musty, cavernous warehouse. My wrists are bound with thick duct tape to the arms of the chair. My knees are also bound, along with my ankles, to the wooden legs. They're taking no chances with my potential escape.

My head hangs low. I can't hold it up. My left eye is swollen shut and my right is blurry. I took a bat to the head just above it. I can't touch the area to assess the damage, but I figure the socket is fractured and it's filling with blood. The simple white tee shirt I wore has been ripped off and TRAITOR carved across my chest with a sharp, double-edged dagger. A rib is broken on my right side. There was an immense *crack* when Boyd slammed his fist into my midsection again and again, the sound like splintering wood. White hot pain turned my stomach inside out. It's now a steady throb. I fear a rib has punctured my lung because there's a stabbing pain in my chest every time I inhale. The King Street Boys want justice, and they want their justice in blood.

Mitch had contacted me the same day we returned from touring with the idea of being bait. The gang has apparently been keeping tabs on me since I ran into Ross at Steve Valentine's retirement party. Mitch advised they were biding their time until an opportunity became available for them to grab me. The Sydney police were going to provide them that opportunity because they needed me. Intel had given them the date and the time of the drug bust, but the location was still an unknown. With a small slimline tracker planted inside the lining of my shoe, I would be the one to provide that last, vital piece of information.

A covert task force should be in motion right now with warrants, raiding homes and member lodgings, bringing in every single member, including politicians, celebrities, and government officials. If everything has gone to plan, this warehouse should be surrounded, the bust netting them Ross, our nefarious leader, Boyd, head of security, and several other high-ranking lieutenants who are in the back room of this warehouse.

I honestly don't know if I'm going to survive this and judging by the grave tone in Mitch's voice when he sent me off with the tracker, he doesn't know either. But there was no choice. I had to go through with it. I *had* to try.

"You think you can just walk away from the King Street Boys?"

The voice is deep. Familiar. It has me lifting my head with effort and squinting my right eye to focus on the man walking toward me. He's wearing a sharp suit and polished shoes. His light blue eyes are cold and cruel.

My reply is a grunt. It's all I can manage.

He gets closer until he stands before me. I gather all the saliva I can produce and spit on his shoes. It coats the expensive Italian leather, the bloodied mess oozing into the finely crafted stitching. It brings me only a small amount of satisfaction.

He hisses and cracks the back of his palm across my face. The assault sends fresh waves of pain rolling through my stomach. He lifts his foot and wipes the mess across the leg of my jeans. Then he takes a step back, out of spitting distance.

Mitch Valentine

I stand there useless as my sister walks toward the building filled with a dangerous nest of merciless criminals. My heart is in my throat.

If I intervene my career will be in tatters and Operation Strike, along with years' worth of hard work, will go bust.

My radio crackles. A solitary word comes through from a familiar voice. A voice that never fails to send heat licking down my spine. A voice of lilting Spanish from a detective in our squad who knows me better than I know myself. "Valentine," she says.

Her tone is thick with urgency, but there's also encouragement. She's imploring me to go. Gabriella Valdez is of Spanish descent, which has given her striking features. Deep, sexy eyes, sharp eyebrows that convey power and authority, and rich dark hair so long and wavy it reaches the small of her back. She's been a detective in our squad for just three short months after years of undercover work with the Vipers, an insidious motorcycle gang that hooked her on drugs and almost ended her life.

She's also the girl I loved throughout my years studying at Charles Sturt University. I convinced myself that my love for her died a slow death when she up and disappeared after graduation. But her reappearance, showing up at my father's retirement party, changes everything.

That love reignited of its own accord like a fuse lying dormant. All it needed was one look, one touch, and that spark caught fire. But I can't think of it now. I can't think of her, or worry about how she's stationed on the far side, long hair in a thick braid, torso strapped with a bullet-proof vest, waiting for the signal to storm the warehouse.

All I *can* think of is that she has my back. She's telling me to go. And she's right. When it comes down to it—this bust, the eradication of the King Street Boys, my career—it all means nothing when it comes to my sister's life.

Mac being here is my fault. I shouldn't have used Romero as bait. Not when I know how much she loves him. And not without telling her. She wouldn't even be here if I had kept her in the loop. I would've expected it of my brothers. There's no reason why she shouldn't expect it of us. I made a mistake and need to apologise. We all do. Mac spent her whole life demanding our courtesy and respect and what we gave her was never enough.

Now it's on me to get her out, but I can't do it alone. I click the button on my radio. "Valdez."

"*Si*," she responds. *Yes.*

My mouth is dry. I'm wrong for asking. But knowing that isn't enough to stop me. "Back me up?"

Her tone is soft when it's usually severe. "*Siempre*, Mitchell Valentine."

Always.

My chest aches with gratitude. Gabriella knows what family means. At least when my career goes down in a blazing trail of condemnation, and demotion after demotion, I can explain that she was simply following orders.

I click the button on the radio to speak. *I love you.* Then I slide it off before the words escape my throat. Now is not the time. But later. Before this day is over, I'm going to remind her that true love never really dies.

Mac

I walk toward the warehouse. I have no plan. I have no idea what I'm doing at all besides not thinking straight. I don't even know what I'm walking into. I'm unarmed, apart from a small Swiss army knife I found in the glove compartment of Jake's car. It's tucked inside the boot on my right foot. I know how to throw it and hit a target, but the blade isn't large. If I want to inflict damage, I need to be close range.

The sun has begun to rise yet the humidity is already intense. A blast of warm air blows down low across the docks. It sets my hair in a whirlwind around my head and across my face. If I hadn't tossed back my head to flick the strands away, I wouldn't have noticed it. But I do. The briefest flash of someone from the right-hand corner of the building, then it's gone. Someone outfitted in skinny jeans, combat boots, and a police issue vest.

Gabriella Valdez.

What is she doing here?

My mind races and my faltering pace slows. If she's here in an official capacity, my eldest brother must be nearby. Along with their respective partners. And if they're here, and Jake is inside with the King Street Boys, I'm walking right into the middle of something huge.

But my legs don't slow their pace. I can't lose Jake. Not now. Not after all this time of being too scared of the future. I was so busy reading everyone else, I didn't stop and take the time to read myself. I *need* him. My hand goes to my belly and my heart screams with fear and yearning. Our baby needs him too.

"We need him," I whisper to the growing life beneath my hand and continue walking. Everything else feels unimportant now. Irrelevant.

"Mac!" It's Mitch. His voice is unyielding and comes from somewhere on my far left. "Stand down."

I shake my head. I don't know how to be the person who sits back and does nothing. My response is scratchy, like sandpaper, and the low wind almost snatches it away. "I can't."

"You can," he orders. "Turn around and start walking to me."

"You heard her. She *can't*." A man appears in the doorway. Just a sliver of him. His light blue eyes are hard and his brows drawn low. A tingle of awareness snakes down my spine. I've met this man before. I know I have. I never forget a face. My eyes lock on his tee shirt like a missile and dizziness engulfs me in a wave. There's blood. Splatters of it. My gaze drops lower. There's a gun in his hand. It's pointed right at me. "She'd rather come inside, wouldn't you, sweetheart?"

The breeze pushes at me, and I realise I've come to a standstill. It's Adam Rossiter. Ross. Eli's brother. He's part of the King Street

Boys? Why? How? Jake was with me that night we ran into him. He didn't say a word. Not. A. Single. Word.

Of course he didn't! cries my inner voice. *What would you have done had you known?*

Something very, very stupid. Oh god, Jake. How well you know me.

"Don't stop now," Adam Rossiter says. "Keep walking."

"Mac!" There's desperation in my brother's voice.

"I'm sorry," I say. It's all I have.

Gunfire pings from my right. From Gabriella. It hits the door. Wood splinters in all directions as Ross pulls further inside the building. His blue eyes burn with cold fire as he aims and shoots right at my feet. I jump. And dust kicks up, spraying my shoes and jeans.

"Try that again," he yells in the direction of Gabriella's position, "and I'll aim a little higher next time!"

My brother bellows a thousand different curses, his frustration evident. The words drown in the sound of thunder. The rumbling is incessant and loud, and it's increasing with every short breath I take. My head turns toward the noise. The only part of the road I can see that leads to the docks is a crest. Bikes are riding over it and down, disappearing behind buildings. Hundreds of bikes.

Holy fuck.

Kelly Daniels has amassed an army of Sentinels, and they're headed this way.

This *cannot* be good.

"Get inside," Ross barks.

I start walking. This is what I wanted. To get to Jake. My stride appears steady and my voice is sharp, but inside I'm nothing but jelly. "Where is he?"

"He's enjoying a reunion."

I step inside. It's dark. I blink several times. Ross snatches me from behind as my sight adjusts. He wrenches my arm behind my back. I cry out, the pain like a sharp knife stabbing my shoulder. The cold barrel of a gun presses to my temple.

"The beautiful and mysterious Mackenzie Valentine," he croons in my ear. His breath is hot and close. I twist my head away and he yanks me back. Another cry rips from my throat. "I knew you'd show up. I know a lot about you. I've watched you. You're quite the enigma. Beautiful, yet an utter bitch. Dominant, yet loyal. Especially to Jake. And now here you are, like a little lamb to the slaughter. Do you think he knows you're here?" he asks, and then keeps talking without expecting an answer. "Let's tell him. He'll be so happy to see you."

Ross shoves me forward. My heeled boot catches on a divot in the cement flooring. I stumble and it tears something in my shoulder. I hold back the moan of pain but tears prick my eyes.

"Keep moving," he growls.

I swallow nausea as I right myself, and force my feet to push forward while I take in my surroundings.

My eyes have adjusted enough to view the cavernous space. It's huge. Almost the size of an airport hanger. It's filled with shipping containers. Old rusted ones. They're set in neat rows, and my gaze slides down each one we pass. I'm trying to scope any kind of exit but there is none.

Ross pushes me forward again, hurrying me along. We reach a wall. It extends through the middle of the warehouse and ends three-quarters of the way along. Almost as if they ran out of material to build a whole one. When I'm shoved around the corner, my legs give out.

Ross lets me go with a shove, and I drop to my knees.

"Jake."

His name is an involuntary whisper from my lips.

I barely recognise his face. Half of it is swollen. The rest is bloodied from cuts. His eye. His *eye*. The white of it is red and blood drips from the corner. It runs down the side of his cheek and splatters to his lap below, little droplets of life leeching from his body. He's strapped to a chair—his legs and arms immobile.

His shirt has been torn from his body and hangs from his waist in tatters. His chest is covered with dirt and sweat and blood. *Traitor* has been carved across his glorious chest in harsh, angular letters.

Tears begin to roll down my cheeks. I can't stop them. "Jake," I sob, louder. The man I love has been tortured and battered and rage burns hot inside me.

His head lifts so very slow, the effort visibly painstaking. He sways as he stares at me. "No," he breathes in ragged voice, his fear visible.

"What is she doing here?"

The sharp question has my eyes snapping to Jake's left. To the man in the stylish suit, perfectly styled hair, and shiny shoes. I shake my head, unable to catch my breath. "Eli?"

Behind him is a large back room with wide windows. There are men inside. At least eight—and all of them muscled and armed. Some are watching us. Others are talking or arguing. There's a table in the middle of the room and on it rests ten hard cases in a matte charcoal colour. One after the other, they line up like little soldier suitcases, closed and awaiting orders.

"For fuck's sake," Eli curses, and those gorgeous blue eyes of his, the same ones that have always looked at me with such kindness and warmth, are colder than the arctic as he glares at Ross. "She's not supposed to be here. We have Jake as a hostage. We don't need Mac. Get her out of here. Now!" he barks.

"Eli, what are you doing?" I ask. My voice sounds weak to my ears.

"Now is not the time," Ross says from behind me. He fists a hand in my hair and wrenches my head right back. I yelp at the sharp burst of pain as Ross leans down and puts his face right in mine. Jake bellows in rage as tears slide down the sides of my temples and into my hair. I hate them. I want to wipe them away so he can't see how much I hurt. "Tell them what you did, you little bitch."

"I didn't do anything, you dumb fuck."

He growls with anger and lets me go, but he does it with an almighty shove. The powerful force of it sends me forward toward the cement floor. My forehead smacks it hard and my body crumples.

"What did she do?" I hear Eli ask. His voice sounds like it's coming from some far away tunnel. I try moving but I can't. My head throbs. The *thump thump thump* eclipses all conscious thought.

"She led an entire legion of Sentinels right toward us!"

"Fuck!" he hisses.

"The bitch needs to die."

"Don't be stupid." Eli's voice sounds panicked. Why does he sound panicked?

"Don't call me stupid, big brother."

"You can't shoot her. It's Mac. I love her. I've always loved her. She belongs with *me*."

"You don't love her. You just think you do." His voice is disparaging. "Besides, no one leaves the King Street Boys. They need to know that if they try leaving, we don't just shoot them, we shoot the ones they love too."

My eyes feel weighted with bricks. I loll to the side and force them open a fraction. Ross is standing over me, gun pointed.

"*I'm* the leader of the King Street Boys," Eli roars and my mind reels. All this time? There's been so much more deception than I can comprehend and the depth of it breaks my heart. "You will do what I say and stand the fuck down!"

"You might be the head of our gang," Ross shouts back, taking no heed of Eli's order, "but it's me they all listen to because you're never there! You're not in it for the brotherhood. You don't care about any of us. You care more about your precious fucking inheritance and about the precious fucking Valentines. Well, newsflash, Brother. You're done with them. Today, they're all gonna die!"

Eli shouts in return as does Jake. Above them both is the roar of motorcycles. *The Sentinals are here,* I think faintly. More shouting erupts. In Spanish. Gabriella?

My brain is in a fog. I manage to turn my head, inch by slow inch. My vision is blurred, but I see her. Gun up, body strapped in armour. She's yelling at Ross to stand down. Everyone is yelling.

Gunfire pops.

"Nooooooooo!" Jake roars.

My body jerks, and I turn my head back as searing pain burns through me like a brushfire. I look up at Ross. Did he shoot me?

The thought barely forms when his body shudders under a bullet. The fire comes from Gabriella's direction. He hisses and turns his gun on her at the same time Eli runs toward me. But Gabriella doesn't stop firing. Her bullets hit Ross in the chest. They slam into him, one after the other. Blood explodes outward in a showering arc and rains down over me. He drops to the ground by my side.

"Mac!"

My eyes shift slowly to Jake. He's twisting and yanking at tape, trying to rip free from the chair. There's an empty metal table on his right and with a frustrated roar, he stands and turns hard, smashing the chair against it.

Jake

The pain is intense. I can't breathe properly, and I can barely see. Mac is on the ground. The bastard *shot her*. He threw her to the ground like she was trash and opened fire, and I sat helpless, strapped to a chair like a trussed-up turkey awaiting my Thanksgiving fate.

Gabriella comes into view, gun up and firing. Ross is pummelled with bullets like they're fists to his gut.

The roller door on my right is wrenched open at the same time. Sentinels and police flood the warehouse. It's utter warfare. They take cover and fire at the multitude of King Street Boys members that flood out from the back room. Bodies move in bursts of speed, and pings of bullets hit steel beams and shipping containers.

Mac is bleeding on the ground in the middle of it all. Rage surges inside me, a veritable tsunami of wrath so powerful it churns red and hot. It burns my throat and my eyes and every fibre of my soul.

I yell her name. Her eyes slide to mine. The green of her irises are dull and her movements sluggish. Using all the strength that remains, I stand and turn to smash the chair at the table, over and over, until it begins to splinter.

"You killed my brother," Eli says in horror, appearing caught between going for Ross or for Mac. His gaze shifts to Gabriella. He doesn't see the flood of Sentinels and police to his right. There's a gun in his hand and it's lax by his side. He looks at it as though seeing it for the first time. Then he lifts it and points it right at her. I lunge toward him, crashing into him, but not before he fires off three distinct shots. *Bam bam bam. One two three.*

Eli and I both go down in the heavy tackle. The distinct *snap* of a bone in my chest renders me breathless as we smash into the cold, brutal floor.

Kelly Daniels

My heart is in my throat the entire ride toward the docks. I barely know Mackenzie Valentine, but I'm already half in love with her. And here she is in love with another dude and having his baby. *I'm such a fuckin' douche.* The first time my heart has ever felt a thump for another female and she belongs to some other lucky bastard.

That lucky bastard happens to be Jake Romero—a childhood friend of my Sentinel brother Fox—so unfortunately I can't shoot him. Or maim him just a little bit, enough to render him useless to another woman.

I want to know what it's like to be with her. Or someone like her. It's not because she's beautiful. It's because she's full of fire. Mac is the kind of girl that when she's in, she's *all in*. An everything or nothing girl. One who can handle death and pain and still remain standing strong by your side.

I killed my old man. In cold blood. Casey knows, as does Grace and my Sentinel brothers. But only a woman like Mac could see through the façade of indifference and into the heart of the scared little boy inside who pulled the trigger. The same one who couldn't bear to hear his mother scream from one more brutal hit or see her buckle under the pummel of her husband's fists. That little boy saw her die, and then he did what he had to do.

That dumb young kid didn't belong in the Sentinels, but he does now. My new reality is hard and cold. There's no place for love.

Our bikes crest over the hill toward the warehouse. My helmet is off and strapped to the back of my Harley because it annoys the fuck out of me. My blond hair is pulled into a ponytail at the nape of my neck. Strands whip across my face and sunglasses as we rumble down the road. Cars pull to the side, getting out of our way. It's clear we mean business. And we do.

Luke and I arrive first. I'm off my bike and running before my brothers even stop behind us. I don't care about the police and their *Operation Strike*. It's all been blown to shit anyway because I hear shots being fired inside the warehouse.

Mitch is running around the side of the building. I follow. The gun from my saddlebag is already resting in the back of my jeans. I tug it out and engage the slide. He doesn't hesitate and runs straight through the roller doors that two police officers wrench up.

"Mac!" he yells. "Gabriella!"

I run in behind him with Fox close behind me. The scene is a slaughter. Bullets are flying from all directions. Mac is down and bleeding profusely from her leg. She's covered in blood, and I can't see where else she's been hit. Gabriella is down too, and Ross is unmoving on the ground, splayed on his side. Jake is beaten and barely recognisable. He's wrestling with another man, struggling to disarm him.

"Cover me!" I shout to Fox and duck low, running toward them as he lets loose a hail of gunfire.

Mitch is two steps ahead of me when Jake's opponent cracks his elbow into what already looks like a broken eye socket on his face. Jake's head smacks back onto the concrete. In that split second of inattention, the man rolls to his side and spies us running toward them. He takes in the Sentinels' cut I'm wearing over my leather jacket and lifts his gun, pointing it at me. He fires but his aim is off and the bullet hits Mitch.

Blood sprays in an arc from his neck, the force of the bullet slamming him backward and into me. I stumble and with my balance lost we both go down. Mac's brother lands on top of me, a river of red gushing from his wound.

"Fuck," I hiss and start dragging my body out from beneath his heavy weight. He's still alive. His breathing is rapid, his chest rising and falling as he sucks in air. I jam a finger in the wound and he shouts a gritty curse of pain. I freeze when a pair of boots reach my line of sight. My eyes draw upward.

"Eli," Mitch gasps, his eyes on the man standing over us.

Eli crouches, dropping his gun. It skitters away, out of his reach. He shakes his head, visibly shaken. "This wasn't supposed to happen."

"It ... was ... always going to lead to ... this," Mitch chokes out.

"You knew about me," he says, his voice accusatory.

"For years," Mitch gasps.

"You never said a word."

"You know what they say ..." Mac's brother chuckles but it's not a happy sound and blood spills from his lips. "Keep your friends close and your enemies closer."

Eli can only shake his head. "My brother is dead."

"Good." Jake's voice is hard and comes from behind him. Eli rises and turns. Jake has no gun, but he holds a piece of splintered wood in his hands. "He deserved to die. And so do you."

Jake swings hard. The makeshift weapon cracks into the side of Eli's head. Skin splits open, and he hits the ground hard. It knocks him out and with the threat contained, it leaves me free to snag the radio from Mitch's gun belt.

With one hand putting pressure on Mitch's wound, I use the other to hit the button and put the call out for more than one ambulance. I'm just about to speak when the sound of sirens render the air. They're already on their way.

Chapter Thirty-Nine

Jake

I toss the piece of splintered wood away, relieved the Rossiter brothers are both down. I was so tired of the threat Ross held over my life for years, and now it's gone. But the ache at what I've done under his orders still remains. I have to live with that, but I'll live with it happily if I know he can never touch anyone I love ever again.

I turn, my eyes finding Mac. She's hurting. When I start for her my ankle is grabbed. I look down. It's Ross. He's not dead like we thought. He manages to yank hard and the unexpected motion drops me to my knees. I twist around, forming a hard fist.

Ross is trying to rise when I smash it in his face. He stumbles backward, hot blood spurting from his nose as he rights himself. The image fills me with grim satisfaction. "I'll kill you with my bare hands."

Mac's voice is steel. "No you won't."

We both turn toward her. She's standing upright, putting all her weight on her left leg. There's a bullet hole in her right thigh. She's wearing black but it doesn't hide the gaping wound and the ooze of blood running down her leg. It's bright and thick. Her face is pale and clammy, but her eyes are raging. There's a gun in her hand. It's Eli's. She must have found it on the ground.

"You already have one death on your hands," she says and before I can blink, she lifts the weapon and shoots. Ross drops, a dead weight, with a single, perfect bullet hole lodged in his forehead. "Now I do too."

"Mac," I whisper.

A choking sob escapes her throat, and the gun drops from her hand. She starts to crumple, as if shooting him was all she had to give and now there's nothing left.

I rush forward, catching her before she hits concrete. Mac sags against me and we both sink to the floor because I have nothing left either.

"Mitch?" she asks, her voice reedy and thin.

I glance his way. Kelly has him, his fingers jammed into his neck to halt the flow, but blood is still seeping. It doesn't look good and my heart sinks. "He's going to be fine," I lie.

"Promise me," she begs, her fingers clutching at the tatters of my shirt.

But I can't promise. Mac watches my mouth open and close and tears leak from her eyes. Instead of giving an answer, I pull back a little and rip the shredded remains of my shirt from around my waist, gathering a long strip to form a bandage. I tie it in a tight knot around her wound, just above the thigh, and she curses in a low, savage growl. "It's okay, it's okay," I soothe, pulling her against me when I'm done, rocking her gently.

"Your face," she sobs against my chest, not even looking at it.

"It's fine," I soothe but it must be a mess. The throb of pain is constant now, and every inhale feels like I'm being stabbed. "I'm fine."

"Gabriella?"

My gaze shifts to the beautiful detective. She lies prone on the floor. Eli managed three shots before I tackled him to the ground. Each one hit her. One in the shoulder and one in her leg, and a final, fatal shot to the head. Luke, a trained paramedic, is taking care of her. My eyes meet his. He shakes his head. She's gone.

My jaw begins to quiver and I lock it down. "Luke is taking care of her."

"Is she okay?"

I draw back and take Mac's face in my palms. There's a deep cut high on her forehead from Ross smashing her head into the cement floor. It's stopped bleeding but her hair is matted with blood, and her face is covered with dried tears and dirt. I swallow the lump in my throat and give her the painful truth. "Gabriella is gone."

Horror fills her eyes and she shakes her head. "No," she replies, her voice adamant. "No she's not."

"I'm sorry."

Her head won't stop shaking and her teeth begin to chatter. "No, no, no, no, no, no!" Mac yanks away from me and I grab her wrists, holding her tight. She doesn't need to see Gabriella like this. A friend she knows and loves. The horror and sickening finality of it is too much. I don't want her living with the image.

"Let me go," she cries and my heart aches.

Mac shoves at my chest, not realising the injuries that lie beneath, and my vision blackens as she breaks free. She crawls her way toward Gabriella, sobbing.

I press my lips together. There's nothing I can do. Luke shuffles backward to give Mac space. She grasps Gabriella's shoulders, lifting her upwards, wrapping her arms around her upper body and holding her close. Gabriella's arms dangle uselessly behind her and her head lolls.

Mac rocks back and forth, holding her, painful sobs tearing from her chest. My eyes burn and my jaw clenches so tight I fear my teeth will crack. I turn to look at Mitch. The paramedics have him now. He's unconscious and being placed on a stretcher.

Kelly has risen to his feet. Blood smears his hands. It's through his hair too, where he's pushed strands from his face. He's taking in the aftermath that surrounds us. Bodies litter the ground. Some of them Sentinels. Some of them King Street Boys. The bitter tang of blood scents the morning air, along with the thick stench of gunfire and devastation.

The paramedics are wheeling Mitch out of the huge roller door when Henry runs in. He gets pulled up short by the police. They're setting up a barrier. The warehouse is a crime scene now.

"Let me through!" he shouts, shoving at them.

While the police are distracted with my best friend, Casey, Travis, and Jared appear and simply walk their way through. The three of them take one look at Mac and Gabriella and they each falter, faces paling.

"One of you go with Mitch," I shout at them, pointing to the stretcher getting wheeled out the other side. Travis runs to his brother and disappears with him out the door. "Mac needs an ambulance too," I say, my voice hoarse as I rise on unsteady legs.

"I'll go direct them," Luke says and jogs off.

I shuffle toward Mac and reach down for her, sucking in a sharp breath.

"I've got her," Jared says, reaching for her at the same time.

"No!" I bark, stubborn. "I need to do this. You take care of ... of ..." My eyes fall to Gabriella. She still rests in Mac's arms.

"Jesus," Jared's voice cracks. He swipes a hand down his face, struggling to come to terms with the unexpected loss.

"I'll take care of her," Casey interjects and crouches. He tries to gently pry the beautiful detective away, but Mac won't let go. She looks up at Casey, her face etched in despair. He's locking his emotions down, but I see grief in his tight jaw and clenched hands.

"I killed her," she whispers, and her face turns to mine. "This is on me."

"Oh, baby, no." I shake my head, struck down with horror. "Don't go there."

Casey prises her white-knuckled fingers from Gabriella's lifeless form, and I take her, praying I'm able to lift her without passing out because I'm damned if anyone else carries her out of here but me.

I squat low and place one arm around her shoulders, the other beneath her knees, and I stand, bringing her with me. The effort costs me and I stagger, dizzy.

"Hold on, Princess," I plead.

Her arms slide up and wrap slowly around my neck as I absorb the steady beat of her heart against my chest.

Reassured, I take one step, then another, each one slow and unsteady. Each one bringing me closer to the big, open doorway. Her hands loosen their grip when I step outside into the warm air and hot morning sun. Then they fall slack. Mac is unconscious in my arms. I blink as best I can, adjusting to the brightness. Evie, Quinn, Grace, and Henry, are all huddled together behind a police line.

"Stay with me, Princess," I say softly.

Evie presses a shaky hand to her mouth, her face ashen when she sees us. Quinn grabs her and they hold each other. Tears stream down Grace's face. She takes Henry's hand in hers and squeezes as I shuffle forward, step by step, determined to carry Mac out of this hellhole and into the light.

The police cart Eli out from behind us, his hands cuffed behind his back. His face appears heavily injured from my strike, but they're showing him no mercy. He's roughly shoved ahead of us and our eyes meet before he looks away.

Elijah Rossiter killed Gabriella Valdez, a police detective no less, and the love of his supposed best friend's life. The judge will throw the book at him. Eli is going away for a very, very long time. That knowledge gives me a very small measure of satisfaction. If Mitch survives, it will give him none at all.

I had no idea he was the real leader of the King Street Boys, but from what I overhead from the Rossiter brothers during my abduction, he was more a figurehead the way a silent partner invests in a business but has no running of the day-to-day operations. It makes sense, considering the King Street Boys were always one step ahead of the police. The gang leader was their inside man on the force. A high-ranking, recently promoted official!

Eli also knows I was Jonah. He knew all along. He and Ross were simply biding their time to use me, knowing how close I am with the Valentine family. I was their 'ace in the hole' and a way for them to get rid of the Valentine's once and for all.

They knew about Operation Strike too. Those cases on the table in the back room? Eight of them were filled with drugs. Two were bombs. After drawing the Valentine's inside, they were going to blow that warehouse sky high.

Only no one figured on Mac. Her unexpected arrival, along with the Sentinals following in her wake, put a kink in their plan and instead of us all being blown to smithereens, we got the jump on *them.*

Mac somehow managed to start a war and finish it all at the same time. There is no weighing the size of the balls this woman carries. Let's just say they're really bloody heavy.

Two paramedics come around the corner as I step outside with my unconscious rescuer. They're jogging toward us, wheeling a stretcher along the cracked pavement. I take a relieved breath and stop, swaying on my feet. They reach us and I lower Mac onto the makeshift bed with infinite care, hesitant to let go of her completely. I withdraw my arms but rather than let go completely, I take her hand in mine.

"She has a gunshot wound to the right upper thigh," I rasp, "and a head injury. She … She …" I choke, unable to get any more out. *She has a wrenched shoulder. And she's lost a lot of blood. She also has a big heart, but she killed a man in there. And now she has a mark on her soul that mirrors mine. She took that. For me. So fix that too,* I want to tell them, but my mouth won't form the words. *Take that away so she doesn't have to live with it the way I do.*

"Romero."

Kelly is standing beside me, his clothes and hands steeped in dried blood. "Your woman ..." he nods at Mac. One of the paramedics is checking her injuries and vitals, the other is prepping her for transport. "She's having your baby, mate."

The ground dips beneath my feet. "She's *what?*"

Kelly's hand grips my shoulder and squeezes. The action keeps me upright while his words reverberate around in my head. "She's pregnant. The paramedics will need to know."

"How do you know?"

"Last night at the end of the party you took off thinking she was doing something with me when she wasn't. I was just some big douche who came on to her not realising what the two of you had. Later that night I found her in the bathroom, sick. I held her hair back while she puked in the toilet. The test was on the bathroom counter, and I saw it. I asked her and she told me it was yours. And that's when she found out you were leaving and came here. For you."

I stare down at Mac. She came here because I abandoned her the first time she fell pregnant with my baby. History was repeating itself and in typical Mac fashion, she was having none of it. She chose to fight for me. She chose to *fight*. For *me*.

"I didn't know," I mumble, trying to process Kelly's revelation. My heart aches with shame for leaving, yet hope unfurls in my chest amidst the pain because I'm going to be a father. Because Mac knew I was leaving and risked her life to stop me. She made a choice, and she chose *us*.

My eyes prickle and hot tears spill down, mixing with the blood and sweat and dirt. After everything we've been through, we've been given a second chance to do this. To get it right. To have a family.

I grasp the wrist of the female paramedic as they begin wheeling her away. She halts. Impatient.

"My girl is pregnant. You need to take care of them both," I plead, my tone urgent. My entire world is bleeding out on that stretcher right now and panic is burning inside me. I feel it rising, hotter than fire. Overtaking me. "Please."

Chapter Forty

Mac

My eyes blink open and the glare from the open window hits. I quickly shut them and turn my head on the pillow of my hospital bed. My body hurts but my heart is in agony.

"Mitch?" I ask, my eyes still closed and my voice rusty from disuse.

Someone will answer. In the seventy-two hours since I've been in hospital, there's always been at least one person by my bedside. Jake has barely left at all. I wish they would all go. Him too. I need ... I don't know what I need. Space to reflect on what I did? Time? A rewind so I can go back and change the past? How far would I go back if I could do that? A few days? A year? Two? Or would I go back to the very start, before I met Jake?

Someone answers, but I'm so lost in thought I don't hear it. "What?"

My hand is squeezed. "He's still in a coma."

The voice comes from Jared, but further away. He's not the one holding my hand. I nod to indicate I heard. The gentle motion causes my head to throb, and I wince. My eldest brother hasn't woken. The loss of blood and a stroke brought on by the injury put his body in distress. And if he knows, deep down inside his soul that Gabriella is gone, I fear he'll never wake. "I want to see him."

Now. Not so I can beg for forgiveness. Asking for that is too much. I just want to apologise while he's still alive. I need him to hear me say *I'm sorry.*

"No." That was Jake, his refusal spoken in a firm tone. He's close. Right by my bed. My hand is squeezed again and his voice gentles. "You're not well enough."

"I want to see him," I repeat, stubborn.

"Mac—"

"Don't." My eyes flare open, hardening on Jake. Half his face is red and purple, the skin tender and swollen. There's a stitched cut above his brow and a split lip he keeps busting open. It's bleeding again. His eye socket didn't require surgery but it's bandaged and the doctors are keeping a close watch on it. I know this because Evie told me. When I asked Jake he simply said he was 'fine.'

"Maybe later in the week," he says softly.

I close my eyes again and turn my head away. I hate looking at him. There's too much kindness. Too much empathy and compassion. Too much goddamn *heart.*

I don't deserve any of it.

"Please go away," I whisper.

"I can't do that," Jake replies. He untangles his hand from mine. The action gives me relief. I don't want to be *soothed.* Except it shifts further down; his warm palm comes to rest on my belly and spreads love through the warmth of his touch. Our baby is in there and she's thriving. Yes it's a girl, which is not an official verdict because I'm only fourteen weeks along, but I just *know.* It's mother's instinct.

"Of course she's thriving," my dad had muttered in his big old gruff voice when I told him. *"She's a Valentine."*

Can you believe it? My dad was taking credit for my little girl's kickass determination to survive. Bullshit. Her grit is all me and Jake. *"She's a Romero,"* I retorted stubbornly.

Dad paled but he put his hand on my shoulder and squeezed. *"Yeah. She's that too."*

To say my parents were thrilled with the baby announcement (inadvertently finding out thanks to my mouthy doctor who thought everyone knew) was to say the earth is round. If Mum had been a gymnast, she would have done a few celebratory backward tumbles with an added somersault for extra effect. Instead, her eyes turned glassy and her hands clutched mine.

"My baby is having a baby," she blubbered while Dad rubbed her back and made gruff, soothing noises to both of us.

"Mum," I muttered, embarrassed at the emotional display and warmed by it at the same time. The best part about my mother is that she would have reacted the same way when I was seventeen.

"I'm sorry," I blurted out.

"For what?" she asked.

"For running away."

Mum shook her head and looked to Dad. They shared a glance that spoke a thousand words, but only to each other. Then she turned to me. *"It was a long time ago. And we weren't fair. We—"*

Dad put his hand on Mum's shoulder and squeezed. She stopped talking.

"There's something you need to know," he said. *"But right now isn't the time."*

"How's our baby doing?" Jake's question interrupts my memory.

"She's fine." My voice is croaky. I clear my throat. "She's better than fine."

"I'll be back later," Jared says in a low voice with a heavy sigh.

My hospital room door opens and shuts and silence returns. It's painful. I feel like I don't know how to be myself anymore. Everything has changed.

"Talk to me, Princess. Please."

There's nothing to talk about. The adrenaline that fuelled my anger over him leaving is gone. Now there's so much pain, and I don't like it. It feels irreparable. My eyes prickle. I squeeze them closed more tightly but a tear breaks free. It drops to my pillow with a *plop*.

Jake doesn't see because my face is turned away from him. "Please go," I whisper.

"Can I get you a drink?"

Goddamn dogged bastard. I turn back his way. Leaning up on one elbow, I reach for the plastic cup of water from my hospital side table and crunch it in my hand. Then I toss it at the wall. It makes a minimal impact before dropping to the linoleum with a pathetic *crackle.* "No. I don't want a fucking drink."

I slouch back down on the bed and face the other way. That was uncalled for. I'm being a bitch but toning it down feels impossible right now. "Why don't you just leave like you tried to do before."

"You don't want me to go. You came after me."

"Only so I could rip your head off for leaving and throw it to the sharks in Sydney Harbour," I mutter bitterly.

Jake huffs with slight amusement. It's a *relieved* sound.

I turn my head. "That makes you happy?"

"To hear you sounding more like yourself? Yes. I'd rather you mad at me than feel nothing at all."

But I'm more mad at myself. And I don't know how to get him to leave. "I'm tired."

"Sleep, then," he replies. "I'll be here."

My lips pinch.

"I'm not going anywhere, Princess. Not ever again."

I ignore the burgeoning sense of peace his words bring me and turn my head to look at the stubborn man. "Fine. Then I'm hungry."

"Lunch will be served soon."

"I don't want to wait," I retort. "I'm hungry now."

"Mac—"

I bring out my ace in the hole. "It's not good for the baby if I don't eat."

Jake swipes at the side of his face that isn't swollen, uncertainty in his expression. "Okay," he says slowly. "How about I go and get you something from the cafeteria?"

"Perfect." I force my lips to curve slightly. It feels off, but he takes it in and nods his head.

He rises to his feet and moves his hand from my belly, leaving coldness in its wake. "I'll be back, okay?"

Jake leans down and presses a warm kiss to my lips. Flutters fill my stomach, and I find myself responding. He draws back and runs his hand over my hair in an affectionate parting gesture before he walks to the door. He opens it with a backward glance before leaving. The door closes with a soft click.

Finally.

I'm alone.

I grab for the buzzer by the side of my bed. My thumb hits the button incessantly. I don't stop until the door flings open, and my worst nightmare enters the room.

Oh fuck.

Houlihan strides in. Soundless nursing shoes somehow manage to slap against the linoleum floor. Her eyebrows are drawn on extra squiggly today, indicating a harried and annoyed appearance. She's having a bad day, and she's clearly prepared for me to make it worse.

I don't disappoint. "I need a wheelchair. STAT."

"You think I'm your errand girl?" Her voice is gravel like a pack a day chain smoker. Houlihan moves to the front end of my bed, where my chart rests in a plastic pocket fixed on the wall. She picks it up in her meaty hands and examines it with pinched lips. She returns the chart to its little slot and her eyes narrow on mine. "You're not going anywhere."

My nostrils flare wide. *Bitch.* "I have a brother in a coma. On fucking life support. You can bet your ass I'm going to get a wheelchair so I can see him or I'll pitch a tantrum so big and loud you'll hear it from the International Space Station."

Her lips pinch harder, but I see her brain ticking over. "Mitchell Valentine?"

My hand snaps out and grabs her wrist, a reflexive action that halts her in place. "You know him?"

After a pause where Houlihan looks at my hand (it's digging into her skin, but I can't seem to let go) and then looks at me, she speaks. "He's on level nine, ward six B, room nine oh two."

My eyes literally tear up with gratitude. For *Houlihan* no less. I blame it on baby hormones. I clear my throat and peel my hand from her wrist, finger by finger. "Thank you."

She leaves and moments later returns with a wheelchair. My eyes round with surprise. "Threaten me again and I'll tear you a new one," she says in her crotchety voice, belying the kindness of her actions. There's no time to respond. Jake will return at any moment. At least with Houlihan seemingly in my corner I now have a fighting chance.

After parking the contraption by the side of my bed, she helps me out. I hiss when I put pressure on my right thigh where the wound is stitched and healing. *That sonofabitch Ross.* Poor Jake is busy worrying about my soul for shooting him. I'm just trying to work out how I can get my hands on his cold, lifeless corpse so I can shoot him all over again. *Sorry, Jake, but my soul is doing cartwheels over the death of that asshole.*

"Don't put pressure on it," Houlihan snaps.

"I'm not," I bark back at her and reach across for my phone.

We bicker the entire trip from my room up to level nine. I'm almost grateful. *Almost.* Because it distracts me from what I have to do. She wheels me through ward six B and toward room nine oh two. My hands white-knuckle the arm rests. I'm pushed through the door and toward Mitch's bed.

Houlihan sets the brake. "I'll find someone else to bring you back down. Some of us have real work to do."

I ignore her parting jibe as I stare at my eldest brother. His skin blends in with the white bed sheets he lies in, and thick bandages wrap around his neck, extending to underneath his right armpit. Deep, dark bruises rest under his eyes, and a ventilator helps him breathe. He's deathly still, not even a twitch to provide the slightest hope.

My eyes prickle and I bring a hand to my mouth, emotion hitting me hard enough to steal my breath. Mitch has always been there for me. Always.

I reach across and take his hand. It feels so lifeless in mine. I close my eyes and see him glaring across the dinner table at me. *"You can't wear that dress. Ever."*

He was the one who orchestrated my return from Melbourne, his eyes burning with the wrath of a thousand suns after I ran away. *"I'm going to fucking kill you."*

"You should have, Stitch," I whisper, swallowing the ache as my eyes crack open, alighting on his prone form. "Because look what I did."

Then there was that time he promised to buy me a new dress after spilling wine on the one I wore to our family dinner. *"You can't buy forgiveness,"* I told him, lashing out.

A sob escapes my throat.

"I'm sorry I interfered in your life," he'd told me. *"We all did. You're our little sister. No matter how strong or capable you may be, it's our instinct to protect you."*

"And look where that got you, you great big asshead!" I rail at him, my voice rising along with my anger. I want to stand up and punch him for doing what he did. For using Jake as bait and not telling me. For coming in after me. For being the best brother a sister could ever ask for.

Instead, I push up out of my wheelchair, putting pressure on my good leg, and I lean across and hug him. My cheek rests on his chest as tears pour down my face. "I'm sorry." My voice cracks. "I'm so sorry."

After taking a deep breath, I hobble backward and stumble into my chair. I'm exhausted and drained, and I need to get out of here. Not just this room. The whole hospital. I can't breathe.

I get on my phone and summon an Uber.

Jake

It pains me to return holding nothing but a dried-out looking ham and cheese sandwich. Mac eats a lot of rubbish. A shitload, really. There's not an hour of the day that goes by when she's not jamming something in her mouth. A burger, fries, Evie's lemon slice, Quinn's peanut butter and white chocolate chip cookies, and those damn redskin lollies that get stuck in her teeth and will likely cause cavities.

You would think her the size of a house with the calories she consumes each day, but her fury burns them faster than a lit match. Even so, she needs to be *healthier*, especially with a baby on the way. This sandwich isn't really the epitome of wholesome food. Maybe I should get some advice from Jared.

I push open her hospital room door and find the bed empty. *Goddammit.*

I turn around and head straight for the elevator. After jabbing the *up* button, I stand and wait. Eventually the doors *ding* loudly and zip open, expelling Travis, Jared, and Evie, the latter slurping her way through a chocolate thickshake. Surely that drink is full of preservatives. There's no way in hell Mac will be ingesting any of the like during her pregnancy.

"She's not here," I tell them, putting my arm across the doorway of the elevator to keep it open.

They halt en masse as I step inside and turn.

"Where is she?" Travis asks.

I point up, indicating she's visiting Mitch. They all step back in, and I press nine. The doors close and the elevator ascends.

Jared reclines against the side wall, hands in his pockets and a scowl on his face. It's directed at me.

"What?"

His voice is accusatory. "You let her out of bed."

My lips peel back in a sarcastic smile. "Oh, that's cute. You think when I told Mac she couldn't get out of bed and visit Mitch that she'd actually listen."

"You shouldn't have left her alone."

My eyes narrow. "She was hungry, Valentine." I wave the offensive looking sandwich in his face. "Was I supposed to let her starve?"

"Enough!" Travis shouts. His face is pained. "We're all stressed and upset right now. Let's not take it out on each other."

"He started it," I mutter, which basically makes me an immature dick.

"You're a dick," Jared retorts, verbalising the obvious.

Travis shakes his head. "I can't believe you two fuckers are going to be dads. God help us all."

Evie unwraps her lips from the straw. "Amen," she adds.

Eventually we arrive at Mitch's room. Mac isn't there. Panic climbs my throat. It feels like heartburn. I rub at my chest.

"Maybe she was going back down as we were coming up?" Evie suggests.

Panic recedes. "You're right. You all stay here and I'll go back down."

I leave them and race back down to Mac's room, but she hasn't returned. I'm standing beside her bed when my phone rings. I tug it free from the back pocket of my jeans. After checking who the incoming call is from, I hit the red *decline* button.

It rings again.

I decline again.

It rings again.

I huff and answer it, putting the phone to my ear. "Jake Romero."

"Sorry to bother you."

"It's fine, but I'm just in the middle of something. Can I call back later?"

"No. I was told to tell you it's urgent."

I swipe a hand down the side of my face. I can't deal with this right now. "How urgent is urgent because—"

"It's *urgent,* Mr. Romero."

A heavy, frustrated sigh escapes me. They wouldn't tell me it was if it wasn't. "I'll be right there."

I send a message to Travis. *She's not here. You need to search the hospital. Get security to check the tapes.* It might seem an excessive step, but this is *Mac* we're talking about.

It takes me forty-five minutes to reach my destination. It usually takes me half an hour, but I have fractured ribs and questionable vision. I rush past reception instead of taking the time to sign the visitor registration log like I usually do. After walking through a maze of turns and corridors, I go through another door which takes me outdoors and along a meandering road. From here there are buggies that can take you to your destination, but I choose to walk quickly. It's not far.

When I reach villa number five oh nine, I open the door with my key and step inside. My father is on his daybed in the living area. It's set on an incline so he's half sitting in front of a window where he can view the gardens that sprawl outward.

When I see Mac beside him, my knees almost buckle with relief. What is she doing here? I had no idea she even knew where my father lived. She's lying in the expensive recliner I bought after getting the shits over the crappy chairs the assisted living facility provided. She has the leg rest up and the back shoved down.

My father's eyes are a little glassy as they watch her rather than the window, and it's then that I realise she's talking.

"And then I told him I only came after him so I could rip off his head and feed it to the sharks."

Dad makes a garbled noise. It's the sound of him laughing and I wonder if Mac realises that. I want to tell her so she understands his response, but I want to keep listening too. I let it go and stand by the door, remaining unobtrusive and quiet.

"It's not funny, Mike," she replies and my brows pull down, puzzled. She *knew* it was him laughing. The only way she could have known was if she'd spent considerable time with him since his aneurysm. "He was going to *leave*. I should've shot *him* instead of Ross."

Dad's garbled sounds grow louder. She's making him laugh *hard*. A lump forms in my throat. Then he speaks. "Maaart knooooorrrk sense."

After years of listening to him talk, I know what he's saying, but Mac—

She snorts, understanding him perfectly. "Nothing will knock sense into that hard head of his."

Dad garbles again.

Oh god, my fucking *heart*.

"Did you know we're supposed to be engaged?"

He jerks in surprise. I haven't told him.

"He wants me to take his name. Can you imagine that? Me? A Romero."

"Pr ... Pr-prooooud," Dad gets out.

He's trying to tell her that nothing would make him prouder than Mac being a Romero. "You'll be my father-in-law, Mike. And a grandpa."

He jerks harder at the second revelation.

Mac pats her belly. "Will you come to the hospital when she's born? My dad can come get you."

"L-l-looove," he answers.

I inhale a shaky breath and my eyes burn.

"M-m-mmmm Miiiiitch," he gets out, "be gord unc unc ... uncle."

Mac's jaw tightens and her voice chokes. "I don't know how I'll live with myself if he doesn't wake up."

I go to step in, but Dad moves a shaky hand toward her. It flops down on top of hers in an awkward attempt at comfort. "T-t tttime. Jake. B-b bbbabyy."

He's telling her that she'll forgive herself in time. That I'll be there for her. And that she needs to think of the baby.

"I told him to get out," she tells him. "I wanted to see Mitch. I wanted space but now ..."

"N-now?" Dad prompts.

"I just want Jake," she whispers. "I blame him for leaving, but I pushed him to do it. We lost a baby once. A long time ago. I was in a car accident. Jake didn't know. I thought he did, but he didn't, and I was so angry at him for not being there. I lost him that day too and it felt like I died. It took me two years to remember how to live again. And ever since, all I could think was that I never wanted to go through that again. I was *scared*. But that's stupid, right? Because I'm a Valentine. We don't get scared. But I was. I still am. And I panicked when I found out I was pregnant again and Jake had gone. So panicked I couldn't think straight or see straight. It was happening all over again. But then Jake said something in my room today that he's never said before."

I hold my breath.

"Wh-wh ..." Dad is trying to ask what.

Mac answers. "I'm not going anywhere, Princess. Not—"

"Ever again," I finish for her.

She lifts her head, startled, her green eyes finding mine. They fill rapidly and she blinks. "You found me."

I want to tell her that I'll find her no matter where she goes, but the truth is that Mac is more slippery than an eel. I'd have better luck finding the secret city of Paititi. "Dad had the duty nurse call me. She told me it was urgent, but she didn't say that you were here. I just assumed Dad needed me."

He pats the bed, indicating to come closer. "Mar-mar-m ... M..."

"Yes, Dad. I asked her to marry me."

His face fixes in a scowl.

"I'm sorry. I should have told you sooner."

"Gr-gr …" He grabs my hand in a tight grip when I go to finish for him. I wait. "Gr-graaandparr."

"And you're going to be a grandpa."

His lips tremble. He slams them together, and his head moves back and forth on the pillow, back and forth, back and forth. He's worked up. Releasing emotion is difficult for him.

"Mike," Mac says in a calm, normal tone, unaffected by his actions. "I'm going to read to you now."

She twists awkwardly in her seat, trying to reach for the cupboard by his daybed. It's always filled with library books, the pages old and worn and read a thousand times by thousands of people. How does she know they're there?

I walk around the bed and crouch in front of the cupboard. "I'll get it," I tell her, opening the door. There's a haphazard pile inside. "Which one are you up to, Dad?"

But he can't answer, his head is jerking around. "The Matthew Reilly one," Mac answers. "The Four Legendary Kingdoms."

I look up at her. "How do you know?"

"I read to him," she says softly. "Every fortnight."

"You …" I can't catch my breath.

"He's family, Jake."

Loyal to the bone. That's my girl. And it makes my heart so full I can barely stand it. I grab for the book. Blindly. Because my vision is blurred. I hand it to her. She finds her place in the story and begins to read. And as her voice carries through the room, slow and repetitive, my father begins to calm.

I don't know how it's possible to fall in love with someone more than once, but I do.

I pull my phone out and tap a message to Travis.

Found her. She's fine. Will bring her back to the hospital in an hour.

After hitting send, I put it away and drag an uncomfortable chair toward my father's side. We both sit there listening to her tell a story.

And for the first time since I met Mackenzie Valentine and went on this crazy ride, I finally feel complete.

Epilogue

Mac

Six months later...

I wake slowly. Deliciously. It's a warm summer morning, and my bedroom window is open. The sheer curtains billow from a delicate breeze. "Crying Shame" by The Teskey Brothers croons softly from the speaker by my bed, right where a thick dark mug of coffee rests waiting for me to rise.

A deep breath fills my lungs. I let it out leisurely, feeling well-rested and happy. Today is the first day of my maternity leave and my first holiday since ... Well it's my first holiday. Ever.

"Mac!" Jared's voice roars up the staircase, ruining my appealing fantasy. "Get out of bed, you lazy beached whale! You're needed downstairs."

"Fuck off!" I shriek back.

The truth is that I haven't woken slowly because I barely slept at all. Who can sleep when your belly is bigger than Mt. Everest? There's no crooning music to gently rouse me either. And no leisurely breaths of air or sweet breeze wafting through my window. The only thing true is my maternity leave starting today.

My bedroom is a sweaty hotbox because I'm the dick that's due to have a baby in the height of summer. A *baby pffft*. An evil being

"

grows inside me. One who kicks and punches and bounces on my bladder like it's a jumping castle of fun. I'm literally being attacked *from the inside out.*

Pregnancy is a total shit sandwich. I'm not glowing and my hair hasn't thickened into a glorious mane. It's lank and damp from sweat and tangled around my neck, choking me like the tentacles of a giant *Architeuthis.*

And I'm not resting comfortably in my own room. Nooooooo. That would be asking too much. I'm in my old bedroom at my parents' house. Why? Because I'm an idiot, that's why.

We gave up our lease with the duplex six months ago. Henry, Frog, and Cooper, bought a loft in the building where Casey, Grace, and Coby still reside. The three twits think the area exudes some kind of badass vibe, and they're hoping it will rub off on them. I eventually had to ruin their ridiculous notion and explain that you're actually born with the badass gene inside you. It's not something you can just *acquire* by association. It's not magical glitter that you sprinkle over yourself at the start of the day.

Not that they listened. No one ever listens to the 'hormonal rants' of a pregnant woman, so I'll just leave it for them to figure out for themselves.

Jake and I decided to have our own house like my brothers and their wives rather than lease an apartment. Though unlike Jared and Evie, who lived in their house while they renovated it, and unlike Travis and Quinn, who moved in to a house they built without finishing the yard, Jake and I are doing the whole shebang. House, gardens, *and* pool. We demolished an old dilapidated house on the same street as Jared and Evie in Bondi and started a new house from scratch.

I figured it would only take a couple of months. All they had to do was pour a slab of concrete for the foundation, slap up a timber frame, some bricks, add a bath or two and a sink, dig a big hole for a pool, add in a few plants and *voila!* Instant dream house!

On that basis, we thought moving in with my parents for such a short period of time would be survivable, but five months later we're still here and I'm hanging on by my fingernails.

Apparently construction workers are lazy. They don't like to work. Sometimes they turn up just for show, eat their lunch at nine a.m. from their lunch boxes like little kids, and act like they've done a hard day's yakka before heading home. They also gossip like you wouldn't believe. I'm guessing it's all the flapping of their gums that leaves them weary after a hard day of pretending to build stuff.

In summary, progress is slow. I show up onsite sporadically, heavily pregnant, and rage at them like a hormonal bitch. It spurs them into action, but they've estimated another three months before we can move in.

My baby shower was supposed to be in the new house. There should be a nursery set up and ready. Instead, I'm two weeks out from delivering Satan and I have nothing.

Well I have Jake, I guess. The asshead who sleeps like the dead. He rolls over in bed and his knee pulls up, hitting me in my side. I grunt. We're getting married. *Today.*

This giant lump of muscled man will be my husband in a few short hours. He was supposed to sleep on the couch, tradition dictating you can't see each other before the ceremony or it's bad luck, but I don't give a shit about the old, musty folklore. Jake promised he would never leave me again, and by god, that means not sleeping apart. Ever. Not even for a single night.

Jake makes an odd snuffling sound. He's slowly rousing. A hot palm finds the hem of my oversized nightshirt. It slides beneath and climbs, rubbing a hand over my colossal pregnant belly.

My heart flutters and despite my shitty sleep, a smile tugs at the corners of my lips.

"You're glaring at me," he mumbles, his eyes still closed.

"I am," I lie, "and I'll continue to do so every morning you wake beside me for the rest of your natural life."

"I already want a divorce," he mutters, his calloused palm lovingly scratching its way across my sensitive, stretched skin.

"You can have the house," I announce. "I'm over it already."

"I'll let you have the cat, then."

"No," I argue. "You can have the cat too."

Our little kitten is a rescue from the RSCPA and a baby shower gift from Henry, Frog, and Cooper, because that's what you buy for someone who's about to give birth to Satan. A mothertrucking *cat*. Satan's spirit animal. They thought looking after the furball would be good training for a *baby*. My friends are clueless wankers. It's lucky they have me around all the time to set them straight.

"Where is it?" Jake asks, his rich brown eyes blinking open blearily. The bachelor party was last night. Jake and all the boys got to imbibe alcohol. Meanwhile, my bachelorette party was two weeks ago and included mocktails and flip-flops on my feet because *cankles*.

"Where's what?"

"Constantine."

That's what we named our kitten. After the demon hunter who literally went to Hell and back. I voted for The Antichrist but Constantine seems to suit the fluffy little troublemaker. She's also completely white, which was thoughtful of the boys. They know how soothing I find the colour.

"I don't know. Do you hear her?"

She's *so* tiny. We had to put a bell on her diamond studded collar—yes *diamond studded* collar. Jake bought it because he's a sucker for Constantine's huge feline eyes. God help us when our girl is born. Jake is going to spoil her until she becomes a complete hellion. Our daughter is going to be precocious and yet utterly endearing. She'll wrap every single one of us around her finger until we're nothing but a twisted mess.

"She's somewhere." I hear her bell tinkling from inside the room.

Jake rolls over and opens the drawer of the bedside table. He rustles around. Finding what he's looking for, he pulls it out and rolls back. It's a small rectangular gift-wrapped box tied with a red bow. He places it on my belly. It sways precariously from its mountainous perch. "Happy wedding day, my beautiful bride."

My cheeks flush with pleasure. Constantine is not the only female he likes to spoil. "You got me a gift?"

He grins, eyes twinkling. "I did. Hurry up and open it before your family storms the bedroom door and drags us out to help with the setup."

We're holding our wedding in the backyard of my parents' house. I'm too heavily pregnant to host anything more extravagant than that. It's why Jared is already yelling at me. He's tasked with twining flowers around the arbour I bought in a fit of fancy and setting out the guest chairs for the ceremony.

"If anyone tries dragging me into the setup, I'll set fire to their clothes. While they're wearing them," I add as I pick up the box in my hands. I've left a million instructions so I'm able to relax today. It shouldn't be hard to follow them.

"You won't be lifting a finger today, Princess," Jake assures me. "Now open your gift."

Lips curved in a smile, I undo the bow and it slides away. A huge bang comes at the bedroom door before I free the lid.

"Macface! Are you up yet?"

It's Evie. She must have arrived early with Jared. The wail of a baby wafts up the stairs. "Fuck," we hear her mutter. "I just want five minutes to see my goddamn best friend on her wedding day."

The sound of her clomping back down the stairs is loud. Their baby, my nephew, doesn't like to be held by anyone else but his mother. He screams holy hell if she sets him down for even a minute. I don't know how she manages to get up and dress for the day let alone shower. It makes me fear for the future.

Jake and I have only two weeks to ourselves before Satan arrives. I plan to make the most of them because Evie tells me her life is basically over now. This means we have just fourteen days left to live before we're sentenced to a hellish existence of poop and puke.

Jake buries his head in my neck, chuckling as Evie departs.

"You think it's funny?"

"Yes." He kisses the skin at the base of my neck. Then another. And another.

A throaty moan escapes me. "That'll be us in two weeks."

His chuckles die a quick death and he draws back. "Now you're just being mean."

"I'm not mean," I argue. "I'm just a realist."

Constantine leaps on the bed. Or tries. Her claws appear on the edge and she lifts her head enough for us to see her ears and desperate cat eyes. She's tried to leap and only got so far. She lets forth an almighty screech, and her bell tinkles wildly as she grapples.

Jake reaches for her and the sheets drop low, revealing his naked torso. "Come here, baby girl," he croons and snuggles the tiny ball of fur into his neck. He drops back on the bed, Constantine barely visible in his enormous hands.

I pause, the box still in my hands as I eye my future husband. His hair is longer now. The ends are golden from our weekends at the beach. He's sporting a short beard too. It's surprisingly soft and I love how it feels rubbing against my skin. Constantine loves said facial hair too. She's rubbing her head against his jaw with adoration in her eyes.

"Open your gift," he urges.

Another bang comes at the bedroom door. Jared yells through it when it's not opened immediately. "They brought the wrong flowers for the arbour!"

Christ. It begins. I sigh. "What *did* they bring?" I call back.

"Red roses."

Idiot. "They're the right flowers."

"But they've still got thorns on them."

All the better to prick you with, Brother dear. "Grow a pair," Jake hollers at him.

"Fuckers," he mutters and disappears.

A gentle knock comes moments later. "Mackenzie, honey." It's Mum. "The stylist is here for your hair."

"Already?" Jake asks me.

My lips pinch. "What do you mean *already*? A good up-do takes time. Do you want my hair to look like ass on my special day?" It's still tangled around my neck. I'd be better taking the scissors with me into the bathroom and hacking it off, but I've been trying to keep it longer for today.

Jake holds his palms up, already surrendering.

"I'm awake, Mum," I call back. "I'll be down soon."

Jake sighs and sits up, Constantine still curled in his neck. He swings his legs off the bed and stands. Entirely naked. It's my turn to sigh. Let's face it, all that tanned, thick muscle is the real gift here. I'll be married to that for the rest of my life.

My future husband stalks to the dresser, tucking our little kitten under his arm like a teeny football. Being so tiny, it makes it appear as though Jake has white armpit hair, and I laugh. He glances over his shoulder, catching me watching him. "Pervert."

I wink. "Takes one to know one."

Pregnancy has surprisingly heightened my libido, and Jake's in turn. He gets mad with lust seeing my belly full with his baby. I figure it's a possessive male trait that dates back to his caveman ancestry.

Dragging my gaze from his naked from, I return my attention to the box and lift the lid. Inside nestles a bracelet set with fire opals. The gemstones catch the light and flame brightly. The beauty of it steals my breath. "Jake," I whisper.

He shrugs as if it's nothing but his expression is one of pleasure. With our relationship being out in the open, Jake is free to buy me whatever he chooses and he does so liberally. He seems to take so much joy in it. "It caught my eye from the store window and reminded me of you. You like it?"

"It's stunning. I absolutely love it. But I love you more."

Jake's eyes crinkle. "To my head tomatoes?"

I giggle and then gasp as Satan punches outward. The saying is one his dad used with him when he was a boy. He uses it freely now. "And back up again."

Jake sets Constantine on the top of my old glossy dresser and goes to open a drawer. The slick surface causes her panic and she tears off, skittering, and slides right down the back of it. The resulting screech is loud enough to burst my ear drums.

"Constantine!" I roll to my side and wrestle my way off the bed. I'm puffing my way over but Jake is already kneeled on the floor, reaching underneath to grab her. She's wedged and he has to tilt his head to the side to see anything.

"Gotcha," he exclaims and drags her out.

She comes out attached to a ratty old envelope. I snatch her up, and she burrows in between my right boob and my belly.

"What's this?" Jake is straightening, the envelope in his hand.

I shake my head. "I don't—" I'm about to say *know,* but then I get a good look at it and see Jake Romero written across the front in childish scrawl. At the time I thought the lettering looked neat and a bit fierce, but now it just appears jagged and silly. "Oh my god."

"What?" Jake flips it over. The back is still stuck down, sealing it closed.

"It's the letter I wrote you when I was eleven."

He looks at me, puzzled. "You kept it all this time?"

"I did for a long while. You left and it felt like the only tie I had with you. For some strange reason it was comforting, but I thought the letter lost. It must have fallen down the back of the dresser and stayed there for years."

Jake slips his thumb beneath the flap and begins to tear it open. I snatch it from him with my free hand; the other is snuggling Constantine. It leaves his hands suspended in the air.

"You can't read it *now.*"

"Yes." He snatches it back and smirks. "I *can.*"

I want to wrestle it from him but my belly cramps. I suck in a sharp breath. *Oh shit.* Not today, Satan. I walk to the bed, turn, and sink down slowly.

"Are you okay?" Jake asks. He has the letter out, but he's watching me, the lines on his brow etched deep with concern.

"Heartburn," I lie.

"You eat too much crap," he mutters, unfolding the page.

"I haven't eaten anything at all yet today. I'm starving." I really am. "I've a craving for pasta carbonara."

Jake's brow arches. "For breakfast?"

Constantine leaps free of my arms and onto the bed. She stalks toward Jake's pillow, tail twitching. After a quick sniff to make sure it's his, she climbs on and claws until she settles in. "Yes. For breakfast."

He shakes his head with amusement as he starts reading the letter aloud.

"Dear Jake.

I'm sorry for what I said. And I'm sorry about your dad."

I'd gone on to write *'you should have told me,'* but then I scrunched up the page and started again. It was none of my business but then again, it felt like it was. At the time I was so confused. But now it's never been clearer. Jake and I are soulmates, and my soulmate had been suffering. How cliché that sounds when I think it. Silly, even. But no matter what, fate knew we were meant to be and kept shoving us together until we figured it out for ourselves.

Jake keeps reading. "Hearing what happened made me hurt, so I know you must hurt too. I don't know how far away you're going, or if I'll ever see you again, but if I do I'll try and be nicer.

And I'll make you a promise. I never break my promises so you must believe in me.

I promise that I'll visit with your Dad, even if you can't. And I'll read to him all the time because books take you to the places you can't go. I can be his family too." His voice wobbles but he continues on. "Because family means no one ever gets left behind. I promise I won't leave your Dad behind, Jake.

Take care,

Mackenzie Valentine."

He looks up from the page, tears in his eyes. "I've never loved you more than I do right now."

"It was a silly letter, Jake. It—"

"Fuck off," he croaks. "It's not silly. It's perfect. Thank you."

Jake folds the page and tucks it inside the envelope. Then he opens the dresser drawer and puts it away with infinite care. After closing the drawer, he turns. "Come here."

"I would, but I've beached myself on the edge of this bed and there's no moving now." No one tells you how you need a crane to get out of bed in the mornings when you're pregnant.

Jake chuckles and walks over to me. He takes my hands and helps me upright, pulling me into a hug. It's not easy with my huge belly in the way, but he manages to hold on tight, his body warm and solid. "Are you happy?" he asks, his face buried in my neck. He's breathing me in, something he loves to do.

"I've never been happier."

He draws back and looks me in the eye, but my arms remain wrapped around his neck. "I know you wanted to work with Jamieson and Valentine Consulting." He knows because I told him. I confessed the need I felt to prove myself. But that need is gone. It died along with Gabriella Valdez. She was a police officer, but she chose to serve and protect out of love, not out of need to prove she could do it. It made me realise that I don't need to prove shit to anyone else but myself and just do what I love.

And I love working with Jamieson. I'll continue working with them for as long as they'll have me. I'm right where I want to be.

"I only thought I wanted to," I remind Jake. "You know that."

"If you ever change your mind, I'd be okay with it. With you working with them. Well ... not okay. Not really. But I'd live with it."

"I'm not going to change my mind."

"Good. I like having you boss us around."

"I like bossing you all around."

Jake chuckles. His lips are still smiling when he ducks his head and kisses me. The pressure of his mouth is firm and his tongue snakes out, licking my bottom lip, demanding entry.

I don't deny him. The kiss turns heated and my fingers tangle in his hair.

"Mac?" *Tap tap tap* at the bedroom door. "The hairstylist," Mum reminds me.

I stand in front of the full-length mirror of my parents' bedroom. Their private space is large. A king bed dominates the room with a large bedhead made of textured fabric. A daybed occupies the area by the window. Mum likes to read there in the winter when the warmth of the sun hits the cushion-covered seat.

Evie and Quinn are sitting on it right now, and Grace and Mum are perched on the edge of her bed. They give a collective sigh at my image. Mum's is heaviest of all. She's in heaven right now. She has a grandbaby to obsess over and another on the way. She has her three daughters-in-law by her side (she adopted Grace into the family a long time ago), and she has me. The hellion child. Though not so much a hellion anymore. Well, maybe a little.

I stare at my reflection. "I look like a whale."

They all protest but it's true. I'm swollen and puffy. I have no jawline anymore. It's vanished because fluid retention has swallowed me whole. My original plan when I eventually married was to wear the beautiful red dress Mitch bought me, but my bloated body would tear it apart. Instead, I wear a strapless ivory dress. The style is empire line, so it fits snug around my boobs and drops neatly to the floor. It's overlaid with intricate floral lace and finished off with little lace-cap sleeves. The dress is elegant and ridiculously expensive, but I couldn't resist.

My hair is done in light, beachy waves and hangs down my back. Two small pieces on either side have been swept off my face and hold together at the back with a jewelled pearl comb. The same one my mother wore on her wedding day. On my feet rest an elegant pair of thin strapped beach sandals in ivory because it's all I can bear wearing.

The overall effect is very romantic when I usually opt for severe, but the change feels perfect, if just for today.

A tap comes at the door.

"Who is it?" Mum asks as the girls hover, twitching bits of my dress into place and realigning strands of hair.

"It's me!" Dad booms.

"Come in," she calls back.

The door pushes open with force and Dad strides in, along with Travis. I half turn to look at them, and Dad's lips mash together. The pride in his eyes is so bright it's a wonder I'm not blinded.

"Everyone out," he barks. "I need to have a talk with my little girl."

"It's a bit late for the birds and bees talk," Travis quips, taking hold of my elbows as he leans in to give me a kiss on the cheek. "You look incredibly beautiful today, little sister."

"Not so little," I grumble. My belly tightens with a cramp and I wince. "But thank you."

His green eyes light with concern. "Are you okay?"

Heat pricks at my eyes. "I'd be better if Mitch was here."

Travis sighs heavily and steps back as I'm hugged in turn by my friends, and then by mother. They step out of the room and the door clicks shut. It's almost time.

"He's not coming?" I ask, looking to Dad.

"No, love." My father shakes his head sadly. "He's not."

I hiccup, but it somehow turns into a sob.

"It's not you," Travis reassures me as Dad grabs my arm in vice-like grip and drags me toward the daybed. "Sit down," he says.

I sink to the edge, wondering how I'll ever get back up again, and I wait, looking up at my father as he gathers his thoughts.

"Mitch is ..."

Struggling.

"Sick. That's right." Dad paces. "He has a cold. Errr flu."

A scowl fixes on Travis's face. "Dad."

"He doesn't want anyone else to get sick. Especially you, Mac, being almost due."

Mitch woke from his coma after several weeks, but only to a minimally conscious state. He had limited awareness that came and went. He came around gradually, but then we broke the news about Gabriella and now it feels as though he's lost the will to live.

He picks fights with me. He picks fights with Jared and Travis. He picks fights with our parents. His rehabilitation is regressing as he slowly, but surely, gives up on life.

Travis shakes his head and crouches, bringing him eye level with me. "Mitch doesn't have the flu."

"I know, Trav," I say softly. "He's not sick. He's broken."

My brother nods. "Deep down inside he wants to be here. He loves you. You're his favourite sibling. He's just not able to take that step yet. He needs more time, and we have to be patient in giving it to him."

Dad stands by Travis and grasps his shoulder, his expression heavy. "Well said, Son."

Bless them both. They don't want to see me upset on my wedding day. "You don't need to worry. I'm fine."

But I'm not. Mitch should have been here, Gabriella by his side in some sexy number that makes all the men's eyes pop from their heads. Instead, he's somewhere hurting, defeated, maybe even drinking, and Gabriella is in the ground.

Her death changed us, and her funeral destroyed us, but we're closer now than we've ever been before. It was attended by more than five thousand people. Police lined the road for kilometres as the procession of her coffin left the church. The Australian community abhors the deaths of those who protect and serve. They came out in droves, standing by the side of the road, solemn, service officers saluting as the procession passed by.

My eldest brother missed it all. Instead, Mitch lay dormant in his hospital bed while thousands honoured her life, oblivious to his loss and missing his chance to say goodbye.

"Out you go now," Dad says to Travis. "I need a private word."

Travis nods and straightens. "I'll see you out there."

When the door clicks shut behind him, Dad takes a seat beside me with a sigh.

I eye him sideways. "You're not really going to give the birds and bees speech, are you?"

He chuckles but the sound is pained.

"What is it?" I ask, wary.

"Did I ever tell you about Aunty Dee?"

Of course he never told us about our aunt Diana, his younger sister, and he knows that. It's a *no-go* topic. She died at the age of eighteen, and she's been a touchy subject ever since. Dad never talks about her with *anyone*.

"You're the very image of her." He hangs his head, studying the floor. My *dad*—the man who kicks ass and takes names and looks *everyone* in the eye when he speaks to them—can't look at me. "The hair and the eyes but most of all, the attitude. Weakness wasn't a word in her vocabulary, just like it isn't in yours. There was fire inside of her and when you were born, it's like she re-lit the torch inside of you."

I had no idea, but it warms me to know I'm carrying my aunt's legacy.

My dad lifts his head and his eyes are filled with the ache of regret. "I loved that fire. It meant no one would ever mess with her. It was going to take her places. So I encouraged it. I fanned the flames. But it was that fire that got her killed. It made her overconfident, gave her too much courage and too much heart. She fought for the underdog with reckless abandon, until one day she stood up to the wrong person at the wrong time, and he didn't like it. Not one little bit. And as she walked to the train station one afternoon after school, he snatched her and he … he …" My dad's voice cracks. He pauses and swallows, looking away again, the memory too much to bear. "He did things to her that no one should ever have to endure."

I reach across and take his big hand in mine, my stomach rolling at what Aunty Dee must have gone through.

"Then you were born, and when I saw that same fire in you, it put the fear of God in my heart." His gaze returns to mine, his expression grave and eyes glassy. "And I tried to smother it."

"Fucking Dick Head school," I mutter.

Dad shakes his head, huffing. "Yes, Fucking Dick Head school. I knew you called it that, by the way. But I convinced myself it could do what I couldn't. I convinced myself it would douse that fire and keep you safe."

"Dad," I whisper.

"That was wrong and I'm sorry."

My eyes burn. "I always thought I was the daughter you never wanted."

"No." His voice is appalled. "God, no. I love who you are. You have a beautiful spirit, and I'm so damn proud of you. You champion your friends and your family. You fight for them and would do anything for them. You went to war for them. You work tirelessly to give them a life you believe they deserve, but it's time to start living the life *you* deserve now." Dad lets go of my hand and stands. He walks to the bedside table where my bouquet of roses rests. He picks them up and turns, a smile slowly forming until happiness lines his face. "Time for you to get yourself hitched."

"You have to help me up first."

He chuckles and my belly cramps again. I'm getting good at hiding it because it kept happening the whole time he and Travis were talking and neither noticed. He takes my hand and helps me upright. Then his eyes crinkle. "Hurry up, love. That baby is going to come out at any moment. Best get that ring on your finger first."

I gasp. "Dad! How did you know?"

"That you've gone into labour? Sweetheart, I may be old, but I'm not stupid. Your mother birthed four of my children. I recognise the signs."

I tuck my arm in his and we leave the room. I descend the stairs and step outside, my father by my side. Henry is on his acoustic guitar by the arbour, and Evie is standing in front of a microphone. They begin my chosen song when they see me—"When I Look At You" by Miley Cyrus—and all our guests stand en masse, turning to watch.

I begin the walk down the aisle, my eyes burning. Jake is standing by the arbour in a navy suit with a red rose boutonniere. He wears a crisp white shirt beneath the jacket, open at the collar. He looks glorious and I remember back to when I broke my arm and likened him to Tim Riggins straight out of Friday Night Lights. We have so much shared history. Who knew that one day the boy who lost his family would marry the girl who smeared spaghetti all over his shirt?

A tear slips out and rolls down my cheek.

Shit. The last thing I need is to ruin my makeup!

Then I pause. Dad stops with me. I hear the slightest falter in Evie's voice and Jake's brow furrows.

"Dad," I whisper through gritted teeth.

"What?" he whispers back.

"We have to go back inside."

"What? Why?"

My voice is a hiss. "Because I think I've just wet myself."

"Holy Jesus," he booms in front of all and sundry. "Your waters have broken."

The music comes to a crashing halt and everyone stands frozen, looking at me. Jake's eyes drop to my belly and back up again, widening with panic. He doesn't yell, but his shocked voice carries down the aisle. "You're in *labour*?"

I grit my teeth. Didn't you hear me before, Satan? I said *not today*.

"No!" I call back, feeling a sticky trickle of fluid run down the insides of my thighs. I wave reassuringly. "False alarm."

Jake's face settles into an expression of relief.

"Bitch, you are *in labour*."

I turn a hard glare on Tim. He's in the aisle seat right where we've paused, and his eyes are on the pool at my feet. A contraction hits me hard and I gasp. My fingers tighten on Dad's arm until I'm sure I've cut his circulation off.

"Dad," I whimper.

Mum comes tearing down the aisle, the elegant fascinator atop her head flying off behind her. "Where's your hospital bag?" she shouts as if I'm deaf.

Travis is right behind her. Jared is right behind him. They start to crowd me. I think my brothers are discussing one of them grabbing my ankles and the other my arms and hauling me out to the car between them. Everyone is yelling. It's goddamn pandemonium.

I rise on my tiptoes, my eyes finding Jake. He's still standing by the arbour, apparently frozen.

"Help me," I mouth.

My plea spurs him into action. His bulky muscle shoves through the throng of friends and family until he's standing in front of me. "Satan's coming?"

I nod, unable to hide the hard evidence. "She's coming."

He exhales, having a *holy fuck* moment. I know how he feels. This thing has to come out of my freaking *vagina*.

"Right." In a single smooth motion, he puts an arm under my shoulders and behind my knees and lifts me. My lace dress trails to the ground, no doubt ruined. He gives me a single look before he carries me out, his eyes crinkling. "Let's do this, Princess."

My labour suite is crammed with hospital staff and family. Mum and Dad. Travis and Jared. Evie and Henry. "Everyone out!" I shriek. "Get the fuck out!"

I turn my head to Jake, my hair damp with sweat and our baby crowning. He's by my side, pale and wobbly. It appears as if a light breeze will knock him over. I grab the collar of his shirt and drag him close so he can see the rage in my eyes.

"Get them all the fuck out of here before I burn this motherfucking hospital to the *ground!*"

Jake doesn't leave my side but the midwife manages to herd them all out the door. Each of them are calling out various words of encouragement as they leave, but I pay no attention. I have a baby half out of my vagina. Their platitudes can go suck a bag of dicks.

"The head is out," my obstetrician announces. "Come look," he says to Jake.

Jake squeezes my hand and prepares to stand, but I hold on for dear life. "If you go down there to see my mangled vagina I will *end you.*"

He sinks back down.

"One more push," the midwife cries.

I slump back in my bed. "I can't."

"Yes you can."

Nope. Fuck you all. I am *done.* I've changed my mind about having a baby. It's too soon. I'm not ready.

Jake squeezes my hand again. "You've never failed at anything you set out to do. Search inside. You've got to find that inner strength and pull it out of you. Don't give up, no matter how much you want to collapse."

"Arrrrghhhhhhhhh!!!" I push hard, rising up on my elbows. "Fuck you! My labour is not a goddamn Eminem song!" I yell on long, pained moan.

"Sorry," he mutters. "That sounded so much better in my head."

The wails of a baby render the air. It sounds like the bleating of a little lamb. "Oh my god," I cry and crumple.

"Congratulations," our obstetrician says with a big grin. He rises from his seated perch between my legs, our baby held up in his hands. "You have a little girl."

Jake stands so abruptly his seat clatters back and hits the wall. His eyes are wide with wonder. "Mac, we have daughter."

Tears are pouring down my cheeks. "And she's perfect."

I watch like a hawk from my pillow as Jake cuts the cord. Then they check her vitals, weigh her tiny body, and measure her length. When we're assured that she's fine, they fold her in a blanket and hand her to Jake.

His cheeks are flushed and his eyes are beaming. He looks to me. "She's so small."

He walks to me and passes her. We've been practising our baby passing already with Evie and Jared's baby, using our nephew as a guinea pig. So his pass is done with relative ease.

I hold my daughter in my arms as the midwife takes photos. Jake puts his arm around me as I look up at her, my smile bright enough to crack the camera lens. Our first family photo.

"I'll go share the news," Jake says, eager like a little kid. "Be right back, okay?"

I spend the ten minutes he's gone staring down at my daughter. "Little Satan, you are early and ambushed my wedding day," I whisper. "I guess this is going to set the tone for the rest of your life, hmm?"

Jake returns. "Look who I found in the waiting room."

He walks in and steps aside. Mitch hobbles through on a cane. My vision blurs. "Stitch."

A smile forces its way to his lips, but his eyes remain lifeless. "I hear I have a little niece."

"You do." I hold up the little bundle for his inspection as he shuffles forward. His rehabilitation includes physical therapy to help him walk again, but his lack of improvement is heartbreaking.

Jake reaches my side and takes our little bundle so Mitch can get a closer look. "Sit down so you can hold her," he urges.

"No." He shakes his head, staring down at my daughter. "I'm good."

"Please," I murmur.

Mitch huffs and stumbles into the seat by my bed. His cane clatters noisily to the floor, and my brother grunts with irritation. Jake plonks little Satan in his arms.

"We've named her Gabriella," I say quietly. "Gabriella Mary."

Mitch's eyes close. Jake takes advantage and leaves the room, giving us a moment. "You don't blame yourself for her ... death, do you?"

"No," I reply, but it's a lie. I do. My mind understands that it's Elijah Rossiter who killed her, but my heart feels differently. It's something I'll live with, but I'll live with it knowing she died doing something she believed in. "Eli killed her." And now he's locked away, awaiting trial. "He was the one who pulled the trigger."

Mitch opens his eyes. There's a spark of something in them. Something I haven't seen for a very long time. It's *resolve*. The kind of resolve that sets the hair on the back of my neck standing on end.

When my brother speaks, his voice chills me to the bone. "And he's going to pay for that with his life."

The End

Other Titles

Fighting Redemption
The End Game

The *Give Me* Series
Give Me Love (Book 1)
Give Me Strength (Book 2)
Give Me Grace (Book 3)
Give Me Hell (Book 4)

FIGHTING REDEMPTION

Ryan Kendall is broken. He understands pain. He knows the hand of violence and the ache of loss. He knows what it means to fail those who need you. Being broken doesn't stop him wanting the one thing he can't have; Finlay Tanner. Her smile is sweet and her future bright. She's the girl he grew up with, the girl he loves, the girl he protects from the world, and from himself.

At nineteen, Ryan leaves to join the Australian Army. After years of training he becomes an elite SAS soldier and deploys to the Afghanistan war. His patrol undertakes the most dangerous missions a soldier can face. But no matter how far he runs, or how hard he fights, his need for Finlay won't let go.

Returning home after six years, one look is all it takes to know he can't live without her. But sometimes love isn't enough to heal what hurts. Sometimes people like him can't be fixed, and sometimes people like Finlay deserve more than what's left.

This is a story about war and the cost of sacrifice. Where bonds are formed, and friendships found. Where those who are strong, fall hard. Where love is let go, heartache is born, and heroes are made. Where one man learns that the hardest fight of all, is the fight to save himself.

THE END GAME

"Professional athletes are pillars of their respective communities. They are heroes in the eyes of boys and girls and are expected to conduct themselves in a manner that positively represents their community."

The public loves a good scandal. Seeing someone fall from the pinnacle of success makes a great headline. No one knows that better than I do. What started out as a promising career in college football, spiraled into scandal and shame. But being a hero is easier said than done. Especially when there are those who expected to see the great Brody Madden fail. I craved nothing except being the best—willing to do anything to prove them wrong. But I went too far, and I tried too hard, and it broke me.

*"At the time of going to print, Jordan Elliott was unavailable for comment."*I met Brody Madden in my senior year of college. An Australian native on an international scholarship, I was the female soccer sensation with stars in her eyes and no room for a hotshot wide receiver with a chip on his shoulder.But a heart bursting with ambition and a driving fire to succeed isn't made of stone. I became his strength, his obsession, and the greatest love of his life. Only I wasn't there when he needed me most.

This is a story about love and a game that takes everything. Where the path to glory is paved with sacrifice. Where pressure makes you, or breaks you, and triumph is born in the ashes of failure. Where two people's end game will change everything.

GIVE ME LOVE

Evie Jamieson, a former wild child, is not only a headstrong, smart-mouthed trouble magnet, she is also a lead singer with a plan. That plan involves relocating her band, including her two best friends guitarist Henry and band manager Mac, to Sydney to kick off their dreams of hitting the big time.

Jared Valentine is the older brother of Evie's best friend Mac and also the man determined to make Evie his. They strike up a long distance friendship which suits Evie because she's determined to avoid the distraction of love, not only because it doesn't fit in with her plan but because twice in the past it has left her for dead. Moving to Sydney however, has put her directly in Jared's path and he has decided it's the perfect opportunity to make his play.

Unfortunately Jared, co-owner in a business that 'consults' in dangerous hostage and kidnapping situations, makes an enemy who's determined to enact revenge. When this enemy puts Evie in his sights, Jared not only has a fight on his hands to make her his own, but also to keep her alive.

Is accepting the love he's so desperate to give worth the risk to both her heart...and her life?

GIVE ME STRENGTH

Quinn Salisbury doesn't think she's cut out for this whole living thing. Even as a young girl she struggled. Just when she thinks she's found a way to leave her violent past behind her, the only thing that's kept her going is ripped away, leaving her damaged and heartbroken.

Four years later, she is slowly rebuilding her life and lands a job as an assistant band manager to Jamieson, the hot new Australian act climbing their way to the top of the charts. There she meets Travis Valentine, the charismatic older brother of her boss, Mac.

From his commanding charm to his confidence and passion, Travis is everything Quinn believes is too good for her, and despite her apprehension, she finds their attraction undeniable and intense.

When her past resurfaces, it complicates their relationship. Instead of reaching out for help, Quinn pushes Travis away, until a staggering secret is revealed that leaves her fighting for her very life.

Torn between running and opening her heart to the man determined to have her, can Quinn find the strength within herself to fight for her future?

GIVE ME GRACE

Casey Daniels has a past forged in Hell. Despite the friends, the endless supply of women, and the muscle car he spent years restoring, it still eats away at him.

Grace Paterson is in Sydney as a temporary bassist for Jamieson, the band Casey handles security for. She's also infuriating, off-limits, and complete irresistible.

A deal is struck, and despite their intense and powerful connection, both think it will be easy to walk away. But life can be more ruthless than either of them imagined. Not only does Grace have a secret she's desperate to keep, Casey has questions from his past that he's willing to do anything to get answers for.

It's not until someone wants one of them dead that Casey realises his love for Grace is the one thing he could never walk away from.

In a story of revenge, betrayal, secrets, and love, Casey will need to reconcile his past with his present, before the future he never knew he wanted is snatched away.

GIVE ME HELL

Mackenzie Valentine is wilful, fiery, and determined to prove she doesn't need anyone. Desperate to break free from the overprotective parents and three older brothers who dictate her every move, she runs away at the age of seventeen to hunt down the only boy who makes her feel alive.

Jake Romero has no choice but to leave the best thing that ever happened to him, taking him down a path that leads to notorious gang, the King Street Boys. When fate throws Mackenzie back in his life, he turns her away in her time of need, knowing he now lives a life in which she doesn't belong. Except his decision has shattering consequences, leading to secrets, lies, and the ultimate betrayal.

Years later, their lives continue to entwine, and when his past returns demanding retribution, Mackenzie intervenes and gets caught in the crossfire, leaving behind a devastation that no one sees coming. Can their relationship withstand the hell it's endured, or is it too late for love?

Acknowledgements

To Terrena. I know you know how much you mean to me but I don't know what I'd do without you!

Tammy I'm not sure how this book would've happened without you. Mac and Jake's story was one I wanted so desperately to get right, and you helped me achieve that. Thank you so much with the research, and the plot, along with being the best beta anyone could ever ask for.

To my editor, Max, as always you make my words look so much better than they were originally. Thank you.

Maree. You're an amazing beta. You provide me with so much motivation and support. And you remind me on the days where it's just not working, that I can actually do this writing thing.

And to all the bloggers and readers who've supported me through this writing journey. Thank you so very much.

About the Author

Kate McCarthy lives in Queensland, Australia.

Facebook:
https:/www.facebook.com/KateMcCarthyAuthor

Instagram:
https://www.instagram.com/authorkatemccarthy/
@authorkatemccarthy

Kate's blog:
http://katemccarthy.net/

Follow Kate on Twitter:
https://twitter.com/KMacinOz

Friend Kate on Goodreads:
http://www.goodreads.com/author/show/6876994.Kate_McCarthy